CATCH THE
LIGHTNING

Tor Books by Catherine Asaro

Primary Inversion
Catch the Lightning

CATCH THE LIGHTNING

CATHERINE ASARO

TOR®

A TOM DOHERTY ASSOCIATES BOOK
NEW YORK

The translations of Zinacanteco texts on pages 78 and 334–5 are taken from the book *Zinacantan: A Maya Community in the Highlands of Chiapas,* by Evon Z. Vogt, Harvard University Press, 1969, pages 649 and 686. Copyright © 1969 by the President and Fellows of Harvard College.

The translation of the Hummingbird text on pages 129–30 is taken from *Of Cabbages and Kings: Tales from Zinacantan,* by Robert M. Laughlin, Smithsonian Contributions to Anthropology No. 23, 1977. Reprinted with permission.

CATCH THE LIGHTNING

A Tor Book
Published by Tom Doherty Associates, Inc.
175 Fifth Avenue
New York, N.Y. 10010

Tor Books on the World Wide Web:
http://www.tor.com

Tor® is a registered trademark of Tom Doherty Associates, Inc.

Library of Congress Cataloging-in-Publication Data

Asaro, Catherine.
    Catch the lightning / Catherine Asaro.—1st. ed.
       p.   cm.
    "A Tom Doherty Associates book."
    ISBN 0-312-86043-9 (acid-free paper)
    I. Title.
PS3551.S29C38   1996
813'.54—dc20   96-21281
                                 CIP

First Edition: December 1996

Printed in the United States of America

0 9 8 7 6 5 4 3 2 1

This book is dedicated to
Sharon Todd and David Dansky,
two gifted teachers
who made a great difference
in my life

Acknowledgments

I gratefully acknowledge the readers who gave me input into this book: William Barton, David Burkhead, James Cannizzo, Louise Cannizzo, Al Chou, Paula Jordan, Frances and Norm Miller, Lyn Nicols, Nicolás Retana, Joan Slonczewski, Bud Sparhawk, and David Truesdale; the Dream Weavers: Juleen Brantingham, Jo Clayton, Suze Feldman, ElizaBeth Gilligan, Lois Gresh, and Brook and Julia West; the people in the research topics on the GEnie SFRT and the Internet who answered my questions; Caltech students Bradey Honsinger, Stacy Kerkela, Jeffrey Miller, Divya Srinivasan, and Shultz H. Wang. My thanks to Shawna McCarthy and Russ Galen at Scovil Chicak and Galen, to Tad Dembinski at Tor, and particularly to my editor, David G. Hartwell. A special thanks to my husband, John Cannizzo, for his love and support.

Contents

I
California

1

Night Thunder

I last saw Earth in 1987, when I was seventeen. The years since then have brought so many changes that the girl I was in Los Angeles seems like another person. But my memory, bio-enhanced now, remains vivid.

I felt the city that night. Although LA never fully slept, it was quiet, wrapped in its own thoughts. Drowsing. Waiting for a jolt to wake it up.

Joshua met me when I finished my shift at the restaurant, and we walked to the bus stop. It had drizzled earlier and a slick film covered the street, reflecting the lights in blurred smears of oily water. Above us a few stars managed to outshine the city lights and pollution, valiant in their efforts to outdo the faint amber glow that tinted the darkened sky. Sparse late-night traffic flowed by, sleek animals gliding through the night, intent on their own purposes.

I could see Joshua's good mood. It spread out from him in a rose-colored mist that shifted with vague shapes, the form of unspoken words. It sounded like waves on a beach, smelled like seaweed, tasted like salt. I was used to seeing and hearing people's emotions, even feeling them on my skin, but smells and tastes came less often. I knew nothing about Coulomb forces then, but it didn't matter: experience had taught me the effect decreased with distance; I would experience it until he moved away. Or until the intensity of his mood faded. I didn't tell him, of course. I didn't want to sound crazy.

We sat at the bus stop and Joshua put his arm around my

shoulders, not like a boyfriend, which he had never been to me, but like the best friend I had known for six years, since 1981, the year Jamaica became the fifty-first state and the Hollywood sign burned down in the hills above LA. Tousled curls fell over his forehead and brushed the wire rims of his glasses. He was my opposite in many ways, his blond curls sun-bright compared to my waist-length black hair. His eyes had always seemed like bits of sky to me, blue and clear where mine were black.

A harsh sensation punctured the bubble of our mood. I had no idea where it came from, only that it cut like a knife.

"Tina, look." Joshua pointed across the street.

I looked. A red sports car was turning off San Carlos Boulevard into a side street. "What about it?"

"That was Nug driving."

Hearing Nug's name was like being hit by ice water. "He can drive down the street if he wants."

"He was watching us." Joshua looked past my shoulder and his face relaxed. "The bus is coming."

As we stood, the bus came alongside us. I got on and glanced back at Joshua. He waved, his hand disappearing from sight as the driver closed the door.

During the ride I sat by myself, leaning against the window. The few other passengers seemed lost in their own thoughts. I wondered if they were going home to their families, to a world they understood.

As hard as I tried to fit, Los Angeles was alien to me. I had grown up in the Zinacanteco village of Nabenchauk on the Chiapas plateau in southern Mexico. I missed its cool evergreen forests, its dry winters and rainy summers. My earliest memories were of my mother, kneeling barefoot at her *metate,* grinding maize in the predawn hours. In many ways, she was a traditional Maya woman. So how, at fourteen, did she get pregnant with me by an artist from Mexico City who visited Nabenchauk to paint the village?

When I was eight, my uncle and aunt died in one of the earthquakes that hit the highlands, leaving behind their eleven-year-old son Manuel. After years of struggling with the decision, my mother decided to look for my father. She took Manuel and me down the Pan American Highway to Mexico City, what I thought then was the edge of the universe. We never did find him. Eventually we ended up here, in the city of sleepless, fallen angels.

The bus stopped on San Carlos Boulevard a few blocks from where I lived. The drugstore on the corner was closed and deserted. I had hoped Los Halcones would be around so I could ask someone to walk me home. My cousin Manuel had died the previous year, just before my seventeenth birthday, and since then Los Halcones had looked out for me. I could almost see Mario jiving with my cousin: *Oye, vato, let's go the show.* And Manuel: *Chale homes. I want to go cruising and check out some firme rucas.* No one was there that night, though.

The Stop-And-Go down the block was still open. I could call Mario. But I would have to wake him up, and I knew he had been getting up early, trying to find a job. The last thing he needed was for me to drag him out of bed at one in the morning.

It was only a few blocks to where I lived. I knew the neighborhood well and most everyone knew me. So it was that I made the decision that changed my life. Maybe I knew, on a level below conscious thought, that something was different that night. Perhaps a neuroscientist could have mapped out the neural processes that prodded my decision, or a physicist could have calculated the changes in the electromagnetic fields produced by my brain. Whatever the reason, I decided to walk home.

I headed down a side street. Old buildings lined the road, tenements and weathered houses. Although most of the street lamps were dark, a few made pools of light on the sidewalk. Cracks in the concrete jagged everywhere, overgrown with grass. Debris lay scattered: chunks of rock, plaster, newspapers, candy wrappings, empty cigarette boxes, fast-food trash blowing along the street or caught up against a building. Somewhere curtains thwapped in the breeze. The smell of damp paper tickled my nose.

When my mother first brought us to LA, we lived in one of

its more meager outlying areas. Although we didn't have much in terms of material goods, she gave us a stable home and more than enough love. After her death, Manuel and I moved here, where we could better afford the rent.

As I walked home, I became aware of an odd sensation. A trickle. It ran over my arms like the runoff from a torrent of warm air rushing by in a nearby *cañon*. But the canyon was in my mind, not in the city.

Two blocks later I saw him.

He stood about a block away, facing the road, a tall man with curly hair. I didn't recognize him. The one working lamp on that stretch of the road was only a few feet behind where I stood, so as soon as he turned he would see me. I knew I should leave, but what he was doing was so odd, I hesitated, stopping to watch.

He held a box that hummed and glittered with color: red, gold, blue, green, purple, silver. Holding it in front of his body, he turned in a circle, his attention fixed on it. From the way he dressed, I would have expected him to be robbing stores instead of playing with gadgets. But then, when Manuel ran with Los Halcones, he dressed that way: sleeveless vest and pants tucked into his boots. This man's clothes were black, though; Manuel had preferred T-shirts and faded jeans.

Thinking about Manuel brought me back to my senses. I backed away, intending to be gone before this guy saw me. But it was too late. He stopped turning and looked up. At first he just stood there, staring. Then he started toward me, his long legs devouring the space that separated us.

That's it, I thought. I spun around and ran.

"Esperate," he called. *"Habla conmigo."*

I wasn't sure why his terrible Spanish made me turn back. I could barely understand him. His voice was strange, too. On *habla* it rumbled with a deep note, like a low tone on a piano. But the warmth I had felt was stronger, flowing over my skin, a river now instead of a trickle.

He had stopped again and was watching me. I watched back, ready to run if he came closer.

He tried again. *"Preguntar mi tu decir."*

His grammar made no sense. *"¿Qué?"*

"Despierto mi." He paused. *"Yo español mal."*

He Spanish bad? That was an understatement. "How about English?"

"Yes." Relief flickered across his face. "Much better." His English was accented, but easier to understand. Every other sentence or so, his voice made that odd sound, like a musical note. They ranged through about an octave, one down low on a piano keyboard.

"What do you want?" I asked.

He held out his palms as if to show he had no weapons. It wasn't reassuring. He could have a knife or a gun hidden anywhere. And he still had the box in his hand.

"Lost," he said. "Help can find you me?"

"What?"

He paused, his face blanking like a cleared computer screen. Then he said, "Can you help me? I'm lost."

"Where were you going?"

"Washington, originally."

I tensed. Nug and his men hung around Washington's liquor store. They all wore black, and wrist guards too, like this guy. I backed up a step. "You're a long way from Washington's."

"Yes." He paused. "I decided not to come down in a continental capital."

Did he mean Washington, D.C.? I wondered if he was on anything. He didn't sound like it, though; his words weren't slurred or wandering, he just didn't speak English that well.

"What's in Washington?" I asked.

"A reception."

I almost laughed. "You're going to a party there dressed like that?"

"This is my duty uniform. My dress uniform is on the ship."

I wondered if he realized how strange he sounded. I hadn't heard of anyone like him in the neighborhood. "What's your name?"

"Althor."

It sounded like a nickname. All of Nug's men took one, though most of them were less creative about it. "You mean Thor? The guy with the hammer?"

"I'm sorry, but I don't know to whom you refer."

Whom? I didn't know people existed who actually used that word. Despite my wariness, I was growing more and more intrigued. I motioned at his box. "What is that?"

"Transcom," he said.

"What does it do?"

"Transmits and receives waves. Right now I scan radio signals." He came closer, showing me the box, and I backed away. As I stepped into the halo from the street lamp, he stopped and stared as if he had just seen me. In a sense he had, since I had only then moved into the light.

"Gods," he said. "You're beautiful."

I kept backing toward the drugstore.

"Don't go." Althor started toward me again.

As soon as he moved in my direction, I took off again.

"Wait," he called.

I stopped. Turned. Looked at him. Why? Something about him was familiar, but for the life of me, I couldn't place it. I felt it too, like tendrils of mist coming off a river. A sense of warmth. Affection, almost. So I hesitated, ready to run but waiting to see what he would do.

Althor backed up to the street lamp so I could see him better. He was tall, about six-foot-four. His eyes were dark, black it looked like, though it was hard to see in the dim light. He had fair skin and curly hair that, as far as I could tell, was the same color as the bronze bracelet my mother gave me before she died. I had to admit he was nice looking. Strange, but handsome. Just because he was handsome, though, didn't mean he was all right.

"You run with Nug?" I asked.

"Who?"

"Nug. You know."

"I do not know."

"You must've seen him around. Tall guy. Anglo. Blue eyes. Buzz hair."

"I don't know this man." He considered me. "You don't recognize my uniform, do you?"

"I've never seen no uniform like that." I winced. "Any uniform." Even now, when I speak seven languages, I sometimes forget to avoid the double negative in English. It seems a strange language, not allowing you an extra negative to make a point.

"I am ****" he said.

"What?"

He said the word again and it still sounded like gibberish.

"I don't understand," I said.

"Literally I think it translates as 'Jagernaut Secondary.'"

"Jagernaut?"

He nodded. "Secondary is similar to what you call a naval captain." He paused. "Actually, it comes closer to your air force. Major, maybe."

"You're a soldier?"

"Pilot. ISC Tactical Fighter Wing."

A pilot! Wariness followed my initial excitement. He didn't look like a fighter pilot. "What's ISC?"

"Imp—" He hesitated. "Space Command."

At the time, I was sure he was a nut case or stoned, or else that he thought I was stupid enough to believe him. "Yeah, sure."

"Why do you think I make this up?"

"Well, I don't run into many fighter pilots on my way home."

Althor smiled. "I guess not."

His smile caught me by surprise. No cruelty showed in it, nor was it a false smile, or the too easy smile of someone who never had reason to cry. It had history to it, complicated history.

I relaxed a bit. "So how come you're in LA?"

He considered me, as if trying to decide whether or not I was a threat. It was funny, really. Five-foot-two me in a fluffy miniskirt threatening six-foot-four him. When he finally answered, I figured that same thought had occurred to him. I had no idea then of the true reason he chose to trust me, nor of the extensive calculations that went into his decision.

"I'm in the wrong place," he said. "Actually, it looks like the wrong time. According to positions of the stars, the date is exactly as I expected. But everything is different." He pointed to the streetlight. "For one thing, I never knew this, that Los Angeles had such lamps."

I blinked. The street lamps were the same as everywhere else in LA: tall antique poles, each ending in a scalloped hook. The glass lamp hanging from the hook was shaped like the bell on an old Spanish mission. Books about California never failed to show them.

"They're angel bells," I said.

"Angel bells? I have never heard this before."

"You really must be new. They're as famous as the Golden Gate Bridge in San Francisco."

Althor frowned. "I've studied American history. If these bells are as famous as you say, I would recognize them."

"Maybe your teacher didn't know LA that well."

"My 'teacher' was a computer chip. It had no record of these bell-lamps." He looked around at the debris-strewn street, the broken windows in the building closest to us, its crumbling steps. "You live here?"

I didn't like him asking where I lived. When I didn't answer, he said, "Why do you live like this?"

I gritted my teeth. "Because I do."

He jerked, as if my anger had struck him. "My sorry. I meant no offense."

After an awkward silence, I said, "So where are you from?"

"Originally, Parthonia."

"Where?"

"Parthonia. The seat of the Skolian government."

"Never heard of it."

"After everything else I've found here, or not found, I'm not surprised." He sat on the steps of the building next to us and poked at his box. "Everything is wrong. The only transmissions I find are at radio frequencies."

I stepped closer to see the box. As he moved his fingers over the panels on its faces, they glowed different colors. He turned over his wrist and pressed the box against his wrist guard. It wasn't leather after all, at least not all of it. Parts were metal, and wires crisscrossed it, what I now know are ceramo-plex conduits, superconducting lines that power a miniature computer web.

"I haven't never seen wrist guards like that before," I said.

"They have a new web architecture." Althor spoke absently, pulling his box off the guard. "At least I can reach my Jag."

"Is that your car?" He didn't look like someone who could afford one.

"My fighter."

"Oh. Yeah." I wondered if he was an actor rehearsing for a movie. More likely his brain had lost a few bolts. But nothing about him tripped my mental alarms and my intuition about people was generally solid.

He held up the transcom. "I've checked radio wave, microwave, optical, UV, X-ray, and neutrino channels. Nothing."

"Why did you come down here to check?"

He shrugged. "The Jag can do the orbital scans."

"I mean, why this street in particular?"

He blinked at me for a full ten seconds before he answered. "I don't know. It seemed—the right place."

"What are you looking for?"

He made a frustrated noise. "Something to make sense. I seem to be in the wrong century. But the date and location, they are both correct. Except this isn't like any Earth I know."

I smiled. "You go to Caltech, right? My friend Josh is a freshman there. He told me about those role-playing games you play. That's what you're doing, isn't it?"

"Caltech? This means California Institute of Technology, doesn't it?"

"I guess so. Josh never calls it that." Now that I thought

about it, if Althor came from Caltech, what was he doing here, by himself, in the middle of the night? He looked more like Nug's friends. Once in high school, Nug and his men had cornered Joshua behind the gym. They tied his hands behind his back and lined up in front of him with their rifles like a firing squad. They thought it was funny. Joshua was so shaken he didn't come back to school for a week. He was afraid to tell anyone besides me, but I told Los Halcones and after that they looked out for him.

"I've heard of Caltech," Althor said. "I never went there, though. I graduated from DMA years ago."

"DMA?"

"A military academy."

The thought of Nug's creeps going to a military school made me want to laugh. Boot camp would be even better. I could just see a drill sergeant yelling in their faces.

But it was obvious Althor was serious. At the time, I saw his words through the filter of my own experiences, which included an intense desire for college and no money to pay for it. If someone had told me back then that someday I would have advanced degrees with honors in both sciences and the humanities, I would have laughed.

I spoke gently. "It don't matter to me if you don't have a fancy degree."

"I do have degree," he said. "It's in inversion engineering."

I smirked. "Perversion engineering?"

He reddened, as if unsure whether I made a joke or he made an embarrassing mistake in English. "*In*version."

I liked that, the way he cared what I thought he said. "So you're supposed to go to a party tomorrow night?"

"It is a reception at the White House for my mother."

"The White House, huh? She must be important."

"She is a mathematician. She has an equation named for her. But that was long ago. For many years she had been ****"

"Been what?"

His face blanked again. Now that I was more tuned to him,

I felt the change. He turned metallic. Then his warmth returned, eddying around us and softening the banks of my barricaded emotions.

"Key," Althor said. "This is the closest translation I find."

That didn't sound like any of Joshua's games. Nor had I ever heard of anyone having their mother, of all people, as a player. "What does she do?"

"Sits in Assembly. She is liaison between the data webs and the Assembly."

"Oh." I had expected something more flamboyant, like sorceress or queen. Then again, maybe "liaison" was code. "Does that mean she's a warrior queen?" I grinned. "That make you a prince? If I kiss you, will you turn into a frog?"

A sleepy smile spread across his face. "Maybe you should find out."

I flushed. I had only meant it as a joke—well, yes, maybe flirting a little. But I wasn't coming on to him and I knew it sounded that way. Why did I keep dropping my guard with him? After only a few minutes he was affecting me more than people I had known for years.

Althor held out his transcom as if he were a vaquero, a cowboy offering sugar to a skittish horse, trying to lure it nearer so he could catch it. "Want to see how it works?"

I stared at the box. One reason Joshua and I had become friends, despite the differences in our backgrounds, was because we both liked gadgets. He enjoyed making them and I liked to figure out why they worked.

"Okay," I said. But I kept my distance.

Althor brushed his finger over a square on the box, turning it silver. "This puts it in acoustic mode." He showed me another side, one with a membrane instead of panels. "Say something."

"¡Hola, box!" I said.

It answered with my voice. "¡Hola, box!"

I laughed. "How did it do that?"

"Your voice makes longitudinal waves in the atmosphere. It

reproduces them." He pressed the box onto his wrist guard and touched another panel. A note rang out. "Frequency 552 hertz." He played another note. "What frequency?"

"The same, isn't it?" I said. "Maybe a little higher."

"564 hertz. You have good ears. Most people can't tell them apart." He made a third note. "This one?"

"Same as the last."

"No. 558 hertz." He pressed several panels and the tone came again, but this time it vibrated like a trilling bird with a whistle in its throat.

"Hey! That's cool." I laughed. "I know what you're doing. Making beats. Me and Josh read about it at the library. Your box is singing those two notes at the same time."

He smiled, seeming more intrigued by my reaction than the beats. "You know what is the beat frequency?"

"Twelve hertz. I can figure out the pitch too." I thought for a moment. "The last one you played. 558 hertz."

Althor nodded. Then he touched another panel. Flute music floated out into the night, as sweet as the down under an owl's wings.

"It's pretty," I said.

He pulled the transcom off his wrist. "Want to try it?"

Did Los Angeles have smog? As I reached for the box, Althor shifted his weight so that his arm moved back in his lap, making me step closer to reach the transcom. I stumbled over his foot, and as I fell into his lap, he slid his arm around my waist. Mortified, I grabbed the transcom and backed away.

"If you come here," he invited, "I show you how it works."

I stayed put. He was sitting on the third step of the stairs, next to the railing, his booted feet planted far apart on the sidewalk and his elbows resting on his knees. Broken pieces of plaster lay scattered around his feet. I wanted to see how the transcom worked, but getting close to him was another story. After considering the options, I sat on the other side of the step so that about two feet of concrete separated us.

Althor leaned over and touched a silver square on the box. It turned gold.

I pulled back from him. "What are you doing?"

"I make it in electromagnetic mode."

"What does that do?"

"Right now, an antenna it makes." He swept out his arm, a gesture including the street, buildings, even sky. "Everywhere."

"I don't see nothing."

"It uses the buildings." He dropped his arm onto the stairs between us, his fingers brushing my thigh. "Augmented by changes in local air density."

I moved my leg away. "I don't feel anything."

"You can't feel it." Althor slid closer. "Besides," he murmured. "There are better things to feel."

His mood was a sensuous river giving off mist, a sensation so unsettling that I dropped the transcom. As it slid out of my hands, my fingers skittered over its surface, making its panels blink. It fell between my legs and landed by the spike heel of my shoe, its panels glowing like gemstones in a river.

A woman's voice burst out of it. "—fourth caller wins two free dinners at Mona's Kitchen. So get your phone ready, folks."

"¡Oiga!" When I reached between my knees and picked up the transcom, my finger touched another square. The woman's voice cut off in midsentence, replaced by a man speaking an unfamiliar language. I jerked my finger away. "What's it doing?"

Althor was staring at where I held the transcom between my knees. It seemed to take an effort for him to pull away his gaze and look at my face. "What?"

I reddened and drew my knees together. "The box. What happened to it?"

"It picks up radio waves." Althor leaned in until his chest rested against my shoulder. He touched a panel on the transcom and it went silent. Then he spoke near my ear. "You haven't told me your name." His river swirled around us, muddling my thoughts. I felt his moods more than with other people, even

Joshua. With Althor it was so intense it almost hurt, or would have hurt if it had been harsh. But it wasn't harsh. It was sensual.

"Tina. I'm Tina. 'Akushtina Santis Pulivok." I had no idea why I gave him my full name. I could always tell when someone thought it was strange and that happened often enough that I had quit saying it.

"'Akushtina," he said. "A beautiful name. For a beautiful woman."

I stared at him. The surprise wasn't so much that he thought it was beautiful, though that was unexpected too; the glottal stop at the beginning of 'Akushtina sounded ugly to most people who didn't speak Tzotzil Mayan. But what really hit me was that he pronounced it right.

Althor picked up a lock of my hair. "So long and soft and black." He had a musky scent, like catnip. "Why are you out here alone?"

I tried to ignore his smell, but it was impossible. Neither of us realized the truth then, that he was giving off pheromones specific to someone with my genetic makeup.

I pulled away from him. "I was coming home from work. My brothers are expecting me." There was no way he could know I had no brothers. "They must be looking for me right now."

Althor tilted his head, like someone struggling to catch a sound he could barely hear. "How do you do that?"

"Do what?"

"Upload to me. Overwrite my thoughts. My web is supposed to be protected."

"What?"

"I can't think." He put his arm around my waist. "You are doing something."

My awareness of him intensified, the textures of his emotions mixing with his actual touch until I couldn't separate them. It was too much. When he bent his head to kiss me, I slid my arms around his neck, acting before I had time to think.

When it came to men, Manuel had been as strict with me as a father. More like a priest. But I still had an idea what went on, enough to realize Althor kissed differently from most. He flicked his tongue over my ear, the closed lids of my eyes, the tip of my nose. When he reached my lips, he kept one arm around my waist and held my head with his other hand, stroking my cheek with his thumb while his tongue came inside.

When we separated, he pushed my hair out of my face. "Where are your brothers?"

I looked at him, feeling the echo of his lips on my mouth. His scent permeated the air.

"Tina?" He touched my cheek. "Are you there?"

"*¿Qué?*"

"Your brothers. Why they leave you to walk like this?"

"They don't." Which was true, seeing as I had no brothers. "I don't usually come out this late."

"Where are you going?"

"Home. Rosa usually gives me a ride, but her car is in the shop." That brought me to my senses, as I realized how strangely I was behaving. I stood up. "I should go."

He stood up next to me. "Already?"

I was afraid to ask for his phone number, thinking he might take it wrong. Earth, in that day and age, was in a state of flux when it came to courting rituals. In some circles, it was accepted for a woman to make overtures to a man. But I had grown up in an environment where that wasn't true.

"Tina?" Althor said.

"I thought maybe—" I paused, leaving him an opening.

"Yes?" He watched me as if I had turned to water and were running through his fingers.

"I— Nothing." I waited a moment, then said, "I have to go."

He started to speak, then stopped himself. "You're sure?"

"Yes."

Again he had that odd look. But all he said was, "Adios, ?Akushtina."

"Adios." I headed for home, struggling to ignore the feeling that I had just made the stupidest mistake in my life.

After I walked about half a block, I glanced back. Althor was still watching. When he saw me look, he took a step forward. I hurried away, crossing the street and then turning the corner. Once I thought I heard a footstep behind me, but when I turned to look, no one was there.

I lived at the intersection of Miner and San Juan streets. As I came down San Juan, it was a relief to see the sagging stairs of my apartment house. Only three more buildings and I would be home.

A pair of headlights flashed on, coming from a car parked on Miner Street. A red car. For a moment, I froze. Then I took off, running for my building.

The driver's side of the car opened and Nug climbed out. Actually, Matt Kugelmann was his name. Tall and lanky, with lean muscles, he moved with an almost feral grace. His head was shaved, except on top where yellow hair stuck up like a scrub brush. Although he was only twenty-four, he looked older. His face had a hardness to it, as if had been baked in a kiln too long. What made him ugly was the way he watched you, as if in his view of the universe your life meant nothing.

That was why I hated him, because people meant less to him than the garbage he sold. He had ordered his people to kill Manuel for stealing crack out of his car. Worse, Nug was the one who sold Manuel his first hit, to "help" him deal with his grief over my mother's death. And of course Nug kept him supplied.

It fast became obvious I wouldn't reach home in time. When I tried to turn and run in the other direction, I tripped in my spike heels and fell, landing in a heap of blue and white ruffles.

A hand slipped under my arm and I looked up into Nug's face. "Hey, Tina," he said.

I stood up. "Hi."

"Just thought I'd make sure you got home okay." He pulled me with him, toward the apartment building. "I'll walk you the rest of the way."

"I'm fine now." As we climbed the steps, I balked, resisting his pull. At the top, I stopped. "Thanks. I'll see you."

"Why you in such a hurry?" He stepped closer and I backed up, into the wall.

"Nug." I pressed into the building, wishing I could disappear. "Go home, okay?"

"I saw you hugging Joshua at the bus stop." He touched the tip of his finger to my cheek. "How come you hang around with that wimp?"

"Don't call him that."

"Why?" Nug sounded genuinely curious. "He doesn't even try to do you. I can't believe it. He must like guys."

I knew perfectly well Joshua liked women, especially tall ones with red hair. "I'm not his type. He likes brainy girls."

Nug laughed, then traced his finger down my neck. "You don't need brains." His leaned his head down as if he were going to kiss me. "You're so damn pretty."

I tried to duck under his arm, but he pushed me against the wall. "You know what you look like?" he said. "Those models in that clothes catalog I get."

The thought of Nug ordering a clothes catalog would have been funny in a different situation. "You mean like the Sears catalog?"

"Sears?" He laughed. "No. From that place in Hollywood, I can't remember the name. Freedman or Frederick's or something. Man, those models look even better than the girls in *Hustler.*"

"Nug, I have to go."

"They got play clothes in there." He reached under my dress and snapped my garter belt. "Like these."

I pushed his hand away. "Cut it out."

"You wouldn't believe what they got. Lace and g-strings and fake leather. I didn't know real girls even wore that stuff." He pushed my purse off my shoulder, then pulled my arms over my head and held my wrists against the wall. "Be nice to me, *chiquitita.* You don't know what Big Daddy might have to do if his little girl is naughty."

"Stop it!"

"You gotta be nice to me." He let go of my wrists. "See, I know stuff."

"Stuff?"

Impatience grated in his voice. "Like you lied about your age to get that job. Like your papers are faked and you ain't here legal, baby. Like if you don't do what I want, I'll just have to talk, you know. You want to go back to taco land? What you gonna do there, Tina? Turn tricks in Tijuana?"

"Don't. You're scaring me."

"Damn it!" He hit the side of the building, shaking off old paint. "Why don't you say, 'Yes, Nug. Whatever you want, Nug'? You always did whatever that shit cousin of yours said, going to Mass every Sunday. I mean, who fucking goes to church every week? Well, he ain't here to keep me off no more. He's gone and he ain't coming back, and neither is your mother, and Los Fuckones can't do shit." He grabbed my shoulders and shook them. "I'm king around here, baby. So don't play hard to get no more."

"No!" I gasped with the force of his motion. *"Stop."*

Something yanked Nug away from me. One moment he was shaking me, the next I was free and stumbling forward. As I caught myself, I saw a startled Nug facing off with someone. Althor.

"What's the matter with you?" Althor said. "Can't you feel how terrified she is?"

"Who the fuck are you?" Nug said.

I didn't stick around to hear any more. I ran inside the building, letting the door bang shut behind me. When I slapped my hand on the light switch nothing happened, so I ran down the hall in the dark, reaching for my keys—

I swore under my breath. My keys were in my purse, and my purse was lying outside where Nug had dropped it.

I went back to the door. Outside, I heard someone falling down the steps. Althor was bigger, but I doubted he had much chance against Nug. He was lucky Nug didn't have a gun.

A car door opened, followed by Nug saying, "You're gonna wish you never fucked with me." The door slammed and the engine started.

I hesitated. Nug wasn't one to leave a fight, not unless he was sure he would lose. But against one man? It made no sense that he would drive away. I eased the door open—and in the same instant someone on the other side pulled it open all the way. I found myself staring up at Althor.

"Tina?" he asked. "Are you all right?"

I backed up and tripped over some debris on the floor. As I fell, I banged into the wall and dropped onto my knees. I pressed my fist against my mouth, trying to make it stop shaking.

Althor came over and knelt in front of me. He started to reach for me, but when I stiffened, he let his arms drop. His face was strained, as if with pain, yet no cuts or bruises showed anywhere on him.

"It's all right," he said. "He's gone." Standing up, he offered me his hand. "I don't understand. Why does your brother treat you like that?"

I stood up and stepped back from him. "My brother?"

"That was one of your brothers, yes?"

"No."

"No? Maybe that explains it."

"Explains what?"

"Why he had no caring of your fear."

"He likes people to be afraid of him. It makes him feel big."

As Althor pushed his hand through his hair, I saw his arm shake. But it wasn't because of his own reactions. I felt what he felt. He wasn't afraid of Nug at all. He was shaking from my emotions.

"How did you know I needed help?" I asked.

"I input it. Even from so far away. Can you always broadcast so strong a signal?"

He was doing it again, saying those strange things. I backed toward the stairs.

Althor looked around at the shadowed hallway with its scarred walls. "I think you should go someplace safe."

"*Está bien*. It's fine." How was I going to get my purse? He was between me and the doorway.

Althor watched me as if I were a puzzle. Then he went outside and got my purse. When he came back, he set it down in the hall and moved off again. Still wary, I grabbed it and backed away. He made no attempt to follow, just watched as I backed up the stairs.

On the second floor, moonlight came through a window at the end of the hall. Junk cluttered the floor and black patches showed on the wall where an old fire had scorched it. A baby cried somewhere, a wail that broke off into softer sobs. Upstairs a man and woman were yelling.

I ran to my apartment and unlocked the top bolt, then the bottom one, then the police lock, then the door. As soon as I was inside, I locked back up. I sagged against the wood and started to shake. Once it began, I couldn't stop. I couldn't even get up to take the few steps needed to reach my bed. I sank down in the darkened room and laid my head against the door, shaking, too tired and too frightened to move anymore.

2

Blue Lace Stockings

I opened my eyes to a sunlit room. It looked the same as always, just my TV table in the center of it and my bed against the south wall. My mother's dress hung above the bed, a *huipil,* a white dress she had woven with wool and feathers. It covered the worst of the peeling paint. Across the room, the east wall made a "kitchen," a counter with space behind it for a stove and refrigerator. A window above the sink let sunlight sift through its gauzy blue curtains.

My watch said 9:00 A.M. That meant seven hours until my shift at the Blue Knight. I changed into a nightgown and crawled into bed. Sleep, real sleep this time, settled down like a quilt.

The sound of a dog barking outside woke me at two o'clock. I went to wash my face, and the bathroom mirror gave a sobering reflection. I looked ten years older. To this day I wonder if that was why Nug was aging so fast, because the strain of his lifestyle squeezed out his vitality.

He was right; I couldn't go to the police, or at least I didn't think so at the time. My family had come to America in 1981, so we were eligible for amnesty under the Immigration Reform and Control Act of 1986. Neither my mother nor Manuel had understood English well enough to keep our file up to date. I was trying to straighten it out, but since I was underage and without a legal guardian, I didn't want to do anything that would draw attention.

After I finished getting ready for work, I opened the door of the apartment—and almost jumped back inside.

Althor was outside, asleep.

He was sitting next to the door, knees drawn to his chest, head resting on them, like an overworked bodyguard who had succumbed to exhaustion. Seeing him in the light, I realized his hair wasn't blond after all. The sun had streaked it gold, but underneath it was purple.

He was older than I had first thought, too, well into his thirties. The previous night I had assumed he was Anglo, but now I had no idea what to think. His skin had a metallic tint, like bronze or gold. It glinted in the bar of sunlight across his arms.

I knelt next to him. "Althor?"

He opened his eyes and blinked.

My mouth fell open. I knew he had eyes; I had seen them the previous night. But when his lashes lifted that morning, all I saw was a gold shimmer. No pupils, no irises, no whites, no nothing. Just the shimmer.

"I don't believe it," I said.

As he looked around, the shimmer rolled up to reveal normal irises. Or almost normal. They were a vivid purple. Stretching out his legs, he rubbed his eyes. Then he looked out the window at the end of the hall. "It's late."

I couldn't stop staring at him. "Why does your skin shine like that? And your eyes?"

"They're like my grandfather's." He turned to me. "He has— I am not sure what is the English word for it. Differences from birth."

Birth defects? I winced, afraid I had offended him.

"Your day is so short." He yawned. "I need to reset my internal clock."

"It's spring. The days are long." I rubbed my finger along his biceps. The gold didn't come off.

He curled his fingers around mine. "Are you all right?"

"Yes. Much better." I took a breath. "Thank you. For last night. I don't want to think what would've happened if you hadn't helped me."

He lifted my hand and pressed his lips against my knuckles,

not kissing exactly, more like biting. It was strange. But nice. I couldn't believe he was out there, though. Back then, even in my wildest imaginings, I would never have guessed the reason why he chose to guard my door that night.

"You were watching over me," I said. "Protecting a girl you don't hardly know."

"Why do you call yourself a girl?" Althor started to reach for me, then paused. When I didn't object, he pulled me into a hug. I held him tight, the curls behind his ears tickling my nose. Closing my eyes, I willed that moment to last forever, as if I could preserve it in amber and take it everywhere I went, to bring out whenever loneliness threatened to overwhelm me.

After a moment, I pulled back my head. "I have to go to work. If I'm late, I'll lose my job."

"Can I walk you there?" he asked.

I laughed, that kind of soft embarrassed sound you make when a person you want to like you acts as if he does. "Okay."

"I am sorry. About last night. I should have asked then."

"I wanted you to."

"You did?" He smiled, his teeth flashing. "I kept thinking, She will say something. But nothing. So I thought you had not the interest. Sometimes I forget how different customs are here. That things are expected from the man which feel unusual to me."

I had no idea how to answer that. So I said nothing, just stood up with him.

When we came out of the building, into afternoon sunshine, his face blanked. Then he said, "It's fourteen hours since I meet you."

"Is that a problem?"

He pushed his hand through his hair. "No."

It was obviously a problem. His disquiet made a pale silver mist around him. Yet despite that, he still meant to stick around. It seemed encouraging. I didn't really believe what he had been telling me about himself. Why would a futuristic fighter pilot lost in the wrong time and place hang around to walk a waitress to work?

As we went down the street, an old Ford drove by. Althor spun around and walked backward, watching until it disappeared around a corner. Then he turned back. "I can't get over it. Another car."

I was about to ask if he was into old cars when I saw something in his hand, a gold box with rounded edges. I had no idea where it came from. His clothes had no visible pockets and it hadn't been hanging from his belt. Its color was changing and its sides becoming more angular. "Is that your transcom?"

He looked down at his hand. "Oh. Yes." He turned his attention to it, making lights blink as we walked.

"My friend Josh makes gadgets like that," I said. "Radios and stuff."

"I doubt he can make a transcom."

"Are you still looking for signals?"

"No. I check my Jag." He paused. "I am check my Jag." He squinted at me. "I checking my Jag?"

I smiled. "I am checking my Jag."

His face blanked. "Yes, that is the correct grammar. I am checking my Jag."

I almost jumped. His voice had come out in perfect English, with almost no accent.

Then his accent returned. "I speak English better than it shows. I just don't use it much. It takes a while to reintegrate the programs."

Reintegrate the programs? "You mean, on your plane?"

"My plane?"

"You said you were a pilot."

"It's not an airplane. It's a ship for space."

I couldn't help but laugh. "Oh, Althor. If you really have a ship, how is it up there while you're here?"

"I sent it back up."

"How?"

He lifted his transcom. "With this."

"How can that box make a ship take off?"

"The hull acts as an antenna. It receives transcom signals on a narrow bandwidth and sends them to the onboard web system."

"And that's flying your ship right now?"

"No. The Jag can fly itself." He glanced at the street with its broken manhole covers. A gust of wind blew pieces of an old newspaper along the gutter. "I think it is more safe in orbit."

"It's not safe up there. The military will find it."

He shook his head. "It has *****"

"What?"

"I think this translates as 'shroud.' It polarizes a molecular film on the hull, causing it to change state, making the hull a nonreflecting surface. It also projects false readings for detection devices at various electromagnetic wavelengths. And it activates an evasion program which monitors a predetermined volume of space around the ship and alters course to avoid objects—" He stopped, staring ahead of us, his mouth opening.

I looked. We had come around the corner, into view of San Carlos Boulevard. "What's wrong?"

"The cars." He motioned at San Carlos. "I've never seen so many in running condition before. This is why the air smells, isn't it?"

I grimaced. "That's right."

"Your trees don't have ****?"

"Have what?"

"Filters. Gengineered molecules that sift pollutants out of the air and convert them to nontoxic chemicals."

"Well, no. It sounds like a cool idea, though."

Up ahead, the bus pulled into the curb at the corner of San Carlos. I started to run, and we made it just as the bus was pulling away. I paid for both of us; not only did Althor have no money, he didn't seem to know what it was.

Everyone stared at Althor as we walked to the back. With his large size, his black clothes, his purple hair, and his metallic skin, he stood out like a neon sign. There were no empty seats, so we hung onto a bar while the bus bumped down the street. Althor gazed out the window, his fascination with what he saw making arcs of light, like translucent arrows circling through the bus. I had never picked up such vivid images from anyone before.

We didn't talk while we rode. It would have been difficult with the way we were bouncing along the street, and I didn't want him to start in about starships when people could hear. He wasn't holding the transcom anymore, but I couldn't see where he put it.

We reached the Blue Knight restaurant at about ten to four. Its canopy snapped in the breeze, and Robert, the doorman, was already at his post. I took Althor around the back. As we entered the building, we ran into Brad Steinham, the manager. He was helping the bartender carry boxes of cans, jars, and other goods from one of the storerooms to another.

"Hey, Brad," I said.

He looked up, started to smile, then saw Althor and frowned. He didn't tell Althor to leave, though. Instead he glanced at me. "You okay? You look tired."

"Yeah, I'm fine." I smiled. "Althor, this is Brad."

Brad put down the box he was carrying and straightened up. Althor nodded, sizing up Brad while Brad sized him up. And Brad *was* sizing him up, literally. He might as well have come right out and asked Althor how much he could bench-press.

Glancing at me, Brad motioned at the storeroom they were clearing out. "We've got leaks back there. Have to move everything before it rains tomorrow." He looked at Althor again and Althor looked back.

"You want a job?" Brad asked him. "Tonight. Seven dollars an hour, to help clear out the storerooms. I need my bartender at the bar."

"You want me to do manual labor for a wage?" Althor asked.

"That's right." He tilted his head at me. "Tina'll be here eight hours. You work that long I'll pay you sixty dollars."

"All right," Althor said. "What you want me to do?"

Brad pointed to the storeroom where the bartender was heaving up a box. "Just follow him. He'll show you where to move the boxes."

Althor went into the room and spoke to the bartender. The man nodded toward a stack of boxes, his face red as he struggled to pick up one of them. Althor picked up two with no sign of strain, moving more like a well-oiled machine than a man. He carried them easily, walking with the bartender.

"Man," Brad muttered. "Where do you find these hulks?" He turned to me. "We won't be able to finish this tonight. If he works out, I can maybe give him a few hours tomorrow."

"Thanks." I hesitated. "You still thinking about hiring Mario full-time?"

It was a moment before Brad answered. "I don't know."

"You said he did a good job that night he filled in for your bouncer."

"Tina, he's got a rap sheet a mile long." Brad exhaled. "Possession of a dangerous weapon. Loaded firearm in public. Carrying a concealed firearm. Assault with a deadly weapon. Felony battery. Attempted murder, for Christ's sake."

I knew how it looked. Most of the charges came from a fight between Los Halcones and Nug's men after my cousin Manuel died. Mario was busted for carrying a Mac-10. The police hit him hard for the gun because they couldn't make the attempted murder charge stick. They also wanted Mario and Nug off the street before the fighting went out of control. Both served time at Soledade, but no one went to jail for Manuel's death. The police never found enough evidence to make an arrest.

"They dropped the attempted murder charges," I said. "Mario's done his time for the rest."

Brad spoke gently. "I'll think about it."

I knew what "think about it" meant. He wasn't going to give Mario a job either.

Brad motioned at Althor, who was headed with the bartender back to the storeroom. "How does he get his skin like that?"

"I don't know."

"And purple hair." Brad shook his head as he walked away. "Sometimes I can't figure what you kids call style."

I watched Althor carry two more boxes out of the storeroom.

"Kid" was hardly accurate. For once I was glad that when I was tired, I looked older than my true age.

At midnight, I found Althor in an empty storeroom with Brad and two waitresses, Sami and Delia. They were sitting on the floor drinking coffee and eating jelly rolls from Winchell's. Brad beamed, and Sami and Delia were flirting with Althor.

"Hi." I stood awkwardly in the doorway, wondering if I was intruding.

"Hey." Brad grinned. "Look at this." He spread his arms, indicating the empty room. "Althor finished *both* storerooms."

"That's great," I said. Althor remained silent as Sami snuggled up to his side, her blond hair falling across his arm. He wasn't paying attention to her, but that didn't mean anything. She was older than me and lovely too. Maybe he wanted me to get lost.

But then he stood up. "Are you finished?"

I nodded. "All done."

Althor barely said good-bye to the others as he left. Nor did he say much while we waited at the bus stop. I wondered if he were irritated at me for interrupting their party. Either that, or he was tired. Then I realized that after clearing out two storerooms in one night, he was probably exhausted.

The bus pulled up and Althor followed my lead, letting me pay for us both. After we sat down at the back, he put his arm around my waist and slid me over to sit against him. I blinked, pleased, and let my head rest against his shoulder.

"I almost forgot." He pulled two bills out from his belt. "Here." ·

It was a fifty and a ten. "Why are you giving it to me?"

"What would I do with it?"

"It's money. Don't you know what money is?"

He spoke drowsily. "In abstract. I never carry it."

"I can't take this." I tried to give him back the bills. "It's yours. You earned it."

"Can you keep it for me?"

"Just until you need it."

"All right." Althor leaned his head back and closed his eyes, letting his head roll until his cheek came to rest against the top of my head. He wrapped his arms around me, as if he were a small boy going to sleep with his favorite stuffed animal. I almost laughed. Closing my eyes, I drowsed next to him, content.

I woke up just in time to ring for our stop. Althor followed me out the back door of the bus, rubbing his eyes.

He was quiet as we headed for my apartment. At first I thought he was bored, that he was walking me home only because he felt he should. I was so busy feeling self-conscious that it took a while for the eddies of his mood to register. Finally it occurred to me that maybe he felt clumsy too. It was an odd thought; he seemed so confident, uncaring of what people thought of him. Except for me. Why?

I watched him rub the small of his back. "I can't believe you moved all those boxes in one night," I said.

"That's what that man Brad said too." He smiled. "Ragnar would say the hard work is good for me."

"Who?"

"Ragnar. Admiral Ragnar Bloodmark. A family friend." His face relaxed. "He's been my mentor since I was a small boy. Like a second father."

It was impossible for me to imagine having not one, but two, fathers. "You're lucky."

"He could never replace my father. My father is a bard. A singer. Ragnar is a military man, and a biomech doctor. He understood when I decided to become a Jagernaut. My father, all he sees is that I might die."

I spoke softly. "That's because he loves you."

Althor's expression gentled, and he brushed his hand over my hair. I picked up a lovely sense from him, as if he wanted to make contact in some way he couldn't define himself, to touch me with a drop of that love both his father and mentor had given him. I caught his fingers and kissed his knuckles the way he had kissed mine that morning. As I let his hand go, his mouth opened slightly, surprise glistening in the air around him.

Although we were silent after that, it was comfortable, neither of us feeling the need to talk. Eventually he started playing with his transcom. Once again, it appeared from nowhere.

"Where do you put that when you're not using it?" I asked.

"In its slot."

"Slot?"

He didn't respond. As he worked with his transcom, his good mood vanished.

"What's wrong?" I asked.

"The Jag, it still has problems."

I wanted to ask more, but we had reached the steps of my building. I stopped, awkward again. "Well. This is it. Thanks for walking me home."

Althor stood looking at me. I hesitated, not wanting him to leave but afraid to go any further.

It was Althor who finally spoke. "I should walk you upstairs." He paused. "To make certain you reach your rooms safely."

I swallowed. "Okay."

As we entered the building, I flipped the light switch. Nothing happened, so we climbed the stairs in the dark and walked to my room with only moonlight from the window to show the way.

I stopped at my door. "Well. This is it."

He glanced around the scorched hall. "You will be safe here?"

"I'll be fine."

"Do your brothers wait inside?"

I hesitated. "I don't have no brothers."

"Then why you tell me you do last night?"

"I didn't trust you."

He touched my cheek. "And now you do?"

My instincts said yes, logic said no. I knew I should listen to the logic. But I was so tired of coming home to that ugly little room alone. "I was thinking . . . you might come in."

Althor slid his hand into my hair, letting his fingers pull through the long strands. "I would like that."

I was so nervous, I kept putting keys in the wrong locks. Finally I got the door open. The electricity wasn't working inside either, so I retrieved my flashlight from the TV table. It made a circle of light around me and left the rest of the room in shadow.

Althor came in and locked up the door. The police lock took him the longest, as he figured out how to set the bar in the floor and brace it against the door. I pointed the light in his direction, shining it on the wall when he turned around so it wouldn't blind him.

"I don't understand," he said. "Why is there no power here?"

"It'll come on in a day or two." I took a stand I had made out of an old birdcage out from under the table and set it next to the TV. When I stuck in the flashlight, it shined on the ceiling.

"Two *days?*" Althor stared at me. "Why so long?"

"Our landlords are creeps. They take forever to fix stuff." I went to the kitchenette and pulled my glass salad bowl off the shelf under the counter. Back at the card table, I set the rose-colored bowl upside down on the stand, covering the flashlight. The glow through the bowl made a dusky rose-hued light. It was pretty, though too dim to see much even near the table.

Althor peered at the makeshift lamp. "That's clever."

"The lights go out so much I had to figure out something."

He stepped closer to me. Too close. It made me aware of how different he was: voice, step, body, clothes, everything was unfamiliar. He had put his box away, but where I had no idea. His clothes lay flat against his body.

He spoke gently. "Sometimes the night needs a softer light." His hand folded around my hair—and that's when I saw the hinge. A ridge ran from the base of his middle finger to his wrist, letting him fold his palm in half, lengthwise from fingers to wrist.

"What happened to your hand?" I asked.

"My hand?"

"It has a hinge."

Althor stiffened, and the air tightened like a sheet of plastic. He withdrew from me, not visibly, but I felt it as much as if he had turned and walked across the room. He spoke coolly. "It had a defect. When I was born. This is how they fixed it."

A birth defect? I flushed, wanting to kick myself for my lack of tact.

Then I had an odd sensation: Althor *reset* his mood, like a computer. He relaxed and hinged his hand from wrist to fingertips, folding it around mine. Bending his head, he slid his other arm around my waist. Then he kissed me.

I knew where we were going, and it was happening too fast. I had always been shy, even with boys my age. I didn't understand why I was acting so out of character. Both of us were, actually. To this day I'm not sure how much of it was the intense pheromones humans with our rare genetic makeup produce and how much was the instinct born of those genetics. Salmon don't think about why they must swim upstream to mate; they just do it. All I could have said that night was that it felt right, as if we blended like colors swirling into paint.

When I slid my arms around his waist, he felt solid and masculine. He nuzzled my hair. "I like your perfume."

"I'm not wearing any."

"It must be you, then." Lifting his head, he nodded toward the bed. "Maybe we should sit down."

"Okay." I couldn't look at him. I was too young and too confused to realize we were dealing with more than normal attraction. My main concern was how to ask if he had protection. Althor had a better idea what was happening, but his worries were about the star-spanning ramifications of his actions. He was making a choice that, for him, would normally have been rigidly controlled by the government, with or without his consent.

He drew me to the bed and sat down, his booted feet planted wide apart on the floor. I stood awkwardly in front of him, between his knees, holding his hands in mine.

"Don't you want to sit?" he asked.

I nodded, too nervous to answer. Then I sat next to him, trying to figure out how to ask what I had to ask. Althor nudged me onto my back and stretched out next to me, sliding his hand up my body, starting at my thigh and pulling up my skirt, then moving his hand over my clothes to my waist. His grip was so big and my waist so small that he closed his hand more than halfway around it. He went up farther and cupped my breast, along with a handful of ruffles, as if I had said, "Sure, you can touch me there," instead of what I wanted to say, which was, "Slow down."

"So pretty," he murmured. "Who would have thought I would end up here with you tonight?"

Ask, I thought. But how? What wouldn't sound stupid? What did it matter if it sounded stupid? Better stupid than dead or pregnant.

"Tina?" He stopped rubbing my breast. "Is something wrong?"

"Do you have a thing?"

"A thing?"

"You know. A condom."

His face blanked. Metallic. He felt like a computer doing a search routine. Then he returned to normal. "I can't find 'condom.' What does it mean?"

"It's so I don't get—you know."

"Get what?"

"Sick."

"I am not sick."

"We shouldn't take chances. Besides, I don't want to get pregnant."

"You can't get pregnant."

"Why not?"

"It's true my ancestors were human," he said. "But they were taken from Earth so long ago, it's unlikely you and I can interbreed."

I almost smiled. I doubted anyone else's man had tried a line like that. "Althor, if you don't have any with you, we have to get some. I'm not trying to lead you on, but I won't go no further without it."

"Is maybe possible I could get you pregnant," he admitted.

"Yeah. Is maybe possible."

"This is not something you would like?"

"Althor!"

"I take it this mean 'no.' You don't want a baby if I am the father."

"Of course not!" I had no way to know that, among his people, I had just done the role-reversed equivalent of a man in my culture telling a woman, "I'm going to bed with you because I want to get laid, but no way would I ever consider you good enough for anything more."

I could tell something was wrong, though. "My mother raised me without a father," I said. "I don't want a child until I know its father will stay with us."

His face gentled and things were right again. I didn't know then that he had already figured out the cultural differences. All he said was, "I have no 'protection.' You have none either?"

"None."

He tilted his head toward the television. "Can we order it from your console?"

"That's a TV. You can't order things from it."

"TV?"

"Wait. I know. I'll be right back." I scrambled off the bed and went to the door.

"Tina, wait."

I turned to see him sitting up again, boots planted wide, elbows resting on his knees. He said, "You will come back?"

That caught me by surprise. That he thought I might skip out, leaving him alone—it seemed an odd idea, more like something I would think about him rather than the other way around. "I'll be right back. I promise." Then I undid the locks and went out into the hall.

Bonita and Harry's apartment was on the same floor, three

doors down. I knocked, praying Bonita answered instead of her husband, Harry.

The door opened a crack. "Tina? What are you doing up so late?" A chain rattled and the door opened, revealing a sleepy Bonita in her nightgown and a fuzzy pink sweater with pearly buttons. A black braid fell over her shoulder.

I didn't know her that well. We said hello when we saw each other, but given the differences in our work schedules that wasn't often. She had always seemed to like me, though.

I spoke awkwardly. "It's—uh—I needed to ask . . ."

She took my arm and pulled me inside. "What's the matter, honey?"

"Nothing. I'm fine. I need sort of a favor."

"A favor?"

"Do you have— I mean, I guess Harry would have them . . ."

"Have what?" She yawned. "It's late, Tina."

I flushed. "A condom."

"Oh." She came wide awake. "Are you sure?"

"Well, it's better than if I don't have one."

"That's not what I meant." She considered me. "Is it your old boyfriend Jake? Don't let him push—"

"It's not Jake." He and I had broken up months ago. "I'm sorry. I shouldn't have woken you up." I felt more foolish by the minute. I backed toward the door. "You go back to sleep. I won't—"

"Wait." Bonita laid her hand on my arm. "Stay here. I'll be right back."

She disappeared into the bedroom and reappeared with a box. She put it in my hands, folding my fingers around it. "Tina, think," she said. "Before you rush into something." Her expression reminded me of my mother. "Why don't you stay here tonight? You can sleep on the couch."

I shook my head. "Thanks, Nita. But no thanks." I backed out the door. "*Muchas gracias.*" Then I was out in the hall and running to my apartment. It was a relief when I heard her door close.

Althor was still sitting on the bed. His curiosity tickled my nose like pepper. When I sat next to him, he eased the box out of my clenched hand. He opened it and pulled out a small square of foil, turning it this way and that.

"What do we do with it?" he asked.

"When it's—well, that's the time. You know. With us and all. That's when you do the thing."

He laughed. "I must be slow tonight. I have no understanding of what you just said."

My face burned. "I'll show you. When it's time."

"All right." He put the foil back in the box and set it on the floor near the head of the bed. As he turned to me, the tickle of his curiosity faded from my skin. He replaced it with a real tickle, the touch of his finger as he trailed it along my arm to my shoulder, then down my neckline.

Althor eased us down to lie on the bed. Holding me close, he worked at the laces on my uniform, pulled and pushed, ran his finger over the holes. But he couldn't get the laces undone. Finally he made a frustrated noise. "Does it come with manual explaining how it works?"

I laughed, a soft shy sound. Pushing my hand between us, I unfastened the laces. After he pulled off the bodice, and the bustier under it, the cool air raised goose bumps on my skin. Then it was warm again, as he hugged me. While he worked on my skirt, I fumbled with his vest, having no more luck than he had with my clothes. I found no hooks, snaps, buttons, ties, or anything. My hand just slid over the leather, or what I thought was leather. It was actually a synthetic material designed to insulate against cold and heat.

He pushed up on his elbow and ran his finger down the front of his vest, popping it open. I had no idea how he did it, but there it was. Or wasn't. His chest was beautiful, muscles and smooth planes, with a dusting of gold hairs. Strange, though. The areoles around his nipples glinted in the dim light, more like metal than the rest of his skin. I touched one, expecting it to be cold. But it wasn't. It just looked like metal.

Althor took off all my clothes except the stockings and garter belt. He kept playing with them, not so much as if he had never seen such clothes, but as if he never expected to meet a woman who actually wore them. To me, they were just the impractical blue lace stockings that came with the uniform. I didn't realize that to him, they were lingerie in a style over three hundred years old.

Watching him undress almost made me forget how nervous I felt. He was gorgeous. His body was all muscles, wide at the shoulders and narrow at the hips. When he lay down again, I told myself I wasn't embarrassed. In truth, I was so self-conscious I could hardly think.

Althor spoke against my ear. "What's wrong?"

I blushed. "I'm okay." Wrapping my arms around his torso, I ran my hands down his spine, from his neck to waist, exploring his muscles, his socket, his—

His socket?

Socket. He had a socket. At the base of his spine, just below his waist. I probed the circle with my fingertips. The opening was less than half an inch in diameter.

Althor kissed my ear. "It's for a psiphon plug."

I had an image of a gas station attendant siphoning fuel into his body. It was too strange. Then, in the midst of my confused whirl of thoughts, Althor started trying to enter.

"Wait." Panicked, I forgot the socket. "Althor, wait. The thing."

"This?" He picked up the foil packet from the floor. "You must show me what to do. I have no data on this stored in my memory."

His memory? I was making love with a guy who thought he was a computer. I wondered if everyone's first time was this strange. I still wonder that, actually. Not too many people lose their virginity to an Imperial Jagernaut.

When I pushed his shoulders, he hesitated, confusion sparking around him like fireflies in the dusky night. Then he figured out what I wanted and sat up on his heels. I also sat up, too embarrassed to look at him. I took the packet and opened it. "Put this on."

"On?"

I touched him. "There."

"Ah. I see." He spoke softly. "You do it."

Somehow I managed it. We lay down again, embracing each other. Being with him didn't feel anything like I had always imagined, though. In fact, it wouldn't even work. Finally he guided himself with his hand—and it *hurt.* I tensed and he slowed down, moving gently, in an easy rhythm. Although I was nervous, I liked that, the way he moved, steady and strong.

The sparks created by his mood intensified, glitters of red, orange, gold, small fires darting against my thoughts. It was disorienting. Although I had always experienced the emotions of others through my senses, it had just been something that happened. Althor directed those sparks as if they were soldiers under his command.

"Tina." His voice was husky against my ear. "Let me in."

Let him in? Hadn't I already done that?

His sparks intensified—

IO path established. The words flashed in my mind. *Upload commenced.*

I jerked, stifling a cry. He kissed me, misinterpreting my reaction, and murmured in a language I didn't understand.

Download. The word flashed by. He had "let me in" as well, to experience his sensations as if they were mine. His peak swelled like a Baja wave during a storm, higher and fuller, until finally he jerked and pushed me down into the mattress with his hips, driving out my breath. The wave broke, hitting us both with the same force, and the sparks around us blended into a blur.

After a while I became aware of the room again. Sparks were winking out one by one, fireflies leaving the beach after the wave receded. Althor lay breathing deeply, thoughts quiet, Baja drowsing in the moonlight.

Eventually he said, "Am I too heavy?"

"It's fine, Thor." I felt ultrasensitive then, like an instrument that had been tuned and then not played.

"Thor?" He smiled drowsily. "No one ever said my name that way before."

"Thor was the god of thunder. He had a magic hammer and he threw thunderbolts at the Earth."

Althor rolled onto his side, fitting my curves into his angles. "I promise not to throw thunderbolts at you."

I smiled. "You just did."

"So do I become frog now?"

"That's okay. You can stay a prince."

He laughed. "You refresh me."

"I do? ¿Por qué?"

"Most people fawn all over me."

I could see why. A lot about him still made no sense, though. I slid my hand around his waist, touching the hole in his spine.

"It's a psiphon socket," he said. "It's how I am installed in the Jag."

"Installed?" You installed parts. Not people.

"The socket connects to the biomech web in my body," Althor said. "I have them in my neck, wrists, and ankles too. They link me into the Jag and, through its Evolving Intelligence brain, into the psibernet."

I had no idea how to respond. "Not many people can do that."

"This is why Jags pilots are so few." He yawned. "You know."

"Know what?"

"Like you." He closed his eyes. "Like me. Not many like us to study it . . ."

Study? I wasn't sure what he meant. "I'm not in school now. But I'm saving for Cal State."

Althor opened his eyes. "You are not in school?"

"Not now."

"No neurotraining?"

"I don't know what you mean."

He stared at me, wide awake now. "Who taught you to control your neural functions so well? Or to manipulate neural webs the way you did mine, on the street last night and here tonight?"

"No one taught me anything."

"You teach *yourself?*"

"Yeah, I teach myself." I thought he was about to do the "sweet, stupid Tina" bit I often heard back then. "What, is it such a big surprise I have a brain?"

"No," Althor said. "Many Kyle operators have a high intelligence, a consequence of the increased concentration of neural structures in their brain."

"Kyle what?"

"You are a Kyle Affector and Effector."

"Oh. Yeah. How did I forget?"

"Tina, I not make this up."

I didn't know how to respond. I thought if I asked questions and it turned out to be an elaborate game, I would look foolish. Or he might be crazy. He didn't sound crazy, though. He was too outwardly directed, too aware of other people and interested in them. He also had a sense of humor about himself. Nor would that have explained the sockets.

I spoke carefully. "What did that mean, the 'upload' and 'download' bit?"

"You saw that? In English?" When I nodded, he said, "My web must be translating for you." He rubbed his fingers over the back of my neck. Then he turned over my hand so the inside of my wrist faced the ceiling. "Yet you have no biomech enhancements."

"I don't even know what you're talking about."

"Gods." He dropped my wrist. "It's a crime."

"I didn't do nothing wrong." I made a frustrated noise. "Anything. I didn't do anything wrong."

"I mean it is a crime you go unnoticed because no one here sees what you are."

"I'm no different from anyone else." Back then, I was afraid that if I admitted otherwise, I would spend my life alone, an emotional freak too sensitive to tolerate human contact.

"It's true," Althor said. "You are a Kyle transmitter and receiver."

"A what?"

He told me that Kyle operators have two microscopic brain organs, the Kyle Afferent Body and Kyle Efferent Body. The KAB and KEB. We also have *paras* in our cerebral cortex, specialized neural structures that humans without our genetic makeup lack. Unique receptor sites in the *paras* respond to a neurotransmitter called psiamine, which only Kyle operators produce.

If you are a Kyle operator, then essentially your KAB picks up electrical signals from the brains of other people and relays the data to your *paras*. The *paras* interpret it for your mind. Your KEB increases the strength and density of the signals your own brain sends out. More exactly, the quantum distribution of your brain couples more strongly than normal with the distributions of other people's brains.

"Your KAB receives signals," Althor said. "Your KEB transmits them."

"What's in the signal?" I asked.

"Whatever is in your mind. Most Kyle operators don't have the sensitivity to decode data as complicated as human thought. Perhaps simple thought, if it's intense, and sent by someone nearby. But usually it is just emotion."

I hesitated. "Sometimes I *see* what people feel. Like a mist. Or sparkles. I hear it or smell it. Or taste it. Or feel it, not in my mind but with my skin."

"This is strange."

"Yeah. And everything you told me was normal."

He smiled. "I meant it's unusual for Kyle organs to interact with sensory input. The neural pathways to your sensory centers must tangle with those to your *paras*. So the emotional input you upload triggers sensory responses."

Just like that, he made a strangeness that had bothered me my entire life understandable. "How can you think you know anything about me?"

"You know how," he said. "You feel it too. Why do you resist?" His voice gentled. "You are beautiful, like light. You shine, so lovely and bright and—and I don't know the words. I am near you and I feel soothed. Healed. I had not known even that I am injured, yet now I am healed."

I squeezed his hand. "You're okay, you know that?"

"I didn't do so much for you, though, did I?" He slid his hand between my legs. "I can still help. Just tell me what you like."

I couldn't talk about it. "I'm fine. Really."

"You're so tense." Althor brought his hand up to cup my cheek. "Do I—" He stopped. "What is that?"

"What is what?"

"Where I touched your face—it made a dark streak." He looked at his fingers. "Is this your time?"

"My time for what?"

"Your menstrual cycle."

Why did he ask so many embarrassing questions? "No."

"Then why you bleed?"

"I'm *bleeding?*"

His face paled. "Tina—you have done this before, haven't you?"

"Done what?"

"Been with a man."

So. The Question. "No." Before he could respond, I added, "But you don't have to worry. I'll be eighteen in five months. Honestly. No one will send the cops after you."

He stared at me. "You're only *seventeen* years old?"

"Yes."

"Earth years?"

"Yeah, Earth years."

"Gods." He flopped onto his back. "I ought to be crack-whipped."

I smirked. "I will if you want. But I've never done that either." Whatever a crackwhip was.

He blinked at me. "I hope not."

"Althor, it was nice tonight."

"It is not done by my people, that an adult take a child to bed."

"I'm not a child."

"Why you say nothing? I would never have done this had I known."

"That's why I didn't say anything."

"You sound older." He shook his head. "When I saw that you had a young appearance, I thought you looked this way because you are small. It seemed charming that every now and then you sounded young. Now I find it is not you sounding young then, but remarkably mature the rest of the time."

I blinked. "Thanks."

He pulled me into his arms. "I'm sorry. Next time I will go slower."

Next time. Relief washed over me. So I hadn't scared him off.

After that we lay quiet. I drowsed next to him, listening to his breathing as it deepened into the rhythms of sleep.

3

The Bullet Man

After my shower, I stood in front of the kitchen window, combing my hair. Water splattered out, cooling my skin and making dark spots on the glass. The sun had just risen and long shadows stretched across the vacant lot next door. The smog wasn't bad yet; the day had a freshness to it, still new. Mounds of rubble cluttered the lot, which was strewn with boards the kids upstairs played with. An old Mustang rumbled by on the road, and a homely dog ran along the sidewalk barking at the dawn.

Turning, I saw Althor sleeping on his back, one leg hanging over the bed so that his foot rested on the ground. The pillow covered his head, leaving his mouth and nose visible. I laughed, not only because he looked funny but also because it was wonderful to wake up with him here.

I eased the strap of my blouse into place. It was my favorite outfit, worn especially for Althor, lacy, with patterns of roses and leaves. The skirt was rose hued, what Manuel had called "the color of a giggling white girl's ass after you slapped it." When I'd asked how he knew that about giggling white girls, and what was she giggling about with him anyway, and how come it was all right for him to do things that he would have threatened to put me in a convent for if I even thought them, he told me to go do my homework.

The electricity was still off, so I made two mugs of hot chocolate on the Sterno plate and carried them to the bed. I pulled the pillow away from Althor's head. "Wake up, sleepyhead."

He grunted and pulled the pillow back.

I laughed, tugging it away again. "You have to wake up. I have an early shift today."

He made a noise of protest. His eyes opened, leaving behind a gold shimmer.

"Hey," I said. "Your eyes are doing that again."

"Hmmm?" As he sat up, the gold retracted, showing his real eyes. "I didn't realize I had fallen asleep."

"You konked out like a log."

"A log?" He peered at the mugs. "That smells good."

I gave him one. "Why does that gold cover your eyes?"

"It's an inner lid. I don't really need it." He cradled the mug in his hands. "The sun on a planet my ancestors colonized was too bright, so they engineered the extra lid to protect their eyes. It comes down when I'm asleep. Or if I feel threatened."

"How come you speak English better now?"

"I do?" When I nodded, he said, "I don't know. Maybe it took a while to adapt to this archaic form."

"Archaic?"

He smiled. "To me, what we're speaking is archaic English. Perhaps my language mods integrated better with my other systems while I slept."

I shifted my weight on the bed. "Don't do that."

"Do what?"

"Talk about yourself as if you're a computer."

"I am a computer." He took a swallow of chocolate. "With such an extensive biomech web, technically I'm not considered homo sapiens. Not human."

I thought of the previous night. "You feel like a man to me." When his expression warmed, it made me wish we could spend the morning in bed. To distract my thoughts, I said, "What does biomech web mean?"

He described the system he carried in his body. He had computer chips in his spinal cord, ones that worked on optics rather than electronics. Fiberoptic threads linked them to his sockets so he could jack into exterior systems like his ship. Other threads connected them to electrodes in his brain cells, letting the chips "talk" to his brain: send 1 and the neuron fired; send 0 and it didn't. It worked in reverse, too, translating his thoughts into binary for his chips. Bioshells around the electrodes protected his neurons, and neurotrophic chemicals policed them, preventing and repairing damage.

A hydraulic system with motors and joint supports, all made from high-pressure bioplastics, enhanced his skeletal and muscular systems. It gave him two to three times the speed and strength of a normal human. A microfusion reactor powered it and his metal-alloy skin helped dump excess heat. The reactor was only a few kilowatts, though; his body couldn't take the strain of anything more powerful.

"Sometimes, in combat mode, my natural brain does almost nothing," Althor said. "Reflex libraries control my actions while my brain 'watches.' " After a moment he added, "It can be unsettling."

"It sounds so strange," I said.

He smiled. Then he "moved."

All he did was touch my shoulder. But it happened so fast I almost dropped the tray. His motion was smooth, but unnatural, as if a puppeteer tugged his arm. He tapped my skin, then drew his arm back to his side, all in a fraction of a second.

"Hey!" I grinned. "That's cool. Do it again."

Zip! In and out, he touched my shoulder.

I laughed. "Can all of you move that fast?"

"Yes. But it strains my natural skeleton. What I have of a natural skeleton." A cloud passed over his emotions. He shook his head. "I try not to overuse the enhanced modes. They're mainly for hand-to-hand combat."

"You're a gadget." I let my gaze rove over his beautiful body. "I like gadgets."

Althor laughed. "I'm glad."

"But I don't get it. Why not just put your brain in a machine, one that doesn't mind a reactor with more power?"

"Who wants to be a brain in a robot?" He grimaced. "Can you see me walking into a diplomatic reception as an armored machine?"

I had to admit, it didn't make for a reassuring image. "Won't they wonder why you never showed up at that party?"

"No one knew I had leave from my squad. It came through after the delegation left. I never did find out what held it up." He swung his legs off the bed. "The Allied president gave the reception in honor of my mother's visit to Earth."

"The what president?"

"Allied. The President of the Allied Worlds of Earth."

"There is no Allied Worlds of Earth. This is America."

Drily he said, "Not the one I was expecting." He picked up his wrist guards from the floor. "Is there a world government here?"

"The United Nations. But they aren't really a government, not like in the FSA."

"FSA?" He fastened a guard around his wrist, attaching it to his socket. "What is that?"

"Federated States of America."

"Federated? Not United?"

"I never heard anyone call it that."

He scooped his pants off the floor, then stood up and pulled them on. "Is LAX operating here? I might be able to get more information there."

"Sure. We've got a lot of airports."

"I meant the Los Angeles Interstellar Spaceport."

I spread my hands. "Sorry. No spaceports."

"Has your Earth colonized Mars yet? The moon?"

"No."

He sat next to me. "And this is the twenty-fourth century?"

"Well, no. Today is April 23, 1987."

"According to the Jag's reckoning, it's April 23, 2328."

The overhead lamp suddenly came on, and the TV blared out the news. Jumping to his feet, Althor whipped a knife out of his boot. The blade flashed like lightning, throwing sparks of light over the walls.

"¡Oiga!" I jumped up and grabbed his arm. "It's all right. The electricity just came on."

When I touched him, he spun around and raised his knife, moving so fast the motion blurred. But he caught up with his reflexes before I had a chance to be frightened. For a moment he stood there, holding the knife over my head. Then he lowered his arm and turned to the TV, where a weatherwoman was telling us today would be sunny, hot, and hazy.

"You okay?" I asked.

"When did you start this picture box?"

"I bumped it last night while I was getting the flashlight." I went over and turned off the sound, leaving the picture. "I guess I hit the 'on' button."

Althor slid his knife back into his boot. "I need to get back to my ship."

I could guess what that meant. Despite what he had said about a next time, I doubted he would hang around. With his looks and connections, I figured he could have most any woman he wanted. I had no idea then just how true that was, but I would have had to be deaf, dumb, and blind not to realize at least part of it.

After being with Althor, I understood what my mother had meant when she said my father and she were the same. She told me his inner soul was as sweet as maize, that it brushed across her like the breath of an owl. She knew him by that touch the first time she saw him. She called it the *ch'ulul* and *chanul,* his inner soul and its animal spirit companion; Althor used words like neuroscience and quantum wave functions. Whatever names they gave it, I knew it was the same.

But my father had never come back.

In Nabenchauk, people lived in large families; elders, young people, married couples with children—all together in houses made from logs, saplings, and thatch palm, built much the way we had built houses for thousand of years, to withstand hurricanes and heat, grief and joy. But my family shrank over the generations, bleached of fertility for reasons none of us knew. I was the last, the sole survivor of a dying lineage. Usually I managed to suppress the loneliness, but after the previous night I knew it would be much worse if Althor left.

"Tina, I'll come back." He pulled me into his arms. "I just have to figure out what's going on."

I laid my head against his chest and slid my arms around his waist, seeking his mind. He was a rush of emotions: worry for his situation, desire for me, memories from a life more privileged than anything I had ever imagined. He was older than he looked, almost fifty. His loneliness made hollows, like empty aqueducts in the desert, so long dry that their sides were parched and cracked. Many women pursued him, but he rarely responded with more than casual interest. It wasn't because he didn't want more. His lovers left him with the same emptiness I had felt with my old boyfriend Jake. He wanted someone who could answer the touch of his mind. Someone like him.

Althor pulled me closer, murmuring in another language. We stood that way for a while, just holding each other.

Suddenly he went rigid. "That's my ship!"

I pulled back. "What?"

"My *ship*." He was staring at the television. It showed a blurry shot of what looked like an aircraft, though it was impossible to make out details.

Althor strode to the table and dropped to his knees, then poked until he found the volume control. A newscaster's voice filled the room. ". . . craft found in orbit early this morning. The Anglo-Australian telescope took this picture when observers detected a change in the scheduled operations of the space shuttle *Challenger*. The shuttle loaded the craft into its cargo bay and brought it into Yeager Military Flight Test Center in California. An unconfirmed source claims it is a hypersonic test plane with orbital capability that malfunctioned and had to be retrieved."

"What the hell?" Althor grabbed at his side, at the waist—and pulled out part of his body.

I almost screamed. For an instant, I thought he had ripped his own flesh. But the rounded cube he held was solidifying into his transcom. On his right side, above the hip, a membrane was closing over a large socket.

"Oh, God," I said. I had almost reached saturation for his strangeness.

He didn't hear me. He was jabbing at the transcom, making lights blink. "I can't reach my Jag."

"You think that plane they found is your ship?"

He looked at me. "They must know it's no plane. They probably recognized its extraterrestrial nature right away." He grimaced. "Gods know what they think. A Jag carries enough artillery to wipe out Los Angeles in a second."

"Why would you bring a ship like that here?"

"I told you. I was going to a party."

"You need a warship to cruise a party?"

"It's *part* of me. I can't just leave it home."

"I thought it was hidden."

"It is. Was." He stood up. "It must be damaged worse than my tests detected. Otherwise it could easily have evaded capture by such primitive forces. But how could my diagnostics miss damage that serious? Only if it were deliberately hid—" He stopped and scowled. "It's probably scared the holy hell out of your military. For all they know, I'm the advance scout of a hostile force."

"You haven't done anything hostile."

"I left an armed warcraft spying on your planet." He shook his head. "They have no idea what they're dealing with."

"What do you mean?"

"Worst-case scenario? They tamper too much with it and the ship detonates. Given the weapons and antimatter onboard, it could take a good chunk of California with it."

I stared at him. "There must be something it can do."

He paced across the room. "I'm hoping it was at least able to disguise itself. It could pass as a planetary shuttle without interstellar capability. Your military probably doesn't yet realize how advanced it is."

"What if you contact the base? Convince them you aren't hostile."

He stopped pacing. "The only way they'll let me near the Jag is if I cooperate with everything they want."

"Can't you do that?"

"I would never willingly divulge information to your military or anyone else. Besides, they still wouldn't let me go. They have no reason to trust me. Why should they?

I watched him uneasily. "What do you think they'll do?"

"Move it to a more secure installation? But that would draw unwanted attention." He considered. "Right now they're probably searching for a mother ship. The longer it takes them to figure out no one is looking for me, the better." He ran his hand through his hair. "If I were in charge at that base, I would make sure we learned everything we could about the Jag, as fast as possible. Capturing the pilot would be a top priority.

He sat down on the bed, propping his elbows on his knees so he could rest his forehead on his hands. As he closed his eyes, I felt his mind straining. I saw it as a translucent image, water on the ground. It lay deep around us but grew thinner as it extended away, until it evaporated into nothing.

"It doesn't work," Althor said.

"What are you trying to do?"

He looked at me. "I fly this Jag many years. I can reach it, in a limited sense, even if we have no physical link. But the farther away I am, the weaker the interaction. It is too much far away for me to reach it now."

"What happened to your English?"

"My English?"

"Your accent got heavier."

His unease shimmered in the air. "I never separated. I left my brain running as a subshell on the Jag's EI."

I blinked. "Its what?"

"EI. Evolving Intelligence. The Jag and I, we are one brain that evolves together. I provide the 'human' component. Creativity. Ingenuity. Imagination." Sweat rolled down his temple. "When I leave the ship, I can centralize my programming into my own brain. I 'put it back' into myself. This is what separating from the Jag means."

"But you didn't do it this time." Because he hadn't expected to meet me.

He nodded. "A large part of my brain is still in the ship."

"But you were fine before. Your English was great."

"I think my mind, it has been in a subshell."

"A what?"

"You know what is a supercooled liquid?" When I shook my head, he said, "If you lower the temperature of a liquid below its freezing point and it doesn't freeze, it is supercooled. Perturb the system and it freezes all at once. My biomech system makes an analogous state to protect me if I am cut off from the Jag. A subshell. But the shell is unstable. One disturbance and it collapses all at once."

"And trying to reach the Jag made it collapse?"

"Yes."

I spread my hands. "I don't know what to suggest."

"I need information. About the Yeager base, to start."

"I'll call in sick today. Then we can go to the library. Maybe we'll find something."

Althor exhaled. "I hope so."

The San Carlos branch of the Los Angeles Public Library was in a small mall, sharing a plaza with the cleaners on its left and a bowling alley on its right. As we crossed the plaza, heat rose from its tiles. The sunlight had lost its freshness. It felt tense, like glass under stress.

I saw the librarian, Martinelli, through the window, a plump man with gray hair and glasses. He was cleaning off the counter where people checked out books. The library was empty except for an elderly couple at a nearby table. As we came in, they were settling down to read the newspaper.

Martinelli glanced up. "Hi, Tina—" He looked past me and

his smile vanished like a cigarette stubbed out in an ashtray.

The elderly couple were suddenly getting ready to leave. Following their looks, I saw Althor standing in the doorway, over two hundred pounds of muscle, dressed from head to foot in black, bare arms bulging, leather guards on his wrists, purple hair uncombed. He looked hardcore, ready for the state penitentiary.

I drew him next to me and spoke in a low voice. "Try to look less threatening."

"How? This is the way I look."

I didn't have an answer to that. We went to the counter and Martinelli came over, giving me an odd smile. "Got a late shift at the bank today, Tina?"

I had no idea what he meant. He knew I worked in a restaurant. I didn't understand why he was giving me that strange smile, either, as if his face were too stiff for it.

Then it hit me. Martinelli was frightened for me. He was trying to give me a way to send him a message if I were in trouble but couldn't talk. I gave him my most reassuring smile. "I'm not working today. This is my friend Althor. From, uh, Fresno."

Martinelli nodded to Althor, and Althor nodded back. Then Martinelli turned back to me. "What can I do for you?"

"Do you have any books on Yeager Flight Test Center?" I asked.

He motioned toward the card catalog. "You can look there. If you don't find what you need, I'll check the computer."

"Okay. Thanks."

I took Althor over to the catalog. As I pulled out a drawer and set it on the table, he sat in a chair next to me. Then he tilted his head toward where Martinelli was working behind the counter. "Why does this man distrust me?"

"He thinks you're one of Nug's friends." I sat at the table. "They come in here and bother him."

"Nug?"

"Matt Kugelmann." After a moment, I said, "He killed my cousin Manuel."

Althor stared at me. "I'm sorry."

Back then, every time I thought I was over Manuel's death it turned out I was wrong. Enough years have passed now that I only remember the good he taught me. He had been as strict as a father: no swearing, no late nights, no alcohol, no cigarettes, no drugs, no running with anyone he didn't like. Nor had he been much on talks about life. But I heard words in the way he treated me, words like respect and loyalty. That was before the crack silenced him. It was his way of dealing with my mother's death, but it took him away from me too.

"Tina?" Althor said.

I swallowed. "It's okay."

"You say this a lot. It's okay you live in a building unfit for animals, it's okay they murder your cousin. It's not okay. You deserve better."

"I'm just trying to get by."

"Where are your parents?"

"I do fine on my own."

"Tina—"

"You're lucky to have a father." I said it too fast, needing to change the subject.

Althor watched me for a moment, but he didn't push. Instead he said, "My father and I spent half the time arguing. Ragnar understood me better."

"He's the admiral who encouraged you to join the military when your father didn't want you to?"

"It was my choice." He shrugged. "My father isn't always rational about Ragnar."

"What does he do?"

"Lose his temper." Althor frowned. "Once, when I was a boy, Ragnar came to see me. He is my doctor, after all. My father, when he saw Ragnar talking to my mother, exploded. My father is most times a calm man. But with an old friend he becomes irrational."

I understand it now: apparently coveting thy neighbor's wife isn't unique to Earthbound humans. At the time, though, I said nothing. For all I knew, it could have been completely different from the way it sounded.

Instead I said, "There's something I have to ask you."

"Yes?"

"Don't soldiers kill people?"

"Yes."

"Have you?"

"Yes."

I shifted in my chair. "How many?"

"I don't know."

"Is that because you were in your ship so you couldn't see, or because you killed so many you lost count?"

"Both." When I stiffened, he spoke quietly. "Tina, people die in wars." He exhaled. "Our enemies executed one of my uncles, the man my parents named me for. Althor Valdoria was a military hero. My father's brother. A part of me wanted to avenge him."

I thought of my cousin. "Revenge is no good. They kill, you kill, they kill, you kill. It never ends."

"If that had been my only reason for joining the military, I would have retired by now. I stay because it's necessary to protect my people. I feel—" He stopped, as if searching for the right word. "Obligated."

In a way, he reminded me of Manuel. "I understand."

"But last night I felt so relaxed with you." He took my hand. "At peace."

"With me? Why?"

"I don't know." He smiled. "After all, you want to make me into a frog."

I laughed. "You'd make a handsome frog." I glanced at the cards I had been flipping around while we talked. "These air force books are mostly in the same place. Why don't you go look while I keep going through the cards?" I took a pencil and paper off the table and wrote down a few call numbers. "Just find those."

"Cards," Althor grumbled. "Paper books. Walk to shelf."

I smiled. "You have a better idea?"

"Go home. Relax. Have the web look up what you want and deliver a microspool. Plug spool into book. Choose font, graphics, and holography." He kept grumbling in his own language, but he took the paper and went to the stacks.

I laughed and bent over the card catalog.

A moment later someone spoke behind me. "Hey, Tina. You got a new boyfriend?"

I looked up. Nug stood there, dressed in jeans and a jacket. String and Buzzer were with him, two guys who looked like their names: String was taller and skinnier than Nug, and Buzzer looked like a stocky old buzzard.

"He's coming right back," I said.

Nug smiled. "New guy, looks like."

I didn't like it when Nug smiled. "From Fresno."

"Fresno?" Nug laughed. "Shit. That's worse than coming from Cleveland."

"What do you want?" I asked.

"Talk nice to me." Nug stepped closer. When I tried to scoot my chair back, he closed his hand around my arm. "What's the matter?" He wasn't smiling now. "You can't take that pretty nose of yours out of the air for two fucking seconds?"

Martinelli spoke from behind the counter. "Leave her alone, Matt."

Nug looked up, his lips twisting in a scowl. But he did let go of my arm. Then he put his hand inside his jacket.

He pulled out a 9-mm. Luger.

Both Martinelli and I froze. Nug stretched out his arm, pointing the gun at Martinelli. "Shut up, old man."

I couldn't believe he was pulling a gun on Martinelli in the middle of the library. I should have known something was wrong, with Nug wearing a jacket when it was so hot.

Nug glanced at String. "Make sure he doesn't bother us."

String ran to the counter and hauled himself over it. Drawing his knife, he tilted his head toward the wall, an area out of our view. Martinelli retreated and String followed.

Nug turned back to me. "Well." He smiled again and it didn't look any better now than it had the first time. "So you got a new boyfriend."

I swallowed. "He doesn't like me talking to other guys."

"That so." Nug stepped closer. "What does he like?"

I leaned back. "Don't."

"Don't," he mimicked. He shoved the gun into his waistband, then pulled me out of the chair and put his arms around me. "This what he wants, *chiquitita?*"

"Stop it!" I lurched away and thudded into Buzzer. He grabbed my upper arms and held me in place.

"Sweet Tina." Nug was gritting his teeth. "We can't have her, can we? She's too pure. You think I don't know, don't you."

I stared at him. "Know what?"

"You never gave me the time." His mood cut around him in angry black and red streaks. "But I gave you slack. I thought, 'She's different. Try harder.' Well, I tried, and you didn't even look at me, like you thought you was too good. Even then I gave you slack. Thought maybe that cousin of yours told you shit about me. I gave you more slack than I've ever given anyone." He pointed at me. "I seen you this morning, slut. I seen you come out with that guy. He there all night, Tina? You fuck him all night?"

"Nug, please," I said.

"What's wrong?" Nug said. "I got everything he has. Maybe better."

I was sure he had sent his men after Althor. They probably pulled him into one of the back rooms. And Nug wasn't stupid. Although we were in a library with a large window, Buzzer's body hid me from view. Anyone outside would see only what looked like Buzzer and Nug talking.

Nug glanced at String and jerked his chin. I heard a thud, metal hitting muscle, followed by a grunt, and the bigger thud of a body hitting the ground.

"Come on," Nug said. "We're outta here."

As they took me to a side door, String jogged up next to us. We came out in an alley between the library and the cleaners. No windows broke the walls on either side, no place where someone might look out and see I needed help. A mist of furious red sparks hung around Nug, smelling like vinegar and soot. Another one of his men was waiting in the alley, a skinny guy named Pits.

"Get the car," Nug told him.

Pits took off, sprinting toward the parking lot in back of the library. Jerking up my foot, I stabbed the spike heel of my shoe into Buzzer's leg. As he yelled, his hold loosened and I twisted out of his arms. I ran for the plaza in front of the library, lurching in my high heels. If only I could get out of the alley. San Carlos was a busy street. Once I was in the plaza, someone had to see me. They had to. I could run into the street even, make a car stop.

Another of Nug's men stepped into view, blocking the end of the alley.

With a cry, I skidded to a stop in front of him. Footsteps sounded behind me, and I spun around to see Nug. Buzzer came up on his left and String on his right, chests heaving as they gasped for breath.

"I'm getting real tired of this," Nug said.

"No!" I said. "People will see—"

"Shut up." He grabbed my arm and threw me back into Buzzer. I tried to scream, but Buzzer clamped his hand over my mouth. An engine rumbled, and an old car turned into the alley from the back parking lot, with Pits driving. He rolled toward us and stopped a few feet away.

Nug glanced at me. "We're going to my place, baby. For a party. All of us." He looked around, then scowled at the guy who had stepped into the alley. "Go find the others."

As the guy took off, Buzzer dragged me to the car and opened the back door. He pushed me down on the seat, on my back, pressing one hand over my mouth and holding my wrists. The other door opened, bringing the greasy auto shop smell Nug carried around with him. Buzzer let go of my mouth, but as soon as I opened it to scream, Nug stuffed in a wad of cloth and covered my mouth with duct tape.

String opened the front door and tossed Nug a rope. "That's all we got."

Nug caught the rope. "It'll do." Leaning over me, he took my wrists from Buzzer and pulled off my bracelet.

I struggled to yank my hands away from him. My mother had given me that bracelet, and her mother to her, and on back for more generations than anyone in our family knew. It could never be replaced.

Buzzer motioned at the bracelet. "Think it's worth anything?"

Nug watched me struggle. "She thinks it is. Maybe we can hock it." He laughed. "Hey, it's a prize. Whoever does her the longest gets it."

I yelled *No!* but all that came out was a muffled grunt. Nug dropped the bracelet on the floor. They flipped me over onto my stomach, and Buzzer held me down while Nug tied my wrists behind my back. When they turned me over again, I clenched my teeth on the cloth in my mouth and jerked up my knees, jamming them into Buzzer's crotch.

"*Shit!*" Buzzer jumped back so fast he hit his head on the door frame. He fell against the door, his fury leaking out of his pores like drops of lava.

The boot whipped up in such a blur, I didn't realize it was a person kicking his leg until the heel hit Buzzer's chest and threw him away from the car. Then Althor hurtled into Buzzer and they spun out of sight. Behind me, Nug swore and opened the car door.

I scrambled out of the car, nearly losing my balance with my hands tied behind my back, just in time to see Althor and Buzzer hit the wall of the cleaner's. As String ran up behind them, his switchblade drawn, Althor whirled around, holding Buzzer by his jacket, kicking his leg up in a move of deadly grace. An unnatural speed controlled his body, as if he were a machine directed by someone else. His anger filled the air with spears of ice only I could see. I didn't know then that it was a programmed emotion, a state-of-the-art defense designed to smother his empathic abilities during combat.

His kick sent String's knife spinning and his heel slammed into String's chest. As String flew backward into the car, Althor threw Buzzer after him. Both men crumpled to the ground, broken and unconscious. I later learned that the only reason they still lived was because Althor's biomech web had calculated that lethal force wasn't needed. The web couldn't completely control his actions, but it helped keep him in check.

Up to a point.

Somewhere, far away but coming closer, sirens wailed. An explosion cracked here in the alley, and Althor staggered back into the wall of the cleaners as if someone pushed him. On the other side of the car, Nug stood with his arm straight out, his Luger aimed at Althor. He had hit Althor's side, at the waist above his left hip, between the edges of his vest and pants. His second shot missed: just as he pulled the trigger, light flashed across his face, making him shut his eyes. Althor had drawn his knife. In my room it glittered; out here it bounced and refracted light in a blinding display of radiance and rainbow colors, like a gigantic diamond.

Althor snapped his wrist and the knife streaked through the air. Nug was already moving, so the blade missed his heart and stabbed his shoulder. As Nug shouted and dropped his gun, Althor ran around the car, straight at him. He slammed Nug against the car, but Nug was smarter than the others; instead of trying to best Althor's strength and speed, he grabbed his vest and used his weight against him, throwing him over his shoulder onto the hood. Althor rolled easily across the car and came down in front of it, landing on his feet.

The sirens were closer now, their wail going up and down, changing in tempo to a faster beat, then back to the drawn-out cry. Althor lunged at Nug and they grappled with each other. With them moving so fast, it was impossible to see who had the knife. It flashed around their bodies, stabbing in a blur of light.

The sirens swelled and pulled into the plaza out front. Pits couldn't get his car out of the alley without hitting the fighters, so he jumped out and took off like fire on oil. I wasn't sure if he was running from Althor or the cops.

Althor stopped moving—and Nug collapsed to the ground in a limp heap. He wasn't breathing.

"Drop the knife," a voice commanded.

Looking up, I saw a policeman at the end of the alley, his gun out and aimed. Althor stared at him. He was standing over Nug's body, his boots on either side of Nug's hips, the knife still raised in his hand. Blood dripped off its diamond-bright edge and splattered on Nug's closed eyelids.

"Drop it," the officer repeated. "Now."

For a moment I was afraid Althor wouldn't respond. Then he opened his hand and the knife clattered to the asphalt.

Footsteps sounded behind me. Turning, I saw a second officer coming up the alley. Another siren was wailing, faint but growing louder. The side door of the library opened, revealing Martinelli with a policewoman. Martinelli's clothes were rumpled and an ugly bruise showed on his forehead.

The woman came over to me and carefully pulled off the gag. "Are you all right?"

I nodded. But I was lying. I had never witnessed a murder before.

"It was self-defense," I said while she untied me. "My boyfriend was protecting me."

"You can give your statements at the station." She tilted her head toward Martinelli. "Go back inside with him." Then she headed toward the others.

As I grabbed my bracelet out of the car, I heard a man say, "Stand up against the wall." Straightening up, I saw the three officers watching Althor. He stared back as if they were enemies, his head turning from one to the other like a well-oiled machine.

"Move it," the first officer said. *"Now."*

I didn't like the way the cops looked, as if they believed they might have to shoot. *Althor!* I thought. *You have to do what they say.* I made an image in my mind showing him facing the wall, ready to be searched.

Althor shot me a look, as if I had yelled in his ear instead of in my own head. A thought brushed my mind, cold and impersonal: *Combat mode toggled off.* Moving slowly, he backed up to the wall of library, still facing the three officers.

"Turn around," the first man said.

Althor watched him, wary and silent. Then he turned, put his palms on the wall, and spread his legs.

The police wasted no time. One picked up the knife, squinting as it flashed in his eyes; the second pulled Althor's arms behind his back and handcuffed his wrists below his guards. No one yet realized he had been shot. Although blood covered his clothes, it could have come from Nug. His vest hid his wound and he didn't flinch even when the officer searched him.

When I stepped forward, intending to tell them he was injured, he looked directly at me. *Tina, no.*

The sound of his mental "voice" startled me into inaction. I stayed put, praying I was making the right decision. The siren I had been hearing swelled in volume, and an ambulance pulled into the alley. People jumped out of it, some striding to where Nug and the others lay, others running into the library.

The first officer motioned to Althor. "Walk out front." He glanced at me and motioned toward the second officer. "You can go with Stevens, miss."

We walked in silence. The traffic on San Carlos sounded distant, as if we were all trapped in a bubble, waiting for it to explode. Two police cars were parked in the plaza. We went over to the first, and Stevens pulled out his keys.

Suddenly Althor whirled, the shimmer of his inner lids snapping over his eyes. As Stevens whipped up his gun, Althor simultaneously kicked up his leg and threw his body at the other officer. His heel smashed into Stevens' chest and Stevens flew over backward, the bark of his gun cracking in the air.

As Althor thudded into Stevens' partner, he lost his balance and fell against the car. It looked bizarre, as if Althor were falling in two directions at once, sideways into the man and backward at the car. Stevens' partner couldn't have thrown him there; Althor had hit him too hard and too fast. The man's head thunked against the car and he collapsed to the ground, unconscious.

Althor's breath came out in a gasp. "Tina, get in the car." He half fell, half dropped to one knee. With his hands behind his back, he grabbed Stevens' gun. Sweat ran down his face, which had paled under the metallic tint. As he lurched to his feet, he worked his cuffed wrists around his body until he was holding the gun at his side. "Can you drive this vehicle?"

"Steal a police car? Are you nuts?" Then I saw the blood pumping out of his shoulder and I knew what had knocked him against the car. Stevens' shot had hit him.

The policewoman called from the alley. "If you take her, you'll only make it worse." She stood half-hidden at the corner of the building, her gun up. Another officer was behind the front door of the library. Neither tried to shoot Althor; they would have risked hitting me.

"Tina, hurry," Althor said. "And get my knife. I can—only carry gun."

I grabbed the knife and Stevens' keys. As I slid inside the car, Althor pulled himself after me and slammed the door. I dumped the knife in his lap, then started the car and jammed the accelerator to the floor. I had no plan, aside from knowing we had to stop the police from following us. Only one idea came to me: I careened across the asphalt—and plowed into the driver's side of the other car. Then I backed up, tires screaming in protest, and sped out of the plaza.

As we drove down San Carlos, I glanced at Althor. He was bleeding, both from the bullet wound in his shoulder and the one that had cut through his side. "We have to get you to a hospital."

"No. They'll see—I'm not human." He swallowed. "If they catch me, go with them. Say I forced you to come."

"No."

"Tina—"

"*No.*" I felt as if I was on a too fast ride at a carnival. But I had no intention of deserting Althor. I owed him. I'll never know if Nug and his men would have killed me after they were done, but even if they hadn't I wouldn't have felt much like living when it was finished.

I swerved into a closed gas station and stopped behind the building. A stretch of lawn separated us from the freeway. "We have to get out of this car. We're too easy to spot in it."

He took a breath. "Put back my knife."

The knife slid easily into its sheath inside his boot. As I straightened up, a runnel of blood ran over my hand. Bluish blood. "Althor, what's wrong with your blood?"

He grimaced. "Is coming out of me."

"I don't mean that. The color is wrong."

"Is fine."

"It's *not* fine." I turned back to the wheel. "I'm taking you to the emergency room."

"No. I'm fine."

I started the car. "It's better they figure out you aren't human than you die."

"Tina, stop!"

As I put the car into drive, words flashed in my mind: *Prepare to download.*

The data hit my mind like water thrown out of a bucket. In only a second, it told me what I needed to know. Althor has a blood disorder similar to sickle-cell anemia. Sickle-cell comes from a mutation in one of two genes that make hemoglobin, the molecule that carries oxygen in the blood. In Althor's anemia, both genes contain mutations, with the result that each of his hemoglobin molecules contains two incorrect amino acid residues. It's like putting the wrong pieces in a puzzle; force them in and the puzzle twists out of shape. Left untreated, his distorted hemoglobin clumps up and deforms his red blood cells. His spleen then takes them out of circulation like bad money, giving him severe anemia.

To fix the problem, his doctors extracted erythropoietic stem cells from his bone marrow and equipped them with a corrected gene that codes for the right amino acid. Blood cells form in the marrow, so when the doctored cells were returned to his body they produced corrected hemoglobin. But the doctors fixed only one of his bad genes. The other not only affects his hemoglobin, it also contributes to his Kyle abilities: "fix" it, and he becomes less of an empath.

Instead they populated his blood with nano-meds, each a protein with an attached spherical molecule. The sphere contains a picochip, a molecular computer that operates on quantum transitions. It directs the activities and reproduction of the med. The protein portion locks onto Althor's hemoglobin, causing it to change shape, making the final adjustment it needs to carry oxygen properly. The meds also have a side effect: when exposed to ultraviolet radiation and nitrogen gas, they turn blue. In his body only a small number exist in the blue state; without a steady diet of photons and N_2 they quickly return to colorless form. Outside, in sunlight and air, many more convert, giving his blood a bluish tinge.

"I won't take you to the hospital," I said when I understood. "But your blood is all over this car. If anyone analyzes it, they'll know you aren't like us."

Sweat dripped down his face. "What do you suggest we do?"

That question shook me. ISC deliberately designs Jagernauts to seem more than human, making them symbols to build morale among civilian populations. Althor hadn't felt much pain during the fight because his biomech web can release nano-meds, similar to morphine, which bind to selected receptor sites in his brain and block impulses that signal pain. His web will release only limited amounts of the med: too much, and he could become addicted or even overdose on it. Seeing him bleeding, at the end of his options, I realized he wasn't invincible. Strong and fast, yes, but also human. Vulnerable.

I got out of the car and ran to his side. As he opened his door and dragged out his legs, he motioned to Stevens' gun inside the car. "Bring that."

"I can't."

He struggled to his feet, holding onto the car. "Bring it."

"I hate guns. They killed my cousin; they almost killed you. I won't bring it."

"We need defense."

"I'll get us protection." I slid my arm around his waist, behind his handcuffed wrists. When he leaned on me, I almost fell; he was more than a foot taller and twice my weight. I nodded toward the freeway. "We're going down there."

I took him down the grassy slope that separated us from the freeway. Although it was only a few hundred yards, it felt like miles. We stumbled together, my heels sinking into the lawn on every step. Finally we reached a tunnel that ran under the freeway. It was dark inside, with names spray-painted on the walls. I took Althor halfway through, far enough from both ends so no one could see us. After trying most of Stevens' keys on the handcuffs, I found one that unlocked them. As soon as Althor was free, he clamped his hand over the bleeding hole in his left shoulder.

I put my arm around his waist again. "I know a place we can go."

He draped his good arm over my shoulders, leaning on me as we continued through the tunnel. It let us out in an empty lot surrounded by a chain-link fence. We picked our way through a clutter of junk: old tires, hamburger wrappings, twists of wire, broken bottles. I guided him over to a tear that split the fence from the ground up to about my height. Bending his head, he managed to squeeze through, but on the other side he had to grab the fence to hold himself upright.

I pushed through the tear. "Are you okay?"

Althor nodded. He spoke in another language, one different from anything I had heard him use before. My mind played games with it, filling in sounds here and there, changing inflections, making the alien phrase into Tzotzil words from the healing ceremony of a Zinacanteco shaman: *Ta htsoyan hutuk 'un:* I shall entrust my soul to you a little.

I swallowed, unsettled by the oddly familiar sound of the words. I slid my arm around his waist and we limped along an alley, our uneven steps taking us over hot pavement beneath a washed-out sky.

Finally we reached a house with a weathered porch. The screen door was closed but the inner door hung open, drooping on its hinges, suspended between the decision to stay attached or to clatter to the floor. Inside, the living room and its couch drowsed in the heat, also a table and bookshelf, and a rug made from what had once been bright cloth.

"Where is this?" Althor asked.

"Mario's family lives here." As he sank down on the couch, letting his head fall back against its beige top, I said, "You wait here."

Although the house was quiet, I knew Mario might be around if he hadn't found a job. I didn't see anyone until I reached the kitchen. Then I froze. Jake, my old boyfriend, was sitting at the table eating a sandwich and reading the newspaper. His real name was Joaquin Rojas, but years ago a teacher had stumbled on the pronunciation of Joaquin, making it sound like "Jaken." People started calling him Jake and the name stuck.

He stared at me with his sandwich halfway to his mouth. Then he smiled and spoke in Spanish. "Where did you come from?"

I thought of Althor in the next room. "Around."

His smile faded as he looked at my blouse. "Tina, is that *blood?*"

A footstep sounded behind me. Jake glanced over my shoulder and the last of his smile disappeared as fast as one of Nug's men running from the cops. He jumped out of his chair and lunged behind a counter. When he straightened up, he was holding a 12-gauge shotgun aimed at the door.

I spun around. Althor stood in the doorway, one hand clamped over his bleeding shoulder while he stared down the bore of the gun.

"Tina, get back," Jake said.

"Jake, don't." I went to the door. "This is Althor. He's with me."

Jake gave me an ugly look. "Since when did you hook up with Nug's garbage?"

I spoke quietly. "He killed Nug. And probably saved my life."

Jake didn't lower the gun. His hostility made granular smoke in the room, with confusion wafting behind it.

A voice came from across the kitchen, deep and rumbling in Spanish. "Who saved your life?"

I turned to see Mario in the doorway of an inner room. He walked into the kitchen, overwhelming it with the massive build that, when he had played football in high school, earned him the name *Destruidor.* Destroyer.

Mario considered Althor. Then he turned to me. "Why is he here?"

"We need your help," I said. "Please, Mario."

He motioned for me to come into the back room. I shook my head, afraid to leave Althor alone with Jake and the gun.

Mario turned to Althor and pointed at a chair. He spoke in English. "Sit down."

Althor sat, giving me a look that plainly said: *I hope you know what you're doing.*

Mario spoke to me in Spanish again, using his no-arguments voice. "I want to talk to you private."

I followed him into his mother's sewing room. When we were alone he regarded me with his protective look, the one that made me feel as if I were his little sister. "What did Nug and them do to you?"

"Nothing," I said. "Althor stopped them."

"Stopped them from doing what?"

"It was nothing, Mario."

"Don't tell me 'nothing.' What happened?"

I swallowed. "They were going to take me in their car. But Althor stopped them."

His face hardened. It was the same look he had worn the day we buried my cousin. Two days later the police found one of Nug's men left for dead in the sewer, the one we knew had fired the gun that killed Manuel. They never found enough evidence to convict anyone, but I had no doubts about who left him in that sewer. I had seen Mario's face.

He spoke quietly. "We'll take care of it."

"No more fighting. Please." When he didn't answer I said, "Promise me."

"I can't do that."

"Mario, please. Nug is *dead.* Who's next?" My voice caught. "You?"

He paused. "We'll see."

I knew that was the closest to a promise I would get. "I only came to ask you to help me and my boyfriend."

Mario scowled. "Who is this guy?"

"His name is Althor." I plunged ahead before he could ask more questions. "After he finished with Nug, the police arrested him. There was a fight. I stole a police car."

"You what?"

"I stole a police car."

"I thought you were smarter than that."

"We didn't have any choice."

"Why not?"

"Just believe me. We had to do it."

"This is one of the first places the cops will come asking questions." He shook his head. "I hide you here, they catch you."

"I just need a car. And your sister's red wig and a blanket."

"Why?"

I touched his arm. "Don't ask. Then when people come with questions you won't be lying if you say you don't know."

He frowned. "This Althor isn't one of us."

"Please, Mario. For me."

As he watched me, his face gentled. Finally he said, "There's keys to my car on the shelf out front. If the car disappears, if it gets ripped off, I don't know nothing about it."

I pulled down his head and kissed his cheek. "You're a prince."

He gave me a half smile, which for Mario is a lot. "If my car gets ripped off, where do you think I can find it again?"

"You remember that party we went to in Pasadena? Look on the street outside the apartment house there."

"Pasadena? What's in Pasadena?"

I went to the door. "I'll never forget you helped us." Then I ran to the kitchen. Jake still had his gun trained on Althor, but he had given him a dish towel to soak up the blood from his shoulder.

"Althor and I have to go," I said.

Jake didn't move. He wouldn't look at me, just kept watching Althor, his face impassive.

"Let them go," Mario said from the doorway.

Jake's hand clenched on the shotgun. But finally he lowered it.

I took Althor back to the living room and grabbed Mario's keys off the bookcase. "Go get in the green car at the end of the alley."

He glanced toward the kitchen. "It's not safe for you here."

"I'll be fine. I just have to get some things." I didn't like sending him out alone, bleeding, but I knew he was the one in danger if he stayed in the house.

Althor frowned, but he went. I ran into Rosa's bedroom. Her red wig was on a Styrofoam bust on her dressing table. I grabbed it and pulled a blanket off the bed. But as I turned to leave, Jake appeared, holding the shotgun down at his side. He stood in the doorway. "Tina, wait."

I stood in front of him, the wig and blanket clutched in my hands. "I can't."

"Are you all right?" He glanced at my blood-stained blouse and brought the shotgun to his shoulder. "If this guy hurt you—"

"He didn't." I wanted to push the gun away. That was why I stopped seeing Jake in the first place. After Manuel died, I couldn't bear the thought of losing anyone else I cared for to violence. Now, with Althor, everything seemed out of control.

"If this guy could finish Nug, you shouldn't be nowhere near him." Jake touched my cheek. "Let us help you."

"I have to do this myself." I pressed my palm against his chest. "But thank you, *hijo*."

His voice softened. "Tina . . ."

I shouldn't have touched him. It brought back that familiar sensation, that bond he and I had shared, what drew us together in the first place. It wasn't necessarily sexual; I felt it with Joshua, too, and it had been even stronger with my mother. Althor had finally given me a word for it. *Empath*.

"Jake, I—I'm sorry. But I have to go."

He watched me, a tangle of emotions hidden behind his stoic face. He wanted to tell me something. Something important. It hung around him in an iron-gray mist. But the words remained unspoken, indistinct shapes in the fog. Instead he said, "You need us, we're here. Just say the word."

I swallowed. "Thanks."

Outside, I found Althor lying in the backseat of the car. I handed him the blanket, then got in the front, scooting the seat up so I could reach the pedals. As he pulled the blanket over his body, I started the car. We backed out of the alley, into the afternoon's fading sunlight.

4

Storm Harbor

It was dark when I pulled onto the shoulder of the road. Trees rustled in the desert wind. Althor sat up, letting the blanket slide off his body. "Where is this?"

"Mount Wilson." I opened the door and a warm breeze wafted in. "There's a place you can hide. I'm going to get a friend. But if I bring you to him in Mario's car the police might trace us." I got out of the car. "Josh showed me a cave up here. Actually, just some rocks that fell together. No one else knows about it."

He climbed out of the car. "I don't think I want to meet more of your friends."

"You'll like Joshua fine."

Althor grunted. He was silent at first, as we picked our way through the pine trees and underbrush. After a while he said, "What is wrong here, that children arm themselves?" The faint moonlight leaking past the branches made his eyes look sunken in hollows.

I spoke softly. "Nug doesn't deserve your remorse. If he could have killed you, he would have done it in a second."

"That doesn't make what happened right." He paused. "And that boy at the house—why the gun?"

I walked for a while, thinking about my answer. "Mario, Jake, my cousin—they're fighting a war too. Like you. Except their enemy is one you never see, one that says you're nothing, nobody, you got nowhere to go, no place in the world."

"You're friend Jake isn't like the others."

"What do you mean?"

"Empath."

"You could feel it?" When Althor nodded, I said, "It doesn't stop the anger. It only makes it hurt more."

"Nothing stops it."

I swallowed. "Seems to me people have to stop killing each other. There must be a better way."

It was a moment before he answered. "I hope we find it."

I felt what he left unsaid. He feared none of us would, neither his people nor mine.

After a while Althor said, "Tell me a story. About your life. A story without anger."

"I'll tell you about my best day. My *quinceañera*."

"*Quince . . . ?* Fifteen?"

"That's right. It's for a girl's fifteenth birthday, a church ceremony and then a dance. Jake was my escort, my *chambelán de honor*. And Manuel—" I swallowed. "I don't have a father, so Manuel walked with me and my mother down the aisle, in church, for Mass. They were all there, my *corte de honor*. My *damas* and *chambelánes*."

"Ladies and lords?"

"That's right. Twenty-eight of them. Los Halcones and my girlfriends." I smiled. "And Joshua too. He looked pretty funny, with his yellow hair and blue eyes. And my mother, she made me a beautiful white dress. The guys wore tuxedos. Can you see it? Los Halcones in tuxedos with blue sashes, or whatever you call those things. Cummerbunds. They pooled their money so they could rent the outfits. I made them promise no weapons." My voice caught. "It was such a beautiful day. It seemed like Jake and I danced forever."

"Why your happiest day make you sad?"

"It's all gone. Everything."

His arm tightened around my shoulder.

I thought of my mother, how she had cried that day. I had felt it, tasted it. Smelled and heard it. She used to tell me ancient tales to explain the bond we shared. Her words painted luminous pictures of the *ceiba,* the axis that exists everywhere: a tree with its roots anchored Olontik, the Underworld, its trunk rising through the Middleworld where humans live, its branches stretching through all levels of the heavens. She believed our minds coexisted the same way the spiritual and material universes coexist through the tree that spans them.

My mother had been a *h'ilol,* a holy woman. She prayed for those whose sickness came from a loss of their inner soul, or from a witch practicing his craft against them. Few women held the title, yet no one doubted her claim to it. Her ability to heal had been legendary. She taught me the prayers, verses to Christ and the *kalvario,* the sacred mountain. She told me about the girl from Chamula who became the Morning Star in the sky, where she swept a path for the sun, just as assistants swept the earthen path for their *h'ilol* during a curing ceremony.

I can still hear her weaving the stories, her voice murmuring in the slumbering heat of a Chiapas night. It wasn't until years later that I realized the curing ceremonies were actually ancient Maya rituals blended with the Christianity brought to us by Spanish missionaries.

A rocky hill loomed on our left, half hidden by darkness and trees. We followed its sloping sides until I found a pile of rocks to one side of it. Two huge slabs stood leaning against each other, creating a small cave with a crack for its entrance. "Through here," I said.

Althor turned sideways and slid into the opening. Inside, he sank down to sit on the rocky floor, still holding the blood-soaked towel over his shoulder. Moonlight silvered him like liquid metal over human metal.

I dropped down next to him. "Are you okay?"

"Yes."

I knew he was lying. "I'll be back as soon as I can."

"Tina—"

"Yes?"

"You will come back?"

That's when it hit me just how much he had to trust me. This was far different from leaving him alone in my apartment. He knew almost nothing about me except that I had violent friends. Yet he had to believe I would bring help, and a safe place for him to recover. If I didn't, he would probably die.

"I'll come back," I said. "I swear it."

I left the cave and ran, stumbling in my heels, back to the car.

It felt as if it took forever to reach Pasadena. After I parked on the street where I had told Mario I would leave the car, I hid the wig and blanket in the trunk. Then I looked around. I had been to Pasadena twice before, once at a party and once last summer to help Joshua move into his dorm.

A tower rose above the houses, its windows lit up like rectangular yellow eyes in the night. I was pretty sure it was the building Joshua had called Milikan Library. I pulled off my shoes and ran toward it, through the streets.

I came out on a lawn in front of a campus. I thought it was Caltech, but nothing looked familiar. Then I remembered. Joshua's dorm was behind the library. I ran across the lawns, past a guy with long hair who stared as if I came from outer space. The dorms were a cluster of Spanish-style buildings surrounded by lawns. As I took the steps in Blacker House two at a time, one thought kept hammering me: What if Joshua wasn't in?

The second floor was painted black, with flames on the walls. Joshua once told me "flaming" meant flunking out of Caltech, and reasons why people flamed were hidden in the wall paintings. I ran past them to room 52 and pounded on it.

The door opened and Joshua stood there, dressed in T-shirt and jeans, tousled curls falling into his eyes. "Tina!" A grin spread across his face. "What are you doing here?"

I took a breath. "I need your help."

He pulled me inside and closed the door. "What's wrong?"

"A friend of mine is hurt. I was hoping he could stay here."

He regarded me for a moment. "All right."

I almost closed my eyes with gratitude. Just like that. It was

Joshua's way. After everything that had happened to him, he didn't trust easily. He chose his friends with care, but once you were among them he was fiercely loyal.

"Do you have a car?" he asked.

"We can't use it. I'll explain later."

He switched off his desk lamp. A book lay open there, and papers covered with equations were scattered everywhere. Glancing at me, he said, "You want some tennis shoes? You better wear a sweater too."

I looked down. I was still holding my shoes and blood covered my blouse. "All right."

His sweater hung around my hips and his shoes slipped off my feet. I crumpled a stocking into each heel to fill the space. Then we went down the hall, past dismantled pieces of electronic equipment, to another room. On its door, the initials *DEI* were made out of old computer chips. As Joshua knocked, I hung back in the shadows.

A guy holding a half-eaten Milky Way bar and wearing a gray T-shirt that said *Confederation, 44th World Science Fiction Convention* opened the door. "Hi. What's up?"

"Daniel, I was wondering if I could borrow your Jeep," Joshua said.

"What for—" He stopped when he saw me. When he realized he was staring, he turned back to Joshua. "Yeah, sure. Just a second." He vanished into his room and reappeared with a set of keys. "Keep it as late as you want."

"Thanks," Joshua said. Then we took off.

The Jeep was open, and as we drove the wind threw my hair around my body. I told Joshua everything, except for letting him believe Althor came from Fresno. I hoped I hadn't made a mistake, hiding Althor on the mountain. Thinking of him alone and injured made the minutes drag out endlessly.

At Mount Wilson, Joshua stepped on the gas. When he finally pulled off the road, I jumped out and ran toward the woods.

"Tina, wait." He ran after me and caught up in a few strides.

We made our way through brush and scraggly trees. They threw shadows across our path, pools of black in the night's darkness. Wind whispered in our hair. The walk seemed to take longer than before, until I became convinced we had passed the cave.

Then I caught sight of the two stones. We ran over and eased ourselves between them, into the hidden cavity. Joshua's flashlight played over the walls—and across Althor's body. He lay on his back on the ground, still and silent.

I knelt next to him, my heart racing. "Althor?"

He didn't answer, and my heart jumped a mile. "Can you hear me?" I asked.

No answer.

"Althor!"

This time his lips moved, words I couldn't hear.

Relief swept over me. "*¿Qué, hijo?*"

"Took out the bullet," he mumbled. "With knife."

That's when I saw it, the bloodied remains of a bullet lying by his arm. I couldn't believe he cut it out of his own body. I didn't see how he stayed conscious. If he lost any more blood, he would be in serious trouble. Even if we could have gone to a hospital, no blood type on 1987 Earth would have been compatible with his.

Joshua knelt next to me. "We have to get him to an emergency room. No matter what he's done, it's better the police catch him than he bleed to death."

"We can't." I laid my hand on his arm. "Trust me. Please. I can't turn to anyone else."

He just looked at me, until I wondered if I had pushed our friendship further than even our strong bond could stretch. Then he exhaled. "Moving him will be hard. He's so big."

I squeezed his arm gratefully. "He can walk."

Althor opened his eyes, his shimmering inner lids glinting in the moonlight as they rolled up. "Can you—clean the wounds?"

Joshua nodded. "We brought supplies."

I touched Althor's forehead. Words flashed in my mind, packets from the dense flow of data along the pathways of his augmented brain. *Connection established. Large coupling constant.*

Coupling. It meant mathematical intercourse, not human. Althor and I were both Kyles, which meant the wavefunctions of our brains coupled strongly, oscillating like chaotic breakers on the neural shores of our minds. Every system of particles can be described by a wavefunction, including the brain. His KEB stimulated thousands of molecular sites on my KAB, millions, even billions. Had he been a less powerful Kyle, the link he set up with me that night could have crippled him, creating massive neural discharges that led to a tonic-clonic attack, like an epileptic grand mal seizure. But Althor took it easily.

I was there, in the midst of a struggle. He was fighting his autonomic system, his heart, lungs, intestines, glands, other internal organs, smooth muscles, blood and lymph vessels. His troops were nano-meds specialized to aid tissue repairs. He regulated blood flow, rushed nutrients where they were needed, changed chemical concentrations, all in a race to outrun the death that chased him through his evaporating consciousness. When we linked, his mind swelled back to alertness like a dry sponge expanding with water, beads of the sparkling liquid jumping into the air and raining down again.

Mitosis. Cells dividing; prophase, metaphase, anaphase, telophase. Cells splitting: 1,2,4,8. Tissue growing. Blood vessels forming. Increase blood flow. 64,128,256. White blood cells; antibodies; infection. Send lymphocytes. Build fibrin. Clot blood. Parenchymal cells: prophase, metaphase, anaphase, telophase. 16384,32768,65536. Bleeding, stroma, bleeding, fibrosis, bleeding, bleeding . . .

"Tina?"

The voice came from far away.

"Tina? What's wrong?"

I opened my eyes. Joshua was kneeling in front of me, his hands on my shoulders. "What happened to you?" he asked.

"I was with Althor." Why hadn't Joshua opened his pack? It still lay closed on the cave floor. "We have to clean him up and bandage him."

"I did. I've been working for almost an hour. The two of you have been in a trance."

I stared at him. Then I looked at Althor. He opened his eyes and he mouthed two words: *Thank you.*

As we drove through Caltech, Althor sat next to me, slumped in the backseat of the Jeep. Joshua pulled into the parking lot outside the Athenaeum, near Blacker House. The lot was empty except for a few cars, chromed beasts sleeping in the dark.

With Joshua and me supporting him, Althor climbed out of the Jeep and limped across the lawn between the lot and the dormitories, what Joshua called the south house complex. We crossed a Spanish-style courtyard to a staircase in Blacker House. With our support, Althor slowly climbed the stairs. The whole time I was straining to hear voices or footsteps, warnings that someone was coming, a student happening on us out of the night.

We reached the second floor without being discovered. At Joshua's room, Althor slumped against the wall. Joshua worked the combination lock on his door, his relief making soap-bubble mists of tangerine light. We had made it.

A door down the hall opened and Daniel stepped out.

Joshua froze. "Hey."

Daniel glanced at Althor. "Josh, can I talk to you?"

Joshua turned to me. "Take him inside." Then he headed down the hall to Daniel.

Uneasy, I took Althor inside and closed the door. It was a single room, cluttered with bits and pieces of lab equipment. A bed stood against the far wall under a window with blue curtains. Shelves were on the left, crammed with books, and the right wall had a sink and cabinets built into it. A computer sat on the desk, along with a haphazard pile of books and papers. Posters of rock stars and scientists covered the walls.

I helped Althor to the bed. As he lay down, I felt sleep drop over him like a heavy blanket cut from the night sky. I sat next to him, wondering what Joshua was doing.

Several moments later the door opened and Joshua came in with Daniel. They both looked grim.

"What's wrong?" I asked.

Daniel closed the door, holding the knob as if to make sure he could make a fast exit. Joshua pulled a chair over to the bed and sat facing me. But his attention was on Althor.

"Is he asleep?" Joshua asked.

"Out cold," I said.

Joshua took a breath. "Daniel saw police sketches of you and Althor in this evening's paper, down in the lounge. The police say Althor's name is Ray Kolvich, that he broke out of San Quentin yesterday, and that he's a PCP addict."

I silently swore. "They're lying."

"Tina, he *killed* Matt Kugelmann."

"It was self-defense."

"Then why can't you take him to a hospital?"

"You wouldn't believe me if I told you."

Daniel spoke. "You better start telling if you don't want us to call the police."

"You know I've always trusted you," Joshua said. "But this— I don't know what to say."

I pushed my hand through my hair. "You know that test plane they found this morning?"

"I heard about it," Joshua said.

"Well, it's not a plane. It's Althor's starship."

"Yeah, right," Daniel said. "This isn't a joke."

"Do you see me laughing?" I asked.

"Is that what he told you?" Joshua asked.

"Yes."

"And you believed him?"

"For good reasons," I said. "Besides, Josh, you saw his eyes."

"I saw something. But it was too dark to tell much."

Although I disliked waking Althor, our choices were limited. I shook his shoulder, but he didn't respond. I tried again. "Althor?"

This time his lashes lifted, leaving a gold shimmer. As Joshua and Daniel watched, the shimmer retracted like a receding wave on a beach.

"Cool," Daniel said. Then he seemed to mentally shake himself. "But it proves nothing."

Joshua glanced at me. "You have to admit, it's probably a birth defect."

Regardless of their outward resistance, I knew they must have had doubts about the news report. Otherwise, they would never have given me a chance to explain, nor would either have spoken with Althor listening. "Think about it," I said. "How could any normal man go through what's happened to him and still be in such good shape?"

"I don't know," Joshua said. "But there must be a rational explanation."

An idea came to me. "I need a pair of scissors."

Joshua went to his desk and came back with scissors. "What are you going to do?"

"Watch."

The bandage went all the way around Althor's body, from below his waist to his chest. I felt around on the right side above his hip. Fortunately the bullet wound was on the opposite side. When I found the dent that marked his transcom socket, I cut away a small square and prodded the skin. Nothing happened.

Althor lifted his hand and pressed his side, fingertips pushing the skin in a circle. A membrane pulled back and the transcom slid out into his hand, leaving a small opening in his body lined with glimmering gold skin.

Daniel leaned closer. "Hey."

"What is that?" Joshua said.

Althor held the transcom in his palm and extended it toward him. "Computer."

As we watched, it changed from a rounded gold box to the hard-edged device with glowing squares. Then Althor brought it back to his waist. He pushed it inside the socket and it molded itself to fit, changing color to blend with his skin. The membrane slid back into place.

"Holy shit," Joshua said.

"That thing must have some kind of nanotech," Daniel said. "Something that lets it alter its composition on a molecular level." He snapped his fingers. "It responds to a change in environment, right? Take it out of your body and that activates its transformation."

"That's right," Althor said.

"The only way you could have a socket there is if your internal organs have been moved out of the way," Joshua said. "And that membrane looks like it's alive."

"Yes," Althor said.

"That kind of nanotech doesn't exist," Daniel said. "Neither does the medical knowledge needed to put a system like that into your body. Not that I've heard of."

I regarded them. "Now do you see?"

Daniel blew out a gust of air. "My mother works at Yeager. She says the shuttle retrieved something called the F-29, a hypersonic test plane that malfunctioned."

"How would she know otherwise?" Joshua said. "Thousands of people work at Yeager. Probably only a handful saw what the shuttle brought down."

My hope leapt. "Daniel, could you get us onto the base?"

He snorted. "Even if I believed your story, which I don't, and even if I could get you a pass, which I can't, there's no way I would do it."

I wasn't really surprised. But I knew it wasn't an F-29 they had found. I rubbed my eyes, trying to clear my mind. "Josh, can we finish this tomorrow? We really need to sleep."

He nodded. "I have an extra blanket in the closet."

"You're going to let them stay?" Daniel asked.

"We can't move him," Joshua said. "He'll start to bleed again."

"Do you know what aiding and abetting means?" Daniel said. "You let them stay, you're committing a crime. If I don't say anything that makes me an accessory."

I concentrated on Daniel, trying to feel what made him tick.

Then I got up and went to him. "Just suppose Althor is telling the truth. Think about it. You're the one who has him to yourself, a man who could answer all those questions you have about space, maybe even make your dreams about the stars come true."

"Don't lay that on me," he said.

"You won't ever have this chance again."

"You're nuts if you believe him."

"You're afraid."

"That's right," he said. "Of being thrown in jail."

"If you don't tell anyone he's here, how will they know?"

"Just because I don't tell anyone doesn't mean they won't find out."

I shrugged. "Tell them we forced you to help us by holding Joshua hostage."

"Why me?" Joshua asked.

Daniel glanced at him. "You know—if I said that, it could keep us from getting into trouble if someone did find out."

"Daniel, just give us a few days," I said.

He looked from me to Joshua. "You trust her?"

"Always," Joshua said. "With my life."

At first I didn't know what he meant. Then an image came into my mind, a memory that wasn't mine: Nug and his men, lined up with rifles. Nug shouted orders like a mock general, making them twirl their guns and aim them at me. It was eerie, because I had never experienced what I was "remembering." Yet I could feel the cords that bound my wrists—

Joshua inhaled and the image cut off, replaced by another. This scene I recognized: I was viewing it from the couch in Mario's front room. All of Los Halcones was there, even Manuel. They lounged against the wall or sat in chairs, some cleaning weapons.

Finally I understood. I was seeing Joshua's memories. I even saw myself, Tina, talking to Mario with an ease that stunned Joshua, as if Mario were a beloved older brother instead of a gang leader. Protection. I wanted them to protect Joshua. And in the end, incredibly, they agreed to do it.

As the image faded, Joshua ran his hand through his hair. Although I had known he was uncomfortable that day I took him to Mario's, I had never realized he felt he was trusting his life to me.

Daniel was watching him closely. Joshua just shook his head. None of us needed special brain organs to interpret that: leave it alone.

So instead Daniel turned to me. "You have two days to convince me. If you don't, we go to the police."

Thank you, God, I thought. "Two days," I said. "Deal."

5

Jagernaut Modes

. . . build new tissue cells. Increase blood flow. New blood vessels—
"Wake up!"

I tried to ignore the shaking and the voice, but neither would stop. Finally I eased out of Althor's mind. He let go as well and sank into a true sleep.

I opened my eyes. Joshua was kneeling over me on the bed, shaking my shoulders.

"Josh, don't." My voice vibrated with his motion.

"Thank God." He let go of me and settled back on his heels.

Late-afternoon sunshine slanted through the window, laying rectangles of buttery light across the bed. I sat up, squinting in the brightness. "What time is it?"

"Almost five o'clock. I was starting to get worried. I couldn't wake either of you up." He motioned at his desk. "I brought you lunch hours ago.

As soon as I saw the cafeteria tray heaped with food, my mouth watered. My next thought was that if someone my size was so hungry, Althor must be starving.

I nudged Althor's shoulder. "*¿Puedes oir me, Leon Dormido?*"
No reaction.

I shook him gently. With his wounds, I didn't dare do it any harder. "Althor?"

Still no reaction.

"Maybe it would help if we sat him up," Joshua said.

"It's worth a try." Kneeling side by side on the bed, we pulled him into a sitting position. "Althor," I said. "Wake up."

No response.

Joshua considered him. Then he lightly slapped his face.

Nothing.

Joshua slapped harder. When Althor still didn't respond, Joshua hit him agai—

Althor's hand shot out and grabbed Joshua's wrist. His outer eyelids snapped open and he shoved Joshua away, sending him flying off the end of the bed.

"¡Hola!" I grabbed Althor's arm. "It's okay. We just wanted you to wake up."

His head swiveled to me. Gold shields covered his eyes. Then he slumped in my arms. He was too heavy to hold upright and we both fell down on the bed with a thump.

Joshua picked himself up off the floor. "Is he awake?"

"I'm not sure." I got up on my knees and leaned over Althor. "Can you hear me?"

His inner lids lifted halfway, making him look like a stoned turtle.

"I think this is the best we're going to get," I said. "Want to try feeding him?"

"Okay." I had to struggle not to grab all the food for myself.

Joshua smiled. "I brought enough for an army. You eat. I'll take care of him."

I could have kissed him. "Thanks."

He got the tray and set it on the bed. As he sat next to Althor's head, I took a tortilla off the tray and held it dangling between my thumb and index finger. "What is this?"

He picked up a glass of orange juice. "You know what that is."

"A big potato chip?"

Joshua tilted the juice to Althor's lips. "You don't approve of our tortillas?"

"No one makes them like my mother." Hers had been big and soft, cooked just right on her *comal*, a round metal plate she propped up over the fire on two old pots and a rock. I could still see her patting the maize dough back and forth, around and around. I had loved that sound. For the first eight years of my life, I had heard it everywhere in the early mornings, every day.

Now it was gone.

I put the tortilla down and took a sandwich instead.

When Althor didn't respond, Joshua pushed open his mouth and dribbled juice into it. At first nothing happened. Suddenly Althor sputtered, splattering drops everywhere. As he drank, his inner lids slid down, turning his face into a mask. After he finished, Joshua took away the glass, turned back to the tray—and froze, staring at the bed.

I stopped eating. "What's wrong?"

He pointed at Althor's waist. "Look."

Althor had bent his arm at the elbow and lifted his hand off the bed. It did look odd, poised in the air, but I doubted that was what startled Joshua. Althor's hand had hinged lengthwise down the center so that his middle and index fingers lay flat against his ring finger and little finger. Actually, "little" finger is wrong; the four digits were almost the same size. With his hand closed they acted like two sets of opposing thumbs, while his real thumb hung free in the air.

His hand moved to the tray and closed around an apple. He raised it to his mouth and ate it, bite by mechanical bite. When he finished, he lowered his arm until his elbow rested on the bed. Then he unhinged his hand, making a V-shape.

Joshua blinked. "What should we do?"

"Maybe he's still hungry." I gave him another apple.

Althor ate four apples, a bowl of squash, and some creamed corn. He wouldn't touch the hamburger. Except for his chewing and moving arm, he lay still the entire time, flat on his back. When he finished, he lowered his arm again and his hand relaxed open. His outer lids closed. Within seconds he was asleep.

"Does he always act like that?" Joshua asked.

"I don't know. I don't think so."

"What if our food makes him sick?"

"He's never said anything about it being a problem."

Joshua hesitated. "You know, you sound different."

"Different how?"

"I'm not sure." He paused. "Your English is better."

I shrugged. "I practice all the time."

"I guess that's it."

We left it at that. Neither of us had any way then to know what was actually happening to my brain.

. . . water cup. Beads of moisture cling to its outer surface, poised to slide down the smooth sides, surfaces swirling with clouds, blue, gray, white, swirling, swirling. A hollow cup, a woman riding a centaur with six legs, four to stand on, two that paw the air . . . Instead of a head, a spout where water pours out, cool and delicious, running in a glistening stream, clear, sparkling . . .

I opened my eyes and looked at the ceiling. The image of the cup stayed vivid in my mind instead of fading, as my dreams usually did. I wasn't thirsty, but I kept seeing cool water pour out of that spout.

Early morning sunshine lightened the room. I had slept on the floor because the bed was too cramped. Joshua had given me a T-shirt to wear last night so I could wash my blood-soaked clothes in his sink. He was already gone, but he had put a blanket over me and left a note with his schedule for the day. I knew he had left to give us privacy; usually he studied all night and slept late. On the bed—

On the bed Althor lay staring at me. He didn't say a word, but as soon as I saw him I knew what he wanted. I got up and went to the cabinets. A quick search turned up a battered cup made from clear orange plastic. I filled it with water and brought it over. He drank it in seconds. Then he lay down again and let out a long breath.

I sat next to him, cross-legged on the bed. "How do you feel?"

"Better." He glanced around the room. "Where are your friends?"

"Studying. Joshua will be back this evening."

Althor nodded and closed his eyes. We had taken off his

clothes to let him sleep more comfortably, and the blanket covered him from the waist down, like a blue stretch of sky. Sunshine filtered through the curtains, drawing gleams from his skin. An old scar showed on his arm and another slashed across his chest. At the time, I had no idea how easy they were to remove. He never bothered because he didn't care.

He looked beautiful to me, scars and all. Sexy too, still sleepy and warm in bed. Leaning over him, with my hands on either side of his shoulders, I kissed him.

His lids lifted, both inner and outer. Then he pushed me away.

I flushed. Had I broken a taboo I didn't know about? Or maybe he just didn't feel like being kissed. He had barely made it back from the edge of death and here I was coming on to him.

But then he said, "The soldier from Troy. We need it, yes?"

"You brought one?"

"Several." He hinged his hand around my T-shirt and tugged at it until I raised my arms. After he pulled it off, I lowered my arms and stared at my hands in my lap, wearing nothing but my bracelet, self-conscious at being undressed in front of him in broad daylight.

He spoke softly. "You're a Raylican goddess." When I looked up, he smiled. "There is an ancient race, almost extinct. You look like their fire goddess." He cupped his hand under my breast and spoke in his other language, the one he had used just before we reached Mario's house, that sounded so familiar.

"What language is that?" I asked.

"Iotic. It's ancient. Few people speak it now."

"How do you know it?"

"My grandmother descended from the Raylicans." He drew me down on the bed, wrapping his arms around me. When I pressed against his side, he lifted the blanket and slid me on top of him. He felt warm and solid. I lifted my head to kiss him—

And saw his face.

He was staring at the ceiling with his inner lids down, making his eyes into shields. It didn't look like the face of a living man. I was making love to a machine.

I rolled off him and sat up fast, holding the blanket around my body. His head turned to me like a mechanized part swiveling on ball bearings. "We have not completed the call." His voice was flat, a dry plain with tumbleweed blowing across it. Reaching out, he curved his arm around my waist.

"No!" I pushed him away. "Don't touch me."

His arm returned to his side. "Why not?"

"Where is Althor?"

"I am Althor."

"I mean the real Althor. The man."

"I am not a man."

I pulled the blanket tighter around my body. "You aren't. But he is."

"I am him."

"Why do you sound different? You're like a machine."

"I am a machine."

"Can't you let Althor out again?"

"I am Althor. How do I make it clear? This is a mode, an incomplete representation of my emotive-mechanical interface. What you call the 'real' Althor is another mode, one currently inoperative." Flatly he said, "This is what I am. If you don't want this part of me, don't ask for anything else."

Just like that. Take all of me or nothing. Perhaps it says something about my life then, that it was easier for me to deal with his killing Nug than with his being a machine. As much as his capacity for violence shook me, I understood it. This was too alien.

But I asked him to accept me as I was: a nobody. As far as I knew, he had no reason to see me otherwise. It seemed hypocritical to expect less from myself than I did from him.

I hesitated. "If we do this—would I be making love to your other mode too?"

"A mode is not a different personality."

"So if I'm here with you, I'm with the Althor I know better?"

"Yes."

I placed my hand against his chest. He felt human. I leaned over him and looked at his face, the shimmering pools of his eyes. You can at least try, I told myself. If you can't handle it, stop.

I lay down and kissed his chest. He moved his hands along my back in measured, mechanized strokes. Then he said, "Resume."

Resume? I didn't have time to ask what it meant. Instead of brushing his lips over my face, he pushed open my mouth and kissed me straight on, too hard, as if he hadn't calibrated the force. Then he rolled over on top of me, bringing us to the edge of the bed. He pulled the condom out of his clothes on the floor and sat up, straddling my hips with his knees while he examined the foil packet.

I couldn't stop staring at him. It was mesmerizing, like seeing someone move by remote control. He was, in a sense; his biochips were directing the hydraulics that controlled his motion. He was a machine, one sensuously beautiful, but still a machine.

"Althor?" I said.

He looked up. "Yes?"

"When you're like this, will you still feel—you know. Making love?"

"Yes." He opened the packet. "There is no reason for my physical sensations to cease because my emotive-mechanical interface is degraded."

I almost laughed. Of all the things I might have imagined about my first lover, I would never have come up with a machine that discussed emotive-mechanical interfaces while putting on a condom.

He rolled it on smooth and slow, latex on gold. I pushed up on my elbows, watching. Who could have guessed it could look so erotic? I cupped my hand around his balls, wondering if he would feel the way he looked, like flexible gold. He didn't. He felt human. Warm and alive.

This time when he lowered himself on me, it was suffocating, not so much because of his size, but because my mind created such strong metallic sensations out of this mode.

Althor pushed up on his elbows. "I am too heavy." He said it as if it were a datum he added to memory storage.

I wondered how he knew. "Can you pick up my emotions in this mode?"

"Yes." He kissed me, once, twice, again, and again, sampling a data set. "I cannot make myself weigh less, however."

"It's okay. You don't have to."

He let himself down again, holding my arms so hard it hurt. I stiffened, and he loosened his grip. Although I didn't realize it then, the damage to his web had caused him to assign incorrect values to data that specified how tightly he could safely hold someone my size. When his systems detected my tension, they recalibrated the numbers.

He rubbed his thumbs over my breasts, moved his hands to my waist, then lower, to my legs. I expected him to do what he wanted, fast and efficient, like a machine. But when he entered, it hurt less than before. I hadn't realized that with biochips controlling his actions, he could calibrate to whatever level of gentleness or urgency he wanted. I began to relax, hugging him tight. His muscles flexed as he moved, his body going back and forth with an exact, unvarying frequency.

Upload, he thought. Metallic sensations flowed through my mind. He touched my cheek. *Download?*

"I don't know how," I said. Before it had just happened. I put my lips against his ear. "Kiss me more. The way you do it, good and hard, like you can't get enough."

And kiss me he did, sampling again, his tongue taking data to fill a new array. I felt how this mode interpreted pleasure, with a hard edge that gripped like a vise. Knowing a man wants you that intensely may be the greatest aphrodisiac ever to exist, far more effective than any chemically produced love potion.

Words flashed in my mind. *Link opened.*

That was when my sensory responses went into overdrive. My brain's tendency to tangle empathic and sensory input strengthens with both the intensity and proximity of the people whose moods I experience. Althor flooded me with his metallic river. It closed around, blanketing my perceptions until I couldn't sense anything else. Suffocating, *I was suffocating—*

Wait! My fingers dug into his back. *It's too much.*

Carrier attenuated, he thought.

The sensations receded to a bearable level and he slowed down, moving with rigid control. Closing my eyes, I tried to feel only him, the living man. But he didn't move like a man. He moved like a well-coordinated machine.

Waiting. The word entered my mind like a prompt.

Waiting? I thought.

Waiting, the prompt came again. He continued with his slow, measured strokes.

Waiting for what? I thought.

Suspend release. His tension built like pressure in an airlock, bowing out the doors.

What does suspend release mean? I asked.

He exhaled in a small explosion of air. *Overriding,* he thought. His movements surged, fast and hard again. I hung on, letting his river sweep me with it this time. He pushed his arm under my waist and lifted me off the bed, pressing us tightly together as we moved. His sweat dripped down and moisture slicked back and forth between our bodies. When his climax broke over us, his muscles spasmed and we both went rigid with the blunt intensity of it.

Gradually the river receded. His grip loosened and we sank back into the bed, he lying with his cheek against the top of my head. Eventually, when our breathing quieted, he slid off me and lay against my side. His body felt warm. Human. As long as I didn't see his face, I could believe a man lay next to me rather than a machine.

"Return," he said.

I opened my eyes. "What?"

He didn't answer. He was fast asleep.

I closed my eyes and my mind wandered. Fragments of his

earlier words drifted in my mind, words from an ancient tongue of his ancestors: *Shibalank, Shibalan* . . .

I opened my eyes. Sunlight still brightened the room, but it had lost its new-morning quality. Distant sounds of people talking came from outside. Glancing at the wall clock, I saw we had slept for several hours and still had a few more before Joshua was due back.

As I moved, Althor's outer lids opened. I propped myself up on my elbow. "Are you all right now?"

"I am discontinuing." He sounded more like a machine than before.

"What's wrong?" I asked.

"My functions are degrading."

"You mean you can't heal yourself anymore?"

"No." His eyes closed. "Access denied."

"What?"

He opened his eyes, this time both inner and outer lids. His face relaxed and his voice rumbled with a heavy accent, familiar and human. "Access denied. This means you ask a question I can't answer."

Relief swept over me. "You're back."

He smiled. "I never went away."

"Does that bother you, that we made love while you were . . . him."

"Him is me. So no, this doesn't bother me."

"Do you remember it all?

"Every second." He grinned. "I can play it back as often as I want."

I flushed. "You're kidding."

"Not at all." More quietly he said, "My sorry if it unsettles. Usually my interface with humans isn't so obvious."

"Aren't you human at all?"

He ran his hand along my side. "I feel what any man feels. The biomech web doesn't take away my humanity. It adds to it."

"Were you born this way? I mean with biomech."

His emotions withdrew like a light switching off. "No."

"Did I say something wrong?"

It was a moment before he answered. "I have—unpleasant memories associated with it." In a more normal voice he said, "I wasn't born with the web, but some of my modifications are at the germ level. The intent is that I pass them to my children." He shrugged. "My doctors don't know if it will work. I'm the first they've tried it on."

I stared at him. "That's horrible. How could they experiment on you?"

"Someone had to be first. I am a good test case."

"No one has a right to make you a 'test case.' "

"Doesn't it occur to you that maybe I want this? That it fixes problems I don't want passed to my children?"

Of course. His anemia. His hands. Other problems too, ones I didn't know about then. "I didn't realize."

He exhaled. "I am maybe too sensitive about it. Or so Ragnar tells me."

"You mean the admiral?"

"Yes. He was my doctor, a brilliant biomech surgeon, head of the team that built my web. When I was small, he helped me learn to use it." Althor smiled. "He used to walk with me while I was learning to use my legs. We talked about so much."

His description puzzled me. I touched the socket in his wrist. "I thought these linked you to your Jag."

"They do."

"Your military wires children to warships?"

Althor stiffened. "Of course not. Jagernauts get their biomech as adults, just before they receive their commission."

It still didn't make sense. But I could tell that if I pushed, it would alienate him. So instead I said, "What did you mean, that you were discontinuing?"

"My web—it's part of the Jag's computer. I am—how to say it? The Jag's web, it comes apart. Because they tamper with it. If its web fails, mine might also. I keep flipping in and out of different modes, probably many more than you realize. The last was more obvious, but others have happened too. Both my web and the Jag did an automatic shutdown when we were cut off, but the tampering still affects me. It's disorienting."

It sounded much worse than disorienting. "Are you going to be all right?"

"I don't know. I need my ship."

"What did you mean earlier when you said we hadn't 'completed the call'?"

"The mod call," he said. "You know what is a subroutine call in software?"

"We studied it some in school."

"A mod call is more sophisticated, but the basic idea is the same."

I gaped at him. "You mean, for you making love is a *subroutine call?*"

"Yes."

"Althor, do you have any idea how kinky that sounds?"

"Kinky?" He smiled. "This means bent?"

"This means weird."

"It is me, Tina. It will never change." He spoke awkwardly. "But you never agreed to the link. My sorry for that. I think the Jag recognizes you as a node in its web now. It may even be augmenting your mind, expanding your knowledge base and vocabulary."

An image of myself with a machine face jarred my thoughts. I stared at my hands. They looked human. They *were* human. If anything, being with Althor made me feel more human, not less.

He touched my breast, folding his hand around it. My body responded immediately, wanting him. But when he tried to pull me down, I resisted. I kept seeing him staring at the ceiling with half-open eyes, a computer having sex.

He spoke softly. "Am I really so repugnant to you?"

"Althor, no." How could he be so empathic and yet also be a machine?

As we made love again, the memory of his machine eyes stayed in my mind. I wondered how long he would remain human.

6

Heather Rose

The only sound in Joshua's room was the television murmuring in the background with a test of the Emergency Broadcast System. Althor sat on the edge of the bed, dressed again, bending and relaxing his arm, the one with the injured shoulder.

The grate of someone doing the combination lock sounded. As the door opened, I jumped up from my chair.

Joshua came in and smiled. "It's just me." He locked the door, then turned to watch Althor. I wasn't surprised to see Joshua's smile fade; it was one thing to have Althor passed out in his room, helpless; it was another to have him wide awake and restless.

"Where is your friend Daniel?" Althor asked.

"He'll be here soon," Joshua said. "He's checking some things."

"Checking what?" Althor asked.

"Yeager Test Cen—"

Althor stood up. "You contacted the *base?*"

Joshua stepped backward, against the door, his face paling.

Althor, I thought. I made an image in my mind of Nug and his men, dressed much the way Althor was dressed, tying Joshua up and playing firing squad with him. I made another picture, one of Joshua tending to Althor while he had been unconscious.

Althor glanced at me. Then he sat on the bed and spoke in a quieter voice. "Why did Daniel contact the base?"

Color came back into Joshua's face. "He called his mother."

"Won't this make her suspicious?"

Joshua smiled. "You mean, that her son and his buddies have an alien stashed in their dorm?"

Althor's forehead furrowed. After a moment, Joshua flushed. "I was kidding." When Althor kept staring at him, Joshua said, "I meant she wouldn't think anything of it. Daniel always talks the business with his parents. They're systems engineers, and he's majoring in computer science. If he bugs his mom about what's going on at her work, she'll just think he's being his usual self."

Althor spoke slowly. "His parents work with web systems?"

"Josh, don't talk so fast," I said. "And don't use so much slang. He's having trouble understanding you."

"Is that what's wrong?" Joshua looked relieved. "Sure."

Another drone came out of the television, rising above the mumbling talk we had been ignoring. Joshua went over and switched off the set. "If I hear 'This is only a test' one more time, I'm going to break something. You'd think we're about to go to war."

"Maybe we are," I said. "With that coup ousting Gorbachev and the new Russian government making noises about FSA spy planes, it's no wonder they're scared."

Joshua walked over me. "It doesn't make sense, starting up the Cold War again."

Althor spoke. "They may know your air force has more than a test plane at Yeager. If they don't get the technology, it will obliterate any balance of power." He shrugged. "Or maybe your governments are working together, setting up a cover. They have good reason to believe they have far worse to prepare for than planetary war."

"Tina said you bled all over that police car," Joshua said.

Althor nodded. "They must know by now I'm not human."

A knock sounded on the door. Joshua jumped, then raised his voice. "Who is it?"

"Daniel," a voice said.

Joshua let him in and locked up again. "Did you talk to your mother?"

"She still says it's a plane."

"You found out nothing?" Althor asked.

"Look, I'm sorry," Daniel said. "But I can't help you. Maybe I do dream about the stars, like Tina said. But what's happening in this country right now is nobody's fairy tale."

"I'm not here in any military capacity," Althor said. "I just want to get my ship and leave with Tina."

Someone outside started doing the combination lock. We all had one second to panic before the door opened.

A girl stood there. She was a few years older than Joshua, a gangly student with green eyes, wire-rimmed glasses, and a glorious mane of tawny hair that fell in waves down her back.

She blinked at us. Then she turned to Joshua. "Do I have the wrong day?"

"Oh shit," Joshua said. "I forgot." He pulled her inside. "Some—uh—friends came to visit." He motioned to the girl. "This is Heather, everyone. Heather Rose MacDane. She helps me with my calculus."

In different circumstances, that would have made me smile. I had never known Joshua to need help with his homework. He was so shy he had never had a girlfriend.

Heather turned to Joshua. "We can study later if you want."

"Yeah. Okay." He looked like a cat jumping from a firecracker.

"Can you help me carry some boxes up the stairs?" she asked. "I left them in the courtyard."

"Oh. Yeah. Sure." Joshua glanced at me. "I'll be right back."

Both Joshua and Daniel left with Heather. When they were gone, I sat on the bed with Althor. "What did you mean about me leaving with you?"

"I want you to come with me," he said. "If we get the Jag."

"Why?"

"I—enjoy your company."

"You want me to leave everything I know, go with you to some universe so different I can't even imagine it, because you 'enjoy my company'?"

"Yes."

"That's nuts. You're more than thirty years older. What happens when you get tired of me? You'll strand me someplace where I'm centuries out of date."

"I wouldn't strand you."

"You say that now."

"I say it now. I say it a century from now." He paused. "That boy, the one with the gun at that house. He is part of why you can't leave?"

That caught me off guard. "You mean Jake?"

"Yes."

"Why do you think that?"

"Because he loves you."

I stared at him. "How do you know that?"

"His mind was practically shouting it."

I tried to sort out my thoughts. "We used to be together. But something has always been missing with him and me." I spread my hands. "I don't know how to explain. We were incomplete."

He spoke softly. "It's like starving inside."

"But with you it's different."

"We're full Kyle operators, Tina. Telepaths, empaths, healers. Do you know how rare that is? Probably we'll never find it again, not like we have with each other." He took hold of my shoulders. "Don't throw that away. Come with me."

"I can't." Although I didn't have the words to explain it then, in a sense I had already changed universes once in my life, when I left Chiapas and came to Los Angeles. Both my mother and Manuel had deserted me, or at least that was how it felt at the time. They left me alone to grapple with a universe I didn't understand, a place where I was alien. Now Althor wanted me to literally leave my universe. He expected me to trust him, a man I hardly knew, who as far as I could see had no reason to stay with me.

I felt him consider forcing my cooperation. Then his mood changed, its sense of threat replaced by a dispirited acceptance. At the time, I didn't believe he would ever have made me go with him. Why kidnap a nobody? I had no way to know how much it took out of him to accept my refusal. A computer would have done the requisite analysis and forced my compliance. Althor didn't. Regardless of what Imperial Space Command may claim about his humanity, or lack of it, the decision he made that day was an act of *human* compassion.

He slid his hands down my arms as if he were holding a wild bird that would fly away if he let go. When he bent to kiss me, I felt his sense of loss in the place where I hid my own loneliness.

Joshua's agitation was a gritty haze. As he locked the door, I swung my legs off the bed and sat up. Next to me, Althor continued to sleep.

"What did Heather say?" I asked.

He sat heavily in his desk chair. "She recognized you both as soon as she opened the door."

"Josh, no! Is she going to turn us in?"

"Well—I don't know." He pushed back his curls. "She's coming back in a few minutes."

"Why?"

"It's hard to tell with her. She doesn't think like the rest of us." His face gentled. "She's brilliant, Tina. She's up there where the rest of us can't follow."

I had never heard him talk this way about anyone. I couldn't help but smile. "It sounds like she means a lot to you."

He flushed. "She's a senior. She doesn't have time for a frosh like me."

Althor opened his eyes. "This is why she has the combination to your room?"

Joshua jumped. "I thought you were sleeping." When Althor raised his eyebrows, Joshua said, "She watered my plants last time I went home. That's all."

A knock sounded on the door. "It's us," Daniel called.

After Joshua let them in, Heather took a chair to the bed and turned it around backward. Daniel stood watching, looking first at her and then at Joshua. A grin tugged at his mouth, and I had a sense that in different circumstances he would have made some comment, teasing Joshua about being "Heather's frosh." Then he glanced at Althor and his smile faded.

Heather settled into the chair with her arms folded across the back, a sheaf of papers in one hand. As Althor sat up, planting his boots wide on the floor, she watched him, calm and unruffled. He blinked at her.

I picked up a lot about Heather at that first meeting. She had an outer toughness, the defenses of someone used to making her way in places where she was outnumbered. But beneath that hard shell lay a softness, a hidden bed of emotions. More than anything else, she exuded an insatiable curiosity.

Right now, though, she looked annoyed. "Josh tells me you claim to have a ship that goes faster than the speed of light."

"I don't have it," Althor said. "Your air force does." His voice made a deep rumbling note on the last word.

Her eyebrows arched. She handed him her papers. "I'm learning complex variable theory. Can you help with this problem?"

I glanced at Joshua, making my "what's going on?" face. He spread his hands.

Althor took the papers. "I don't know why you think I can help."

"Just wondering," she said.

He glanced through the papers. "This is inversion theory."

"Inversion?" She leaned forward. "What's that?"

"What happens when you go faster than light." Althor lifted the papers. "This is—I don't know the English word. Treatment with no acceleration. No tensors."

"I've never heard it called inversion," Heather said. "But yes, that's what I get when I put faster-than-light speeds into the equations of special relativity."

So. It was a test.

"I'm an engineer," Althor said. "Not theorist. It's been almost thirty years since I studied this and I never did that well in it."

"That mean you can't do it?" Heather didn't look surprised.

Althor blew out a gust of air and frowned at the papers. He asked her what some symbols meant, then sat reading. After a while he put the sheet on the bed and went to the next page.

"This has a mistake," he said.

"Where?" Heather asked.

He pointed to an equation. "The ratio is upside-down."

The sweet scent of her surprise drifted through the air. It wasn't because of the mistake; I was sure she put it there on purpose. But she hadn't expected Althor to find it. "You're right," she said.

He continued to study the papers. As he found other mistakes, the fragrance of her astonishment filled the room.

Althor indicated the last page. "A factor is missing here."

"That line is all right," she said.

"You left out a two."

She took the page from him. "Oh. You're right. I did."

I smiled. "See? He knows what he's talking about."

"All it shows is that he can do Heather's math," Daniel said.

She regarded Althor. "So you claim your alleged ship can do what those equations predict."

"Essentially," he said.

She leaned closer. "Starting from sublight speeds?"

"Well, yes," Althor said. "How else?"

She practically pounced. "That's impossible. You can't get past light speed. Time stops. Mass and energy become infinite. Length shrinks to zilch, zip, nada. Besides, even if you could get through light speed, superluminal travel has so many problems it could fill a book."

"You don't go through light speed," Althor said. "You go around it."

"Yeah, right," Daniel said. "The hyperspace bypass from Cannes to Hell."

Althor blinked. "What?"

"He means he doesn't believe it," Joshua said.

"Light speed is just a pole in the complex plane," Althor said. "To go around it, you leave the real axis."

"Mathematically that might work," Heather said. "But physically it makes no sense."

"It makes sense," Althor said. "You add a **** term to your speed."

"A what term?" Joshua asked.

"It means—" Althor paused. "I don't know the English word. Ortho-real."

"Imaginary," Heather said.

"Yes," Althor said. "You add an imaginary part to your speed."

"What's imaginary?" I asked.

"Square root of a negative number," Joshua said.

"Oh, come on," Daniel said. "Imaginary numbers aren't real. You can't add an imaginary component to your speed."

Althor scowled at him. "Tell this to the million starships doing it."

Heather didn't look convinced either. "Doing it how?"

"You rotate through complex space."

"Of course," Daniel muttered. "The ol' complex space rotation."

Heather shook her head. "Making speed complex may remove the singularity at light speed, but even if you get to superluminal space, you still have trouble. For one thing, you could go back in time."

"Going pastward is no problem," Althor said. "It looks like you go forward in time, but in ship made from antiparticles flying from your destination to your departure point."

"That's the lamest thing I've heard yet," Daniel said.

Althor's reaction caught us all by surprise. He rose to his full height, towering over Daniel, his fists clenched. "You say I am crippled?"

Daniel stepped back. "Well—no. I didn't mean that at all."

Althor stood there, fists knotted at his sides, while we all stared at him. Then I had the sense he reset himself, as he had done the night I asked about the hinge in his hand. He drew in a breath and sat on the bed again, letting his fists relax.

No one spoke. I could almost hear the others thinking *This man committed murder.* I was sure Althor had no intention of hurting them, but they had no way to know that.

After a moment Althor spoke to Daniel. "My sorry."

"Uh—yeah," Daniel said. "Sure."

Heather spoke carefully. "Althor, what you describe about going into the past—that was written about in some early papers on tachyons. It's called reinterpretation. Bilaniuk, Deshpande, and Sudarshan had articles on it. Feinberg too."

"Then why do you act so surprised at what I say?"

"Because no experiments ever supported those theories." Despite her wariness, her curiosity made a bouquet of flowers, each bloom giving off a different scent. "If you go into the past you get hit with paradoxes. You could stop yourself from being born."

Althor shook his head. "What happens in one reference frame must happen in all of them. If I stop myself from being born, everyone in every frame must observe it, as specified by the Lorentz transformations. That includes *my* frame. Since it's stationary relative to me, I always observe myself traveling into the future, even if I travel into the past relative to, say, the planet where I was born. So if I could stop myself from being born, I would have already seen it happen. And I didn't."

"I know," Heather said. "That's the paradox."

"There is no paradox," Althor said. "You can't do something in one reference frame and not do it in another. Don't think of time as linear. It exists all at once, just as all space exists together. If I go backward in space relative to one observer and forward relative to another, the people who see me going backward can't observe something inconsistent with what the people who see me going forward observe. The same is true for traveling in time. If I stopped my birth, it would happen in every observer's frame. But it didn't. Not in mine. I can go into the past, but I can't do something my ancestors didn't already experience."

"You're saying our existence is predetermined," Heather said. "I can't believe that."

Althor shrugged. "Given initial conditions and all forces, the classical equations of motion determine your position for all times. How is that any different?"

"Classical mechanics has rules," Daniel said. "So does quantum mechanics, or any other description of the universe. They make sense. If you go faster than light, you can go anywhere. Or anywhen."

Althor leaned forward. "They make sense because your everyday experience involves moving in different directions in space, not time. Superluminal travel isn't some magic time machine. For someone to observe you going pastward, both your speed and theirs must obey specific mathematical relations. And you're going *fast*. By the time you travel back to your birth, you're a long ways from Earth. How do you get home? If you reverse the sign of your velocity, you'll no longer be going pastward relative to Earth. It's a mess."

"You're in this universe before your birth," I said.

Althor blinked. "Actually, I'm here before the Althor of this universe was born. But he's not me."

Heather's fascination curled around him like a heavy-leafed vine. "Maybe you're on the wrong Riemann sheet."

"The wrong what?" Joshua asked.

"Riemann sheet," Heather said. "It's a mathematical representation designed to make multivalued complex quantities into single-valued functions."

Daniel scowled. "You're doing it again."

"Doing what?" Heather asked.

"Talking so no one understands what the hell you're saying."

She thought for a moment. "A Riemann sheet is like a clock. The face has a cut in it from, say, the center to the twelve. The hands go around from midnight to noon, then slide through the branch cut to a second clock underneath. It's the same as the first clock, except it goes from noon to midnight. At midnight you go back to the first clock. The more complicated the function, the more clocks you stack up."

"Riemann sheets are just math," Althor said. "They don't really exist."

"How do you know?" Daniel asked. "You're claiming imaginary universes exist."

Joshua spoke. "Althor, maybe when you did this inversion thing, you fell through a branch cut and came out on the wrong sheet. Like Heather's second clock. Same time, different phase."

Althor considered him. "Do you have a history text?"

Joshua pulled a green book off his bookcase and gave it to him. Althor flipped through the pages, stopped to read, flipped more, read more. Every now and then his face blanked into his computer mode.

"Find anything?" Heather asked.

"I'm trying to match what's here with the history files in my web." He scanned a page. "A lot is the same, even down to details. There must be a parallelism between the universes. But it's not identical. Like here—the Greeks migrated south later on this Earth. There is no record at all in my files of this Egyptian 'Desert Conquest.'" He went to another section. "And Zoroaster was born later here."

"Who?" Joshua asked.

"Zoroaster. He founded a Persian religious system prior to Islam." Althor read some more. "The development of Messianic religions was also delayed." He looked up. "You date your years from the birth of Jesus Christ, yes?" When Joshua nodded, Althor said, "He was born 339 years later here than in my universe."

Heather motioned at the papers he held. "Those equations need two Riemann sheets. Maybe your universe is the first and we're on the second."

"Actually, the equations need an infinite number of sheets." Althor lifted the papers. "These are incomplete. They don't have James corrections."

"James corrections?" Heather asked. "He must not have discovered them here yet."

I smiled at Joshua. "Maybe you're going to be famous." When Althor gave me a questioning look I said, "Joshua's last name is James."

"It wasn't a Joshua James," Althor said.

"Oh." Joshua looked disappointed.

Heather said, "You're asking a lot for us to believe this is more than a game," but her garden of curiosity was blooming all over the room.

Joshua put his hand on her shoulder. "Just think of what we could learn."

The moment he touched her, I knew he was wrong about her having no interest in him. Her fragrances curled into his hair, accompanied by the pulse of a drum, the song of an oboe. For the first time I noticed the way his T-shirt hugged his torso *just so,* the way his jeans clung to his hips—

I jerked, breaking away from Heather's mind. Neither she nor Joshua noticed. She smiled up at him, her look far softer than anything she had for the rest of us. Joshua stood waiting for her answer, oblivious to the effect he was having on her.

Heather sighed. "Okay, Josh. Let's see what we can do."

7

The Hummingbird

T*ina?*" The voice called in the dark, low and urgent. "*¿Eres tu aquí?*"

I lifted my head. Althor lay asleep beside me and Joshua was snoring on the floor.

"*¡Tina! ¿Puedes oigame?*"

I looked out the window. Jake Rojas stood in the courtyard below.

I kept my exclamation to a whisper. "Jake! How did you know I was here?"

"Why else would you come to Pasadena, except to see Josh?"

Behind me, Althor sat up and slid his arms around my waist. I heard a rustle from the floor and turned to see Joshua standing up, rubbing his eyes. He came around the bed and leaned out the window. "Jake? Wait just a second. I'll bring you up."

Joshua threw on a coat and left the room. A minute later he appeared in the courtyard. He and Jake shook hands, then took off running. It was only a moment before the door opened and they came inside. Jake glanced around the room as if he didn't quite know what to make of it.

I regarded him. "Is everything all right?"

"We been worried about you." He glanced at Althor, then back at me. "First the cops came asking questions. Then the FBI. Then some guys who wouldn't say nothing about who they were. It took me this long to get past the men they have watching us."

"That test plane the shuttle found is Althor's," I said.

Jake considered Althor like he didn't believe it. Then he looked at me. "Nug's funeral was yesterday."

I tried to feel regret for Nug's death. But I kept remembering my cousin Manuel, how he used to laugh and swing me around when I was a little girl. From Althor, I felt a remorse Nug didn't deserve.

After the silence became awkward, Jake spoke to me in a gentler voice. "I need to talk to you private."

I wasn't sure where we could find privacy. I didn't know what Joshua and Daniel had told the other students on the hall, but I had a sense they all knew Joshua was hiding people in his room; in such a close-knit community, it was hard to keep a secret this big. I felt a sense of excitement in the hall—and also one of fellowship. Joshua and Daniel were two of their own, and as long as we were here on their approval, apparently the others accepted us as well.

"We can go out in the hall," I said.

Althor took hold of my wrist. "No."

"I need to do this," I said.

"I'll go with you," Althor said.

Jake tensed. "Like hell."

Althor scowled at him. "It's none of your business."

Jake gave him a look that could have burned rubber off a tire. "She told you she's going, *cabrón.* So let her go."

If Althor knew what Jake had called him, he showed no sign of it. He must have understood, though; his biomech web can translate *bastard* into hundreds of languages.

"Althor, I'll be all right," I said.

The cords in his neck tensed. But he nodded and let go.

It was quiet when Jake and I stepped outside. After I closed the door, he raised his arms in that familiar way, ready to hug me. He stopped himself and let his arms drop. "I've been crazy trying to find you."

I swallowed, unsettled at how much his presence affected me. Apparently I hadn't turned off my feelings as well as I thought. "I'm all right. Really."

"I had to warn you." He paused. "And to say good-bye."

"You're leaving?"

"I wanted to tell you at Mario's." Anger tightened his voice. "But you were with him."

"Where are you going?"

"Arizona, after the cops let us leave town. My stepfather, he says there's a job for me in his garage if I want it."

I knew it was a good decision. His mother lived in a small town with almost no people at all, let alone gangs. "What made you decide to go?"

"I'm tired, Tina. Tired of coming closer and closer to—I don't know what." He exhaled. "I went to Nug's funeral."

"Why?"

"I don't know." After a moment he said, "Maybe because I'm glad it wasn't me." He touched my cheek. "No more guns, baby. If that's what it takes to bring you back, I'll do it."

I felt caught on an edge, poised between two universes, literally and figuratively. Jake offered everything I wanted: a predictable world, stability, a mate like myself, or at least more like me than most anyone else in LA. Althor offered chaos, choices I barely understood, let alone sought.

"I don't know what will happen," I said.

"That's what I came to warn you about." He shook his head. "Those people, they don't stop asking questions. We haven't told them nothing. But they aren't going to give it up. They'll find out you and Josh are friends. They'll come here."

I had believed a dorm room at Caltech was the last place anyone would look. To this day I wince when I think how close the false sense of security came close to ruining us. "We owe you."

"I didn't come here to help him. Just you."

"I won't forget it." I took a breath. "But I have to see this through with Althor."

It was a moment before he answered. He spoke in a gentle voice. "I know. You always stand by your man. But when it's over—if he—if you—" He paused. "You know my mom's number in Arizona."

"I'll call, Jake. If I'm still—" Still what? Free? Alive? I had no idea how the situation with Althor would end.

"If you can." He kissed me. *"Adios, mi hija."* Then he was gone, running down the steps and into the night.

"Breaking into computer networks is illegal," Heather said. We were all standing in Joshua's room: Althor and me, Joshua, Heather, and Daniel. Heather and Althor faced each other like fighters in the ring.

"But you can do it." Althor made it a statement rather than a question. He motioned at Daniel. "He has her password."

Daniel stiffened. "I told you I don't."

"You're lying," Althor said.

"What, you know what's in my brain?" Daniel demanded. "I told you I don't know the password to my mom's account." The lie of that surrounded him in an orange haze, droning like a maddened bee.

"It's irrelevant," Heather said. "I'm not fooling with any network at Yeager Flight Test Center."

Althor spoke in a too-quiet voice. "I need your help."

I shifted my weight. I had already seen, at the library with Nug, what happened when Althor felt backed into a corner.

Heather paled, but she didn't back down. "You claim you're some futuristic fighter pilot. You told Tina you brought a warship here that could blow California to smithereens. Then you expect me to break into a military network and falsify records so you can get onto a secured base? At the least you want me to compromise this country's security by letting an escaped killer loose in Yeager. If your story is true, you're asking me to risk the safety of a world."

"Where else can I go for help?" Althor asked.

Heather pushed her hand through her hair. She walked to the window and looked out at the courtyard. When I glanced at Daniel, he averted his eyes. Even Joshua wouldn't look at me.

Finally Heather spoke. "If I did help you—and I'm not saying I will—but if I did, the best I could do, and that's only with Daniel's help if he's willing, is get us on the base."

Hope jumped in Althor's voice. "Just get me there. I'll do the rest."

Heather turned to him. "What is it you would do?"

"Leave," Althor said. "And never come back, if I have a choice."

"What do you mean," Joshua said, "if you have a choice?"

"My ship might be too damaged. Or what brought me here maybe can't be reversed." Althor grimaced. "If this is true, my only real choice is to die in space or come back to Earth. This Earth."

For an instant, as he spoke, his mental armor slipped and I felt his fear. He clamped down his barriers immediately, but he was too late. I knew how vulnerable he felt. To him, this Earth was primitive, even savage; he feared he would die a painful death far from home. In fact, the process had already begun, though I didn't know it then. The longer the team at Yeager worked on his ship, the more they damaged his brain.

Both Joshua and Heather picked up traces of Althor's turmoil. Joshua's forehead furrowed, as if winged by a bullet he hadn't seen coming. Heather looked as if she were struggling to catch whispers that flitted out of hearing. I understood then what drew her and Joshua together. It was the same thing that made Joshua and me friends, that drew me to Jake, and especially to Althor. Empath. Like sought like.

Heather spoke to Althor. "If I help you, there's a price. A ride in your starship."

Daniel grinned. "Yes!"

"This is no game," Althor said. "If you get killed, no magic potion will make you alive again."

"If you're telling the truth," Heather said, "this is a chance we'll never have again."

"The inversion drives have a malfunction," Althor said. "If I get home, I have no intention of returning here. I might not get home a second time."

"Take us out as far as Mars," Daniel said.

"No," Althor said.

"No ride," Heather said, "no security pass."

Althor muttered in his own language, but I didn't need to recognize the words to know he was swearing. I also felt Heather's and Daniel's doubts hovering behind their bravado. I laid my hand on Althor's arm. "This may be our only chance."

He exhaled. Then he spoke to Heather. "*If* we reach the ship, I'll take you in orbit around Earth."

"Deal," Heather said.

Moonlight sifted through the curtains and silvered the room. Outside, crickets sawed in the night. I sat with Althor on the bed, unable to sleep. The others had gone to prepare for our trip to Yeager and we couldn't turn on the light when the room was supposed to be empty. Althor was silent, brooding; with the perfect vision of hindsight, I realize now that he knew he might be killed during his attempt to recover the Jag.

After a while he said, "Tell me a story."

"What would you like to hear?" I asked.

"I don't know." He lay down and put his head in my lap. "Any story."

My voice slipped into the lilting style I had learned from the best story teller I knew. "This tale was told to me by my mother, Manuela Santis Pulivok, told to her by her brother, Lukarto Santis Pulivok, who heard it from a traveler in Santo Tomás Chichicastenango. It is the story of the Ancestral Hero Twins." I paused for effect. "Before the birth of the twins, their father and uncle offended the Lords of Death. The two men made a great commotion while playing a ball game in a court above Xibalba, the Underworld where the Lords of Death lived. So the Lords took their lives, sacrificing them for their offenses. They buried the uncle under the ball court. The skull of the father they hung in a gourd tree, a warning to humans that they should be wary of offending the gods. This happened before the birth of the dead man's sons, Xbalanque and Hunahpu—"

"Where did you hear those names?" Althor sat up. "Shibalank. Quanahpah."

"It's pronounced Xbalanque. And Hunahpu."

"Where did you hear them?"

"Originally, it comes from the *Popol Vuh,* an ancient holy book of the Quiche Maya."

"What made you think of it tonight?"

"You asked me to tell you a story."

"But why did you think of this one in particular?"

"I don't know. Why are you so upset?"

He watched me intently. "Just before we made love yesterday I told you a quote from Iotic. It was about the great beauty of a woman called Shibalank."

"Xbalanque was a man," I said. "But I remember now. Some of the words sounded familiar. I guess that's why I thought of this story."

"Tell me more."

"The daughter of a Lord of Death found the skull of the ball player hanging in the gourd tree. It got her pregnant by spitting into her hand."

Dryly he said, "I can think of more pleasant routes to fatherhood."

I smiled. "Is that like your story?"

"Shibalank and Quanahpah were twin sisters. They founded the first two houses of the ancient Raylican dynasties."

"Xbalanque and Hunahpu were twin brothers."

Shadows and moonlight played across his face as he tilted his head. "These legends, among my people they are over six thousand years old. By Earth reckoning."

"It must be coincidence then. Maya civilization isn't that old."

"This is what you are? Maya?"

"My mother was." I hesitated. "I don't know about my father."

He considered me. "Our scholars believe my ancestors come from somewhere on Earth. How else we have DNA almost identical to human DNA?"

"I don't know."

"Tell me more of your story."

"The Xbalban god was enraged by his daughter's pregnancy." That was no surprise to me, after seeing my mother's life. "She escaped to the Middleworld, where the grandmother of the dead brothers took her in. The woman gave birth to twin boys, Hunahpu and Xbalanque. They became great ball players. One day they played in the court where their father and uncle had disturbed the gods. They too angered the Lords of Death. But they survived every trial the Lords put before them, even returning to life again after letting themselves be killed. Finally, wanting to know how the twins overcame death, the Lords of Death demanded the brothers kill them and bring them back to life. So the twins killed them. But they didn't bring them back to life."

"This is not so smart of Death," Althor said. "To insist to die and be made alive again."

I laughed. "I guess not."

"Can you tell me more? Other stories?"

"There's the hummingbird story. I especially liked that one when I was little." I concentrated on the words, translating them in my mind from Tzotzil into English:

> *The hummingbird is good and big.*
> *So that's the way it is;*
> *There were workers in hot country;*
> *They were burning bean pods,*
> *The fire could be seen well, it was so tall.*
> *The hummingbird came,*
> *It came out,*
> *It came flying in the sky.*
> *Well, it saw the fire;*
> *Its eyes were snuffed out by the smoke.*
> *It came down,*
> *It came down,*
> *It came down so that they saw that it was big.*
> *Don't you believe that it is little, it is big.*
> *Just like a dove, its wings are white,*
> *All of it is white.*

I say they tell lies when they say that the hummingbird was little,
The men said it was very big.
Then they recognized how it was,
For none of us had seen it,
We didn't know what it was like.
Yes, it says "Ch'un ch'un" in the evening,
But we didn't know what size it was.
But they, they saw how big it was,
They saw that it was the same as, the same size as a hawk,
Having to do with the father-mother,
"One leg" as we call it."

Remembering the words made me miss my mother. To this day I can see her in my mind, her beautiful face rapt as she recited the lines. She loved telling stories, even acting them out with her hands.

Althor was staring at me. "How old is this story?"

I shrugged. "I don't know. It's a Zinacanteco myth."

"What is *father-mother?*"

"It was the best translation I could think of for Totilme?il, the ancestral gods."

"The hummingbird is a god?"

"No. Just a messenger for the gods."

"This story is not about bird," Althor said.

"It's not?"

"It's a starship."

I laughed. "Oh, Althor."

"It came flying out of the sky? It was big and white? This is how hummingbird looks?"

"Actually, no," I admitted. "Hummingbirds are tiny and dark."

"They make this sound 'ch'un ch'un'? They stand on one leg?"

"Well—no."

He watched me closely. "A civilization must grow from roots.

What are Maya roots, six thousand years ago?"

"Stone-Age Indians, I think."

"Could this hummingbird story have roots six thousands years old?"

"I doubt it."

He regarded me. "In our tales, the sisters come to Raylicon on the Star Path. It is a black fissure in the stars."

"There's a Maya legend similar to that."

"Our scholars think it describes the trip my ancestors took from Earth to Raylicon."

"But who took them? And why?"

Althor spread his hands. "If a starfaring race did exist six thousand years ago, one that could transplant a race from one planet to another, they are long dead and vanished."

It made no sense to me. "Why would anyone move a bunch of Mesoamerican Indians to another planet?"

"The ancient Raylicans carried a pure strain of the Kyle genes." The moonlight caught glimmers from his skin. "Perhaps the race that moved them intended to concentrate Kyle traits. That pure form is almost extinct now. It shows up only in descendants of certain Raylican high houses."

"Like you?"

"Yes. Like me."

"You think the Maya are your ancestors?"

"Maybe."

"Althor, you look about as Indian as a cotton swab." Actually, that wasn't true. But his metallic hues were far lighter than my skin.

"Indian?" Althor asked. "Is that what you are?"

It wasn't actually a word I used for myself. Nor did I feel comfortable with Latina; it sounded too much like *Ladino,* the descendants of the Spaniards who conquered the Maya. Mejicana, maybe. Chicana was what I had always checked off on forms.

"I'm probably mestiza," I said.

He blanked again, then said, "Mixed blood."

"Yes. Half Spanish descent and half Maya."

"You look like my grandmother. I look more like my father."

His father. I've always wondered if I look like mine. Do we sound alike, laugh alike, think alike? I wonder if he asked my mother to come with him when he left Chiapas. Perhaps she refused as I refused Althor, too afraid to chance the unknown.

My voice caught. "It's all dreams anyway." I took off my bracelet and gave it to him. "This is the truth. It's been passed from mother to daughter for generations, from mother to son if there was no daughter to inherit it, and from father to daughter. It's all I have. Someday I'll give it to my daughter."

Althor pulled me into his arms. "Come with me, Tina. Don't stay here. The loneliness will kill you."

"No." I laid my head against his chest. "I can't."

He pushed me back, gripping my shoulder while he shook the bracelet in front of my face. "Why is this so important? It's just a damn ring of metal."

"It's all that's left of my clan." I didn't know how to put into words what it meant. As long as I knew my father existed somewhere, I could hope to find him someday, once again to have a family, a heritage, a clan. Althor was asking me to give up that dream. And for what? An uncertainty so total it was a nightmare.

But he wasn't looking at me anymore. He was staring at the bracelet.

"What's wrong?" I asked.

"I need a light."

He crossed to Joshua's desk and took the desk lamp, then sat on the floor and leaned over it. When he switched it on, gold light filtered around him like a leak in the darkness. I went over and sat next to him. He was holding the bracelet under the lamp, turning it over and over, running his fingers along the faint hieroglyphs engraved inside it.

"What are these symbols?" he asked.

"Mayan glyphs. They're just a copy, though. The bracelet isn't old enough to be authentic. The ancient Maya didn't make jewelry like that, either."

"Why do you have this?" he asked. "And your mother, and her mother, and on back? Inheritance on Earth goes through male lines, doesn't it?"

"Not always. I don't know why we pass it from mother to daughter. That's just the way we've done it."

"Raylicon was a matriarchy."

"What does that have to do with my bracelet?"

Althor showed me the hieroglyphs. "The inscription inside. It's Iotic."

I stared at him. "How can my bracelet have your language on it?"

He spoke softly. "Maybe because Iotic was your language before it was mine."

"On my bracelet? That makes no sense."

"It's not a bracelet."

"It's not?"

"It's a fitting for the tubing on the exhaust of a Raylican transport shuttle."

My mouth fell open. "What?"

"The shuttles are ruins on the shore of the Vanished Sea in the Sleeping Desert." His face gleamed in the lamp's glow. "They are the oldest artifacts on Raylicon, dating from six thousand years ago. These shuttles, they are not built for humans. The proportions are wrong." He turned the bracelet in his hand. "I have seen others of these. On the transports."

"A bronze bracelet in that good of condition *can't* be six thousand years old."

He shook his head. "It's not bronze. It's an alloy called cordonum, made atom by atom using nano-bots to place the particles. It endures much better than bronze."

"Mayan glyphs like that didn't exist six thousand years ago."

"I don't know how," Althor said. "But it is Iotic. The ancients brought the language with them, a remnant of their lost home." His voice caught. "Before tonight, I had no past. Do you know what that means? My ancestors ceased at six thousand years. Now you may have given me a past." He swallowed. "When I may never be able to return home again."

"Althor, no." I pulled him into my arms. "Don't say that."

He turned out the light and held me. We sat there for a long time, rocking back and forth in the silver night.

8

Lightning Jag

The Mojave Desert rolled by as Daniel drove his Jeep down Highway 14. Dry land stretched out for miles, gray green and dust yellow, feathery strands of ocotillo plants reaching out fingers and prickly spikes of mesquite patching the land in earthy colors. Tumbleweed blew across the road, rolling lumpily, and the sky was a pale blue plain above us. Although it was only eight in the morning, heat already shimmered on the asphalt.

Even with a hat pulled over my hair, the wind still snapped out blond curls from my wig and threw them around my head. I pushed at my glasses, trying to settle them on my nose. I felt stupid wearing a business suit. Anyone who saw me would surely know I was a fake.

Heather had loaned me the suit and wig. Joshua found Althor a stage beard left from a play put on by the chemistry graduate students, and Daniel dug up a boring blue suit for him. We dyed his hair blond. So now Althor sat in the Jeep with his blue jacket across his knees, tie loosened and collar open, his newly yellow curls dancing in the wind. He squinted and raised his hand to his eyes, but he stopped himself before he rubbed anything.

"Are the contacts bothering you?" I asked. When he cupped his hand to his ear, I raised my voice. "Heather's eye lenses. They still bothering you?" The contacts turned her green eyes blue; on Althor, it was more of a blue-violet color.

"Everything blurs," he said.

Heather turned around in the front and looked at the three of us—Althor, myself, and Joshua—scrunched in the back. "Can you see enough to walk?" she asked him.

Althor rubbed under his eye. "I think so."

"Try not to rub your face," I said. "It makes the gold show." I took a bottle of foundation out of my purse and touched up the gold streak under his eye. I had to be careful: if I used too much makeup, it would show, making people wonder why this macho guy in a conservative suit wore it; if I used too little, it wouldn't cover the shimmer of his skin.

Daniel pointed to a sign: ROSAMOND BLVD. YEAGER MILITARY FLIGHT TEST CENTER. NASA-AMES-DRYDEN RESEARCH FACILITY. Under it, a second sign in faded letters said EDWARDS AIR FORCE BASE.

"Edwards." Althor snapped his fingers. "I recognize this. They renamed it?"

"In honor of Chuck Yeager," Daniel said. "After he died."

"In my universe," Althor said, "General Yeager lived well past the 1980s."

Daniel turned onto the exit. Other cars came behind us and more were on the road ahead. We drove through land dotted with blue and yellow flowers, and the orange glow of California poppies. Then we crossed a dry lake bed and entered a wrinkled-blanket terrain covered with yellow flowers that spilled every-where like paint.

After about six miles, we reached a security checkpoint. Lines of cars waited; both lanes were backed up, as well as a third made by coming off one usually used by traffic leaving the base. As we waited, Daniel looked back at us. "This is the West Gate."

"Does it always have so many security police?" Althor asked.

"Security police?" Daniel asked.

Althor motioned toward the booth, where harried guards were trying to deal with the rush hour traffic. "The guards. There are at least six of them."

"Milcops," Daniel said. "Usually there's only a couple. All you need most days is a sticker on your car and they wave you through." He eased the Jeep forward as the milcops let another car through.

"How many people work here?" Joshua asked.

"About 5000 military," Daniel said. "Maybe 6000 civilian and 8000 contractors."

Heather whistled. "Sounds more like a city than a base."

"Do you think the guards know why security has been increased?" I asked.

"I doubt it," Daniel said. "They don't have any need to know."

We moved forward again, again—and it was our turn. Daniel pulled alongside the milcop and held up a JPL badge. When Joshua elbowed me in the ribs, I opened my purse and took out the MIT badge they had fixed up for me. I sat stiff in my seat, certain the milcop would realize we were fakes.

Thorough planning had gone into this attempt. Heather found a file in the Yeager system about a group expected at the base later in the day, specialists brought in to study the "test plane." We came early because the specialists weren't scheduled to arrive for several hours. Despite our careful work, though, too much could go wrong. At least that was how I felt. Althor was hard to read; I later learned he had switched into a combat mode used for special operations. The others were tense, quiet—and eager. The previous night, during our planning, Daniel had said that if we pulled this off, it would be ten times better than the time students took over the computer running the scoreboard at the Rose Bowl and changed the teams to Caltech and MIT.

The milcop looked over our badges and asked for our on-site contact. As Daniel gave him the number, I held my breath. The milcop went into the guard booth and picked up a phone. I watched through the tinted glass, trying to stay calm while he spoke to whoever was on the other end.

He came back out. "They're waiting for you up at North Base," he said, waving us through.

And that was it.

As we drove away from the guards, Joshua blew out a gust of

air and Heather closed her eyes for a moment. We rode through gently rolling hills, headed west with a line of other cars. After a few minutes, we reached the main base. It was the size of a small city, but with a practical look about it, too functional for a college, too sedate for an industrial complex. Other cars were pulling off the road, but we kept going, straight on through the base and back into the desert.

Althor made a strange sound, a small explosion of breath. Turning to follow his gaze, I saw a distant scaffolding out in the desert, one that resembled an unfinished skyrise about eight stories tall. In a different direction, a gleaming silver airplane was mounted on a pedestal, like a fat rocket with short wings and a needle nose. It looked familiar, but I couldn't place why.

Althor was staring at the plane. "That's an X-1."

Heather turned around in the front seat. "A what?"

He pointed at the plane. "An X-1. A real one."

"Yeah, it's an X-1," Daniel said.

Althor grinned. "I've read about them. I never thought I would see a real one, though. Does it still fly?"

"I don't think so," Daniel said.

Althor indicated the scaffolding. "What about that lift? Is it for the space shuttle?"

Daniel glanced at it. "That's right."

" 'The Six Million Dollar Man,' " I said.

"What?" Althor asked.

"It's an old TV show," I said. "The opening showed the crash of a plane that looked like that X-1."

"That was actual NASA footage," Daniel said. "The real pilot survived."

Heather was watching Althor. "It must seem dull compared to what you've seen."

Althor laughed. "Aircraft are never dull. I've liked them since I was old enough to shoot a rocket in the air and watch it come down."

Heather smiled, and Joshua's surprise made yellow loops in the air. It was the first time any of them had seen Althor laugh.

Daniel turned onto North Base Road. Another security check-point lay ahead, across from a temporary trailer. We stopped and a milcop looked our IDs over, comparing them to a list on his clip-board. He motioned to a small lot by the road. Two other cars were parked there, with milcops going over them. "Pull in there." He tilted his head toward the trailer. "While we inspect your Jeep, you can get your site badges."

"Sure thing." Daniel sounded relaxed, as if he did this all the time. I still wonder how he managed it. True, he had been to the base before with his mother. But to say the circumstances of our visit were more difficult is an understatement.

Daniel parked and we climbed out of the Jeep, smoothing our wind-blown clothes and hair. The heat blazed. Neither Daniel nor Althor put on their jackets, but Althor let me fix his tie. As I pushed up the knot, he muttered something about "bizarre bar-baric custom, tying a rope around your neck." I smiled. I knew a lot of twentieth-century types who agreed with him.

Inside the trailer, a man behind a counter checked our IDs. Althor stood at the back of our group, tall and silent, dressed in his conservative suit, blending with the scenery. To fit our parts, the rest of us needed to look older. Heather and I managed with business suits and makeup, and Daniel with a coat and tie, but nothing we did helped Joshua. Heather finally changed his age to twenty-two in the file, and we kept our fingers crossed that they would take him for one of those brilliant types who can earn a Ph.D. practically as a kid. It wasn't that far from the truth.

The man finished with Daniel and turned to me. "ID."

I handed him my MIT card, certain he would find a mistake. But he just typed at his terminal and gave me back the card. He took Joshua's next and typed again. Then he stopped and peered at the screen, his forehead furrowing.

We all tensed. I felt it, like plastic pulled tight around us.

The man glanced at Joshua. "Chakrabarti? That's an Indian name, isn't it?"

Joshua regarded him with innocent blue eyes. "Yes, sir. My mother was Swedish."

He gave Joshua his ID and motioned us all toward a doorway. "Marjorie will take your pictures and give you badges."

I tried to relax as the photographer snapped our pictures. But I kept wondering if this was how it felt to have mug shots taken. Incredibly, she just gave us our Yeager badges and let us leave. We walked outside into searing sunlight, with the Mojave Desert stretching out around us.

The milcop waved us over to the Jeep. "You're all set," he called. Daniel raised his hand in acknowledgment. Everything was fine until Althor halted in the street, his fingers pushing against his temples.

We stopped next to him. "What's wrong?" Joshua asked.

When Althor didn't respond, I pulled on his arm. "Come on."

For the first time Daniel's outward cool slipped. "We can't stop here."

Althor dropped his hand. "**** * ***"

I stared at him. "What?"

"***** * * *"

Heather swore under her breath. "What's wrong with him?"

The milcop walked over to us. "Is there a problem?"

Heather pulled a tissue out of her purse and blew her nose. I thought she was nuts—until I saw the milcop turn his attention from Althor to her. "What's the problem?" he asked.

"Hay fever." Heather sniffled. "The pollen is killing me."

"You and half the base." The milcop shook his head. "Some people do fine with over-the-counter treatments. But if it's already causing you trouble, you may want to see a doctor. Spring is hay fever hell here."

Heather smiled wryly. "Thanks. I'll look into it."

He nodded and headed back to his post. As we started walking again, Daniel spoke to Heather. "How did you know about the hay fever? You sound like you really have it."

"I do." Heather grimaced. "He wasn't kidding about hay fever hell."

Joshua was watching Althor. "Are you all right?"

"Yes," Althor said.

"What happened?" I asked.

"The Jag." Althor's accent was stronger now. "We're close to it. I tried to reach it. It's damaged. Some from before, but also some new." Sweat sheened on his forehead. "What they're doing to my brain—I can't—I'm losing ability to integrate functions."

"What's going to happen if they don't stop?" Daniel asked.

"I don't know." Althor walked faster. "I don't want to find out."

We took the Jeep up North Base Road. As we neared North Base, its three hangars grew out of the desert. They were gorgeous, shaped like cylinders with rounded roofs, each painted a different background color: blue, green, yellow. Their most striking feature, though, was the murals on them, colorful scenes of aircraft soaring through the sky.

"Hey." Joshua was staring at the hangars. "Cool."

"Your air force makes pictures on hangars?" Althor asked.

"Why not?" Daniel said.

"Never seen it," Althor said.

We parked near an office building. Across the lot, a walk-through security check broke the expanse of a chain link fence. We headed for the checkpoint, wind ruffling our hair. Heather sneezed and blew her nose.

Daniel went first at the security check, holding up his badge. The milcop took it, looked at the picture, looked at Daniel, and nodded for him to go past.

I stepped up and held up my badge. After the guard checked it, he considered me. "How long have you worked at MIT?"

Stay calm, I told myself. "Three years."

"What's a byte?" he asked.

I heard it as "bite." I concentrated on him, trying to guess why he would ask such a strange question. All I could pick up was that he didn't think I looked like a computer whiz.

"It's part of a computer," I guessed.

He waved me past and let the others by with a badge check

and a nod. Then we were through, and staring around at North Base. It didn't look like much, a few buildings baking under the sun. The lake bed stretched out beyond it, parched dry.

Daniel glanced at me. "You're lucky that guy didn't know much about computers."

"What do you mean?" I asked.

"A byte isn't part of a computer. It's eight bits. Eight ones and zeros."

"She convinced him," Joshua said. "That's what matters."

Althor looked around as we walked. Milcops in berets and green camouflage uniforms patrolled the area with dogs. Squat vehicles rumbled by, each one like a cross between a small tank and an all-terrain cockroach. "They have a lot of security," he said.

"The ThreatCon is probably Charlie," Daniel said.

Althor looked at him. "What does that mean?"

"ThreatCons are for possible terrorist aggression. Alpha is situation normal. Bravo is the next step, then Charlie. Delta would be a full base lockdown." Daniel grimaced. "If you get your plane, you can bet this place will go to Delta."

Heather was going through the papers they had given us in the trailer. "We're supposed to go to a security briefing. No, wait. That's this afternoon. Right now we see our contact. Dr. Robert L. Forward."

"Hey," Joshua said. "He won the Goddard Prize in 1981."

"Goddard Prize?" Althor asked. "What is this?"

"An award in rocket science. He got it for work on antimatter propulsion."

"If they've already discovered the Jag uses antimatter propulsion," Althor said, "they may realize it has interstellar capability."

"Does that matter?" Heather asked.

"Sooner or later they will realize I'm here without a mothership." He grimaced. "I'd rather they thought someone was looking for me."

We came around the corner of a building, into view of the hangars. Up close they were even more impressive, murals drawn in bold detail, showing fighters soaring in cloud-streamered skies, above lush countryside or desert landscapes. The yellow and green hangars were closed. Blue was open, but a canvas hung in its doorway, weighted to keep wind from blowing it around. A fence surrounded the structure, with a guard booth and gate where it met the hangar. Scaffolding supported by cement dividers towered next to the hangar.

"That's odd." Heather indicated the milcops with dogs patrolling inside the fenced area. "They have no guns."

"It's a precaution," Althor said. "They don't know what happens if bullets hit the ship."

"You sure it's not going to blow?" Heather asked.

Althor exhaled. "No."

Then it happened. As someone left the hangar, a gust of wind grabbed the canvas and flipped it into the air—revealing the beauty inside. The Jag looked like an alabaster sculpture, its hull a blaze of white in the sunlight slanting into the hangar. Its lines were so clean, it seemed ready to leap off the ground and soar into the air by itself.

The canvas fell back in place.

Heather whistled. "That's something." Daniel and Joshua's faces mirrored her reaction.

"Is so close," Althor said. "If I could just reach it."

Two milcops waited at the hangar security check, a man and a stocky woman, both armed with handguns. We showed our badges again, Daniel first. The woman nodded him through and he went to the gate, waiting for us. As the man turned to Heather, the woman checked my badge. I stood as still as possible, trying to look innocuous.

She nodded. "Go on."

The man was checking Althor's badge. He seemed to take forever, peering at the picture, then at Althor. As the woman let Joshua by, I went to the gate and waited with Heather and Daniel, trying to relax.

Finally the man passed Althor through. Daniel took out his copy of the key-card they had given us at the trailer and turned to the gate. A box that resembled a telephone keypad hung on it.

While the milcops watched, Daniel swiped his card through the slot on the box and typed his code into the keypad. He pushed on the gate and we waited, hot desert wind fluttering our hair.

Waiting.

Daniel muttered under his breath. "Must have made a mistake."

Heather spoke in a low voice. "Try again. I think you get three times before an alarm goes off."

Daniel swiped his card and entered the numbers again. This time when he pushed, the gate opened.

In. We were in. Althor's face showed no reaction. But his heart jumped so hard it registered on my senses like the clang of a mallet on a gong.

As we headed for the hangar, a call came from the milcops behind us. "Wait there."

We all froze. Heather turned, somehow managing to look casual. "Yes?"

Both milcops came over. The man spoke. "Don't forget to change into the white coveralls before you enter the craft. You'll find them in the locker inside." He paused, studying Althor. "Sterile environment, you know."

Althor nodded. "Of course."

"Well, then." He considered us. "Go on ahead."

As we turned back toward the ship, relief poured over me. A few more moments and we would have what we came—

"Wait," the woman said. When we turned, she was frowning at Althor. "What's on your face?"

"My face?" he asked.

"There." She pointed to where sweat sheened his temples and soaked into his hair. "That. It looks like makeup."

"It's lotion," Heather said. "He has poison ivy."

The woman continued to watch Althor. "I don't see any rash."

"It's covered," he said.

Reaching up, she rubbed his temple. Her fingers came away smeared with foundation—and a gold streak showed on his face.

I felt the milcop's explosion of recognition. I doubt she recognized him from the sketch on the news; it strained credibility that she would associate a leather-clad tough with a bearded, blue-suited scientist. More likely, milcops assigned to the ship were given descriptions of Althor, complete with the oddities, including his gold skin.

She grabbed for her gun, but Althor moved faster, with enhanced speed, whipping up his leg while he threw his body forward. It took him a bare second to knock them both out. As they crumpled to the ground, someone outside the fenced area shouted.

Althor grabbed Daniel's arm and ran for the hangar, yanking Daniel along, nearly dragging him. We ran after them. What else could we do? He obviously meant to use Daniel as a hostage, which hadn't been part of our deal, but unless we intended to desert him now and let the milcops detain us, we had no choice but to follow his lead.

As we veered around the scaffolding, three milcops ran out from the hangar. None was armed, but they brought two dogs with them, a black one and a lean red monster. One of the milcops shouted, and the dogs bounded toward us.

Althor threw Daniel to the side. The dogs hit Althor full force and they fell to the ground, the dogs tearing at his suit, trying for his neck as he wrestled with them. Moving in a blur, he heaved them off his body. They hit the asphalt hard, and the black one lay there, eyes closed, breathing raggedly. The red dog lifted its head and tried to climb to its feet.

As Althor jumped up, Daniel backed away, toward the scaffolding. He didn't get far; Althor grabbed his arm and swung him around to face the milcops. He slapped his knife flat against Daniel's neck.

The knife's brilliance shattered the sunlight. The red dog growled, on its feet again, but a command from a milcop stayed it. Daniel stood stiff as a board, sweat running down his face. Grabbing my arm with his free hand, Althor backed toward the hangar, pulling us both with him.

We ran straight into the concrete dividers that held up the scaffolding. Although the Jag was only a few yards away, it might as well have been across the base. The canvas swung open on the side farthest from us and a group of people in white coveralls appeared with another milcop. Rather than take them to the man-gate on this side, near us, he pulled the chain-link fence away from the far side of the hangar and took them out that way.

The milcops in front of us squinted in the glare from Althor's knife. A man with hair cut so close to his head that it looked like yellow dust spoke. "We don't want to hurt you."

"Move away from the ship," Althor said. "Or I kill him."

"We don't want anyone hurt." The milcop had a soothing voice. But something bothered me. Had his attention flicked to a point behind Althor?

I glanced back and saw a man with an M-16 coming through the scaffolding. He gave me a reassuring nod, apparently assuming I was a hostage. In truth, he was right, though at the time I didn't see it that way. I turned around, trying to look as if I were going along with him. But I spoke to Althor under my breath. "A man is coming up behind us. He's two steps—"

Althor whirled and kicked up his leg, thudding his heel into the man's chest with an accuracy that suggested he already knew the milcop was there. The guard crumpled and Althor lunged over the dividers, still holding Daniel and me, forcing us to scramble with him. As Heather and Joshua threw themselves over the barrier, something whizzed so close to my head that it brushed my hair. We fell on our stomachs next to the unconscious milcop. Bullets hit the dividers, sending concrete chips flying into the air, and the barrier split into a network of cracks.

"Stop shooting," someone shouted. "You'll hit the ship!"

Althor grabbed the fallen guard's M-16, studied it for a second, and fired over the dividers, spraying the area with bullets. The milcops scattered, most running for the hangar's cover. They released three more dogs, and as we crawled behind the dividers the beasts bounded toward us, growling, fangs showing. Althor fired and one dog dropped, then another, then the last. I bit my lip, trying not to cry out as the animals died.

Clenching the M-16 in one hand, Althor played his fingers

over the transcom in his body, its display lighting up his side. A shriek burst out of it, one that continually changed pitch and quality, going too high to hear, dropping into audible range, then down so low that I felt rather than heard it, then back into hearing range. I later learned it was working in conjunction with components and convoluted waveguides within his body. The scaffolding around us began to shake. Beams creaked like racehorses straining at the starting gate, and with a groaning snap, one of the supports broke free, flying away from the structure.

The scaffolding buckled. We lunged to our feet, running for the Jag while metal and wood fell around us. I didn't understand Althor's purpose; the collapsing structure was more danger to us than to anyone else. People were shouting, someone saying he couldn't get off a clear shot. Someone else ordered him not to shoot, that the bullet might rebound into the hangar. I realized then that the chaos was helping more than hurting us.

An edge of something hit my head and I stumbled, the world going dark.

"*No!*" Althor grabbed me around the waist, half carrying me as he ran. A milcop appeared in front of us. My dazed brain saw his movements like a high-speed parade of snapshots: he raised his M-16; Althor's boot hit his arm; the gun barked; shots went wild over Althor's head; the milcop collapsed as Althor barreled into him. The canvas on the hangar loomed in front of us—

And we stopped.

Four milcops stood there, their backs to the canvas, only a few yards away, their M-16s trained on Althor. He stared at them, his inner lids glinting in the sunlight. He still had his gun, but if he tried to aim and fire it, we all knew the milcops would shoot. He might get off one round, but not before they fired. And they were too close to miss.

The man with dust-blond hair spoke to Althor. "Drop your weapons."

Althor touched the transcom in his waist, silencing it. His face was impassive, but I felt his frustration like steel bands. I picked up something else, too, an emotion less easy to define. Fear? Some, yes, but this was different. Longing. To stand this close to the Jag and be unable to reach it was physically painful to him.

"We don't want to hurt you," the dust-blond man said. His awe felt like velvet on my skin. He would shoot Althor if necessary, but he didn't want to. None of the guards was supposed to know what Althor was, but they had guessed. This one wanted to *talk* to him, ask a hundred questions, not as an interrogation, but to speak to our first visitor from beyond Earth. He wanted to understand why Althor looked human, why he was here, how his ship worked. He wanted Althor to help us fly to the stars.

Actually, two of the milcops felt that way. The third was just doing his job. The fourth, a man with a clenched face, made me uneasy. He saw Althor as a threat beyond imagining. Had he and Althor been alone, he would have shot Althor point-blank with no qualms at all, certain he was protecting Earth. Fear made his thoughts vivid: he disagreed with the decision to place no explosives on Althor's ship—better to risk losing the Mojave Desert than the entire planet.

Voices came from behind us. Glancing back, I saw a line of milcops several yards away. One, a woman, was speaking into a walkie-talkie, making a report. Dispirited, I turned back. The dust-blond man was still talking in his soothing voice: *drop your weapon, release your hostages, come with us.* As Althor let the M-16 slide out of his hand, I closed my eyes. It was over. Done. We were caught.

"Whoa, *shit*," a voice yelled. "It's alive!"

I snapped opened my eyes. Everyone was staring at the hangar entrance. The wind had lifted the canvas again, kept lifting it, in fact, higher than seemed reasonable, given the weights holding it down. Then I realized it wasn't wind pushing that canvas up.

Althor couldn't go to the Jag, so it was coming to him.

It rolled out fast, straight at us. The milcops scattered, running to keep from being crushed. As soon as the man with the clenched face was clear, he spun around and fired his M-16 at the ship.

"Don't *shoot* it!" someone shouted.

Althor ran for his ship, dragging Daniel and me with him, so close to the Jag that my hand rubbed it. The hull had a pebbly texture, like a golf ball. A hatch sucked open and Althor lifted me off the ground, literally throwing me inside. I slid across a deck of glowing blue tiles and plowed into a pile of computer print-outs. Althor shoved Daniel after me, then jumped inside while Daniel rolled out of the way. Heather and Joshua scrambled in just before the hatch sucked closed like the shutter on a high-speed camera.

As I jumped to my feet, an explosion rocked the ship and flung us across the cabin. Althor's injured shoulder smashed against a bulkhead and I felt agony sear through him, so intense he almost blacked out. But he didn't falter. He pushed into the cockpit, squeezing between the bulkhead and pilot's seat. Papers, pens, and calculators lay strewn over the console in front of him. He sent them flying with a sweep of his hand and shoved himself into the seat. It snapped an exoskeleton around his body in a form-fitting mesh, bringing an array of panels to his fingertips.

Then it touched his mind.

Althor gasped. At least, that was the audible sound. In his mind, he screamed. His link with the Jag shattered. I only picked up a ghost of his pain, but even that almost sent me into shock.

Another explosion hit the ship, a dull boom against the hull. The force of it threw me into Daniel and we fell with an impact that sent my breath out in a gasp. Scrambling back to our feet, we grabbed handholds in the bulkhead, hanging on with Heather and Joshua.

Althor quit trying to reach the Jag through his web and spoke in his own language. A screen in front of him glittered blue, swirling with lines and speckles. Then a three-dimensional image of the scene outside appeared.

Some of the milcops had backed away from the ship, staring at it with a mixture of fear and wonder. Several were struggling with the clenched-face man, trying to wrest away his gun. He flipped one over his back and knocked out another, tearing away from them long enough to throw something at the Jag. As another blast shook the ship, I saw the dust-blond milcop fire his M-16—not at the Jag, but at the man with the clenched face. The man went down, clamping one hand around his knee.

Althor was still speaking to the Jag, low and fast. The ship hovered at the edges of his mind, extending probes here, there, making brief connections, withdrawing if Althor flinched, strengthening the link if he didn't.

A rainbow appeared in the holo of the scene outside, super-imposed over it. As the colors swept across the milcops, they clapped their hands to their ears. From my link to the Jag, I picked up what happened: the ship was using membranes in its hull to make sound waves painful to human ears. The rainbow was an image the Jag produced in the holo of the scene outside to show the waves: red for maximum density, purple for minimum.

The milcops backed away. Several were already out of the en-closure and sprinting for an office building, one shouting into a walkie-talkie. They had no way of knowing what the Jag was about to do. Attack? Explode?

When the rainbow reached the fence, it turned muddy. That blurring quickly spread back into the enclosure, making the col-ors run together and fade. I caught a message from the Jag: it was missing something—an instruction set—equations for dealing with certain boundary conditions. Its corrupted system was mis-reading the interference created by the fence as an instruction to turn off the sound.

Nor could Althor get the Jag to move. It had stopped about halfway out of the hangar. He asked for a grid of some kind, but whatever routines the Jag needed to process that com-mand weren't functioning. Finally he touched a disk on his exoskeleton, entering commands manually. The grid appeared, a three-dimensional lattice superimposed on the scene outside. A blazing red dot swept through the image, outlining the hangar walls—

With no warning, the hangar exploded. Debris flew every-where, hurtling through the air. The remaining milcops inside the enclosure took off, scrambling over the nearest section of fence. Some dropped to the ground, protecting their heads with their arms while debris flew above them. A block the size of a door came at the Jag. In the holomap, it looked like it was shooting straight at Althor. When it crashed against the outside hull, it appeared to shatter only inches away from his face.

Then the hangar was gone. The Jag stood free under open sky.

A loud rumbling started, vibrating the deck. Outside, the last of the milcops jumped to their feet and ran like wind in a hurricane. One man tripped over a chunk of debris and another hauled him up, dragging him until he could run again. The Jag's rumbling built, growing stronger and louder.

Althor swiveled his seat around and regarded the four of us. "Some of the launching routines are—I don't know the word. What you call 'off-line,' I think."

"Can you fix them?" Heather asked.

"They fix themselves. It will take a few seconds." He turned to me. "I need hostages. But not four. If you—" He stopped. "If you want to go, you must leave now."

This was it. He might escape or he might die, but either way he was leaving. Words stuck in my throat. I couldn't say what he wanted to hear. I couldn't go with him.

When I didn't react, Althor's face became an emotionless mask. Swiveling his seat around, he turned back to his controls. The airlock sucked open.

"Hurry," Althor said. The rumbling from the Jag's engine became more insistent. "I must leave."

I went to the airlock. I was making the choice Jake had offered, at Caltech, taking safety and the known against my fear of the unknown. I thought I could live with it: Jake was also an empath, a Kyle operator, not as strong as Althor, but still an empath.

But I couldn't forget Althor's words: *It's like starving inside.* Being with Jake was just enough sustenance to stay alive.

I turned around. "Wait."

Althor remained intent on his controls. He had turned into a machine again, whether on purpose or because he had no control over it, I didn't know. His voice was flat. "I have no time to wait."

"Take me too," I said.

The airlock closed. "You will come with me?" he asked.

"You have to promise." I swallowed. "Promise you won't strand me in some universe I don't know, where I can't understand anything."

He swiveled his seat to face me. "I will promise this, if you promise to be my wife."

I couldn't understand why he wanted it, given how little we knew each other, but there it was. "I promise."

"Swear that you will connect to no other network," Althor said. "Local or remote."

"I don't underst—"

"Swear. Or I will not take you."

"But you were the one who asked—"

He regarded me with shielded eyes. "I was too closely integrated with my emotional functions then. In this mode, I have higher clarity of thought."

He was lying. I knew it then and I know it now. I saw the orange flicker around his body. But he was in control now and he meant to get what he wanted.

"And you?" I asked. "You'll promise the same for me?"

"Yes," he said. "You have access to my systems. You are in my mods, nets, memories, and files. Your influence has migrated to all of my processors. No virus scanner can remove such a thorough invasion of my systems without destroying their integrity. If you come with me, the fact of your presence will continue to rewrite my code, penetrate memory locations, alter functions."

My thought then was: *What am I getting into?* But I had no time to think it over. "You have my word. I won't betray you."

"I trust your word. I will take you."

Just like that. A switch in his brain changed from one setting to the other. He turned back to his ship, dropping our conversation as if swapping to another node. I went back to the others, embarrassed at having such a strange, personal conversation in front of an audience.

The link between Althor and the Jag strengthened as the ship found more locations in his web it could safely access. Their communication was too fast to follow now, a dance of verbal, vocal, and manual messages. They were merging. Except it wasn't only them. I was trapped in their link.

A growl sounded behind us. Turning, I saw two panels open down from a bulkhead like drawbridges, three feet wide and four feet long. White material covered each panel and filled the cylindrical hollows they had uncovered.

"Get in the cocoons," Althor said. "All of you."

As I stepped toward the hollows, I overheard a message from the Jag about aircraft "scrambling from Nellis." My foot touched a panel and the material on it snapped a ropy arm around my leg. It yanked, and I fell across the panel. Other ropes snaked around my body and dragged me into the cavity, maneuvering until I sat facing outward with my legs stretched out. The cottony material covered everything except my nose and eyes, and the panel sank into the deck until my legs lay in a rectangular depression filled with a silky white cocoon.

"What the— Shit!" Daniel jerked as a rope of cocoon silk pulled him down. He fell across my legs, his knees thudding into my thighs. He thrashed as the cocoon crammed him into the hollow with me, but the harder he fought, the tighter it wrapped around him.

"Daniel." I struggled underneath him. "I can't breathe. You're too heavy."

"Sorry," he muttered. He slid his arms around my waist and we maneuvered into a more tolerable position, with me in his lap and our legs stretched out. His embarrassment left a sharp astringent scent in the air. In the other cocoon, Joshua and Heather had their arms wrapped around each other, looking far more content with their close quarters.

"Daniel," I said.

"Look, I'm sorry," he said. "I can't help this."

"I know. That's okay. Do you know what scrambling means? Aircraft scrambling from Nellis?"

"Where did you hear that?"

"The Jag told Althor."

"Nellis is an air force base near Las Vegas," he said. "Scrambling means they have chase planes in the air, probably an umbrella over Yeager flying a loose 'flagpole' around the base and surrounding area. They'd chase off any aircraft trying to find out what was in that hangar."

I swallowed. "And stop anyone trying to take off?"

He exhaled. "Yes. I wouldn't be surprised if they have a squadron airborne at all times right now. Maybe twenty-four aircraft working in waves, six new to launch each time six land."

"Do you think Althor can get past them?"

He spoke uneasily. "I don't see how."

From the cocoon, only a corner of the holo in the cockpit was visible. It was enough, though, to see a blast of flame sear the area around the ship, followed by clouds of exhaust that billowed over the debris-strewn asphalt. The rumbling grew more insistent and the deck tilted, pressing us back into the cocoon.

The Jag lifted into the air. Althor's link with it slipped—no, *ripped.* He made no sound, but I felt the scream he bit back. I later learned his damaged links with the Jag were stimulating neurons in his brain that registered pain. He wasn't actually being hurt, but the messages his brain received interpreted it that way.

The Jag hung a few yards above the ground, its thrust balancing gravity. Billows of exhaust filled the holo image; whatever stealth systems the ship had obviously weren't functioning. Yet despite all that excitement, the ship barely managed to wobble over the fence. It climbed higher and cleared the next hangar, blasting the roof into oblivion. We made it out over a taxiway— and the thrust quit.

We dropped in a sickening lurch. The engines kicked in, cut off—and we hit asphalt with a jarring impact. It shoved the air out of my lungs as if I'd been kicked in the ribs. Althor's hands flashed over his controls, his voice running a stream of commands. Instead of trying to take the ship straight up again, he taxied across the asphalt, engines roaring. We turned onto a long road and sped up until it felt as if a huge, invisible hand pushed us into the cocoon. The ground fell away—no, we leapt away from the base.

Static came from the cockpit. ". . . immediately," a crisp voice said. "I repeat, land your craft immediately."

"My intent is not hostile," Althor said.

I heard an indrawn breath and voices crackling in the background. The crisp voice spoke again. "Then land your craft and release your hostages. If you refuse, we can only assume your intentions are not to the benefit of this country. Or planet."

Messages flashed in my brain, data sent from the Jag to Althor. Most of it was in Iotic, but bits and pieces came in English. Whether the Jag deliberately translated or was automatically adapting to my mind, I didn't know. But from the familiar words and the images the ship produced, the situation became clear: a "ceiling" of fighters was holding us down. We were flying in a low circle while the Jag searched for a hole in the ceiling.

"If I land," Althor said, "I am your prisoner."

"We have no wish to harm you," the man at the base said.

"Why should I trust you?" Althor asked.

"Trust has to begin somewhere. You ask us to trust that you aren't hostile. Prove it."

I felt Althor's anger crackle, felt the words *I don't have to prove anything to you* on his tongue. He bit them back. Instead he said, "Call off your fighters."

"You violated our airspace," the man answered. "With an armed warcraft. If you refuse to land, we will be forced to use whatever means necessary to stop you."

"If you fire on this craft," Althor said, "it will be considered an act of hostility by Skolian Imperial Space Command."

Another voice came on the radio. This man was excited, barely able to contain his words. "We don't want to hurt you! We want to talk to you. What is your Space Command? Are your people coming here? How do you know English so well?"

Althor spoke carefully, choosing his words with help from a translator that whispered in his mind. "My commanding officers know where I am. If you persist in holding me, they will interpret it as a hostile act."

The first voice came back on the radio, clipped and cold. "We have found no trace of another ship in this system. Your craft was damaged and abandoned in orbit."

"I've already contacted the mothership," Althor said.

"No indication exists that your craft transmitted any message."

"Then your search was too primitive," Althor said. I knew he was stalling.

"Land now," the voice said. "Or we will fire."

Throughout the exchange, the Jag was sending Althor updates on its web. Most of its weapons and navigations capability were off-line. With Althor's help, it was fixing itself, but it wasn't easy. It couldn't have sent any message anywhere, and Yeager was calling his bluff.

"They ought to be more afraid of what will happen if they don't let him go," I said.

"You think if they captured a MiG, they'd let it go?" Daniel asked.

"This isn't a EuroEast airplane. It's from another star."

"And its pilot knows English? Looks human? Leaves his ship spying on the planet? Kidnaps a woman and commits murder as practically his first acts on Earth? They must be scared shitless."

"You agreed to help."

"I'm just trying to make you see why those chase planes will fire on us."

I spoke softly. "Daniel, we could die."

He swallowed. "I know that."

"But you still wanted a ride."

"Hell, yeah. When will I ever get this chance again? Besides, they'll do everything in their power to get Althor back alive."

"I hope you're right," I muttered.

In the cockpit, Althor was trying to negotiate. "You've damaged my craft. I may not be able to land."

"Can you eject?" the crisp voice asked.

"Not all five of us."

A message from the Jag flashed in Althor's mind. In the same instant, pressure slammed my chest, flattening me against Daniel.

"Holy *shit*." The voice came from what the Jag identified as a chase plane. "Look at that mother go!"

The pressure grew worse, crushing us. Spots danced in my vision. Darkness closed in, withdrew, closed in again.

The pressure stopped as suddenly as it had started. Daniel slumped forward, his head against mine, and a red drop of liquid floated past my face. Twisting around, I saw that his eyes were closed. Blood from his nosebleed floated through the air in wet spheres.

Turning back, I saw Althor floating toward us. It was eerie the way he moved, as if he were underwater. His tie drifted, its end curling in the air. I struggled to breathe, but I couldn't get enough air. I looked past Althor to the holo that showed outside the ship—and I passed out.

9

Psiber Fight

I think she's waking up," Heather said.

I rose through the darkness toward her voice.

"Tina?" Althor asked. "Can you hear me?"

I opened my eyes. A trio of faces looked down: Heather, Althor, Daniel. They crouched around the cocoon, holding handles on the bulkhead, hair drifting about their heads. Daniel's nosebleed had stopped and Heather looked fine. Althor had taken off his tie and jacket, and the outline of his vest showed under his shirt. His contacts and beard were gone. Fresh blood stained his shirt, and though he showed no outward sign of discomfort, I picked up the throbbing pain in his shoulder.

The slice of the cockpit visible from the cocoon showed only a bulkhead. The holo had vanished. I wanted to look again, convince myself the stunning image I had seen was real. Earth. The turquoise ball had hung against the stars like a jewel in the Milky Way's glittering swath.

A mechanical pencil drifted by my nose and my hair swirled in a black cloud, freed from its wig. I tried to get up and floated out of the cocoon.

"We're in orbit," I said.

Althor caught me around the waist. "Just barely."

"Will you turn on the holomap again?" I asked.

"The what?" Heather asked.

"Holomap," Althor said. "In the cockpit. It was showing Earth."

"How did you know to call it a holomap?" Daniel asked me.

"I don't know." It hadn't occurred to me to call it anything else.

Althor picked me up as if I weighed nothing, which I guess I did. He pushed against a bulkhead and we floated toward the cockpit, nudging aside debris that drifted in the cabin. I finally saw Joshua; he sat in the other cocoon, eyes closed, face pale.

"What happened to Josh?" I asked.

"He's fine," Althor said.

"He looks awful."

"He's sick." Althor pushed into the cockpit. "It happens to some people in free fall. Heather threw up too. You and Daniel both passed out. The oxygen mix in your cocoon was wrong."

He slid me into the pilot's seat, and it molded its exoskeleton around me. Control panels shifted in to fit my smaller size. A visor lowered over my head, hieroglyphs scrolling across it in a stream, but I pushed it back up, feeling trapped. Prongs poked the base of my spine and neck, trying to plug into nonexistent sockets. Even without a direct link to the Jag, though, I felt it more now. Cool. Impersonal. Puzzled. It wasn't sure what it had caught.

Its exchanges with Althor murmured in my mind: we could go no farther until it repaired navigation and thrusters. We had been lucky to make it this far, into what it called a low-polar orbit. Althor had rigged a temporary fix to the shroud, enough so that we were, for the time being, hidden.

The Jag was also eavesdropping on Earth. The authorities apparently believed it was a scout of some kind. The ship picked up fragments of an argument, someone warning against shooting us down, that they didn't know what would happen if the craft exploded. Another voice overrode it, giving orders to shoot.

Behind the transmissions, the Jag's report on Earth-based weapons droned in my mind: *Theater High-Altitude Air Defense, Patriot PAC3, Light Exo-Atmospheric Projectile, RAPTOR/TALON, HEV* . . . It went on like a chant, the Jag digging up identities of what—to it—must have been centuries-old defense systems that might not even have the same names in this universe. Althor asked a question and it answered, something about certain missiles being ground-launched, unable to reach us.

Althor "stood" wedged between the pilot's seat and the forward controls, facing toward the cabin. It seemed a strange position for a pilot to take, but it didn't really matter; the ship uploaded what he needed into his brain no matter what direction he faced. The process wasn't as efficient as when he plugged into the Jag, but it still worked. The ship's web sent out electromagnetic signals, most in the infrared, and Althor's sockets acted as IR receivers.

A yellow legal pad with notes scribbled on it was drifting next to us. Althor sent it floating back into the cabin. "Can you clean up the junk in here?" he said to someone behind me. I leaned around and saw the others floating there, watching us.

"Sure," Heather said.

"Put it in the cocoons," Althor said. "They will transfer the debris to a holding cavity."

As they went to work, I tried to get out of the pilot's seat. "I should help." The seat, however, had other ideas. It refused to release me.

Althor brushed my hair away from my forehead, where the scaffolding had hit. "I think you need to sit for a while. This is a bad bruise."

"I'm okay."

His expression gentled. "Humor me, then."

Joshua spoke. "Althor, do you have a bag?"

I looked back. Joshua was floating in the center of the cabin, his face pale. Althor took one look at him, then opened a panel in a bulkhead and pulled out a tubelike device.

Heather floated over to Joshua. She spoke in a low voice meant only for him, but the Jag picked it up and transmitted her words to my brain.

"What's wrong?" Heather asked.

"I'm sorry," Joshua muttered. "I think I'm going to chuck up everything."

"Why are you apologizing?" She reddened. "You held it longer than I did."

Althor went over and gave Joshua the tube. "Astronauts with far more training than you two get sick. It's nothing to be embarrassed about."

Joshua smiled wanly. "Thanks."

Althor returned to the cockpit and opened a bulkhead. He took out a bowl with a cluster of small domes attached to its inner surface and fastened the domes to various of the forward control panels. One by one a prong extended from the top of each dome, glowing with red light.

He unbuttoned his cuff and rolled up his sleeve, revealing his wrist guard. It was an odd image, a man in a conservative shirt wearing what looked like a gang member's black leather guard. It's an apt image for a Jagernaut, though; controlled violence governed by the tenets of civilization. Their empathic traits combine with their enhanced combat abilities in a dualism that, at its best, produces officers who choose to live by a demanding code of honor, balancing their destructive abilities with a strong sense of ethics. It is also the reason why their suicide rate is so high; empathy and warfare don't mix well.

He turned the inside of his wrist down and pressed his guard onto the prong on a dome.

"What are those?" I asked.

"Web mods." He lifted his wrist, bringing the dome with it. On its flat side, which had been flush with the control panel, the tip of a tube glowed red.

He told me the red light was a laser. It swept over a micromesh inside the control panel, producing a diffraction pattern. The condition of the software and equipment controlled by that panel determined the shape of the mesh, and hence its diffraction pattern. The domes digitized the diffraction data and sent it to the miniweb in Althor's wrist guard, which dealt with minor errors and referred more serious problems to his biomech web. For minor damage, it made fixes by sending commands to the dome, which translated them into a diffraction pattern for the panel. The panel responded by changing its associated systems until the mesh configuration they produced gave a matching diffraction pattern.

"For more extensive damage," Althor said, "the domes act as diagnostic tools."

"What do they tell you about the Jag?" I asked.

He grimaced. "That it's a mess."

"You got away," I said. "That's the important thing."

"Boy, did he ever get away," Daniel whooped. "He left those Jinn-19 jet fighters in the dust."

Althor plugged the dome back in. "I'm not away yet."

The Jag continued to murmur in my mind: . . . *exceeded range of St-IV . . . Polar orbit, 500 kilometers . . . navigation systems corrupted . . . WARNING: ARROW systems deployed . . . radar directed/inertial update . . . IR terminal homing . . .* Throughout it all, the ship kept poking my brain, like the host at a party searching out the identity of a stranger who had showed up.

A siren screamed.

The cockpit lit up like a Christmas tree. Panels snapped away from my body, jerking forward to Althor. The crippled computer couldn't control them, and they ended up pushing him down on his knees so that he was wedged between my legs and the forward controls, facing away from me. He didn't waste time untangling me from the seat, just yanked the panels around his body. The cockpit changed shape to make him its focal point with me riding piggyback. In the cabin behind us, I heard the others getting into the cocoons.

The Jag tried to strengthen its link with Althor, but his mind recoiled—so it blasted its messages into my mind: *WARNING: shroud failed. WARNING: XB-70 aircraft carrying SRAM Rotary launchers. WARNING: air-launched missile approaching.*

The cockpit disappeared.

I was in space, in a gigantic gold lattice of human-sized cells. I still felt the pilot's seat, but the virtual reality was so vivid that the lattice seemed real. Earth hung below, sea blue and turquoise, showing North and South America scantily dressed in clouds.

Data scrolled inside the cell on my right. As soon as my attention shifted to it, the cell swelled to fill my field of view. Information flooded through it and my brain: missile trajectories, construction, tracking systems; Jinn-19, KC-135, a slew of acronyms I didn't understand. It came far too fast to absorb. How did Althor process it all?

As I thought of him, the data flood receded, shifting back to the edge of my view. Several cells in front of me, a violet pulse formed. The Jag sent new data: *height, 194 cm; weight, 114 kg; eyes, purple; hair, purple; humanoid class, gamma—*

It was Althor. The Jag was showing a representation of him.

A beacon swept the grid and played across my cell, probing it. Then it blinked out and the flood of data stopped. In front of me, the violet pulse elongated, forming arms, legs, a head. When it finished, Althor stood there, facing toward the Earth, his body made out of violet light. Representations of the approaching missiles appeared within the grid as red blips. The Jag had responded to my confusion, finding a way to present the data in a form I could absorb.

Six minutes to impact, the Jag thought.

Althor hurled a white orb at the missile swarm, and it streaked through the lattice. I noticed a gray blur at the edge of my vision. In response to my attention, it moved into view, expanding into the detailed image of a satellite with an FSAF insignia on its hull. A turret swiveled on it and a beam stabbed out, highlighted in white by the simulation. The Jag reeled off statistics: *coherent radiation—long range—impact in one second*—and the computer-generated image of the laser beam splattered around our cell locations like liquid over a giant bubble.

Ninety-four percent of incident energy absorbed or deflected by plasma shield, the Jag thought. In response to my confusion, it poured on more data: the "shield" was a plasma that deflected X-rays. That meant, however, that it was also opaque to electromagnetic radiation at lower frequencies. At the one point where the plasma intersected the hull, an observation probe extended through the shield, one advanced enough so that even moderate exposure to X-rays couldn't cook it.

The orb Althor had hurled reached the cloud of blips, missing the outermost missiles but catching one in the middle. The orb vanished, along with three blips. It was eerie to see them disappear in silence, without even a flash of light.

No gas exists in space to be heated into a fireball by an explosion, the Jag told me. Then: *Eighty-nine percent of incident X-rays absorbed or deflected by plasma field.*

The bombs may have made no sound, but Earth responded with an explosion of words. The pilot of a chase plane yelled, "Jumpin' crickets, that baby ain't no fucking *scout.*" More reactions poured in as surface bases registered the explosions. Some urged a stop to the missile launches; others urged they be stepped up. One thing was certain: they were scared. This "baby" didn't need a mothership; it had its own fangs.

Althor hurled another orb at the missiles. He had trouble with his aim; as soon as the orb started through the lattice, it was obvious it would go nowhere near its targets. He tried throwing another, with even worse results. The orbs tried to home in on the swarm, but either their tracking systems were also damaged or else the approaching missiles had some way of throwing off pursuit.

A gold rod in the "roof" of Althor's lattice cube became supple, like a vine, and coiled around his wrist. When he raised his arm to throw another orb, the vine tugged, correcting his motion. The link between his mind and the system solidified—and Althor gasped with pain. As his cry echoed through the lattice, the vine snapped away from his wrist, flailing like a broken rubber band. His image faded into a smudge of purple. It reformed quickly, but with distorted and blurred edges.

Missile tracking systems failure rate at 64 percent, the Jag thought.

Jaaaag. Althor's thought phased in and out. *Traaansferrrr to naaavigaa . . .*

WARNING: the Jag thought. *Navigation systems failing.*

Jag, I thought.

A fiber detached from the lattice and coiled around my head. *Attending.*

Can you show me what's wrong with navigation?

The lattice underneath Althor's feet lit up, highlighting the rods that formed edges of the cube. Except they were no longer rods. They had become great twists of gold rope. Unraveling rope.

Althor let go of his orbs and grasped the navigation "rope," clutching the ends to keep them from raveling. The orbs floated away from him, meandering around his grid cell.

Navigation control restored, the Jag thought. *Weapons interface corrupted.*

Dropping the cords, Althor grabbed at the orbs. As his hand closed on one, the Jag thought: *Weapons interface integrity recovered by 21 percent. Navigation systems failing.*

I reached forward. Shimmering with blue light, my arms stretched across the lattice, longer and longer, until they reached Althor's cube. I took hold of the cords at his feet.

Navigation integrity restored, the Jag thought.

Althor spun around. *Tina! Get out of the system! This could damage your brain.*

Get the bombs, I thought. I pulled back to my grid cell, bringing the navigation cords. They dragged along my arms until the shimmering blue skin broke and swirls of electronic bits dripped onto the grid.

Althor whirled back around. He hurled more orbs, and they streaked toward the warheads. With the missiles closer now, it took less time to reach the swarm. Most of the orbs missed, but they came around and went after the missiles again, homing with better accuracy than before.

More red blips disappeared. Only two remained.

Missile tracking failure at 84 percent, the Jag thought.

Althor swore and yanked down a rod from the lattice above him. It split in two, one half coming away in his hands while the other lengthened until it reformed the cube's edge. The half in his hands grew, molding into a massive gun. Even as it formed, he was bracing its bulk against his shoulder.

Then he fired. As a beam shot out from the virtual representation of the gun, the Jag poured out stats: *focused beam, 2.2 MeV, antiprotons . . . particle penetration into nucleus . . . excitation from bound to unbound state*—and the beam hit the approaching blips.

They disappeared. Just like that. Quiet as a night on the desert. With a gasp, Althor sagged to his knees.

Missile launch from XB-70 craft in quadrant sixteen, the Jag thought. Another swarm of red blips appeared in the lattice.

Althor struggled to his feet, hefting up his mammoth gun. He moved as if the virtual weapon were too heavy to lift. His image wavered, then became distinct again.

Tracking systems inoperational, the Jag thought.

NoOoOoO. Althor's protest vibrated.

Switching to backup, the Jag thought. Then: *Unable to access backup modules.*

I'll DOOOooooo it, Althor thought. He reached toward a group of gray cells behind the gold cubes where we stood. His arm pulled out longer, longer—

And stretched so thin that it detached from his body. It dropped through the lattice as a dead weight, bits of memory pumping out the stub on his shoulder. His image distorted, then melted onto the grid like wax pooling at the base of a burning candle. His virtual scream curled through the grid, fading as his image dimmed.

I was alone with the warheads.

JAaAaAaG! My cry bounced everywhere.

A thread coiled toward me. *Attending.*

Is Althor dead?

Commander Selei has discontinued.

What does that mean?

Commander Selei has discontinued. Then: *My EI functions are degraded. I have lost autonomous capability. You must input commands.*

Commands? *Get us out of here,* I thought.

Navigation degraded by 94 percent. Backup inaccessible. I cannot execute command.

Then blow up the bombs.

Tracking systems inoperational. Weapons/navigation interface corrupted. Backup inaccessible. I cannot execute command.

I didn't want anyone executed, including us. *Can you make us invisible?*

No. Shroud nonfunctional.

What's wrong with it?

The codes that control it are corrupted.

Show me in a way that I understand.

Look up.

I looked. A sky hovered within the lattice. *What is that?*

A representation of the code.

I could "see" the errors. They showed like cracks, a mess of fissures that turned the sky into a giant jigsaw puzzle.

Fix the sky, I thought.

Specify 'fix.'

Make some plaster.

Specify 'plaster.'

Like mortar. To repair the cracks in the shroud.

The shroud consists of energy fields, projections at various electromagnetic wavelengths, modulation of hull properties, and evasive maneuvers. It cannot crack.

I pointed at the jigsaw puzzle sky. *Make plaster to fix that.*

Specify nature of replacement code.

I don't know how. Can't you?

Damage to my web has deposited data in the wrong memory addresses and erased crucial links.

What does that mean?

I am too injured to properly rewrite my own code.

I concentrated, submerging my mind more deeply into the Jag. Although I didn't realize it at the time, I was lending it my Kyle abilities to augment its EI brain. In a sense, I was helping it heal much as I had helped Althor. All I understood then was that it needed ideas on how to fix its "sky," suggestions that might help as it struggled to rewrite its damaged code.

The plaster must be thick enough to fill cracks, I told it. *But thin enough to not interfere with how the sky works.*

After a pause, it thought, *I am only able to reconstruct part of my code. Probability of successful operation raised from .04 to 11 percent.*

Eleven percent wasn't enough. But the swarm was so close now. We couldn't have more than a few—

Estimated time to impact is ninety-three seconds, the Jag thought.

Think! I told myself. *Jag, the plaster must bend without breaking, if the sky needs to bend, but must be strong enough to keep the sky together. It must be smooth enough so it doesn't interfere with operation of the—the lattice. It must be—* Be what? *It must be able to change consistency to adapt to changes in the sky.*

Probability of successful operation raised to 43 percent, the Jag thought. The cracks in the sky went white, filled with putty. Nothing else happened. *Estimated time to impact is twenty-two seconds.*

The first of the red blips reached the unit cell of the lattice where Althor had stood—

And—?

The missile disappeared.

What happened? I asked.

Waveform modulation reduced to 13 percent.

What does that mean?

We cannot withstand another direct hit.

Direct hit!? I had neither seen nor felt anything.

Estimated time to next missile impact is eleven seconds, the Jag said.

I heaved on the raveled navigation cords, kicking the Jag into a course change. I had no idea where we went, only that acceleration hit us, shoving Althor's body into my knees. The missiles hurtled through space where we had been only a moment ago.

I cannot withstand the stress of our present acceleration, the Jag thought. Then: *Air-launched missiles from European quadrant.* Another swarm of red blips appeared, coming from the direction of the EuroWest.

Jag, I thought. *Sand the plaster on the sky. Fix the damn thing.*

Replacement code applied.

A cloak of darkness fell over the mindscape. The lattice shone gold against black velvet, and the pack of missiles racing toward us glittered like sparks.

Shroud functional, the Jag thought.

I yanked the nav cords again, kicking us into another course change, gritting my teeth as the acceleration increased. *Can the missiles find us?*

Yes. Our exhaust is visible. WARNING: navigation systems failing. WARNING: if we continue to accelerate, the stress will weaken my structure past the point of recovery.

Fix our course and get rid of our exhaust, I thought.

Course change implemented, the Jag thought.

The force pushing Althor against my legs vanished and the navigation cords stopped disintegrating. The most damaged sections of rope began to weave back together.

Are we safe now? I asked.

No. I estimate the probability of a hit in the range 8–27 percent.

That's better than before.

This is an accurate statement.

Let me see Althor.

Commander Selei is discon—

I meant, let me out of this lattice thing.

Released.

Gradually I became aware of the cockpit again. My mind felt bruised. Althor was slumped over the forward controls. Looking around, I saw Daniel wrapped in one cocoon and Heather and Joshua clinging together in the other.

I turned back and laid my hands on Althor's back. *Jag. Is he alive?*

He is discontinued.

I don't know what that means.

His processing units have ceased operation. His brain no longer responds to input.

I tensed. *You mean he's brain-dead?*

No. His neural activity has not ceased. He is dormant.

Can we help him?

I can reboot his brain.

Will that hurt him?

Each time he overextends himself, it exacerbates the damage. Until repaired, his human/psiber interface should be used for no more than amplification of his link with you.

Why only with me?

The interaction between the two of you is not synthetically created, the Jag thought. *It would exist without his web. Enhancing that link should not further corrupt his systems. It may aid his repair processes.*

Why?

You are a healer. You can exert biofeedback control over your own body and to some extent, through your Kyle centers, to those of others.

Like my mother. *How much can I help him?*

I do not have enough data to quantify your Kyle rating.

My rating?

I am unable to determine a numerical value.

Oh. I wondered if Althor had suffered brain damage from what happened in the lattice.

Yes, the Jag thought.

How bad is it?

He can function. With proper treatment, he will heal.

If you reboot him, will it damage him any more?

No.

Do it.

The lattice reappeared around me. Then it blanked completely. No grid, no Earth, no sky, no nothing. Just black.

Althor groaned, stirring against my legs. Hieroglyphs scrolled through the blackness in my mind, white on black. The Jag murmured in Iotic; apparently Althor had made it the system default. The lattice reappeared, along with Earth. The displays again poured through the lattice in a confusing flood of symbols rather than the pictorial input I understood better. Althor's violet image shimmered into view, this time facing me, directly in front of my cube.

Are you all right? I asked.

He spoke in his own language.

Resetting language mod, the Jag thought.

I blinked. Who was I talking to, Althor or the Jag?

We are the same, Althor said. With the Jag translating, his English was perfect, or at least as perfect as the odd English the Jag used. *How did you repair the shroud?*

I guessed, I thought. *It did most of the work itself.*

That's an impressive 'guess,' Tina. His image rippled with violet light. *You should never have been subjected to that battle. I'm sorry.*

What about you? I didn't want to think what it must be like when he fought people instead of machines. Did he feel them wanting to kill him? Did he feel them die?

Althor's image dulled. *Yes.*

How do you bear it?

There was a time when I wanted so much to be a Jag pilot I could almost touch it. He exhaled. *I fast learned there was no glory in it. But it is necessary.*

I spread my hand across his chest, blending my blue with his violet. *I have to believe a better way exists to protect what we love than by killing people.*

He answered softly. *Perhaps someday we will find it.*

The attack left us subdued. For the rest of the trip, Heather, Joshua, and Daniel floated quietly at a holoscreen, watching space reel by outside the ship. As Althor worked on repairs, I monitored the lattice, letting him see it through my mind. Earth continued to search, but for the time being the shroud managed to camouflage us.

Eventually Althor stopped working. As he put away his tools, I said, "Did you fix the problem that brought you here?"

He shook his head. "I need to do more work. But I want to move away from Earth, find somewhere safer. First, though, I return my hostages." He touched the exoskeleton surrounding my body and it opened, freeing me to leave the chair. "You can ride in the cocoon on the way down. Once we're away from here, I'll fix the co-pilot's seat for you."

I pushed out of the seat. Daniel, Heather, and Joshua were floating in the cabin behind us, listening.

"You're going to let us go?" Joshua asked. Althor nodded and relief flashed across their faces. After the way he had changed the "rules" of our deal at Yeager, I understood their wariness.

"Your military will debrief you," Althor said. "Tell them I threatened to kill you if you didn't cooperate. And that I've kept Tina as a hostage. This should protect you."

Daniel spoke uneasily. "Joshua could never pull it off. He's a terrible liar." Joshua scowled at him, but didn't refute the statement. Anyone who knew him knew it was true.

"It's not a lie." Althor spoke quietly. "If necessary, I would have killed any of you."

I knew he had never intended to kill them. But they believed him, and that was what mattered. If they believed it, whoever questioned them would as well.

The sun was setting when we reached Caltech. We appeared out of nowhere, hanging next to Milikan Library, washed in a red-gold glow from the sunset. Wind battered the area as we came down, and students ran from the blast, shouting or pointing. Exhaust blistered the grass into oblivion and huge clouds billowed around the craft. Papers and books scattered everywhere, dropped by their owners or torn from their arms.

As soon as we were down, Althor jumped out of his seat and strode to the airlock. We had little time; even if we hadn't yet been detected, it wouldn't be long before fighters were on their way here. As we scrambled out of the cocoons, Althor opened the airlock and warm air flowed into the cabin. Outside, several hundred yards away, a growing crowd of people stood watching the ship.

Joshua turned to me, and we reached out together, pulling each other into a hug. "Tina—" His voice caught. "Good-bye."

A tear rolled down my cheek. "I'll miss you."

"You take care of yourself." He squeezed me, then let go and joined the others at the airlock.

Althor spoke quietly to them. "I thank you. For my life."

"Good luck," Daniel said. "To both of you." Heather and

Joshua both nodded. They all jumped down from the ship and ran across the cooling ground.

As we rose back into the sky, I watched them from a holo-screen. They looked up after us, surrounded by a crowd of people, their upturned faces receding in the twilight.

10

Inversion Interlude

Saturn wheeled above us, a golden giant banded by butterscotch stripes. Hundreds of rings circled her, like bronzed grooves on a record. Althor put us in orbit around the moon Rhea. I floated at a holoscreen, staring at Rhea's mother world, turning my bracelet around my wrist as I thought of my own mother.

"Got it!" Althor said. His legs and hips were floating in the air. The rest of him was hidden in an open bulkhead.

"Did you find what's wrong?" I asked.

"It's the engines." He maneuvered out into the cabin and floated in front of me, his body at an angle to mine. "Both the inversion drives and shroud were affected."

"Can you fix them?"

"I think so." He smiled as he watched me fiddle with my bracelet. "This is much more attractive as jewelry than a piece of plumbing."

I hesitated. "I always wanted my daughter to have it."

He understood what I didn't say. "Tina, I have wanted for a long time to be a father. But I can't make promises. It is true, we are similar. But maybe not enough."

"Is there a chance?"

"I think so. We need to ask the doctors." He touched a square on a bulkhead and a tall panel slid open, revealing two slinky space suits.

"You're not going outside, are you?" I asked.

"The Jag's self-repair functions are degraded. I need to do some work." He stripped off his clothes, smiling when I blushed, and hung them in the locker. When he put on one of the suits, it molded to his body, far more svelte than any twentieth-century space shuttle suit.

In fact, a shuttle space suit was to Althor's environment skin what a horse and buggy was to an Indy 500 race car. Shuttle suits needed seven layers, starting with nylon lining, then a garment that removed heat and waste gases by circulating chilled water through tubes. From inside out, the actual suit had a Mylar pressure bladder, a Dacron pressure restraint layer, a Neoprene layer for micrometeoroid protection, aluminized insulation, and an outer protection layer. The helmet was like a fishbowl. Gloves with silicon rubber fingertips made handling tools viable and attached to the suit via metal rings that contained ball bearings to let the wrists rotate. The astronaut wearing it maneuvered using a gas-jet-propelled unit that resembled a big backpack. The suit also had cameras, tethers, lights, solar shield, computer, microphone, and boots. Even without the maneuvering unit, it weighed 113 kilograms.

In contrast, Althor's suit was like a second skin. Its power module fit into his belt. The hood hugged his head, except for the transparent glassplex in front of his face. Nano-sized robots packed the skin: multiple bonds made robot arms, chemical groups rotating around single bonds acted as gears, molecular spheres served as ball bearings, aromatic groups formed plates, and so on. A dense mesh of fullerene tubes acted as a muscle system, one far stronger than human tissue. Nano-bots converted energy absorbed from contractions into work needed to stretch the skin. The bots' picochips formed a web that gave the skin a crude brain. A film on its outer surface acted as a solar collector and also transmitted pressure data to the picoweb, which directed bots to manipulate the inner surface so Althor "felt" what he touched. The picoweb also recycled wastes and directed the bots to perform repairs.

Althor's lips moved inside the helmet. "I'll be back soon." He took his diagnostic equipment and went to the airlock. The inner door irised, leaving behind a glimmer, as if a soap bubble hung in the opening. The outer door hissed open as the inner one closed. The timing was wrong; it sounded like the outer opened before the inner closed. Yet I neither heard nor felt any loss of air pressure.

When Althor was outside, I said, "Jag?"

Attending.

I had expected a verbal response. "How do you link to my mind so easily?"

The quantum probability distribution of your brain is currently maximized in the same spatial location as that of my processors. As a result, our overlap function is large.

I tried "thinking" to it. *What does that mean?*

Our effect on each other gets stronger as we get closer together. Right now you are inside of me.

Then why does Althor need to plug into you? I asked.

His system allows far more extensive interactions than can be achieved without a physical or electromagnetic link.

Is he all right out there?

Yes. Watch. A holo of Althor appeared on the screen showing him skimming along the hull. His suit glittered as he changed direction. *The sparkles are my representation of gas-jet spurts made by his suit,* the Jag thought. *The suit plugs into his sockets and he directs it by thinking where he wants to go.*

I thought of what it had said about Althor using his biomech links. *Is that safe?*

It may aggravate his neural injuries. However, the audio and manual controls were deactivated by the specialists at Yeager. The neural link works because they had no idea it existed.

Althor attached his equipment to the hull and went to work, bathed in Saturn's golden light. When I concentrated, I could "hear" the Jag monitoring his mental conversation with his suit, as if the ship considered Althor a valuable piece of apparatus.

Yes, the Jag thought. *He is mine.*

Its? I had no idea how to interpret that. Did the Jag see me as a rival?

The word "rival" has no meaning in this context, the Jag thought.

*He has a need for you. It is in your best interest to treat him in a man-
ner humans consider appropriate for the mutually agreed upon mating of
your species.*

Don't worry. I will.

Good. We are understood.

After what felt like eons, Althor headed back. As soon as he
was inside the cabin, I floated across the cabin and plowed into
him, my momentum sending us into a spin. Grabbing me around
the waist, he opened his helmet and pushed it back, laughing the
whole time.

"What's so funny?" I asked.

He grabbed a handhold and stopped our spin. "Will I get this
reaction every time I come in an airlock?"

I laid my head against his chest. "Just don't go out there
again."

"If I did my work right, I won't have to."

He put away his suit and dressed, then went to the cockpit
and ran more tests. I floated nearby, watching him.

Jag, can you bring the co-pilot's chair up again?

Yes. The seat rose out of the cockpit deck, squeezing in next
to the pilot's seat as bulkheads shifted position to make room. Its
exoskeleton lay open like butterfly wings; when I slid into the seat,
the mesh folded around me, molding to my limbs to allow freedom of movement.

"Do you know Heather's last name?" Althor asked.

"MacDane, I think."

A holo about six inches high appeared on the flat shelf in front
of his seat, a fiftyish woman with gray-streaked hair. Hieroglyphs
scrolled along a reflective strip on the bottom edge of the holoscreen.

"Entry," the Jag said. "Heather Rose MacDane James. Nobel
Prize in Physics, 2027 A.D. Developed James Reformulations of
relativistic theory, making possible Allied development of the inversion stardrive."

"Hey," I said. "That's Heather."

"Full entry," Althor said.

More people appeared: a slender man with an achingly familiar face and three girls ranging from about four to twelve. The Jag reeled off data about Heather's birth, life, education, and work. Then it said, "Husband, Joshua William James. Children: Caitlin MacDane James, Tina Pulivok James, Sarah Rose James."

As my mouth fell open, Althor smiled. "A good name they gave their daughter." He leaned forward, concentrating, and at first I thought he meant to bring up another holo. An odd look passed over his face, as if a spirit walked over his grave.

"What's wrong?" I asked.

"What?" He glanced at me. "Nothing. We just need to go."

So. This was it. "Okay."

We moved away from Saturn smooth and steady. Althor activated a holomap to show our progress. It couldn't show the actual ship; instead the Jag rendered an image based on its data about itself, one essentially indistinguishable from a genuine record of our progress.

Then I noticed a strangeness. The Jag was becoming less streamlined. "We're squashed."

Intent on his controls, Althor spoke in his own language and the Jag translated. "A blunter design is better after we invert."

I hesitated, wanting to ask more but concerned about interrupting his work.

"It's all right to ask," Althor said. "I'm swapping."

Although I had felt his mind swapping among different nodes in the Jag's web, I hadn't yet realized I had become another node, one he switched to when resources freed up. As Althor worked, the Jag answered my questions. It told me that if subluminal observers could record our flight, they would see our length shorten as we approached light speed. After we inverted, our length would increase, until at 141 percent of light speed it would have the same magnitude as when the Jag was at rest relative to its observers. At greater than 141 percent, length extended.

"On this jump," the Jag said, "we'll probably reach thousands of kilometers."

I whistled. "You mean, I'll see Althor as thousands of kilometers long?"

Althor smiled, and the Jag spoke. "Relative to you, I am at rest. So you see no change. I alter my shape to minimize my area relative to other reference frames."

I wondered why the Jag was speaking instead of using a neural link. I know now it was because Althor couldn't join our mental conversation until he healed. At the time it didn't occur to me that a computer would have its responses programmed—or would program itself—to take its primary user's feelings into consideration.

I motioned at the holomap. "The constellations look like they've shifted."

"We're speeding up," Althor said.

The Jag spoke. "Forty-two seconds ago, we accelerated at one hundred times the force of gravity for a period of thirty seconds. We are now traveling at 10 percent of light speed."

I laughed. "You're kidding."

"Why would I 'kid'?" the Jag asked.

"Wouldn't acceleration like that kill us?"

"We went into quasis."

"What?"

It described how the ship and everything in it formed a system, a collection of particles described by a quantum state, or wavefunction. If even one particle changed one property—position, momentum, spin, and so on—its state changed. Quasis, or quantum stasis, prevents *all* state changes. The Jag didn't freeze; its particles continued to vibrate, rotate, and otherwise move as they did during the instant quasis went into effect. But they couldn't make transitions. In theory, a system in quasis becomes infinitely rigid on a macroscopic scale. In practice, the process isn't 100 percent effective; extreme or rapidly changing forces can weaken it.

We had survived the missile hit at Earth because the Jag put us in quasis. A missile can tunnel through an object in quasis, that is, pass through without affecting it, by going into complex space.

Often, though, the projectile detonates, its momentum going into electromagnetic energy, complex space, or its own debris, which may or may not tunnel through the quasis object. No quasis is perfect, so particles in the object may also absorb momentum, causing damage.

Althor indicated a red star on his holomap. A gold halo appeared around it—and the star "jumped." In fact, all of the stars moved, converging toward a point in front of the ship. The color of the one Althor had highlighted changed from red to green.

He glanced at me. "We just came out of stasis. We're at 40 percent of light speed now."

My mouth fell open. "I didn't notice a thing."

"Your neural cells can't change their molecular state either. So you can't think a new thought during stasis."

The stars jumped again, and again, converging toward a single point. The highlighted star had turned a deep violet, almost too dark to see, and the display read 60 percent of light speed.

"How close do we have to get to light speed before we can invert?" I asked.

"It's a balance," Althor said. "Entering complex space is like detouring around an infinitely tall tree by leaving the road and entering an unfamiliar forest. The less time we spend in the forest, the better. So we go as near to the tree as we can before we leave the road; that is, we push as close to light speed as possible. Too close, though, and our increased mass uses too much fuel. It's like trying to ride up the trunk of the tree. So we don't go that close."

The stars jumped again. The highlighted star was no longer visible, its color shifted out of optical range.

Then the Jag turned inside out.

That's how it felt. We stayed inside the ship because the rest of the universe turned inside out with us. In the holomap, the stars jumped apart again, red-shifting back to normal colors. At first I recognized none of the constellations. After a moment I realized they were there, but flipped into inverted positions.

"Hey," I said. "That's why you call it inversion. Because of the stars."

"The term comes from a conformal mapping," the Jag said. "It was proposed by Mignani and Recami in the mid–twentieth century for generalized Lorentz transformations in four dimensions."

Althor smiled. "That means yes, it's an inversion."

"How fast are we going?" I asked.

"Only a hundred thousand times light speed," he said.

Only? "That sounds pretty fast to me."

"In superluminal space no upper limit exists on speed," he said. "We can never go slower than light speed, though."

"What about all that stuff about going into the past?"

The Jag answered. "According to James theory, it is impossible to arrive at our destination before leaving our departure point. However, during inversion we can travel pastward or futureward. In theory, I can optimize our trajectory so that no net time elapses in subluminal space, assuming time passes at the same rate in both the place of arrival and departure. Due to accumulation of errors, however, I estimate ten hours and fifty minutes will actually elapse." It almost sounded annoyed by its inability to match the theoretical limit.

"Where are we going?" I asked.

"Epsilon Eridani," Althor said.

"Is that where you live?"

He shook his head. "It's only about eleven light years from Earth, a quick jump, all I'm willing to risk on this faulty engine. The Allied Worlds of Earth have a station there." He paused. "I should warn you: we may end up in a universe where neither of us belongs. Or the ship may detonate when I try to reinvert."

I swallowed and nodded. As we decelerated, the constellations contracted to a point. Then the universe turned right side out and we were subluminal. I exhaled in relief as the stars settled back into their normal colors and positions. An orange sun lay in front of us, its brightness muted by the holomap.

A man's voice crackled from the com. "Imperial Jag, this is Epsilani Station. Please identify yourself!"

It wasn't until I felt Althor's flood of relief that I realized how much he had feared he would never see home again. He couldn't even answer at first. He just sat with his hands gripping a forward panel.

"Imperial Jag, respond," the voice said. "We are a civilian base. I repeat, we are civilians here. Please state your intent."

Althor took a breath. "Epsilani, this is Commander Selei, Jagernaut Secondary, ISC Sixteenth Squadron. I have a damaged ship and request docking."

"We have facilities available, Commander. Are you requesting quarters?"

"Yes," Althor said. "Repairs too."

"We'll do what we can," the man said. "We're just a science station, though. We've never seen a Jag out here."

"I understand."

"Do you need anything else?"

Althor touched his bandaged shoulder. "A doctor."

"We'll have one meet you at the dock."

"There is one other thing."

"Yes?"

Althor glanced at me. "Can anyone there make a marriage?"

Silence. Then: "Could you repeat? I'm not sure we picked up that last bit."

"A marriage. Can anyone there perform one?"

"Well—yes, I'm sure we could rig up something."

"Good." Althor watched lights blink on his controls. "I am receiving your docking signals. We're coming in, Epsilani."

II

Universe II

11

Epsilani

The planet Athena grew on the holomap, a gas giant banded by blue and red stripes. She had at least seven moons, and thin rings colored like caramel taffy and blueberry ice cream. From our direction of approach, the Epsilon Eridani space station, or Epsilani for short, looked like no more than a tiny strip of metallic tape "above" the great globe of Athena.

As we drew nearer, the "tape" resolved into a wheel. Its small size disappointed me; I had hoped for something more dramatic. A mirror-bright disk above it reflected sunlight onto the station, where more mirrors picked it up, sparkling in the black of space. The wheel rotated serenely, six spokes radiating from a central hub. A stem extended down from the hub and a stationary grid curved out from it like sepals on a flower. The wheel continued to grow as we came in, until its "stem" resolved into a chain of spheres that resembled beads, or linked seedpods, with a small bud at the end. In fact, the entire station resembled a rotating, wheel-shaped blossom.

"It's beautiful," I said. "What are all those things under it?"

"The grid is a radiator," Althor said. "It bleeds off excess heat. The hub is where we'll dock. The smaller spheres under it are probably manufacturing plants." He motioned to the rim of the wheel. "That torus is the habitat where people live."

The wheel continued to grow, until it filled the holomap. A tiny speck appeared, coming toward us from the hub—and then I realized the "speck" was a ship. My perception of the station changed, dizzyingly, like an optical illusion. Only distance had made it appear small. The wheel was more than a mile in diameter.

Althor indicated the approaching ship. "That's a Faraday drone. It will transfer us inside the plasma core."

"The what core?"

"It's a well of electrons, about one thousand coulombs' worth. It holds the habitat at a potential of fifteen billion volts. The design is based on a classic NASA study."

He motioned in the direction of the star, Epsilon Eridani. "It's protection, against cosmic rays and solar fluxes. The plasma repels particles and keeps radiation at a safe level."

The drone came in closer, until it blocked our view of the station. As it matched its speed to ours, its front end opened like a blossoming flower.

"Hey," I said. "It's swallowing us." All the holomap showed now was the interior of the drone, a metal cavity braced with giant struts. If I hadn't known the drone was moving, I would have thought we stopped.

The Jag hummed with talk from Epsilani and Althor answered, something about accepting data on a com channel. The holomap switched to a view showing the drone's approach to Epsilani, one apparently recorded from within the station. The drone had closed again and looked like an unopened flower bud.

Althor pointed at the map, indicating a feathery stem on the bud. "That's an electron gun. It bleeds electrons into the well to equalize the potential between us and the station."

The bud spurted exhaust. Through my link to the lattice, I caught a message from the station, something about compensating for a "wind" created by repulsion of positive charges on the drone and station. As the Jag adjusted to my brain, it was coming up with more and more creative ways to present data, so that I "saw" the message as an iridescent insect winging its way through the lattice. A swarm of bottle-blue flies hummed in with data about how plasma density variations were controlling instabilities in the shield. When I concentrated, more datoids appeared, flying in and out of the grid, clustering in cells, buzzing to new locations.

We had just about reached the station's hub. The drone opened its petals and they locked into the hub like a flowery jigsaw puzzle piece. An unfamiliar voice said, "Docking complete, Commander. We're all set."

"Got it," Althor said. He switched off the com and turned to me. "Before we go any further, I need to talk to you."

His expression made me uneasy. "Yes?"

"I'm not certain what situation we're facing. My ship was severely damaged before I reached Earth and I don't know why." He pushed his hand through his hair. "I don't know this station or these people. For now, I would prefer none of them know my identity, that is, that my parents are members of the Imperial Assembly."

"What do you want me to do?"

He took my hand. "Reveal as little as possible. Other than that, just follow my lead."

I squeezed his hand. "All right."

We left the ship, drifting through the airlock into a circular chamber. Except for a console in a bulkhead and a hatch across from us, the area was completely bare. Panels around the walls of the chamber bathed us with light and heat.

"Bacterial contaminants detected," a pleasant voice said. "Request permission to proceed with decon."

"Go ahead," Althor said.

I glanced at him. "Contaminants?"

"Everyone carries bacteria and other organisms," he said. "The decon web thinks some of ours might be dangerous to Epsilani's ecosystem."

"Does it want us to scrub down?" I smiled, imagining us together in the shower.

He laughed. "Unfortunately, no. It just releases nano-meds into the air."

"Like the ones in your blood?"

"Similar. Except the carrier molecules kill bacteria."

"Decon complete," the voice said. "Welcome to Epsilani."

Across the chamber, the hatch opened, and six people floated in. The man in the center was almost as big as Althor, a bit heavy around the waist, with graying temples and a confident air. A second man floated at his side, tall and angular, with jet-dark skin. Four guards accompanied them, two men and two women, what looked like security police. They too cut tall figures, and each wore a weapon, a tube with a black grip and a snout, which I later learned shot only sedatives.

The leader moved with the ease of someone comfortable in free fall. "Welcome, Commander Selei." His voice sounded odd, vaguely British, but unlike any accent I had heard before. "I'm Max Stonehedge, Director of Epsilani Station." Stonehedge indicated the second man. "This is Bob Kabatu, our expert on Skolian physiology."

As Althor nodded to them, Kabatu grinned. "Hello, Commander." He too had an unfamiliar accent, what I later learned was a dialect spoken in an African country that didn't exist in 1987. His smile faded as he looked at the blood-soaked bandage on Althor's shoulder and the bruises on his arms.

Stonehedge glanced at me. "Perhaps you'd like to introduce us to your . . ."

"Fiancée," Althor said.

"Ah. Yes." Stonehedge smiled at me. "Hello, Ms. . . . ?"

"Pulivok," I said.

Kabatu spoke up. "Commander Selei, it looks to me like that shoulder of yours is still bleeding. I'm guessing here, but I'd say it hurts like hell."

Althor paused. "It is a bit—stiff."

"Maybe we should go straight to the med center," Kabatu said. "We can save formal greetings for later."

Althor spoke carefully. "All right."

We all floated across the chamber, accompanied by the security officers. The hatch let us out into a much larger sphere, the interior of the hub. A group of people were flying around in it, doing a gymnastics class. They tumbled through the air, laughing, shouting, flipping in wild rolls that would have broken bones on Earth. Some of them called to Stonehedge and he waved back.

We crossed to another hatch, one that let out onto a passage circling the hub. The "wall" on the other side of the passage slid past, part of the rotating station. We floated with it, faster than the rotation, until we reached a pair of doors in the moving wall.

Stonehedge pressed a set of colored triangles next to the doors. They opened, and we floated into an elevator. It was more pleasant than I expected. A downy rug covered the floor and art made from delicate strips of coppery metal hung on the walls. Light diffused through a white ceiling bordered by intricate designs of parrots and bonsai trees.

We drifted upward when the elevator first moved, but after a few moments we floated to the side. Gradually our weight increased, until we settled to our feet. It felt as if we were going "down," but we were actually riding outward, to the rim of a wheel. A slight pressure pushed us sideways, making it an effort to stand up straight.

Stonehedge told us about the station, a research center built to study the Epsilon Eridani system. Epsilon Eridani was a K star, more orange than Earth's sun and only a third as luminous, with about three-quarters the mass and 90 percent the diameter. The station was a joint effort by Europe, Japan, several African countries, and the United States. United. Not Federated. About three thousand people lived in the station then, mostly adults with a growing number of children, a long way from their goal of ten thousand.

Stonehedge was easier to understand once I grew used to his accent. Although he used unfamiliar idioms, his English resembled mine more closely than mine resembled that of people three hundred years in my own past. English had become the language of science among the Allieds, extending a trend that began in the twentieth century. As humans moved out to the stars, they standardized the language, hoping to facilitate communication among increasingly diverse populations separated by light years.

The director's spiel was well rehearsed and obviously one he enjoyed giving. His enthusiasm for his station came through in every sentence. He also tried to draw Althor out, with little success. Althor did loosen up when Stonehedge got into engineering details of the station. It was different from when he and Heather talked theoretical physics; Althor had seemed informed then, but uncomfortable, out of his milieu. With practical applications he came into his own. He was a rocket man. He liked to get his hands on concrete problems and work them out.

They built Epsilani using titanium from Athena's moons. Large sections of the station were constructed via metal-vapor molecular beams, which essentially sprayed metal atoms onto large balloons. The vapor was doped with molecular robots, each consisting of molecule-sized carbon threads plus a spherical cage carrying a picochip. The bots also served as a substrate for the chemical process that wove the tubes into the titanium. After the bots finished their construction, they remained in the composite, forming a station-wide picoweb that repaired damage. If a dust particle or small meteor pierced the station, the web dispatched nano-bots to fix it.

Stonehedge told us that Epsilani's wheel was almost two kilometers in diameter and rotated at one revolution per minute. Humans could function at faster rotations, but the Coriolis forces bothered some, causing motion sickness and disorientation. Coriolis was responsible for the sideways push we felt in the elevator. The spokes also carried cables and heat exchangers that connected the habitat to external power supplies and the radiator.

When I felt about as heavy as I did on Earth, the elevator stopped. We had reached the torus, the living habitat for the colonists. The doors opened—and we stepped out into a wonderland.

A platform circled the station spoke we had just left. The spoke itself rose up behind us, through the roof of the torus far above us. I had expected the habitat to be metal surfaces and functional equipment. Instead, Epsilani resembled the Japanese Tea Garden in San Francisco. A long park about a hundred yards wide stretched in front of us, gradually curving upward, until in the distance the upper surface of the torus cut off our view.

A river ran along the center of the park. It looked odd, as if the water ran "up" the curve of the torus. In truth, the station's rotation makes each point along the river essentially perpendicular to gravity, so it doesn't really flow uphill. Delicate bridges arched over the water and trees spread their branches in leafy shelves. Lush gardens were everywhere. On either side, the park sloped up the "walls" of the torus. Houses were built into the slope, terraced affairs with many windows, patios, and even open roofs. The colonists didn't need roofs, after all, other than for privacy; they could make every day perfect.

Panes of dichromesh glass ran around the upper surface of the torus, and mirrors directed sunlight through them, so that it streamed into the park. Here and there people walked along paths. A few rode bikes, sleeker models than in my universe, but still bicycles. Dogs ran in and out of the bushes. In fact, animals were everywhere: prowling cats, red or blue birds, a rabbit bounding out of a glade. Water rippled in a nearby pond as a fish jumped up in a spray of drops.

Stonehedge told us that when Epsilani reached its target population, it would be self-sufficient. Entire sections of the torus were devoted to agriculture, and the colonists' precise control of the weather let them plant crops continuously. Numerous animals lived in the habitat, pets and livestock both. The colonists mined chemicals and metals from Athena's moons. The station had an oxygen and nitrogen atmosphere, at a humidity of about 40 percent, with a lower nitrogen partial pressure than on Earth. Photosynthesis regenerated the oxygen and removed extra CO_2. The colonists recycled everything. Tailored nano-meds broke down waste products and aided crop and livestock growth.

I gazed out at the plain. "It's lovely."

Stonehedge gave me a gentle look. "Yes. It is."

Kabatu motioned toward several buildings half a kilometer up the torus. "That's the medical complex. My office is there."

"We walk?" Althor asked.

Glancing at him, I saw the paleness of his face. New blood showed on the bandage covering his shoulder, red with a tinge of blue.

"No. We'll ride." Kabatu frowned at Althor and held up his hand. "Don't bother to argue, Commander. Those are my orders."

I almost smiled, impressed by how fast Kabatu figured out how to deal with Althor. I knew Althor didn't want to walk, but he was too stoic to ever admit it.

Kabatu nodded toward a rail that ran the length of the plain. "We'll take the mono-hoot."

"The what?" Althor asked.

Stonehedge smiled. "It's a ground-based monorail system. Someone, I forget who, said it was a hoot that we gave it such a grandiose moniker as MagRail. So we call it the mono-hoot."

Althor's mouth curved up, as if he might laugh. He didn't, though. I wondered at his wariness. The longer we spent on Epsilani, the more I liked her people. My intuition said they were exactly what they seemed: hard-working colonists who enjoyed showing off the fruits of their labor.

Still, how would I know what undercurrents swirled around us? I was treading water, struggling to float in a sea of new impressions.

Kabatu's office was sunny and cramped, its walls covered by consoles, cabinets, and equipment. He sat Althor down in a reclining chair and removed the bandage on his shoulder. One look at the wound was enough to crease his face with concern. Reaching out, he grabbed a mechanical arm off the wall. It hummed in response, and a line of yellow lights appeared, stretching from the first of its three elbows to the seven jointed "fingers" at its end. Kabatu touched the third finger and it lit up. Directing the light at Althor's shoulder, he gently probed the wound.

Althor jerked away. "What are you doing?"

"Stay still," Kabatu said. "I'm imaging the injury."

"You don't have to touch me to do that."

"This probe gives better detail." Kabatu waved his hand at the wall. Turning, I saw holos rotating in front of a screen, views of Althor's torso: the muscular system, in bands of red; his skeleton, shown in ivory; his cardiovascular system, with the arteries carrying oxygenated blood highlighted in red and the veins and pulmonary arteries carrying deoxygenated blood in blue; his nervous system, fibers branching out from his brain and spinal cord; immune system; and internal organs—heart, lungs, parts of the digestive and endocrine systems. One view showed a complex web, its conduits and "organs" highlighted in metallic colors.

"You've got biomech in there." Kabatu whistled. "Holy saints, man, you're riddled with it."

"You have a problem with this?" Althor asked.

"I've just never seen anything like it." Kabatu withdrew his probe and set the arm back onto the wall. "How did your shoulder get hurt like this?"

"Gun."

"What kind of gun?"

"Gunpowder gun. Metal bullets."

Kabatu's mouth fell open. "Who shot you with that?"

"It's not your business."

"Sorry. I'm just surprised. How did you get the bullet out?"

"Cut it out."

"Good Lord, why?" When Althor frowned, Kabatu held up his hands. "None of my business." He dropped his arms. "Here's the situation. I can fix the damage to your natural body. But your biomech is another story."

"It's self-repairing."

Kabatu nodded. "Yes, I can see it's trying to seal off the damage. But there's too much disruption for it to fix, Commander Selei. You need new components, including some bioengineered units. There's no way I can do that here. Even if I had the resources—which I don't—I've never seen a real biomech system before, much less worked on one. You need an ISC medical facility and a trained team of biomech surgeons."

Althor didn't look surprised. "But you can repair the rest of me?"

Kabatu nodded. "I'll give you some muscle and nerve builders, with anesthetics for the pain. Avoid using the biomech functions, though."

"I understand."

Kabatu cleaned Althor's wounds, using a solution dispensed by the robot arm. Next he sprayed the wounds with a mist that settled into the injured areas. At the time I assumed it was an anesthetic, but it actually contained several species of non-meds to aid the repair work of those his body already carried. He bandaged Althor with a material that molded to his body, changing color and texture to match his skin. After the bandages settled into place, it was almost impossible to distinguish them from his real skin.

"Give it a couple of cycles," Kabatu said. "It should heal by then."

"Cycles?" Althor asked.

"Earth days," Kabatu said. "Thirty or forty hours should do it."

Only two days? At first I didn't believe it. Then it occurred to me that compared to circumventing the speed of light, healing bullet wounds in two days was trivial. Yet I found it disorienting. The Jag was completely outside my previous experience, but I understood wounds and their healing. That one visit to the doctor made me more aware of the differences in Althor's universe than everything about the Jag.

Kabatu took us back to the room where Stonehedge waited with the security officers. Althor's wariness made a blue haze punctuated with glints of light. Again, I wondered at it. It seemed to me that the people here had more reason to be apprehensive of a Jagernaut than the other way around. At least they spoke English. Once we reached Althor's people, I would no longer understand even the language.

I reached for Althor's mind, but it was like hitting a wall. I didn't realize then that he had barriered it. At his command, his biomech web could release neurotransmitters that damped signals sent by his KEB. If his web released too much of the chemical, or for too long, he became groggy and eventually passed out. But for short periods, he could make it difficult even for another empath to pick him up.

After we left the hospital, Stonehedge took us to a cluster of terraced buildings. He stopped at an attractive house, airy and light, with many patios. "These are reserved for visiting scientists or dignitaries." He glanced at me. "We can arrange for separate quarters if you like."

"This is fine," I said.

Althor considered him. "Allied contracts, properly performed, are binding with my people and Traders. Do you have a person here who can authorize such a contract?"

"I'm not sure what you're asking," Stonehedge said.

"Contracts," Althor said. "Social contracts."

"Ah. Yes. You asked to see the chaplain." The director nodded. "She can perform marriages legally binding across all political boundaries. We can set it up tomorrow." He paused, glancing at me. "If all parties agree to it and are of legal age."

"We must take care of it now," Althor said.

"You can't," Kabatu said. "You need blood tests and genetic screening."

"You have the results from my exam," Althor said.

"For you, yes. But not for Ms. Pulivok."

"We can do tests later," Althor said. "Now we sign the contract."

"Wait," I said. This was all moving too fast.

Stonehedge spoke gently. "You don't have to do anything you don't want."

I tried to read Althor's face, his colors, his moods. I didn't understand why he was pushing so hard, or what they meant by "political boundaries." My attempts to reach him were no more successful than before, but they were oversensitizing my KAB, producing a hyperextended awareness of everyone around me. I even glimpsed the scene through someone else's perceptions, either Stonehedge or Kabatu. Until that moment I hadn't realized how fragile I appeared next to Althor. The mere act of our standing together made it look as if he were trying to intimidate me.

"It's all right," I told Stonehedge. "I'm just not used to the way you do things."

He considered me. Then he spoke into a band around his wrist. "Nancy?"

A musical voice came out of the band. "Here."

"We're at the house. Can you come over?"

"Right away," the woman said.

"Great. Out." Stonehedge smiled at me. "That was Chaplain Ming. She'll be happy to answer your questions."

"No." Althor took hold of my arm. "We'll speak to her together."

I pried at his fingers. *Althor? Your safety routines aren't working. You're holding too tight.*

He blinked and let go of my arm. *I'm sorry.*

"I think that's up to Ms. Pulivok," Stonehedge said.

Behind him, I caught sight of a slender woman crossing a bridge on the river. Black hair hung in a ponytail down her back, swinging as she walked. Large almond-shaped eyes graced her face. Long, lithe, and tall, she looked about thirty-five.

In fact, when I thought about it, everyone I had met in Althor's universe looked between thirty and forty. It makes sense to me now. In 1987 people lived longer than they had in, say, 1687; three hundred years down the road humans have learned even more about how to slow aging and extend life spans.

When the woman reached us, Stonehedge introduced her as Chaplain Ming. "We thought Ms. Pulivok might like to talk to you," he said. "Prepare for the ceremony."

Althor glanced at me and shook his head slightly. I hesitated, feeling his concern that we not be separated. But I also knew this might be my last chance to talk privately with someone who spoke a language I understood.

Ming smiled at me and spoke in a voice as rich as cornstalks heavy with ripe ears nodding in a breeze. "We can go inside, if you like."

With a silent apology to Althor, I said, "Yes. I would like that."

Althor stiffened. But he didn't protest. I went with Ming into the house, entering a living room with delicate screens for walls. The chairs, sofa, and tables were all made from pale ceramics and burnished metal lace. No wood or plastic showed anywhere.

As we sat on the couch, Ming said, "Ms. Pulivok—"

"Tina."

"Tina." Her voice was like music. "Why are you so afraid?"

"What makes you think I'm afraid?"

"You seem so uneasy. Dazed."

That was an understatement. Even if Althor hadn't asked me to hold back, though, I would have said nothing about being three hundred years out of place. I was afraid it would sound like I was raving. "I just wanted to ask some questions."

"Certainly."

"Why are you all so uncomfortable around Althor?"

She tensed. "His name is *Althor?*"

"Does that bother you?"

She hesitated. "I realize the name Althor is popular now, since the last war. Selei has never been common, though. To hear of an 'Althor Selei'—" She gave me a wry smile. "You have to admit, that combination would throw anyone into an induction loop."

I blinked, confused by her idioms. After a moment, she said, "Tina? What's wrong?" She hesitated. "Are you with him of your own free will?"

I frowned. "Yes. Why does everyone keep asking that?"

"Because you look frightened. And you're so young."

"I'm not that young. I'll be eighteen in a few months."

She stared at me. "You're only *seventeen?*"

I was fed up with being treated like a child. I hadn't yet realized that the lengthening of life spans had moved the definition of adulthood to an older age. After all, thousands of years ago humans generally married and bore children at an age that, in 1987, was considered childhood. Nor was it just a function of era; in Zinacantan, girls tended to marry younger than in Los Angeles. In Althor's universe, those trends continued. Physical maturity was no longer enough to make an adult; life had grown too complex, both technologically and socially.

Nor was it just my age. Although in 1987, I was small for an American woman, I was average for many places in the world, including Zinacantan. But heights had been increasing, and that trend continued into Althor's time. To the people in his universe, someone my size tended to look childlike regardless of age.

"Where I come from in Mexico," I said, "I'm not considered a child."

Surprise flickered around her. "You're from Earth?" When I nodded, she said, "We thought you were Raylican."

"No. I'm Maya."

"The Raylican resemblance is astonishing." She smiled. "Who would have thought an extinct people on Earth would so resemble an almost extinct people halfway across the galaxy?"

I stared at her. "The Maya are *extinct?*"

"Well—I thought so. Don't you know?"

I leaned forward, suddenly cold. Ming kept talking, words of concern, but I couldn't hear. A roar buffeted my ears. Extinct. My people were extinct. My last tie to Earth was gone. I struggled to breathe. I couldn't hear, couldn't breathe—

"—hyperventilating!" Kabatu's voice cut through the noise in my head. "Move back!"

"Get out." That was Althor, furious. "All of you."

As my head cleared, I looked up to see the room filled with people: Ming, Althor, Stonehedge, Kabatu, security officers. Althor sat next to me—and waves of concern rolled out from the others. Gentleness and compassion have never been traits associated with Jagernauts, a perception encouraged by their military bearing and combat versatility. It's ironic, given that they are empaths, but their appearance belies the facts. The unease of the people watching us turned into the bright sparks of surprise when Althor drew me into his arms, murmuring words of comfort.

"Max." Ming spoke quietly to Stonehedge. "I need to talk to you."

The director nodded, and they disappeared into another room. Kabatu and the security officers stayed, the guards watching Althor, their hands resting on their guns.

Althor brushed a tendril of hair away from my eyes. "What happened?"

"Ming—she told me the Maya are extinct."

He exhaled. "I'm sorry, Tina. I also thought this must be true. Why else haven't my people seen yours and realized where we came from? But I didn't want to say anything, not until we had a better idea."

Stonehedge returned with Ming, their moods creating translucent clouds of apprehension. Ming stood in the doorway, but Stonehedge sat on the couch, bringing himself on the same level as Althor, far enough away so he didn't intrude on Althor's space, on the opposite side of Althor from where I sat. I felt the effect of his choices immediately: Althor perceived him as less of a threat.

Stonehedge spoke carefully. "Commander Selei, none of us wishes to interfere with your private life. But please understand how this looks. An Imperial Jagernaut arrives at a remote Allied science station with a damaged ship and injuries, bringing a frightened child he insists on marrying despite her reluctance." He spread his hands. "We need more information before we can perform the ceremony."

Althor watched him, his face expressionless, metallic and cool. Calculating. He was trying to decide how far to trust the director.

A beep came from the band around Ming's wrist, and she glanced at Stonehedge.

"What is it?" Althor asked.

Stonehedge said, "I asked my people to find anything they could on any Skolian man with your name, appearance, or military identification."

Althor tensed. "And?"

Ming touched a square on the wall and swirling lines appeared on a wall-to-floor holoscreen. A life-sized holo formed, showing two people. The woman was slender, with green eyes as vivid as the sun on a leaf in the forest. Her black hair, long and straight, was pulled into a twist on her head; from the highest point, it cascaded down her back to her hips. She had an emerald-and-ice beauty, her face curved in perfect lines, like a marble statue.

The man made my breath catch. His shoulder-length locks matched the color of Althor's natural hair exactly. Although his skin wasn't metallic, his features were Althor's, more refined and less blocky, but otherwise the same. His hands had no thumbs, just four thick fingers about the same length, with a hinge down the back of each hand.

Ming read a line of Skolian hieroglyphs scrolling along the holoscreen's edge. "The holo was taken two years ago. They're standing on a dais with other dignitaries during a speech given by the Imperial Assembly Voice. The woman is Dyhianna Selei." She looked at Stonehedge. "That's her, Max. The real deal. The Assembly Key."

Stonehedge glanced at Althor. "Who is the man?"

After an awkward silence, in which Althor just looked at the director, Ming read off the answer. "Eldrin Jarac Valdoria. He's Selei's nephew." She touched a panel, bringing up a menu. Another touch, and she had a new stream of hieroglyphs. "He's the oldest son on the Skyfall side of the lineage. Right now he's first in line for one of the Triad Keys. In fact, according to this, he would have become the Web Key when his father died if the Traders hadn't captured the Third Lock. And look at this—he's the older brother of Althor Valdoria, the war hero."

"Turn it off," Althor said.

Ming touched a panel and the holo vanished. Everyone in the

room watched Althor, their emotions moving in currents: wonder, incredulity, fascination. The moment stretched out like taffy being pulled, its silence broken only by a distant hum of machinery.

Then Althor said, "Dyhianna Selei and Eldrin Valdoria are my parents."

The moment cracked open, no longer taffy, instead a dam releasing water, chilly and bracing. Stonehedge let out a whistle. "Why didn't you want to tell us?"

"You've seen my ship," Althor said. "That damage is no accident."

"Our techs agree," Stonehedge said.

"It had no problems before I took it to ISC headquarters," Althor said.

Kabatu leaned forward. "Are you saying your own military sabotaged it?"

"I don't know." Althor paused. "I was scheduled to attend a diplomatic reception on Earth."

Comprehension swept across Stonehedge's face. "Which gives you good reason to suspect the saboteurs had connections with the Allied Worlds of Earth."

"That possibility has occurred to me," Althor said.

"I can assure you," Stonehedge said, "that no one here is in any way hostile to you or any member of your family."

Althor regarded him, his mood metallic again. "You must allow us to marry."

Ming spoke quietly. "The closer the two of you become, the more of a target that makes Tina. Isn't she safer now?"

"No," Althor said.

"I'm sorry," Stonehedge said. "But a girl her age needs her guardians' permission to marry. Until we have that, we can't do anything."

Althor shook his head. "Tina has no identity. You won't find her in any database. If assassins take my life, she has nothing. I gave her my word I wouldn't leave her stranded. The Selei name will give her both a family and protection."

Kabatu whistled. "That it would."

Only I saw the orange light that flickered around Althor. The color of deception. It wasn't that his words were false; he did fear assassination and intended to honor his promise to me. But that wasn't his only reason for wanting the contract. He was also guarding his own interests.

"I don't have any guardians," I said. "They're dead." Centuries dead.

Stonehedge pushed his hand through his hair. "If we can verify that, I might be able to sign in their place. I'll have Legal check into it."

Ming was watching me closely. "Are you positive this is what you want?"

Althor's thought came into my mind: *Perhaps I should leave. I think she wants to make sure you're agreeing freely and not because my presence intimidates you.*

I couldn't process her words with Althor uploading to my brain. As I shook my head, the Jag thought, *Carrier attenuated.* Mercifully, my hyperextended awareness of Althor and the others receded.

"Tina?" Ming said. "Are you all right?"

I nodded. "Yes. And yes about marrying Althor. It's what I want."

"Have you had time to make preparations?" When I shook my head, she smiled. "I probably have a dress you could borrow, if you'd like."

"We don't need to change our clothes to sign a contract," Althor said.

Kabatu snorted. "You're not selling her real estate in the Orion Nebula, man. You're marrying her."

I thought of my mother's wedding dress, the *huipil* hanging in another universe and time. "Althor, I'd like a dress."

He folded his hand around mine. *I'd rather we didn't separate.*

Stonehedge chuckled. "Commander Selei, I can show you around the station while they do all that."

"What?" Althor turned to him, his confusion buzzing like an

agitated bee. I could actually feel the fragmentation of the neural subshell that allowed him to converse with people while his brain interacted with another psion.

The Jag's thought brushed past me. *Althor, your interface is degenerating. I need you back here to do more work.*

"Commander Selei?" Stonehedge asked. "Are you all right?"

"I've a minor biomech problem," Althor said. "Nothing serious." To the Jag, he thought: *I can't do anything when you take me down for repair work. I won't leave Tina alone with them.*

My analysis yields a 98.9 percent probability that these people had no link to the assassination attempt on your life.

I don't care, Althor thought. *I'm not trusting her with anyone while you turn me off.*

Stonehedge was speaking to Althor. "Can we do anything to help?"

"No," Althor said. "I mean, I'm fine."

A thought from the Jag coiled around me, discreet, hidden from Althor. *Tina? Can you convince him?*

Didn't you already fix him? I thought.

I didn't have enough time to stabilize him. My patches have been decaying since he left. Disruption of his language ability and higher reasoning is minimal, but increasing. Motor coordination will go next, then internal organ function. Ultimately, he could die.

Doesn't he realize the danger he's putting himself in? I asked.

Yes. He did not wish you to know.

"I recommend rest," Kabatu was saying to Althor. "And food. For both of you."

"We can provide dining arrangements," Stonehedge said.

Althor suddenly spoke in a cold voice. "Doctor Kabatu, you can put that clip away." He crossed the room so fast, I barely had time to catch my breath before he was looming over the doctor, holding a blue med clip in his hand.

Kabatu looked at his empty hand, then back up at Althor. "I had heard Jagernauts were fast, but I had no idea." He blinked. "Why did you do that?"

Althor was studying the clip, essentially a sliver and firing mechanism. "This is set for . . . Perital. Perital?" He scowled at Kabatu. "Who are you planning to knock out?"

"No one." Kabatu paused. "I loaded the syringe when we first learned you were coming on board. As a precaution. I took it out just now to deactivate it."

Althor's wariness intensified. I detected no deception from Kabatu, but that was no guarantee it didn't exist; empaths have a heightened ability to pick up emotions, but it is neither infallible nor always straightforward. Still, my sense was that Kabatu told the truth.

The Jag sent me a thought. *I had already estimated a 98 percent chance that he would have taken such a precaution for exactly the reason he gives.*

Okay. I got up and went over to Althor. "You can go back to the Jag. I'll be all right."

Althor looked down at me, his hair disarrayed, his face creased with strain. "Tina—"

I took his hands. "Please."

He wrapped his arms around me, his hands clenched with tension. A snap sounded by my ear. Althor let go, and I drew back to see him staring at the broken remains of the clip in his hand. The sliver stuck out of his palm.

Althor looked at Kabatu. "Give me the antidote."

"It was on one of the clip's other settings," Kabatu said.

"Then get a new clip."

Kabatu stood up. "They're in my office—"

"The console." Althor's words slurred. "Or nano . . . take only . . . seconds . . ."

As Althor fell backward, Stonehedge jumped to his feet and brought up his arms, catching him under the armpits. The director stumbled under their combined weight and hit the couch with what had to be a jarring impact against his legs. Then he eased Althor down on the floor.

"Damn," Kabatu muttered, stepping over Althor's outflung arm. He knelt next to him and took a cylinder from his belt. The cylinder unrolled into a reflective tape, which he lay across Althor's neck. Symbols scrolled across it and small holos appeared, rotating to show views of a man's body.

I knelt next to Kabatu. "Is he going to be all right?"

"He'll sleep for a few hours." Kabatu exhaled. "I really was about to deactivate it."

"It's all right," I said. "Can you take him to his ship?"

Stonehedge spoke behind us. "Take him to the hospital."

"No." I got up, facing the director, wishing I were bigger. I felt like an otter challenging a bear. "He has to go to his ship. It's repairing him."

"Repairing?" Stonehedge smiled. "That's an odd way to put it."

"Max, she's right." Kabatu stood. "If he's malfunctioning, his ship is better equipped to work on him. I wouldn't even know where to start."

"You talk as if he's a piece of apparatus," Stonehedge said.

"Jagernauts are," Kabatu said. "We don't know much about them; Imperial Space Command keeps it under wraps. But I've never heard of one with as much biomech in his body as this man. Especially his legs. *All* of it is biomech. None of his own bones at all."

"All right," Stonehedge said. "Have the techs let the ship know he's coming." He paused. "Unless it knows already?"

"I doubt it," Kabatu said. "Kyle interactions fall off with distance, and his ship is at the hub. It's unlikely even human Kyles could communicate across so much distance. I don't see any way the EI brain in a ship could."

"Selei isn't just any operator," Stonehedge said. "He's Rhon."

I watched them curiously. It was my first indication of how much more advanced Althor's people were in the Kyle sciences than the Allieds realized.

"I doubt a Rhon psion could do it," Kabatu said. "But who knows about the Rhon? From what I understand, you can get tossed into prison just for making a holo of one of them." He glanced at Althor. "I doubt it would go over well if the Imperial authorities found out one was sprawled unconscious on our floor while we discussed Kyle interactions."

Stonehedge winced. "No, I doubt it would. You better take him to his ship."

Within moments, four medics arrived. They suspended Althor on a floating stretcher and sped out of the house, accompanied by Kabatu.

Tina, the Jag thought. *You must do something else.*

Yes?

Make sure they notify no one about Althor's arrival. No one must know he still lives.

What about his commanding officers?

No, the Jag thought. *I calculate a 99.5 percent probability that the assassins have a link to ISC. A 99.9 percent probability exists that they have high-level access to the galactic nets. If he uses either the psiber or spacetime webs, he may alert them that he survived. I will take you both to a planet owned by Althor's family. From there we can use secured channels set up precisely for crises such as this.*

I wasn't sure that sounded better. *How do we know someone in his family isn't in with the assassins?*

I calculate a 99.999 percent probability against it.

What makes you so sure?

They are Rhon, the Jag answered, as if that explained everything.

"Ms. Pulivok?" Stonehedge asked. "Why are you staring at me?"

"I was thinking about the nets," I said. "Please don't tell anyone Althor is here. If the assassins discover he's alive, they may try to kill him again."

Stonehedge nodded. "Don't worry. We won't."

Good, the Jag thought. Its intensity lightened, almost as if it were experiencing relief. *And I will see if I can civilize your groom.* It uploaded an exaggerated image of Althor to my mind, a Jagernaut growling at everyone in sight, his hair in wild disarray, his uniform splitting at the seams. *It may be hopeless. But I will try.*

I laughed, then stopped when Stonehedge gave me an odd look. After that the chaplain took me to find a wedding dress.

Ming lived in a terraced house, with plants hanging from eaves and balconies. Metal lace decorated the walls. In the bedroom, the quilt on her bed shimmered with designs of parrots and bonsai trees. Silhouetted against a pink sunrise, the birds gleamed in iridescent green, blue, gold, and red. The cloth was holographic, letting the designs extend out of the cloth. Three-dimensional holoart glowed on the walls, showing pagodas, gardens with cultivated flowers, trees shaped into statues. A gust of wind started in one picture and blew around the room through the others, even though each image showed a different scene.

Ming rummaged in her closet. "I have something from my friend's cousin—here it is."

She took out a simple dress, about knee-length, made from white lace. The cloth was holographic, its glistening rainbows shimmering above and within the lace. It made me think of the dress my mother had sewn for my *quinceañera*.

"It's lovely," I said.

Ming smiled. "You can have it. I'll never wear it."

I swallowed, touched by the gift. "Thank you."

"Would you like some time to rest before the ceremony?"

"Actually—I wondered if you would mind answering some questions."

"Certainly." She motioned me toward a table. "I'm hoping you can help us understand too."

I sat down with her. "Understand?"

"A Rhon heir shows up running from assassins and asks us to marry him to a child he says has no identity. We can't help but wonder what's going on."

"I don't know." Although Althor had told me about his family, I had no feel yet for what it meant. "I still don't really even understand who he is."

Ming described what she knew, telling an ancient story of a dying people. Five thousand years ago the Ruby Dynasty controlled a starfaring empire. For star drives, they looted the ruined shuttles beached on the Vanished Sea, all that remains of the mysterious race which stranded humans on Raylicon. The Ruby Empire rose and fell three thousand years before the birth of Christ. It was one of humanity's most remarkable—and fragile—achievements.

They developed star travel before they had any grasp of the physics. Then they went searching for their lost home. They never found Earth, but they did settle many planets. Necessity forced them to learn genetic engineering, both to adapt colonists to new worlds and in an attempt to expand their gene pool. But their empire was too fragile to survive; they had neither the scientific background nor the population needed to sustain such accelerated development. So it collapsed, stranding the colonies for over four thousand years.

Desperation finally drove the Raylicans back to the stars. They were dying, succumbing to a gene pool too small to remain viable. They hoped an influx of genes from rediscovered colonies would save their race. But the colonies had either perished—victims of inbreeding—or else self-induced genetic drift now divided them from their lost empathic kin. Kyle genes often produce lethal abnormalities; the colonies that thrived did so because their gene pools had lost the empathic traits.

The Kyle genes didn't disappear completely, however. Althor's parents are Rhon psions, a class of Kyle operators named for the geneticist Rhon. The Rhon project was dual-pronged: using DNA derived from the Ruby Dynasty, Rhon engineered for increased empathy and produced Althor's family; using other DNA, he engineered for increased pain resistance and produced the Trader Aristos.

Aristos are the reason genetic research on Kyle operators is now illegal. In a sense, they are reverse empaths. They can receive input, but their "receiver" is abnormal: it picks up only pain. The signal must come from an empath, someone whose brain amplifies it enough for the Aristo to receive. An Aristo's brain, in trying to lower his or her sensitivity to pain, relays the signals to neural centers that register them as pleasure.

"Do you think the Aristos are the ones who tried to kill Althor?" I asked.

"I doubt it," Ming said. "They would probably give anything to capture him alive." She spread her hands. "Maybe someone wants to stop the marriage. Essentially he's asking us to establish a treaty between his government and ours, the kind that usually take years to arrange."

"Why should my marrying him involve a treaty?"

She smiled. "It's one of the oldest stories in the book. Two powers establish an alliance through an advantageous marriage."

Her comments puzzled me. I didn't know then that Althor's people view lineage as more durable than government. The Raylicans have spent six thousand years struggling to survive their infertility. During that time their empire rose, collapsed, and rose again. To them, fertility is the most enduring symbol of a union. Two centuries ago the Imperial Assembly arranged a marriage between Althor's mother and an Allied man. The contract for that union was a treaty that filled a library. Although the marriage eventually failed, the treaty remained in effect until the last Skolian-Trader war, when Earth betrayed the Imperialate.

Was it truly betrayal? That depends on your point of view. During the war, Althor's aunt, Sauscony Valdoria, commanded the Imperial fleet. As per terms of the treaty, she sent the most vulnerable members of the Rhon to Earth, for protection. After the war the Allieds refused to release them, fearing it would restart the star-spanning destruction. What made it even more galling was that the Traders agreed to release their most valuable prisoner of war—Althor's father—in exchange for the son of the late Trader emperor.

"An Imperial special operations team eventually freed the members of the Rhon being held on Earth," Ming said. "But we almost went to war over it. The Raylicans themselves may be dying, but their Imperialate thrives, especially with the influx of genes from Allied immigrants. The only reason they don't over-throw us is because, small as we are, we're almost big enough to tip the balance of power toward whoever allies with us."

I considered the implications of her words. "Althor's parents are both Rhon, aren't they?" I searched for a tactful way to put it. "They're both—close."

"It's called inbreeding." Ming exhaled. "It's not my place to judge. Inbreeding is one of the few ways the Rhon can reproduce themselves." She considered me. "Do you know your Kyle rating?"

"I don't understand what you mean."

"It's an exponential scale. Ninety-nine percent of humans are between 0 and 2. Those who test higher than 3, about one in a thousand, are empaths. A rating of 6 qualifies a person as a telepath, about one in a million. Only one in ten billion rates as a 10. The scale starts to break down above 11 or 12. Rhon operators—like Althor—are rated as 'Rhon' instead of by a number because their ratings are much too high to quantify. The Rhon are also rare to the point of extinction."

That took a moment to absorb. "He thinks I'm a telepath. But before I met him, I never picked up much."

She nodded. "I've heard it's not unusual, in a link between two or more operators, for the stronger to expand the abilities of the others. But even without him I bet you have a high rating, at least four. Perhaps even five."

Four. Perhaps five. I had never thought of myself as special in any way before.

After Ming left me to rest, I lay on the quilt, reaching for the Jag . . .

Attending, the Jag thought.

How is Althor? I asked.

Asleep. I'm still working on him.

I've been wondering about Kyle operators.

I can make my library available to you.

Will it distract you from your work?

No. The index is a minor automated function. It requires no attention. A menu formed in my mind:

Index
Help
Exit

Index, I thought.

I closed my eyes and a library seemed to appear, a room of ceiling-high shelves crammed with books. A librarian who looked like Martinelli seated me in an armchair. In response to my questions, he brought books or else sat in another chair and talked to me. He made images in the air, detailed pictures to illustrate his words.

Several hundred Kyle genes exist. They are alleles, or alternate forms, of normal genes. Mutations. Like most mutations they do more harm than good. Fortunately they are almost fully recessive, which means that they show almost no manifestation unless you inherit copies from both parents. People who carry one Kyle allele and one normal gene are normal, but those with paired alleles often have problems. Anemia. Missing limbs or organs. Lung or heart disease. Abnormalities in nerve, muscle, or circulatory development. Brain damage. Kyle fetuses often die within weeks of conception. Those that survive rarely live long enough to reproduce.

Kyle genes survive in human gene pools because they help people who carry them *unpaired.* It's the same reason sickle-cell anemia persists; not only do carriers with one normal and one sickle-cell allele show few signs of the disease, they are more resistant to malaria. People with unpaired Kyle genes rarely manifest harmful mutations, but they do show slightly heightened empathic responses. It aids parenting, and their offspring also tend to associate positive qualities with parenthood, becoming parents more often on average than in other groups. Gene pools maintain an equilibrium: Kyle genes survive, but empaths remain rare because of debilitating effects produced when the genes pair up.

The Rhon carry some form of every Kyle allele and every one of those alleles is paired. So how are they healthy? It depends on many factors: control sequences in genes; stretches of DNA known as *introns;* positioning of genes on chromosomes; how many alleles are present. One allele alone might cause an undesirable trait to be expressed; the presence of another might suppress it. The genes are also pleiotropic, which means they do more than one thing. In rare cases, an empath can be born healthy, or almost healthy, like Althor. Problems still exist, though. Suicide was once the leading cause of death among higher-rated Kyles. Even now, when psiberneticists can train empaths to mute the onslaught of other people's emotions, it remains a problem.

Jagernauts have protection; their biomech webs can release a drug that suppresses psiamine, the neurotransmitter needed to interpret empathic input. In other words, they can "block" emotions. The web provides only limited amounts of the drug, however; otherwise it interferes with the Jagernaut's ability to function. Empaths without biomech can still block emotions, though less effectively, by using biofeedback to suppress the psiamine. I learned to do it at an early age, without realizing it, by imagining a mirror that reflected emotions back to people, or a fortress around my mind, or a blinding white light.

Everyone has a KAB and a KEB. Normal genes produce enzymes that limit growth of the organs. People with paired Kyle genes can't make the enzymes properly, so their KAB and KEB keep growing; instead of a few active molecular sites, they have thousands, even millions. The probability of someone like Althor being born—a healthy Kyle operator with billions of active sites on his KAB and KEB—is unlikely to the point of impossibility.

But nature is patient.

Humans have settled over three thousand worlds: Traders on fifteen hundred, Althor's people on nine hundred, Earth on three hundred. Three trillion people. Multiply that by the centuries humans have known how to search out Kyle operators and the numbers become even more daunting. In all of those people, the entire complement of Kyle genes has twice been known to match up and create a healthy psion. Those two men were Rhon psions. One, a giant with metallic gold skin, fathered Althor's mother, and also her sister, who is both Althor's aunt and his paternal grandmother. The second man was Althor's paternal grandfather. Althor's maternal grandmother was a result of the Rhon project. His grandparents produced healthy children because they came from different gene pools and because their DNA had, through natural selection, determined ways to suppress harmful traits.

Still, the Rhon are like genetic bombs waiting to explode. The most severe mutation is the CK complex. It formed early on in the Raylicon population, from radiation exposure they suffered when they looted the ruined star shuttles. Althor carries CK. The librarian assured me that sex made him safe, and didn't understand why I smiled at the phrasing. Sex chromosomes, it said. Men are male because they have one X and one Y chromosome. Women have two X chromosomes. In the female, only one X is fully active in each cell; otherwise we would get a double dose of genetic activity. But even on a dormant X, a small number of genes express—including, unfortunately, CK. It occurs only on the X and has no homologue on the Y, so no male can ever carry it paired. When unpaired, CK is harmless and suppresses other mutations.

When paired, it kills the embryo.

Because CK suppresses other mutations, Raylicans with only one CK gene had a survival rate far higher than those without it. So the complex became more and more common despite numerous attempts to eradicate it, until eventually all Raylicans carried it. As a result, CK paired up in one out of every two females conceived and the number of surviving girl children plunged.

When they saw what was happening, the women without CK tried cloning themselves using their zygotes, or fertilized eggs. A single-celled zygote is *totipotent:* all of its DNA is active, so it can grow into a human being. The same is true of the two cells made when the zygote divides; separate them and they make identical twins. Two divisions gives quadruplets and three gives octuplets. Sixteen doesn't work; the zygote loses totipotence after three divisions.

Embryos with Kyle DNA are different; the more Kyle genes, the sooner the embryo loses totipotence. Most Raylicans are lucky to produce twin clones. For Althor's family, even twins fail. If the cells are forced to develop anyway, the resulting clones have no empathic abilities and suffer severe abnormalities. After several attempts to produce Rhon twins ended in tragedy, it was declared illegal to experiment on Althor's family, a belated attempt on the part of an Imperialate ethics committee to protect them from less scrupulous forces in their government.

But that research led to advances. Geneticists learned to "wake up" dormant DNA in cells that had lost totipotence. Now—in theory—they can use *any* cell to make a clone. They take out the nucleus of a fertilized egg and replace it with a reawakened nucleus. Waking up DNA is tricky, though, as is finding a suitable egg. For Kyle clones, the egg must come from an empath or else the clone fails. With the aid of female empaths in rediscovered colonies, the Raylicans can clone themselves, but as yet their success rate is too low to fend off their eventual extinction.

For Rhon psions, the reactivated nucleus is simply too sensitive to its environment. All clones fail. After bruising debates with the ethics boards, one group tried cloning Althor's aunt by putting a nucleus of her reactivated DNA into her mother's egg. It failed. So they laboriously reconstructed the egg that produced her, building its DNA unit by unit. Even that clone failed. Perhaps someday science will succeed, but so far the results have been disheartening.

Why is it so important to produce more Rhon? The Assembly uses them for the psibernet that binds Imperial Skolia together. Any telepath with a biomech web can access the net, but only Rhon telepaths have the strength to power it. Without them, the psibernet would cease to exist.

Even if a method of cloning the Rhon is found, however, it will only provide a partial solution. Psiberspace obeys the rules of quantum mechanics, including the Pauli Exclusion Principle, but applied to quanta of thought rather than light or matter. Just as no two fermions can ever have identical quantum numbers, so no two minds in the link that powers the psibernet can be identical. So having ten clones of the same person is no help. Even breeding back into the line isn't useful after one or two generations; in addition to the ethical questions involved, the greater the inbreeding, the more similarities among offspring.

The library also gave me chilling facts the Imperial Assembly never made public. Contrary to popular belief, Rhon never made a Rhon psion. He fast realized that unless he found a way to eliminate the harmful effects of Kyle genes, he would never create a diverse, robust population of telepaths. That was why he experimented with pain tolerance; a gene that affects the brain's recognition of pain also prevents production of an enzyme that limits KAB growth. So carriers of that gene tend to have both a larger KAB and lower pain resistance.

Rhon tried to separate the effects, raising pain tolerance without losing the enhanced KAB. To avoid complications, he chose subjects who carried only the Kyle gene of interest. They had no genes for the rest of the biological machinery needed to produce a Kyle operator and so weren't empaths. Because only one gene was involved, it looked like a good test case. His group labored for years, their work exemplary, monitored at every step by an ethics board.

The problems weren't obvious at first. The humans Rhon created looked odd, with red eyes and glittering black hair, but that was mild compared to what genetic fiddling had produced in some colonies. Almost everything went as anticipated. His creations did indeed have the hoped for combination of increased pain tolerance and enhanced KAB. Just one unexpected twist turned up; their KAB detected only signals produced by pain. At the same time, their brain was receiving the order *increase pain tolerance*—so it routed the pain signals to its orgiastic centers.

That one glitch changed interstellar history.

When Rhon realized what happened, he understood the implications far better than the well-meaning committees regulating his work. His insistence that these new humans be killed appalled the ethics boards. While the debate raged, Rhon's creations—the soon-to-be Aristos—murdered Rhon, stole or destroyed his records, and set out on their own.

A race with no qualms about causing human suffering can wreak havoc in a gentler universe. Only after the Aristos reached a population of several thousand, when they began to "step on each other's toes," did their expansion slow. But those few thousand, within a space of decades, founded a brutal empire.

They also continued Rhon's work, trying to create super-empaths. Why? The stronger the empath, the stronger the signal that person sends, and so the more intense the pleasure response it evokes in an Aristo. They breed empaths for sensitivity and beauty, call them "providers," and seek them with a drive as strong as their need to eat or sleep.

Eventually they succeeded in their ultimate goal: they created two Rhon telepaths, a male and female for breeding. The youth, when he realized his future, killed himself. The female reached adulthood and escaped, murdering her creators to avenge her mate. She also destroyed every record she could find of the work that led to her birth. To this day she is the only known Rhon psion successfully created in the lab.

That woman was Althor's grandmother.

Jag. I thought. *That's a terrible story.*

Yes, the Jag answered.

Althor's parents are so closely related. He's lucky he turned out normal.

The Jag paused. *He does have a chromosomal abnormality. An extra Y chromosome.*

You mean he's XYY?

Yes.

Don't people with extra sex chromosomes have problems? I thought of the children we hoped to have. *Like sterility?*

XYY males are not infertile. Nor do they pass the extra Y to their offspring.

But?

They tend to be taller on average.

That's all?

The Jag paused. *As a group, they are below average in intelligence.*

Althor isn't. He was a rocket scientist, in fact, or a rocket engineer.

You are correct. Most Kyle operators are above average, due to their extra neural structures.

Is that all that's different about him?

The Jag paused again. *A significantly high proportion of human males in prisons tend to have the XYY genotype, particularly the population above six feet tall.*

A half-remembered news report I had heard in my own universe came back to me. *Because they're more aggressive. More violent.*

Yes.

Althor isn't that way. I knew as soon as I said it that it wasn't true. When the Jag didn't respond, I said, *He's not criminally violent.*

No. He's not. It isn't all genetics, either. Upbringing, personality, and environment all affect personality development.

Why are you telling me this?

A number of the simulations I have constructed to model your future yield the following as a solution: you will find the Pilot's aggressive tendencies unacceptable.

You think I'm going to walk out on him.

Yes.

Then you're using the wrong data.

My data sets for you are small, the Jag agreed. *I augmented them by extrapolating behavior patterns developed from algorithms applied to gamma humanoid females with a phenotype that approaches yours.*

Does that mean you guessed, based on what I look like?

Essentially.

Who did you compare me to?

You appear Raylican. So I extrapolated behaviors of females from the Ruby Dynasty. However, models incorporating these data become unstable. In fact, the most stable simulations employ patterns opposed to those of a Raylican female. Such a woman would seek a lack of aggression in the male. You appear to seek the opposite.

I blinked. *I never thought about it that way before.*

Given your small size and nonaggressive nature, combined with the subcultures that have formed your environment, your criteria for mate selection are logical.

Then you know I won't dump Althor.

I will add your input on this matter to my models. Its response had a curious sense of lightening, like relief. It made me wonder just how far the Jag would go to protect its pilot.

12

Star Union

Ming opened the door onto a panorama of stars: rubies, topazes, sapphires, opals. I stood with her in the doorway of the Observation Deck. Only the wall behind us was opaque; the rest of the room was dichromesh glass, a bubble extending "below" the wheel of the station. A crystalline pulpit stood across the chamber, silhouetted against the starscape. A lacquer box sat on it, and a vase with a rose. Next to them a book lay open, a real book, paper and leather, an antique. I had requested Ming use it because her electronic holobook didn't feel right to me for this ceremony.

People filled the chamber, standing around and talking. Kabatu was there, wearing a blue jumpsuit like Ming's, with NASA and Allied Worlds shoulder patches. Stonehedge stood near the pulpit, also in uniform, with medals on his chest. Gold glimmered on his clothes like reflected starlight.

Then I realized the glimmer didn't come from the stars. The scene had so overwhelmed me, and Althor looked so different, that it was a moment before I realized he was standing next to Stonehedge. The metallic gold cloth of his uniform glistened. It was also holographic, creating sparkles of gold light that gave it a shimmering depth. The style was simple, a long-sleeved pullover with horizontal ribbing across his chest that made his shoulders look even broader, and pants with a line of darker gold running down the outer seam of each leg. The pants tucked into knee-high gold boots polished to a mirror shine. A sword hung at his waist, sheathed in gold, its point arcing back in a curve.

As Ming walked with me into the chamber, Althor glanced

in our direction and did a double take. He looked like I felt: dazed. This had all happened so fast. Ming took me over to him, then went to stand behind the pulpit. Althor kept staring at me, until finally Stonehedge pushed him. Blinking, Althor stepped in front of the pulpit. When Ming cleared her throat, he and I stopped looking at each other and turned to her.

It had taken Ming and me a long time to find a ceremony I recognized. We finally dug up a Catholic wedding over three hundred and fifty years old, dated even by my standards. It surprised me that she could read Mass; I didn't know then about the charter of the Allied Worlds Interfaith Council, which provides for Inspace Chaplains, religious leaders who serve the diverse populations of space habitats and colonies, where access to well-established religious communities isn't yet available.

We sent the ceremony to the Jag for Althor's approval. Although the Jag sent back his agreement, I suspected Althor never actually saw it. I had felt his mind slumbering as the Jag worked on him.

Althor and I stood in front of the pulpit, bewildered, trying to pay attention while Ming read the ceremony. I thought of home, of the people I would have liked to share this day with, of Manuel and my mother.

"Tina?" Ming said.

I suddenly became aware the ceremony had stopped. "Yes?"

She tilted her head at Stonehedge. "He won't go with the term."

"It's illegal," Stonehedge said, his voice low enough so it didn't carry to our audience.

"Tina picked it," Althor said. "If this ceremony is the one the Jag received, then it was her choice."

Stonehedge scowled at him. "You didn't read your own wedding ceremony?"

"I couldn't," Althor said. "The Jag just woke me up."

"Max, it *was* her choice," Ming said. "She insisted, in fact."

"It's *illegal*," he said. "We're pushing the law as it is, claiming we're her guardians. I can't authorize a lifetime term for a seventeen-year-old."

"Don't you all marry for life?" I asked.

"Not at your age," Stonehedge said. "You can set up a ten-year contract, maximum. At the end, you can renew for ten more, if you want. By the time the second renewal comes around, you'll be of legal age to decide if you want to spend the rest of your life with this man."

"I think we should let them do it," Ming said. "The legal definitions don't apply to this situation."

Stonehedge's exasperation sparked in the air. But when Ming gave him a questioning look, he waved his hand. "Go on. Finish."

She backed up a few lines. "In sickness and in health."

"In sickness and in health," Althor repeated.

"As long as we both shall live."

"As long as we both shall live."

After I repeated the vows, Ming went on. She read the passage for exchanging rings even though Althor and I had none to give each other. Then she opened the lacquer box—and took out a gleaming gold band. As my mouth fell open, she handed it to Althor.

Althor blinked at the ring. "What do I do?"

Ming smiled. "Say, 'With this ring I thee wed, and plight unto thee my troth.' "

His face blanked into computer mode. "I do not find this phrase." He came back to normal. "What is 'pleat into thee trough'?"

"Good question," Stonehenge muttered. "At least he didn't say 'bleat.' " When Ming gave him a sharp glance, he held up his hand as if to fend her off.

" 'Plight unto thee my troth,' " she told Althor. "It means you pledge to marry her. You put the ring on the third finger of her left hand."

Althor slid the ring onto my finger. "With this ring, I pleat unto thee my truth."

I put my hand over my mouth, trying not to laugh. Ming gave me a second ring, one made from soft gold metal. Eighteen-karat gold, as it turns out. I swallowed, stunned by these beautiful gifts they were giving us.

"Thank you," I said. Althor nodded his thanks as well, a curl of hair falling in his eyes.

I slid the ring onto his finger. He wiggled his hand, hinging it back and forth, examining the gold band. When he finished, Ming read the Mass, and more blessings and prayers. As the station rotated, Athena moved past our view like a stately goddess. It all had a dreamlike quality, as if we were floating through stardust.

When Ming started the final blessing, Althor must have realized she was almost done. While she was in the middle of a sentence, he turned, put his arms around my waist, and kissed me. For a moment, I was too startled to react. Then I kissed him back.

"Don't mind us," Stonehedge said.

Ming laughed softly. "I guess we can skip the rest. You may kiss the bride."

After that, everything blurred. Stonehenge introduced us to the guests: scientists, administrators, colonists, military personnel. All the time the stars wheeled by outside the bubble, their glorious parade hypnotic in its immensity. The haze from Althor's uniform blended with the golden haze of exhaustion my mind created, until I was moving through a dazed golden fog.

Eventually Kabatu rescued us, spiriting us off to a quiet chamber with a bench running around the wall and a console table in the center. After he left, we sank down on the bench together.

"Finally," Althor said. "I never know what to say at formal things like that."

I laughed. "You didn't need to say anything. They all just wanted to look at you."

His voice softened. "When I first saw you, with Nancy Ming, the light from the doorway behind you was making a halo around your body." He rubbed the lace of my dress. "And the way this sparkles—it was unreal. You looked like an angel."

"I thought the same about you."

"That I looked like an angel?" He laughed. "I've been called many names, but never that."

I smiled. "That you look like a hero."

"Hardly."

"You do to me."

"That's why they make us wear these clown suits." He motioned at his clothes. "ISC uses computer simulations and psychologists to design our dress uniforms."

I traced the curve of his sword. "Even this?"

"Actually, that's mine. I inherited it. It's a ceremonial sword from the Abaj Tacalique. They gave it to my grandfather at his wedding to my grandmother."

I stared at him. "Abaj Takalik? That's a Maya city. Near Guatemala. Its ruins are two thousand years old."

"A city?" His mouth opened. "The Abaj I know is a fraternity formed six thousand years ago to guard the Ruby Dynasty. Now they're sworn to protect my family."

"Bodyguards?"

He nodded. "It's primarily a ceremonial position. My parents have Jagernauts as bodyguards. But the Abaj still swear fealty to the Ruby Dynasty." Dryly he added, "Even though we haven't ruled anything for five thousand years."

"The Jag told me about the psibernet, how it needs your family."

"It takes three Keys to power it. My mother is the eldest, liaison to the Assembly. My Uncle Kelric is the military Key. He also commands the Imperial fleet." He paused. "The third Key, my grandfather, died about fifty years ago. My father should have taken his place. But the Traders captured the third Lock."

"How can you capture a lock?"

He smiled. "It's a control base, actually. My father would link into the power center of the web there. The Traders can't use it because they have no Rhon psions, but they don't want us to have it either."

At the time I didn't connect what Althor was telling me with what Ming had told me earlier about the exchange of prisoners that freed Althor's father after the last war. That exchange took place before the Trader officials involved knew their military had captured a Lock. I've often wondered what they would have done had they realized they possessed both a Lock and a Key. Would they have refused to give up Althor's father, even though the youth they were trading him for was their future emperor?

"You should build another Lock," I said.

"How?" He spread his hands. "My ancestors took the technology from the ruins on Raylicon. We've figured out the star drives, but we still don't understand their psibertech."

"I don't understand. Why is the psibernet so important?"

He leaned forward, elbows on his knees. "It lets us communicate almost instantaneously across any distance. The only alternatives are to send interstellar messages via electromagnetic waves, which travel at light speed, or via starship, which brings in relativistic effects. With relativity, you are never sure when messages will arrive. Inversion is the worst. *During* inversion, signals you send to other inverted ships can arrive any time, even before you send them, or not until the end of the universe." He turned over his wrist, showing me its socket. "The psibernet bypasses all of that. As fast as I can form a thought, any telepath in the net can pick it up. The speed at which information moves through a military machine is vital. Imagine a large, slow warrior and a small, fast opponent. The Traders could crush us if they could catch us. But they are too slow. So we survive."

"David and Goliath." I smiled. "It's a story about a boy who defeated a giant."

He exhaled. "I wish we could defeat them. Now that they have a Lock, all they need is a Key and the giant will have his speed. There are eleven of us in the Rhon. Eleven potential Keys. Four women and seven men." He suddenly looked like a boy caught with his hand in the cookie jar. "I am the youngest. The most insignificant."

"Jailbait, huh?" I smirked. "Maybe you're not old enough for me to marry."

As he laughed, a knock sounded on the door. Kabatu looked

in. "Commander Selei? Max wondered if you wanted to get the contract specifications done now."

"I'll be right there," Althor said.

After Kabatu withdrew, I said, "Are you going to work on the treaty?"

He shook his head. "That will take months of negotiation between the Allied Congress and Imperial Assembly. We and the Allieds have been dancing around this for decades. All four Rhon females are married, so both sides have long expected to arrange the marriage of a Rhon male with an Allied woman having a high Kyle rating." He gave me a guilty look. "Given my minor status compared to my uncles, my name never came up seriously. No one expected a Rhon marriage this way, unplanned, unannounced, un-everything."

I began to understand why he had pushed so hard for it. If Ming was right, that my rating could be as high as a five, I had value to Althor's people despite my low social status. Any children he and I had would be Kyle operators, probably even telepaths. My genes came from a different pool, a different universe even, so a good chance existed that the Kyle alleles he and I carried differed enough to minimize unfavorable traits.

In retrospect, I also see why he insisted I take no other husbands: Imperial law allows polygamy. And Althor was last in line for any arrangement with a Kyle woman. So he leap-frogged the hierarchy and made sure he would have no competitors.

"Right now I want to ensure that certain provisions are in place," he said. "I have a few lands, a little wealth, a minor civilian title. All that goes to you if—" He paused. "If anything happens to me." Fatigue creased his face. "I have to get word to my family. Meanwhile, I'm going to leave you with the Abaj on Raylicon. They will protect you."

"No!" I stared at him. "You can't leave me alone."

He put his arms around my waist. "I don't want you exposed to this. I'll arrange with Stonehenge to secure our contract here until I send for it." In a subdued voice he said, "If I'm killed, he will forward it to both the Assembly and Allied Congress."

"No. Althor, don't say that. No one will kill you."

"I hope not." His expression softened. "Especially not now, when I have so much more than I did before."

After Althor left, I returned to the Observation Deck to look at the stars. It was quiet now, the people and remains of the wedding gone. In the wash of starlight, I prayed for Althor. Don't let him die, I thought. I petitioned the meld of Maya and Spanish deities I had learned as a child: the Father, Son, and Holy Ghost; the Vashakmen, who hold the world on their shoulders; the Totilme?iletik, our ancestors; Ix Chel, both the moon goddess and the Virgin Mary. I had no incense to offer, but white candles still burned in the chamber. I asked the spirits to forgive my poor showing for the rituals and prayed that they let no lightning knock out parts of Althor's soul.

Lightning and thunder: it was how I saw Althor. So I also prayed to Yahval Balamil, the Earth Lord, who uses a landsnail's shell to hold powder for his thundering skyrockets. His essence lives in water holes and caves, including around Nabenchauk, my home, Lake of the Lightning. I added a prayer to ?Anheletik, who seeps out of caves as a mist, or comes as lightning; and to ?Anhel, god of thunder and rain. For good measure I ended with a prayer to Thor, the Norse god of thunder and war. Granted, it was out of place, but it seemed like a good idea.

Eventually I left the Observation Deck and walked through the park. The mirrors outside the station had rotated to reflect sunlight into other areas of the torus, leaving this section in night. Starlight shone through the windows, as bright—and as hard— as gems.

13

White Lace Abduction

Someone shook my shoulder. I opened my eyes, seeing a gold blur. Gradually it resolved into Althor. Behind him, holos gleamed on the walls in our bedroom, red and gold desert scenes, soothing images that had dimmed when I lay down earlier.

I spoke drowsily, my eyes closing again. "Are you finished with Stonehedge?"

"As done as we can be for now." He lay next to me. "You and I have maybe six more hours before we leave."

"Ummm . . ." I rolled close to him. "Good."

He pulled at the tie at my neckline. "I think I can do this one without a manual."

I laughed, sleepy and warm. I couldn't get my eyes open, though. So I lay against him, half asleep. His cheek slid down my shoulder, and his mouth closed around my breast, suckling, warm and sensuous. I tried to wake up, but I couldn't focus. It felt like cotton filled my brain. So I let my thoughts drift. No need to think.

After a while, Althor slid his hand under my dress and pulled off my panties. I drifted in a half dream, vaguely aware of him trying to stir a reaction from his new bride.

Finally he laughed. "Tina, wake up! It's our wedding night."

"Hmm . . ." I made an effort to open my eyes. "You switched modes again."

"I did?"

"Your accent came back."

"I thought the Jag stabilized it." He kissed me. "I guess not."

"Maybe it—ouch!" My eyes snapped all the way open.

Althor pushed up on his elbows. "What's wrong?"

"The hilt of your sword just jabbed me in the stomach." Now that I had my eyes open, I realized he was still fully dressed. I laughed. "You haven't even taken off your boots."

He grinned, sitting up as he tugged his pullover over his head. He dropped it on the floor, then undid the sword and set it down on the pullover. When he lay down again and began kissing me, it felt wonderful. But . . . something was wrong. Something was missing. Or muted.

Then it hit me. The golden haze created by my exhaustion was gone. I still saw the sparkling effect of his dress uniform, but that was all. My own naturally produced light show had disappeared.

I stopped kissing him. "Althor, did you hear a thud outside?"

He lifted his head. "What?"

"A thud. Outside."

"No, I hear no—"

We both heard it that time. Someone had opened the door to our house.

Althor jumped off the bed and grabbed the sword. Heavy footsteps thudded in the living room. As I got off the bed, pulling down my dress, he nudged me toward the back wall. "Stay behind me."

The door he faced was the only entrance. He moved toward it, pulling his sword out of its sheath as the footsteps came closer—

And an arm brought a gun around my body, a weapon bigger than any assault rifle, made from mirrored metal. The stock lay against my abdomen and the barrel jutted up my body, between my breasts, its tip resting under my chin. I felt something behind me, human-shaped, but larger and hard like metal.

"Althor," I whispered.

He turned, and as soon as I saw the look on his face, I knew we had run out of luck.

The door opened, revealing four giants, each over two meters tall. They resembled robots, human-shaped but heavier. The flexible mirrored surfaces of their bodies reflected the room's holoart. Their heads were ridged metal helmets with screens where a nose should have been. Each giant wore a metal waistband with a power pack and boots with six-inch treads. Three of them carried guns that looked the way the one pressed against my body felt.

They had Stonehedge. A bruise purpled his face and more covered his arms where they showed through the torn cloth. The right sleeve of his uniform had been ripped completely off and a patch was fastened to the inside of his elbow.

I know now that the mirrored giants were mercenaries wearing armor, but at the time I had no idea what they were, other than terrifying. Because they look like robots, people call them warrior droids, or just waroids. Although they have neither the speed nor agility of a Jagernaut, they have more power, and the advantages of being a walking fortress.

Althor stood in the middle of the room holding a ceremonial sword made from soft gold, facing metal giants with guns that could, in one shot, do more damage than fifty case-hardened swords. He looked at the waroids, at me, back at the waroids. Then he dropped the sword.

"Lord Selei." The voice came from a waroid across the room. It sounded eerie, as if it were filtered to remove identifying nuances.

"Don't hurt her," Althor said.

"We have no interest in your wife," the waroid said. "Cooperate and she will live."

"What do you want?" Althor asked.

"Turn around. Put your arms behind your back."

As Althor complied, the waroid opened a compartment in his armor and pulled out a cord with lights flickering on it. He didn't come near Althor; he simply let go of the cord. It fell to the ground, snapped across the floor to Althor, and climbed up his legs to his wrists. Then it unraveled into a mesh and bound his hands together. I thought it was alive. In truth, a binding mesh is as insentient as a rock. It works on nano-bots with sticky molecules that either cling or slide on surfaces, depending on their state.

When the mesh was in place, the waroid approached and prodded Althor forward by pushing his shoulder with the tip of his mammoth gun. The one behind me removed his gun and moved to my side, taking hold of my arm. Its footsteps were silent as it walked, instead of thudding, but other than that it was identical to the others. It led me forward, following the others, who were bringing Althor and Stonehedge.

The waroid who had spoken appeared to be the leader. As we walked, he touched a panel on his armor and his boots became silent. I understood then: they had deliberately made noise when they came in, drawing Althor to the door while they sliced through the back wall, probably with black-market nano-bots that dissolved metal.

Outside, it was still night; the line of dawn that moved down the curving plain of the torus wasn't yet visible. We walked through the starlit parks in silence. Nothing moved. We passed a man and woman sprawled unconscious on the ground next to a bench, then a dog sleeping under a tree, then a dead mouse.

When we reached the spoke, the leader pressed a pattern into the elevator panels. Nothing happened. He tried again, with no success. Turning to Stonehenge, he said, "What is the combination?"

Stonehedge just looked at him, his face set in firm lines.

The leader raised his arm and backhanded Stonehenge across the face, slamming him into the waroid behind him. "What is the combination?"

"Go to hell," Stonehenge said.

The leader motioned to another waroid. As it approached Stonehenge, the director tensed. But the waroid only examined the patch on his arm, the material that sheathed its fingers flexing like a mirrored skin. Then it straightened up. "Try now."

The leader regarded Stonehenge. "What is the combination?"

Stonehedge spoke in a clenched voice, as if fighting the words. "Triangle, square, four, circle, circle, red, four, three, eight, green."

The leader entered the combination and the spoke doors opened. After the nine of us crowded inside, the doors closed and the car began its journey to the hub.

We later determined that the moment Althor had contacted Epsilani, a message had gone out, sent by a sleeper virus that infected their web. The sleeper didn't awake until Althor's message came in, and after performing its function it destroyed itself. It didn't succeed in removing every trace of its existence, though, either at Epsilani or elsewhere. It had infected all of the nets, Allied and Skolian, even Trader.

As we rode inward, our weight decreased. When we were weightless, the doors opened onto the passage that circled the hub. We floated to the decon chamber, through the hub, past the drifting bodies of unconscious colonists.

I felt the Jag now, or more accurately, I felt its absence. It was quiescent, like a sleeping beast. I understood then why my brain was like cotton. The waroids had shut down the Jag, and because of my link to it, they had unknowingly affected my brain as well. When we entered the decon chamber, the holomap by its console showed a pod moving from a large ship outside the station toward the Jag's docking chute.

Two waroids waited by the entrance to the chute, standing on the deck rather than floating. Our guards were settling onto the deck as well, their magnetized boots fastening to its surface. Althor's guards stood like giant statues, holding his arms as he floated between them. My guard also stood with his feet planted, his hand gripped on my upper arm. I drifted next to him, holding down the hem of my dress.

The leader was watching the holomap. "How long until the ship is loaded?"

"It should only be a few more minutes," one of the waroids said. Her voice had a curious sound, flat and inhuman, but with an accent. I didn't recognize it as Skolian at the time, but I saw Althor stiffen when she spoke.

The leader considered me. "What are your connections?" he asked.

I swallowed. "My what?"

"Leave her alone," Althor said.

The leader's head swiveled to him. "Why can't we find this wedding contract of yours?"

"Stonehedge probably lost it," Althor said. "It's just a supplement contract."

"Supplement? What does that mean?"

The Skolian waroid answered. "It's a euphemism. It means she's his concubine."

The leader looked at me. "I can see the motivation for this." Using the tip of his gun, he pushed aside the neckline of my dress, partially uncovering my breast. "Yes, I see can see the motivation."

Althor struggled in the grip of his guards. "Don't touch her!"

Another waroid spoke. The authority in his manner came through even the filtering of his voice, as did his Skolian accent. He indicated Stonehedge. "Get rid of him."

The leader nodded. He motioned at a different waroid and it took a med clip out of its armor. As it fired the clip, Stonehenge tensed, a strained look passing over his face, as if he wondered whether or not he was about to die. Then he slumped, his body going limp. When I realized he was only unconscious, I almost gasped with relief.

The leader swiveled his head to the Skolian waroid who had wanted Stonehedge knocked out. "What is it?"

"Selei is lying," the Skolian said. "He could have as many concubines as he wants. He's never taken one."

"Everyone has his needs," the leader said.

The Skolian made an odd sound, like a filtered bark of laughter. "Oh, he does, you can be sure. When he applied to DMA, he failed a test in his psychological battery of exams because it suggested he spent too much time fantasizing about sex, enough to distract him from studies. The admissions board let it go, though."

"Then why do you dispute his claim about the girl?"

"It doesn't fit his profile. For lovers, he selects women who are his equals. Not concubines. You must remember, this man descends from a rigidly matriarchal culture."

"That was five thousand years ago," the leader said.

"True. But traces of it remain."

The leader's head swiveled to me. "I would hardly call this frightened child his equal."

Althor was watching the Skolian waroid intently. Even without my empathic sense, I could guess his thought: Who was this, who knew more about his confidential records than Althor knew himself?

"Sir," another waroid said. "The pod is in position on the Jag. We're ready to leave."

"Leave my wife here," Althor said. "You have me. You have what you came for."

"You want us to let her go?" the leader said.

"She's of no use to you. And she can't identify any of you."

"She pleases me," the leader said. "You aren't going to need her anymore."

Althor clenched his fists. "Touch her and you'll regret it."

The leader walked around him, his boots hissing as they attached and released from the floor. "You're in no position to make threats."

"With what you must be getting paid for my kidnapping, you could have any woman you want," Althor said. "You don't need her."

"You must have had a reason for marrying her, Rhon prince."

"Just look at her. It's obvious why."

"I don't believe you." The leader motioned to the waroid holding me. "Bring her."

We went into inversion soon after leaving Epsilon Eridani. No one talked to us or answered our questions. When Althor and I tried to speak to each other, they told us to be quiet. They didn't talk much even among themselves. Their main intent seemed to be getting their job done.

The cabin was cramped. Nine waroids crewed the ship, each

reclining in a control seat, with visored helmets over their heads. Exoskeletons enclosed their bodies, bulkier models than on the Jag. Althor was two rows in front of me, bound to his seat from neck to toe by a mesh. They hadn't bothered webbing me, just tied my arms and legs to the seat.

Jag, I thought. *Wake up.*

No answer.

Althor? Can you hear me? Again, no response. Cotton filled my brain.

The trip stretched into a daze of silence and fear. Twice Althor tried to twist around to see me, and both times the pilot told him to stay still. After a while, the visored helmet on my seat came down. Lights blinked and hieroglyphics scrawled across its inner surface. Odd symbols appeared, in strange patterns of color and symmetry. Sounds pinged or echoed eerily. A cloying mist blew against my face, clogging my nose . . . sleepy . . .

I stirred once, almost waking, aware again of strange patterns, smells, and sounds in the helmet. A tube was in my mouth, giving fluid every now and then. I swallowed, never knowing if the taste would be bitter or sweet.

I woke up when we reinverted and was relieved to find the helmet retracted. A murmur in unfamiliar languages went on between the waroids and the ship. It was all verbal or visual; no one seemed linked into this ship the way Althor linked to the Jag. We accelerated, were weightless for a moment, then accelerated again. When the g-forces let up, a bell clanged, followed by several jolts.

The waroids stirred, preparing to leave the ship. One untied me and helped me out of the seat, its armor hissing like a pump releasing air. Althor was standing at the front of the cabin, his arms bound behind him, flanked by guards. He watched me, his face creased with strain.

We disembarked onto a black plain that stretched for miles in every direction, until it faded into a metallic haze. Low buildings were visible in the distance, square and blunt, lava-black. Cranes hooked their way to hundreds of feet above the plain, bent at odd angles, with gigantic chains hanging from their tips, un-

moving chains, as still as everything else. We were inside a structure so large that its ceiling formed a "sky." Overhead, two halves
of a gigantic dome were closing. A sliver of black sky showed
through the narrowing opening, then disappeared as the doors
silently came together.

The low gravity gave our walk across the plain a dreamlike
quality. The building we approached resembled a black box, long,
wide, and low. A slab in one wall rolled to the side, uncovering
a membrane that irised open, leaving a shimmering hole. When
we walked through the shimmer, it felt as if a soap bubble clung
to my skin.

The room inside could have been the interior of a polished box
made out of black marble veined with red. Tables, benches, floor,
walls, ceiling: all were carved from one gigantic block of stone.
The waroids had Althor sit on a ledge jutting out from one wall.
One of them questioned him in an unfamiliar language. The
leader listened, standing with his legs planted wide and his arms
crossed, his armor reflecting the red-veined marble so that he
looked like an obelisk.

Althor refused to speak. Finally the leader motioned at my
guard. The waroid pulled me over to the leader, who pushed me
against one of Althor's other guards.

The leader spoke to Althor. "You will cooperate, I assume."

Althor looked at me and his composure slipped, his face creas-
ing with strain. "Yes. I'll cooperate."

His guard resumed the interrogation. Althor answered in the
same language, his sentences terse, his face once again impassive.
Apparently the leader didn't believe whatever he was saying. After
several moments he motioned to the doctor who had knocked out
Stonehedge. The doctor walked forward, opening a compartment
in his armor and removing a metal tape. Althor tensed as his
guards took hold of his arms and pulled back his head. But the
doctor only placed the reflective tape against Althor's neck. Data
scrolled across it in English, rather than the hieroglyphics Skolians used, and holos of a man's torso formed. One showed a complicated web with disruptions around the left shoulder.

A waroid behind us spoke. "Sir, we're getting the signal. They've docked and disembarked."

The leader swiveled his head. "Go meet them."

"Right away."

I glanced at the waroid who was leaving. Getting a signal from what?

The doctor spoke in English. "His biomech web is damaged." Moving with care, he peeled the false skin off Althor's shoulder, uncovering the healing wound. When he removed the bandage around Althor's waist, it revealed the transcom socket. He pressed the skin around it and the transcom slid into his gauntleted hand.

The door behind us rumbled again. Turning, I saw the waroid who had left return with a man and woman. At nearly seven feet tall, with a muscular physique, a gun hanging from her belt, and a mirrored carbine in her hands, the woman was obviously a body-guard. The man was also well over six feet tall, with a lanky build and silver hair. He walked over to us, bringing a sense of authority with him.

"So, Althor," he said. "We see each other again."

14

Ragnarok

Ragnar?" Hope and apprehension chased each other across Althor's face. I recognized the name. Admiral Ragnar Bloodmark. Althor's mentor. His second father.

Bloodmark looked down at him. "I'm afraid we have a problem."

Althor's face closed again, hiding his emotions. "What kind of problem?"

"You're supposed to be dead."

Although Althor's composure didn't slip, even my deadened empathic senses couldn't miss his reaction. He faced a betrayal that shook the foundations of his life. But all he said was, "I'm not."

"So I see." Bloodmark turned to the mercenary leader. "I've received the offer, and it is acceptable. We uploaded the rendezvous coordinates to your ship."

"I still don't like it," the leader said.

"We tried it your way." Bloodmark motioned at Althor. "This is the result. He still lives and the Allied-Skolian negotiations continue."

"Is that what this is about?" Althor asked. "Our reestablishing diplomatic relations with the Allieds?"

Bloodmark glanced at him. "I truly am sorry, Althor. I am, in my own way, fond of you."

A chink of bewilderment showed in Althor's defenses. "Then why? Why are you doing this?"

"There are those of us," Bloodmark said, "who find it unacceptable that our existence as a coherent society—our very lives and liberty—are bound to the whims of an unstable family that is dying out as we watch." He paused. "Some of us see alternatives."

Althor tensed. "What alternatives?"

The admiral paced away from him, hands clasped behind his back. "Four hundred and fifty years." He turned around. "This is a long time to fight a war."

"If we don't fight the Traders," Althor said, "they'll conquer us."

"Probably."

"Then you know we need an alliance with the Allieds."

"We tried that." Bloodmark paced in front of Althor. "Your dear mother's legacy to our two governments. A failed marriage and a flawed treaty." He stared at the far wall. "Your lovely mother." He turned to Althor. "And when we needed them? They betrayed us. They held our prize jewels—your family—hostage." He held up his hand, a tiny space between his thumb and index finger. "This close, Althor. We came this close to fighting a war with our 'allies' on the heels of our last war with the Traders."

"If you consider my family 'prize jewels,' why kill me?"

"I didn't say I was going to kill you. Prize jewels, after all, are worth a great deal of wealth. But right now, we have a more important question. This mysterious marital contract of yours." Bloodmark waved his hand at me. "With this pretty, if inappropriate, child, who, if I understand correctly, comes from Earth."

Althor stiffened. "It's a supplement contract."

Bloodmark snorted. "Althor Selei, who barely deigns to acknowledge the reams of spectacularly beautiful women who throw themselves at his bed? You've always chosen women as partners. I find it hard to believe you would suddenly take a concubine."

Althor shrugged. "That's your problem."

"Why can't we find the contract?"

"I don't know. Maybe Stonehedge misfiled it."

"Shall I use drugs?" Bloodmark asked.

"It won't do any good. I've nothing to tell you."

"Sir." The mercenary doctor spoke. "His biomech web can release antidotes to truth serums. If it doesn't have the antidote, it can flood him with tailored neurotransmitters to make him forget or misremember information."

Bloodmark spoke softly. "Don't lecture me on biomech webs, Doctor. I designed the prototype Commander Selei carries in his body."

Even filtered, the doctor's voice sound subdued. "Yes, sir."

Bloodmark turned to the leader. "What have you found out about her?"

"Nothing," the leader said. "She can't be from Earth. No record exists matching her description, retinal pattern, voice signature, fingerprints, or brain scans."

"Then where is she from?"

"One of the frontier worlds, I would guess, someplace that hasn't kept up records."

"Kyle rating?" Bloodmark asked.

"Almost nothing," the leader said. "We ran scans during the flight out here. She's barely an empath. Maybe a two on the scale."

Barely an empath? I glanced at Althor in time to see a puzzled look pass over his face, then disappear.

"You're sure?" Bloodmark asked. "Shipboard scanners aren't designed for Kyle tests."

The doctor spoke. "It isn't as good as the equipment in a lab, but if she had any significant Kyle ability, we would have found some indication."

Bloodmark nodded. He turned back to the leader. "Your assessment?"

"At first I thought Selei was lying about it being a supplement contract," he said. "After her tests, though, I'm inclined to believe him."

The admiral turned to another of the waroids. "Your assessment?"

"I agree." It sounded like the Skolian who had known Althor's military records. "She doesn't seem to have much to offer aside from—the obvious."

Bloodmark came over to me. "You've been very quiet during all of this."

"I want to stay with Althor," I said.

He spoke softly. "I would be careful what you ask for. You may regret it."

"Why?" Althor asked. When Bloodmark didn't respond, Althor said, "Damn it, Ragnar. Answer me."

The admiral turned slowly, his expression hardening. "For decades I have answered to your family. Bowed to you. Kept my place. Even though morally, intellectually, psychologically, emotionally, and physically I am your superior. No, Althor, I will never 'answer' to you again."

"Is that how you saw it?" Althor stared at him. "Gods, I've looked up to you since I was a boy."

Bloodmark's stiff postured eased. "I truly am sorry it had to be you. You are—more tolerable than other members of the Rhon."

"You couldn't have been faking your friendship," Althor said. "We're telepaths. We would have known."

"And I'm not."

"Not a telepath?"

"That's right."

Althor blinked. "That matters to you?"

"To me?" Bloodmark gave a curt laugh. "No. Only to you. Your family." Bitterness tainted his voice. "You consider yourselves so superior. But you're not."

Althor gave him an incredulous look. "That's not true."

"Isn't it?"

"No. How could you have felt this way without our knowing?"

"Oh, I think your father suspects. Never the full extent of it, but he has far less affection for me. You should have listened to him more, Althor, instead of mouthing off every time he said a word."

Althor swallowed. "I don't believe you felt this way. I would have *known*."

Bloodmark shrugged. "You would be surprised what a bio-mech genius can simulate with his own web. At disguise, I am a master." He considered Althor. "I am proud of you. Of all the systems I've designed, you are the most splendid. It is true that bio-mech demands a high toll: the operations, the danger of parts growing incorrectly, the years of training, the chance of rejection, the security clearances, the price even in our humanity—it is pro-hibitive, to say the least. But it is worth it. We are a superior species. That day before your eighth birthday, when you took your first step—that was the day I knew my work with you would succeed. My tears then were as real as those your parents shed."

"Don't," Althor said.

"But have you ever thought of the price Imperial Skolia paid for your repair?" Bloodmark came closer to him. "In human terms? Terms such as, say, the planet Far Shore? I was born there, you know. A rough place. Half the population is starving. On a planet with three billion people." His voice hardened. "The cost of a juice pod on your homeworld would be enough, on Far Shore, to feed a family for days. What it cost to make you a whole human being—that could have fed Far Shore's entire population for a year."

Althor stared at him. "You think my family should feed Far Shore?"

"I don't hold your family responsible for feeding planets. I do find it a sad commentary that the Assembly considered one hideously deformed child more important than the population of an entire planet."

The mercenary leader spoke. "What do you mean, 'hideously deformed'? We're promising to deliver a healthy Jagernaut."

"Deliver where?" Althor said.

Bloodmark turned to the leader. "He's quite healthy, I assure you."

"If there's a problem," the leader said, "we damn well better talk about it now."

"Althor is as physically perfect as human science can make a man," Bloodmark said.

"Human science?" the leader said. "What the hell does that mean?"

"Ragnar, stop," Althor said.

Bloodmark glanced at him like a sculptor admiring his work. He turned back to the leader. "He was born with that face. A beautiful child. And that magnificent Rhon brain of his. Unfortunately, that was all he had." He made a disgusted sound. "Any other two people as closely related as his parents, with such a proclivity for genetic defects, would never have been allowed to breed. But not so for the Rhon. No attempt to make more of them is too desperate."

"What was wrong with him?" the leader asked.

"Stop it." Althor stood up, hands still tied behind his back. His guards grasped his upper arms roughly, holding him in place.

"He was born without legs," Bloodmark said. "Left arm and hand deformed, lower right arm missing. One kidney, and that defective. Only part of one lung. Defective heart. Defective liver. Skeletal sections missing. No spleen. Only partial digestive system. He had a stomach, though. You could see it every time you looked at him. He was missing entire portions of the right side of his body." He grimaced. "It was disgusting."

"Christ." The leader motioned at Althor. "And now he looks like that?"

Bloodmark nodded. "We removed him prematurely from the womb because he had more chance of surviving in an artificial environment where we could work on him. We studied his genes to determine what he might have been without his—defects. And then we rebuilt him into that human. It took ten years to make him whole, and another ten to ensure the biomech grew properly with the rest of him."

Althor said nothing, just stared at Bloodmark. He looked as if he had been kicked in the stomach.

"I don't like it," the leader said.

The doctor spoke. "Commander Selei is sound, sir. It's true, he does carry more biomech than any other case I know of. It's rarely done on children; only in situations like this when it's their only chance of survival. But all Jagernauts have webs, so it's assumed we'll be delivering biomech." He walked over to Althor and pointed out his shoulder, as if Althor were an expensive piece of equipment. "My concern is the damage to his web." He indicated the transcom socket. "This will also need a replacement unit, one without weapons capability. Otherwise, the socket will spoil." He tilted his helmet down to the admiral. "These problems could cause rancor."

Bloodmark nodded. He spoke to the leader. "We'll offer to renegotiate, so it doesn't look as if we are trying to cheat on the terms."

"Damn it," Althor said. "Cheat *who?*"

Watching him, I had a feeling he knew. But I had no idea. One thing I had no doubt about, though: Bloodmark didn't want to answer. It was a long moment before he turned back to Althor—and said:

"We're selling you to Kryx Iquar."

At first Althor didn't react. He just stared at the admiral. Then, slowly, he sat down.

"Who is Kryx Iquar?" I asked.

Althor looked at me. "The Eubian Trade Minister."

"Who are the Eubians?" I asked.

"We also call them Traders," Bloodmark said.

My heart stuttered. "You're *giving* Althor to *them?*"

"Not giving," one of Althor's guards said, turning her helmet toward me. "Trading. For more frigging wealth than the yearly gross product of the entire Allied Worlds."

Althor was finally starting to react. "Ragnar, gods, *why?*"

Bloodmark sat next to him and spoke more quietly, as if revealing the full extent of his betrayal allowed him to drop the defensiveness that had masked his guilt. "A fake Allied extremist group is claiming credit for your abduction. After the trade takes place, the Eubian ministry will announce they purchased you, and how. The Allieds will of course condemn the action.

Apologies and disclaimers will proliferate. But the damage will be done."

Althor stared at him. "That will destroy any hope of any alliance between our people and the Allieds."

"Yes. It will."

"Ragnar, you're going to start a war."

"Actually, I'm trying to end one."

"How? The Traders have the third Lock." Althor swallowed. "They can use me as a Key. Once they have that, we lose our advantage over them."

"Advantage?" Bloodmark snorted. "We have lived with four hundred and fifty years of hostilities. Every time it erupts into full-scale war, it devastates billions of lives."

"You would rather the Traders conquer us?"

"Favorable terms are being arranged." The admiral sighed. "Your family is flawed, Althor. I've seen firsthand what it does to hold a handful of humans responsible for such a crucial portion of our defense. Even if your family were the epitome of human perfection, it would destroy you. Shall we draw this out in a long, bloody war? Better to cut our losses now. I learned long ago when to order a retreat."

"How can you believe that?" Althor asked. "We've served the Net for five centuries. It's growing stronger, not weaker. And with help from the Allieds, we'll have a chance of recovering the third Lock."

"The net is growing," Bloodmark said. "Bigger and stronger are not the same. Even with three Keys, the job of powering and maintaining it was almost impossible. Now, with just your mother and your uncle, it's killing them. How much longer can this continue? The psibernet will collapse; not today, not tomorrow, but soon."

Althor's fists clenched behind his back. "You want to be on the side you think will win." When Bloodmark didn't answer, Althor said, "You're a fool. The Traders don't want 'terms.' They want to own the Imperialate and Allied Worlds. Period."

"'Own' is a relative term. Most Trader subjects live comfortable lives." Bloodmark stood up. "And when the Imperialate becomes part of the Concord, a select few of us will have a more—honored status. The freedom to pick and choose from among choicer options."

I could guess where Bloodmark was going: Althor's mother was the choicest "option" of all. I don't think Althor saw it then; he was too close to the situation. But he understood the rest of what Bloodmark meant. He spoke in a cold voice. "What you mean is the freedom to own people." When the admiral didn't answer, Althor said, "Did it ever occur to you that our citizens don't want this choice you plan to make for them?"

"It has already been made." Bloodmark spoke more gently. "If it helps any to know—we intended your Jag to explode when you reinverted on approach to Earth. The group that supposedly arranged your kidnapping would have claimed credit for the destruction. We had doubts this was as effective as an arrangement with Kryx Iquar, the other option we laid the groundwork for. And it certainly wasn't as lucrative, to put it mildly." He paused. "But it had the advantage of not requiring we hand you over to the Traders."

"Is that supposed to make me feel better?" Althor asked.

Bloodmark sighed. "Althor, I would have preferred it be someone else in your family. But you are, I am afraid, the least-well-guarded member of the Rhon."

Althor just turned his head away. Bloodmark watched him, then walked back to the mercenary leader. "Contact Iquar's people. Inform them of the damage to Commander Selei and renegotiate the deal. The damage is relatively minor. Allow only correspondingly minor changes in the agreement."

"What if they won't go with that?" the leader asked.

"They will," Bloodmark said. "They want him. But be careful. I want no rancor."

"Understood."

"And kill the girl," Bloodmark said. "She's seen too much."

"No!" Althor stood up. "She won't try to escape."

"Contact my ship when you've settled on terms," Bloodmark told the leader.

"Yes, sir."

Bloodmark headed for the airlock, where his bodyguard waited. I stared at him, feeling sick, unable to absorb the full import of his words.

"Ragnar!" Althor's composure dissolved. "Gods, man, don't do this to her."

Bloodmark paused in the airlock, still facing away from Althor. After a moment he glanced at the leader. "Let her stay with him until we return."

Then he left.

I closed my eyes, aware only of my heart pounding. An armored hand touched my elbow. As I opened my eyes, a mercenary nudged me froward. A slab of stone opened outward from the wall, revealing a stone hallway.

They led us through a maze of marble tunnels. Our trip ended in a bare room that looked like the interior of a seamless polished box. After the waroids returned to the hall, beyond Althor's reach, the leader stood in the doorway, his armor reflecting the walls, black with red veins. He spoke in his language and lights flickered on the mesh that bound Althor's wrists. Gathering itself back into a cord, it whisked off Althor. It sped across the floor to the leader as he opened a compartment in his armor, then climbed up his body and snapped into the compartment.

"You have several hours before we leave," the leader said. "You can stay with your wife until then." He stepped back and the wall closed.

Althor just stood there, rubbing his wrists, staring at the smooth wall. Then he drew me into an embrace. "Gods, Tina. I'm sorry. I'm so sorry you got pulled into this."

I hugged him around the waist, my face buried against his chest. As he bent his head over mine, a pressure pushed against my mind.

Tina?

Louder, I thought. *I can barely hear you.*

We are sure to be monitored in here. His thought faded. . . . *musn't find out . . . only Stonehedge knows . . . treaty . . . your Kyle rating? I don't understand . . .*

It's the Jag. I tried to shout the thought. *It did something to me.*

Althor tilted up my head so that I was looking into his face, but I still picked up nothing. He kissed me, bringing us even closer together. . . . *y yo te amo. ?Akushtina.*

"And I you," I whispered. *Te amo. I love you.*

His voice caught. "As long as we both shall live."

15

The Cylinder

Our cell was exactly what it looked like: a hollow cube with no exits, at least not any we could find. So we sat against one wall, arms wrapped around each other, staring into the empty interior of the cube.

After a while, I said, "I'm sorry about Bloodmark."

Althor swallowed. "So am I."

"What he said—about rebuilding you . . ."

"It's true. In fact, he underplayed it."

"It's incredible. You're beautiful."

It was a moment before he answered. "I've never lost the sense I formed in my childhood, that my body is hideous." He hesitated. "Does it bother you?"

I looked up at him. "No."

He touched my cheek. "I still carry the genes. If I have children with a woman who carries the same alleles, they could be born like me. Or worse. At least my brain was intact."

"Then you should have children with someone who doesn't carry them."

His voice caught. "Like you."

I laid my head against his chest. "I don't want to die."

"Gods, Tina, I wish they would take me in your place."

"I don't want you to die, either."

"Nor I." We sat silent then, out of words, staring at nothing.

Some time later I became aware of his body shaking. I looked up and saw tears running down his face. "Althor—" I touched the wetness on his face.

He spoke softly. "I loved him like a father."

"I'm sorry." I kept saying that. It sounded so useless. Apparently all my prayers had done no good at all. True, Althor wasn't going to die. I was. What they were doing to him was worse than death.

"Do you believe in God?" I asked.

"Yes." He stroked my hair, his voice damp like his face. "More than one, actually. Our supreme being isn't a 'god,' though. She's female."

"Then why do you say 'for gods' sakes.' "

"It's the English translation of a Skolian idiom. Literally it means 'for the sake of any above-spirits that may notice me.' The spirits don't have a sex."

"Can you pray to your Goddess?"

He laid his cheek against my head. "I tried. She doesn't hear. Or maybe she doesn't exist. Maybe Ixa Quelia is no more than the desperate mythology of a dying people."

"Ix Chel?"

"Ixa Quelia."

"Ix Chel is the Maya moon goddess."

"Raylicon has no moon, other than in our legends, probably brought by our ancestors from Earth. Ixa Quelia is the goddess of fertility. Fire. The night. Life."

Life. No wonder he thought she hadn't heard.

Eventually we dozed, half awake and half asleep. After a while I became aware of voices. Opening my eyes, I saw mirrored armor filling the room. Admiral Bloodmark stood in the doorway.

As Althor and I stood up, Bloodmark spoke. "We've been in contact with Iquar's people."

Althor tensed. "And?"

Bloodmark motioned at me. "Iquar wants her too."

"No!" Althor pulled me against him. "She's not even an empath. Your people tested her."

"We sent him holos." Bloodmark shrugged. "He wants both of you, as compensation for our delivering damaged equipment."

"Ragnar, don't do this to her. Let her go."

Bloodmark came forward, through the forest of waroids. "At least this way she'll live. You may even get to see her." He glanced at the mercenary nearest him. "Bind him."

They shouldn't have come into the room when Althor's arms were free, no matter how much they thought they had subdued him. He lunged at the nearest waroid, moving so fast that his reflection in its armor became a gold smear. He grabbed its mirrored arm and swung it around, hurtling its bulk into two others. They crashed together and toppled, the grating clang of their armor echoing off the polished stone walls.

Then he went after Bloodmark.

They blurred. Two human machines in battle. Althor's attack threw them forward and in the low gravity they sailed at a wall, feet off the floor. Bloodmark twisted, knocking Althor off balance, but Althor used the admiral's momentum to wheel him around. They hit a waroid, still grappling with each other, but as fast as the mercenary reacted, Althor was faster, shoving against it so that he and Bloodmark spun away before it could grab him. Althor and Bloodmark wrestled together, feet skimming the polished floor as they tried to throw each other.

The waroids shouted, strange filtered calls. Three aimed their weapons, tubes with bulky handles. But they didn't shoot, not with Althor and Bloodmark locked together and moving fast. The fighters hit a wall and rebounded, moving like flashes of moonlight on sea waves at night, silver and black, blurred water rolling on a shadowed beach. They crashed past me, coming so close that I felt the heat generated by their reactors.

They lost their balance, and Althor swung Bloodmark under him as they hit the floor. For one instant they made a frozen tableau, Althor with his hands around Bloodmark's neck, strangling him—

The shot came as an explosion of compressed air. It hit Althor in the chest and threw him backward, wrenching him away from Bloodmark. Four waroids shoved him against the wall, pinning his arms and legs. Althor swore and tried to pull away, but four human fortresses were more than he could overcome.

Bloodmark stood up, rubbing his throat. "Is there any more damage?"

The doctor pulled out his med clip and stepped over to Althor. As Althor struggled, one of the waroids pulled back his head, exposing his throat.

"Don't knock him out," Bloodmark said.

The doctor swiveled his helmet to Bloodmark. "It will make him more manageable."

"Iquar's people want his reaction time slowed," Bloodmark said. "He's no good to Iquar if the only way to control him is to knock him out. You'll need a neural suppressant that affects his reflexes without diminishing his empathic responses. If sedatives are in his system, it could affect your treatment."

"I understand." The doctor replaced the clip. While the other waroids held Althor's head back, he pressed his tape against Althor's neck and the rotating holos appeared. "A few more optic threads around the shoulder region ripped. But the damage is minor. It should repair itself before we rendezvous."

"Good," Bloodmark said. "Now restrain him properly this time."

They bound Althor's wrists, then took us back through the building. Four waroids flanked Althor, one on each side holding his upper arm. One walked with me, silent except for the hiss of its armor every now and then. I wondered what it became when it took off the armor. A man or woman with a normal life, family, friends? It was impossible to imagine.

We left the building and crossed the glassy plain, moving in the low gravity with dreamlike languorous steps. As we walked, the quality of the light changed, becoming softer, like starlight. I looked up. Far overhead, the dome was opening, revealing a black sky studded with stars. They resembled jewels, their colors far more vivid than when seen on Earth. In fact, they were as bright as on the holomaps in the Jag—a view created by the near vacuum of space.

"Wait!" I stopped walking, my heart pounding. "We have to go back. To the building. We're losing air."

The waroid grabbed my arm, forcing me to go with him. Ahead of us, Althor twisted around to look, then stumbled as his guards yanked him forward.

Bloodmark slowed down to walk with me. "There is plenty of air."

I pointed at the dome opening above us. "Not out there."

"Can you see a glint of light, like a curtain?"

By squinting, I could just make out a familiar soap-bubble shimmer far above us. "What is it?"

"A membrane," Bloodmark said. "It holds in air."

I later learned a molecular airlock is a modified lipid bilayer. Nano-bots dope the membrane, each an enzyme plus a picochip. Applying an electric potential causes the enzymes to alter shape and lock onto receptor molecules in the membrane, changing its permeability. One setting makes it impermeable to gasses, air and water vapor in particular. When we walked through it, our bodies became part of the interface. Its cross-linked structure and picochips remembered its previous form, so it could regain its shape after we passed through.

Bloodmark spoke quietly. "If it makes a difference to you, I am glad you are going with Althor. If Iquar lets you see him, that may make it easier on Althor."

I clenched my fists. "I don't see how you live with yourself."

"There are times when we must do what seems cruel to avoid a greater evil."

"Who gave you the right to decide?"

His voice hardened. "Who had the right to condemn us to centuries of war?"

"Don't you know what you meant to him?" I wanted to hit him. "Is this how you would treat your son?"

"My son is dead." Bloodmark spoke numbly, lost in the memory. "He was ten. About the same age as when Althor started to live a normal life. A task force of Eubian agents infiltrated a base near a city where he lived with my Elder Wife. The Traders meant to be in and out within a matter of hours. They were discovered. Near a park. My son was playing there. He was caught in the cross fire. Shot by our own people." His voice had a deadened quality. "An accident. A tragic accident."

Softly I said, "And now you're going to make Althor the sacrifice for that accident?"

He stiffened. "My son has no connection to Althor."

Ahead of us, the waroids reached the ship. As they took Althor inside, we came up to them. The leader spoke to Bloodmark. "You'll hear the results on the news broadcasts."

"Very good," Bloodmark said.

"You're not coming with us?" I asked.

"Of course not," Bloodmark said. "When the exchange takes place I will be seated at the Assembly. I have an invitation to dine with Althor's parents afterward." He paused. "I imagine I will be with them when the news comes over the broadcasts. I will do my best to console the shocked and grieving parents."

I gritted my teeth. "You bastard."

"Whatever you may think of me, I am doing what I believe best for my people."

A waroid pulled me toward the ship. I looked back to see Bloodmark standing with his bodyguard, alone on the field, hands clasped behind his back, silver hair gleaming in the black landscape.

The mercenaries tied us into our seats again and lowered the visored helmets on both of us. I didn't know what Althor's did, perhaps began dosing him with biomech suppressants. In mine, the mist curled around my face and I drifted into a fitful sleep.

I woke when something poked my lips. Opening my eyes, I saw a waroid pushing a tube from the framework around my head into my mouth. The mercenary had pushed back my visor and was floating in front of me.

"Drink," she said. "Come on, girl. It's just water."

I opened my mouth and the tube clicked into place. Liquid ran cool and sweet down my throat. Someone asked a question in another language and the waroid said, "Her dehydration wasn't critical. Otherwise it would have activated an alarm."

When I finished drinking, I opened my mouth and the tube clicked back into the framework. The waroid still floated above me, watching. Maybe she didn't have enough to do. More likely she was making sure the merchandise remained in good shape. Didn't want to deliver dehydrated goods. Freeze-dried. Instant Tina. I tried to laugh, but it came out as a sob.

"What's the problem?" someone said.

"Damned if I know," the waroid watching me said. "None of her monitors show anything."

Someone said, "She's crying, idiot," and someone else muttered, "Sometimes I hate this job."

The woman in front of me snorted. "You won't hate it when pay time comes. We'll be some of the wealthiest people alive. Hell, we'll be fucking richer than some planetary governments."

As a murmur of agreement washed over the others, the pilot said, "Approaching reinversion. Prepare for transfer."

Movement rustled through the cabin as the mercenaries settled into their seats. The exoskeleton on mine closed and a holomap appeared above it. The map showed the stars blueshifting in discontinuous jumps, converging to a point. Holographic hieroglyphs scrolled under the display, my first indication that Skolian languages are three-dimensional, one dimension containing most of the information, the other two adding subtleties and complexities.

We reinverted smoothly. After the stars redshifted to normal, a tiny bar appeared in a corner of the holomap. Gradually it swelled in size, revealing itself as a rotating station, what I later learned was called, simply, the Cylinder. It had an extended torus, making it a double-walled cylinder. Instead of a hub, a nonrotating tube extended down its hollow center, flaring out into a pod at each end to give it a fluted appearance. A massive ring of thrusters circled the neck of each pod.

The Cylinder grew to fill the holomap. Lights scintillated on it, either fixed or racing in necklaces of green, gold, silver, blue, and violet. Glitter drifted around the fluted tube. We came in closer, until the holomap could no longer show the whole station;

closer still, and structures on its surface resolved, cranes, spires, and towers; even closer, and structures within the structures resolved, like fractals repeating their pattern at higher magnifications. Closer yet, and only a pod on the closest end of the fluted tube was visible. The glitter had grown into specks—

With a mental lurch, I realized the "glitter" was ships. Huge ships, with multiple sections, bristling with turrets and antennae. Finally I absorbed the station's magnitude: it was thousands of times larger than Epsilani. The pod before us was opening, like a massive flower with sharpened petals. As we passed under those petals, I realized the pod could hold a hundred ships our size.

New voices came over the com, speaking yet another tongue, one with a harsh sound. Input for the holomap switched to a site outside the Cylinder, allowing us to see our ship inside the open pod, like an insect in a Venus's-flytrap. A robot arm unfolded from the pod's inner surface; when fully extended, it stretched the length of the mercenary ship and more. As it opened its skeletal fingers, a cargo door on the ship rolled open. With no atmosphere to carry sound, the whole process was eerily silent. The claw entered the cargo bay—and came out with the Jag in its skeletal grasp. A huge door in the surface of the pod slid upward and the crane withdrew inside with its captive starfighter. The massive door closed, leaving a smooth section of hull.

Althor spoke, his voice groggy, as if he had just woken up. The pilot answered, something about the Jag being transferred to Iquar.

The ship docked, entering a chute in the neck of the pod. My holomap shut off once we were inside. A shudder vibrated through the ship, a sense of something huge clamping onto it. When the vibration stopped, someone said, "We're secure."

I stirred, and my hair drifted in lazy coils, swirling into my face. The waroid on my right climbed out of her seat and stood up, her magnetized boots planted on the deck. She freed me from the seat, then pulled me up and held onto my arm to keep me from drifting away. My limbs felt numb, the sensation returning in pins and needles.

At the front of the cabin, several waroids were holding Althor while another locked his hands behind his back. He stood watching me, his face creased with fatigue. Despite my deadened brain, I sensed traces of his fear.

We disembarked into a large chamber. After decontamination, we floated out into a huge bay with swinging catwalks and decks made from crisscrossing strips of red metal. A rail ran through the area, terminating at the decon chamber. Two transport cars waited on it like bullets molded from bronze, their noses pointed away from the ship.

The mercenaries split us up, taking Althor in the first transport and me in the second. The car had no frills, just a seamless metal interior with four seats and a web console. Two mercenaries sat in the front and one in the back with me. As a low hum started, mild acceleration pushed us into our seats.

I can't say how long the ride lasted; maybe twenty minutes, maybe an hour. It felt interminable. I sat shivering in my seat, wishing I had a coat. Concentrating on the cold kept me from thinking about whatever waited at the end of our ride.

The car finally slowed to a stop, and a clank vibrated through the metal. The door opened and a woman stared in at us. Large and angular, with a jutting jaw and broad shoulders, she looked as strong as an ox. Her gray hair was pulled back in a twist, with wisps curling around her face. The brown jumpsuit she wore had no patches on it, nothing to indicate she had an identity.

Behind her, I glimpsed an open area the size of a three-car garage with a high roof. Rows of consoles filled it, running perpendicular to the rail. As we stepped out of the car, gravity pulled at us, almost as much as on Earth. Tiles covered the deck, black metal diamonds edged with silver. No windows showed anywhere, just a ceiling and walls the deep blue color of the sky just after the sunset cools. The area looked like a minor control center: operators sat encased in exoskeletons, lights glimmered on consoles, and holomaps rotated in the air, three-dimensional views of equipment, the Cylinder, and hieroglyphics.

People moved about the consoles, some dressed in blue or gray uniforms, but most in brown jumpsuits like our guide. After Althor disembarked from the other car with three of the mercenaries, the Trader woman led us through the control center. Everyone stared at us. More accurately, they stared at Althor. I later learned that Kryx Iquar, the Eubian Trader Minister, had made no secret of his triumph. He had achieved the coveted grail, capturing a member of the Rhon, a prince who was both a psi-bernet Key and the ultimate provider.

A man waited for us at the back of the control center. He wore the uniform of an officer in the Eubian navy: gray tunic with red braid circling the cuffs, gray pants with a blue stripe down each leg, black boots. The insignia on his left shoulder showed a black puma leaping out of a red circle, clawed forelegs extended, teeth bared. Althor glanced at the patch, then grimaced and turned away.

At the officer's command, an oval section of the wall shimmered. It was a modified molecular airlock: when opaque and stiff, they served as solid barriers; when soap-bubble thin, they allowed entrance while guarding against air loss. We walked through the shimmer—into a forest glade.

The emerald-lit clearing was a few yards wide, surrounded by trees with branches that met overhead. Distant bird calls trilled. Purple flowers hung in the foliage like gaudy tiger lilies and a downy green carpet curled around my feet. A carpet. In a jungle.

I looked around. The oval doorway behind us had vanished, replaced by trees. I saw what looked like several large rocks within the trees, but on closer inspection they resolved into control seats with exoskeletons. We were inside a holoart creation, similar to the pictures in Ming's room on Epsilani but far more elaborate.

The naval officer was staring at Althor. When Althor glanced at him, the Trader dropped his gaze, either awed or intimidated, perhaps both. He seemed a normal person, with graying hair and blue eyes. Age lines showed around his eyes and creased his forehead.

On the other side of the glade, the trees vanished, revealing another oval doorway. Three people stood there, two men and a woman. As they entered the chamber, the forest reappeared behind them. The woman and one of the men had brown hair and blue eyes, but the second man's hair was darker, almost black. His eyes were the color of rust. I later realized he was a taskmaster, a member of the highest caste among the Trader slaves, probably the illegitimate child of an Aristo with one of his or her providers.

Althor watched the rust-eyed man, and the Trader stared back in unabashed fascination. Then he seemed to mentally shake himself. After conferring with the naval officer, he came over to me and spoke in the harsh Eubian tongue.

I swallowed. "I don't understand you."

Glancing at the mercenary holding my arm, he repeated his words. The waroid tilted his helmeted head down to me and said, "This is Lieutenant Azez. He requires your identification. Your name."

I looked up at Azez. "Tina."

"Tain-ya." Azez nodded. He walked back toward Althor, staring again, as if Althor were a magnet he couldn't escape.

In fact, Althor mesmerized all of them. If he cared, he showed no sign of it. He stood between his guards, his face impassive. Azez spoke to him in Eubian and he answered in the same, the harsh syllables incongruous on his lips.

Then Azez walked "through" the trees. It was bizarre, as if he passed through a ghost forest. Looking more closely, I was able to make out a console disguised within the holos. Azez leaned over it and spoke in a tongue I hadn't heard before, one with an elegant sound, smooth and lilting, what I now know is Highton, the language of the Aristos, the Trader ruling caste. After a moment Azez returned to the glade and motioned Althor toward a seat, apparently offering to let him relax. Althor just shook his head. Beads of sweat were running down his temple.

We waited. And waited. Several times a Trader or mercenary made a comment, but other than that we all just stood there.

Finally the oval across the room reappeared, this time revealing a man and woman. Everyone in the chamber bowed, except for Althor and me. I had no idea I was expected to do it, and Althor clearly had no intention of bowing to the newcomers.

Seeing them made my skin crawl, though I didn't understand why at the time. They had the kind of perfection that comes from being able to afford any features, any physique, any life you want. They were tall even for Althor's universe, the woman long-legged and well curved, with a sultry beauty; the man broad-shouldered and narrow-hipped, so handsome it seemed unnatural. What struck me most, though, was their coloring: black hair with a crystalline glitter and red eyes, like rubies.

The woman walked to Althor, gazing at him as if he were a prize she coveted, one she would have killed for if she thought she could get away with it. She spoke in Highton, her voice rumbling. Despite the elegant words, she still sounded threatening, as if she were promising him a velvet-draped bedroom in hell. The man in the doorway watched the exchange with a detached fascination, smiling slightly when unease flickered over Althor's face.

The woman turned to her companion and bowed. He walked forward, relaxed and confident, arrogance in his every move. Everyone else in the room bowed, but he paid no attention; he and Althor stared at each other, fixedly, as if they were carrying out some ritual, vying for control. Their appearances heightened the effect; both men had the same height and build, one gold, the other red and black, like two opposed aspects of a supernatural being. Despite the handicaps Althor brought to the contest—a prisoner, half-dressed, hands locked behind his back—the Trader still couldn't dominate their interaction.

The woman spoke again, formally, a phrase ending with "Kryx Iquar."

So. This was Kryx Iquar. The Eubian Trader Minister. The man who had bought us.

Althor and Iquar watched each other, caught in silent combat. Except something was wrong. Althor was falling, *falling* . . .

The floor came up and hit my body. I heard a flurry of words and realized the floor hadn't moved; I had fallen. Althor spoke in

Eubian, his voice intense, urgent. I lifted my head to see him fighting in the grip of several mercenaries, struggling to reach me, his face for the first time revealing his fear.

Iquar knelt in front of me. Looking into his red eyes, I shuddered, remembering the gruesome sense of falling. Mercifully it had receded, muffled by whatever deadened the rest of my Kyle senses. I sat up, pushing my hair away from my face, my hand shaking.

"They tell me you speak English," Iquar said.

I closed my eyes, so relieved to hear a language I understood that a chill ran up my spine.

"Look at me," Iquar said.

I opened my eyes in time to see a frown flash across his too-perfect face. He stood up. "She is in shock." He spoke in Highton and people answered, voices tempered with the fear of those who knew they had angered someone they must always please. Althor watched from across the chamber, still held back by the waroids, his face strained.

As the gray-haired woman helped me to my feet, the other Trader woman came over, murmuring in their harsh language. The waroid next to me took hold of my arm and pulled me toward the wall where we had entered the chamber.

"No!" I tried to pull away. They were taking me away from Althor, my only anchor in this confusing, terrifying universe.

Althor was fighting as well now, trying to yank away from the mercenaries holding him. "Let me go to her!"

The glistening oval appeared in the holo-trees and the mercenary pulled me toward it. As I struggled, I screamed Althor's name. I could hear him fighting behind me.

"Let her *go!*" he shouted.

The waroid dragged me forward, my heels scraping through the cloud-carpet. Then we were through the oval and the chamber closed behind us, leaving me outside and Althor with Kryx Iquar, both of us caught in a nightmare.

16

Lord of Pain

I once dreamed a dream, centuries ago in LA. It was simple, really: I went to Cal State Los Angeles and earned a BA in accounting. I made friends who carried books instead of guns. That was my dream. That was all I asked for.

I got a lot more.

The room lights were low. I lay on a bed, dimly aware of the gray-haired woman moving about.

Some time later I pushed up on my elbows. My head swam and everything blurred, as if I had been drugged. The room was circular, carpeted in blue, with colors swirling on the walls. Someone had taken off my dress and covered me with a blanket, one deeply blue, as soft as a dream. Across the room, the Trader woman dozed in a reclining chair.

A black table stood nearby. The pitcher on it was delicate, a flower with petals that came together on one side in a spout. Condensation ran down its sides to the table, where it disappeared, and a cup shaped like a blossom sat next to it. I tried to reach for the cup, but my arm shook too much. I collapsed back onto the bed, too drugged to function.

The woman appeared and leaned over me, laying her hand against my cheek, then my forehead. Although she didn't smile, her touch was gentle, like a nurse's. She poured some water for me and I gulped it down.

I gave her back the empty cup. "Where is Althor?"

She shook her head. Then she tugged my arm. At her insistence, I climbed off the bed, groggy and dazed. She took me to the wall and spoke, evoking an octagonal portal with a soap-bubble membrane that clung to us as we walked through it. A pool filled the misty chamber beyond. Mosaic tiles made delicate patterns on every surface in the room, whirls of gold, violet, and green. With the woman's help, I eased into the scented pool. I was too dizzy to do much besides sit, listing to one side in about two feet of water.

The woman left. A moment later, she returned with two bowls. Kneeling by the pool, she nudged me back up and gave me a handful of translucent pastel beads. I gazed at them, letting the little spheres pour into the water, too drugged to care what happened to them. After two more tries with the beads, both unsuccessful, she made an exasperated noise. She stripped off her clothes and climbed in next to me. To my dazed brain, it all seemed surreal. She had two belly buttons. Two umbilical cords. If it was a birth defect, Iquar apparently didn't consider repairing it worth the trouble.

She took a handful of beads from one bowl and squeezed her hand, then opened it to reveal a frothy pastel lather. A sweet scent drifted up from it, blending well with the fragrance from the water. She bathed me from head to toe and washed my hair. The beads from the larger bowl made a cream that removed body hair. She took all of it off me, except the hair on my head, eyelashes, and eyebrows. It seemed bizarre at the time, but then, to a woman from three hundred years in my own past, my shaving my legs and armpits would probably have seemed just as bizarre.

She helped me swim toward the far end of the pool. As we drew closer, a fountain resolved out of the mist. She stood me on a dais under it and water fell over me, plastering my hair and sheathing my body. After it rinsed away the lather, she had me swim to the edge of the pool and climb out. As we stood next to a mosaic of waving fronds on the wall, warm air blew out of tubes hidden in the design, soft and hypnotic, drying our skin. Then the woman put her clothes on and led me back to the bedroom.

Someone had cleaned my dress. It had a honey-sweet fragrance, how I imagined ambrosia would smell. I tried to thank her, but she didn't understand my words and showed no interest in my hand motions. Instead, she went to a console against the wall and called someone. So I lay down on the bed again, drowsing as I listened to the harsh murmur of her voice.

After a while she got me up again. This time we left the room. We followed an octagonal corridor with a floor of crisscrossing bronze strips that felt cool under the bare soles of my feet. Octagonal arches appeared at periodic intervals, glowing with gold light. I looked for a window, a portal, anything to show an "outside," a familiar sight, trees or houses, animals, some buoy in this buffeting ocean of strangeness. Los Angeles seemed so distant now, like pieces of someone else's life.

I never saw a window. Eventually we came to a dead end. The woman spoke and the usual shimmer appeared, this time in an octagonal doorway. She led me through it and across a small chamber to a second doorway. The room beyond was large, the first wasted space I had seen, or so I thought at the time. In truth, the pool was also a luxury; she could have simply sprayed me with nano-bots that acted much the same as soap, gathering particles of dirt into the interior of lipid micelles.

Everything in this room—walls, floor, furniture, art—was patterned from gleaming bronze, copper, and amber octagons. A divan stood in the center, behind a table, and pillars hung with bronze scarves rose behind it, their gauzy cloth rustling in air currents.

Kryx Iquar was sitting on the divan.

He didn't acknowledge the woman as she bowed and left the room. When we were alone, he spoke in English. "Sit down."

When I started to sit in a chair at the table, he shook his head. I hesitated, confused. Then I realized what he wanted. Gritting my teeth, I stepped past the table and sat next to him on the divan. A gauze scarf drifted across my face, then fell away.

Iquar took my chin, tilting my face up. "Exquisite."

"Where is my husband?" I said.

He took hold of my shoulders and turned me right, then left.

"Your holos don't do you justice. You really are like a Raylican. Except your nose is smaller. Is your appearance real?"

"Real?"

"Did you have it altered to make you look this way?"

"No." I wished he would stop touching me.

He didn't, though. Instead he dropped his hand to my breast and felt the nipple through the cloth.

"Don't!" I hit his hand away.

Hitting him was stupid. You don't strike one of the most powerful human beings among three interstellar civilizations. But he only laughed. Leaning back on the divan, he put his arm around my waist and jerked. I sprawled forward on my stomach, my hair flying out like a spray of black silk across the coppery divan, which I realized was actually a bed. Scrambling to my knees, I tried to pull away. He yanked me down again, still laughing as he flipped me onto my back.

"You never finished your wedding night," he said. "Don't you think it's time?"

"No!" I tried to roll away from him.

He raised his hand over me. "Hold still."

I swallowed, staring at his hand, and froze.

Iquar spoke to the air. "Darius, attend."

"Attending," a voice said. It reminded me of the Jag, but with a harsher voice.

"Initiate stim cycle, lab bay five."

"Initiated," the voice said.

Nothing happened. Nothing, except Iquar closed his eyes and opened his mouth, as if he were concentrating on something neither audible nor visible. He exhaled, a sound barely heard but familiar somehow.

Junkie. I knew that look. Like a junkie in snow heaven. A feather of hope brushed my fear; if he were doped up enough, perhaps he would forget about me.

He didn't.

I've tried, in the years since, to understand why the emotional scars of that night took so long to heal. Fear, confusion, pain—it

could have been any of that. Or perhaps it was the way he lay there
for so long after he reached his physical peak, groaning in a euphoric daze, as if he were having sex in another reality. He held
onto me as if I were a touchstone for the physical world while he
existed somewhere else, doing what, I had no idea.

Some time later he said, "Darius, attend."

"Attending."

"Discontinue stim cycle in lab bay five."

"Discontinued."

Iquar sighed and closed his eyes. Within moments he was
asleep. When I tried to ease into a less awkward position, he
awoke and raised his hand over me. "Lie still."

I froze. After watching me for a moment, he seemed satisfied.
He lay down and fell asleep again.

So I stared at the gauze over the bed, listening to him breathe,
trying not to move while he slept. I discovered another part of
being owned, along with the fear, anger, and loneliness. It was
also boring as all hell.

When I awoke later, I was back in the room with the gray-haired
nurse. I don't remember much about that time; I was drugged
again, and crying, asking for Althor. She tended my bruises, murmuring words of comfort, and eventually I slept again. When I
woke, she gave me water and medication that put me back to sleep.

The next time I woke up, I felt almost normal. The past few
days seemed a fevered nightmare. The nurse was in her recliner,
watching a holo projected above her chair. It looked like an ad-
venture story, with people riding odd animals and speaking the
harsh Trader tongue.

As I sat up, she turned off the holo. She asked a question and
I spread my hands: another of our stimulating conversations. She
made a call on her console and talked to someone. Then she helped
me dress and we left the room, once again heading out into the
octagonal corridors.

This time we went to a command center. A huge one. Hundreds of people worked at its consoles, hurrying back and forth,

or sitting in control seats, encased in exoskeletons. Voices hummed, both human and mechanical. Banks of equipment packed the area and holomaps rotated everywhere, showing views of the Cylinder, its attendant ships, and stars. Some traced exhaust from the thrusters, highlighting it in colors. In an area at the back, above the commotion, there was a dais with three control seats. Two were empty.

Iquar sat in the third.

The nurse took me to him, then bowed and left. Iquar motioned toward one of the control seats. "You look more optimized today."

I climbed into the chair. Optimized? It makes sense to me now, given this universe where computer webs are so much a part of the human experience that people can't imagine how the "primitives" ever survived without them. At the time, the comment left me at a loss for a response.

Iquar smiled and sat back, closing his eyes. He had that stoned look of euphoria again. "Althor has been asking to see you."

I almost jumped forward. "How is he?"

"We are taking him to the CMC base in sector Z. We have the Lock there."

"Can I see him?"

He didn't answer. After being ignored for several moments, I gritted my teeth, then sat back and watched the droning activity below.

Eventually Iquar said, "They tell me your marriage is a supplement contract."

I glanced at him. "That's right."

"Good."

Up until then, I had been too overwhelmed by events to absorb the full situation. But it was finally sinking in. A war was about to start between the Imperialate and the Traders, one where the Traders had both a Lock and Key. Goliath had his speed. Worse, the shaky alliance between the Imperialate and Allied Worlds would fall apart with news of Althor's abduction. It was a second betrayal, added to the first, and this time the damage might well be irreparable.

Except. A treaty already existed. Hidden in the Epsilani web, our marriage contract was the answer, the cement to mend a cracking fortress.

At the time, I didn't understand the symbolic power of our marriage. I brought fresh Kyle bloodlines to the Rhon, and so in a sense to all Althor's people. It was like a gift from Earth to the Imperialate, one that compensated for their previous "betrayal." My youth gave even more poignancy to the symbol. Althor's race, the Raylicans, were old. Tired. Dying. To them, and so to all Skolians, a symbol of vitality meant more than any politics. My contract with Althor went further than a treaty: it could also heal deep wounds between the two civilizations. But only if Stonehedge could deliver it into the right hands.

Iquar spoke languidly. "Do you know what a dry socket is, Tina?"

I glanced at him. "No."

"It can happen if you lose, say, a molar. A dry socket is a hole in the gums, with nerve ends exposed to the air."

"It sounds painful."

"It is." He paused. "It is possible to mimic that sensation all over the body. You cover it with a mesh. Probes on the mesh connect to nerves within the body. When activated, each probe produces an effect similar to a dry socket."

I stared at him, too stunned to move or speak. Would he really do that if I angered him?

Sometime later, he said, "Do you know how many people I own?"

"No."

"Guess."

I hate this conversation, I thought. "A hundred."

He laughed. "A hundred. How quaint."

"Ten thousand?"

"No."

"I don't know."

"About one hundred billion."

How could anyone own one hundred billion people? What did he do with them?

"Darius would have to run inventory to obtain an accurate number," he said. "But I own one hundred and three planets. Actual populations vary widely, of course, but one billion per planet is a reasonable average." He looked at me. "They live, for the most part, normal lives. That's the key, you realize. People rarely revolt when they're comfortable."

"What if they revolt anyway?"

"I get rid of them."

I swallowed. "Why are you telling me this?"

"Look at your husband's people. The Skolian Imperialate." He snorted. "They named it after his family. The Ruby Dynasty. Did he tell you that? His full name is Althor Vyan Selei kya Skolia." His voice hardened. "We are stronger than they, Tina. When time evens out the currents of power, it is we who will be in control. You would do well to remember that."

I didn't have a response for that. After watching me for a moment, he sat back and closed his eyes, still with that euphoric expression. I sat stiff and silent.

After a while my attention wandered to the people in the command center. Every now and then one glanced at me, then quickly looked away. It was easy to read their faces. They might as well have stood up on the consoles and shouted: *Thank God it's you up there and not me.*

Most of their work seemed involved with running the Cylinder. It was speeding up, preparing to invert, using weeks to do what a Jag managed in seconds. At several consoles, engineers modeled station designs, preparing to build new habitats for Iquar to rule. Most of the models weren't stable. One, a long tube with end caps, appeared stable at first, but then its rotation wobbled, growing worse and worse until the entire structure began somersaulting end over end.

"You realize," Iquar said, "that legally, by anyone's laws, I'll own you and Althor for the rest of your lives." As I looked at him, he opened his eyes. "Just in case the thought of trying to leave crossed your mind."

"Slavery is illegal in the Imperialate and the Allied Worlds," I said. No one had actually told me that, but I had no doubt it was true.

He smiled. "That may be. But the Paris Treaty requires your governments to return our property. I have full documents for my purchase, duly executed and recorded. In a case such as—oh, let's say, the loss of a Rhon prince—the refusal to return property could be considered an act of war."

I didn't believe the Allied Worlds or Imperialate actually signed an agreement that required them to return escaped slaves to the Traders. "What treaty?"

"You really are slow-witted, aren't you?" Iquar laughed. "The perfect concubine. Exotic, breathtakingly beautiful, scandalously young, and as stupid as a brick."

I gritted my teeth. I didn't care how powerful or genetically improved he was, the only difference between him and Nug was that Iquar lived in a universe where he could run amok.

"Perhaps I will let you see Althor," he said. "Would you like that?"

I almost jumped out of my chair. "Yes."

"Very well. Darius, suspend stim cycle in lab bay five."

"Suspended," Darius said.

Iquar stood up. "Come."

He took me down an octagonal corridor and stopped after only a few yards. Then he opened a portal. We walked through its shimmer into a lab crammed with instrumentation, both in its open areas and on the walls. I barely noticed any of it. All I saw was Althor.

"No." I felt as if the world had dropped out from under us. "God, no. Please, no."

A framework held him suspended about five feet off the ground. His clothes were gone and a mesh covered him from neck to toe. He was staring at the ceiling, breathing in gasps, his voice rasping as if his throat were torn raw. Sweat dripped off his body and pooled on the floor, then disappeared.

He didn't know we had come; his ragged breaths covered the few sounds we made as Iquar pulled me inside. Iquar touched a panel on a console, and the framework holding Althor rotated, raising his head so he was looking straight at us.

"Iquar, no." His voice rasped. "I don't want her to see me like this."

The Trade Minister went to the framework and smiled. "I've brought you a present."

Althor swallowed, sweat running down his face. "Don't do this."

"You wanted to see her. You told me yourself."

"Not like this."

I felt as if the room were whirling. Dry sockets. I thought of Iquar in his drugged daze, enjoying himself, being *provided* for, and I wanted to run him through with a stake. I whirled on him, bringing up my fist to pummel his chest. "You've been doing this to him—all this time!—you *bastard.*"

He easily caught my arms. No longer smiling, he jerked me around to face Althor. "Take a look, mighty prince. What's yours is now mine." He sounded like he was gritting his teeth. "For five hundred years your family has made a mockery of us. No more."

Althor spoke hoarsely. "We never did anything to any of you."

"No? You were bred for us. Your inferior family, instead of providing for Aristos—as is our right—mocks us with your 'Imperial' Skolia." He shook me so hard my vision blurred. "Here's your sweet fresh life. A symbol of new beginnings, at least for one man. His lovely concubine. Well, choke on this, provider. You can watch while I use up her charms and throw her away."

Althor swore at him, straining against the framework that held him, his lips drawing back in a snarl.

Iquar's face changed again, becoming affectionate, like a lover's. He spoke in a soft voice. "Darius, resume stim cycle."

Althor's mouth formed the word "No." But it never came out. Instead his entire body went rigid.

And he screamed.

The universe turned into a chaos of screams, Althor's screams. I stumbled toward the framework, trying to reach him, but Iquar yanked me back. Grabbing my arms, he heaved me onto a lab bench and shoved me flat on my back. As he reached for the ties of my dress, my head filled with Althor's screams, his cries ringing, ringing, *ringing*. Iquar looked as if he had shot up the strongest drug in creation, soaring into a high so intense he would never come down. Every time Althor screamed, Iquar groaned with the release of it.

JAAAAAAAAAG! My mental cry cut through the layers of cotton in my mind, propelled by the force of Althor's agony and my own terror. *PROTECT!*

Emergency wake-up toggled, the Jag thought.

17

Lightning's Vengeance

y mind blasted wide open. It all came back, the emotions, the sensations—

And I was *FALLING.* I plunged into the hole where Iquar's capacity for compassion should have been, whipped around and around like a cork in a whirlpool that poured into the fetid sewer of his mind.

The neutrons of Althor's mind fired their message again and again: *pain.* His KEB amplified and broadcast it, and Iquar's abnormal KAB picked it up, his thalamus routing the signals to the orgiastic centers of his brain. He and Althor were locked in a gruesome link: Kyle and Aristo, empath and anti-empath, provider and sadist.

Except now Iquar was staring at me, his face contorted with ecstasy. "You! *You're one of them!*"

I could barely hear his shout. Noise filled the lab: Althor's screams, alarms, other sounds my mind produced out of the chaos. Lights flashed everywhere like a carnival gone mad, red and amber all over instrumentation panels and the walls, until I wasn't sure what came from my mind and what was real.

"Darius!" Iquar shouted. "Stop cycle!"

Althor's screams broke off in a gasp. But the din in the lab kept on, shrill and raucous. Iquar shouted into the band around his wrist and a voice answered, then cut off so abruptly that Iquar just stood there, staring at his wrist. I didn't need to understand the words to know what had happened: somewhere, somehow, disaster had broken out on his Cylinder.

"*You* did this," Iquar shouted at me, his voice barely carrying over the noise of the alarms. He yanked me off the table and dragged me to the console. With a sweep of his hand, he ripped a tube off a lab sink and tied my wrists to a loop on the console. "You'll pay for it." He stretched out his arm, pointing at the framework that held Althor, his face turned lurid by the lights flashing in the lab. "I'll put you in that for hours."

Then he left, running through the octagonal doorway. It solidified after him, leaving us trapped in the lab bay.

"Tina." Althor's hoarse shout barely registered above the noise. "Get me out."

I yanked at my bonds. "I'm tied to the console."

His thought came into my mind, echoing with aftershocks of pain. *Are you linked to the Jag?*

Yes!

It's out of control! It's firing an arsenal designed for relativistic combat inside a space station. You have to make it stop, or this entire station will blow.

I could feel the Jag's anger, a cold rage unlike any human emotion. *Jag!* I thought. *Stop! You'll kill us. You'll kill the Pilot!*

Its lattice appeared in my mind. The Jag accessed my optic nerve and the lattice jumped out so that I saw it superimposed on the laboratory, glowing gold.

You and Althor must come to me, it thought.

He's still locked into Iquar's machine, I thought.

Probing Cylinder web system.

I was sure it had no chance of breaking into the Cylinder web. Even then I knew the system must have been designed to fend off attacks. But I and everyone else underestimated the Jag. Its rage pushed it further than anyone knew it could reach, and it tore open the Cylinder web like hands ripping gauzy filaments.

The mesh rolled off Althor's body. As the framework released him, his feet dropped to the floor and he grabbed a strut to keep from falling. For one moment he stood staring at me. Then he limped to a wall and opened a locker. He pulled out his clothes, the gold pants and boots of his uniform. As he dressed, lights continued to flash and sirens to scream, fierce and urgent.

Then he came over to me. The whole time he was untying my wrists, he kept whispering, "Tina" over and over. When I was free, he sank to his knees by the console.

I dropped down next to him. *We've got to get to the Jag.*

I can't walk under my own power, he thought. *I'm going to let my web take over.*

No! It will hurt you. The Jag told me—

Tina, this is the only way. My hydraulics will move my body. As long as I'm conscious, they can keep going. He touched my face. *Just don't be afraid. I may seem inhuman to you.*

I trust you.

He kissed me. Then he changed, his face becoming impassive. *Combat mode toggled.* His thought was cold, metallic.

Althor stood up, moving with a surreal smoothness, like a well-oiled machine. The Jag's lattice was tied to my vision, so it "moved" with me as I stood next to him. But I had no idea how to operate the grid environment.

Transfer control to me, Althor thought.

Transfer will aggravate your neural damage, the Jag thought.

Override safety, Althor thought.

Control transferred.

As control of the lattice switched to Althor, my view of it dimmed into a translucent ghost image. He grabbed my arm and we ran to the door. But it refused to open. Data poured through the lattice. The Jag turned the flood of information into surreal images that I saw as ghosts overlaid on the lab, swarms of fluorescent insects buzzing, humming, and clicking, streaks of bottle green and beetle red. Their legs became razor-sharp disks that spun under their bodies. The swarm exploded outward and dove into the lab's web. New data poured through the lattice as the swarm razed the web system into shreds.

The doorway reappeared. As we ran through it, the lattice vanished, replaced with a ghost schematic of the Cylinder. It looked like a pipe with a fluted tube down its middle and spokes, all of it ragged, as if scoured by acid. The image filled the corridor and moved with us. Two blips showed our progress, and a blazing red dot gave the Jag's location, fifty kilometers away in a bay on the inner hull of the torus.

A beam stabbed out from the dot, across the interior of the Cylinder, and sliced down the opposite side, adding a new acid-groove to the pipe. *Annihilator hit on defense platform VDT 2,* the Jag thought.

The schematic came with us as we ran down the corridor. Every time we passed under an arch, it turned red and an alarm blared. More than once we ran through clouds of gas visible only on the schematic. Both Althor and I passed out for several seconds each time, and his biomech web faltered. Much longer, and it would have begun to shut down, but with his enhanced speed he reached clear air in time. He held me around the waist, carrying me when we passed out.

We ran straight into the barrier. It gave like a wall of elastic and snapped back, throwing us into a heap on the crisscrossed floor. Neither of us had seen the faint shimmer filling the arch. Molecular airlocks, it seems, can also be made impermeable to people.

As we scrambled to our feet, a robot came out of a passage beyond the membrane, a metal and ceramic skeleton with equipment mounted on its gaunt frame. We spun around, ready to run back the way we came—and saw three waroids striding toward us, their mirrored surfaces reflecting the hellish light from the arches.

Cylinder security web breached, the Jag thought. *Membrane modifications initiated.*

The waroids rammed into a barrier and it snapped them back. As they fell together with a crash, Althor shoved me against the corridor wall, out of the line of sight between him and the waroids. Then he spun around to the barrier that had stopped us. The robot had deactivated it and was rolling forward. Althor kicked up his leg, and when his boot punched the robot's chest, its instrument box imploded in shards of ceramic and glass. In the corridor, the waroids were up again, two of them pressing their hands against the membrane that separated them from us while the third worked at a wall panel.

An octagonal portal appeared in the wall next to me—and revealed a red-haired man, one of Iquar's military men, a slave-made-naval-officer who held his favored position only as long as he pleased his superiors and they pleased Iquar. He held a massive laser carbine, the same kind of mirrored gun the mercenaries had carried.

The officer shouted at Althor—and aimed his gun at me. In that same instant Althor kicked up his leg, stretching out his body with a deadly grace to bridge the distance between them. His boot hit the carbine and it spun out of the man's hands, flying up into the wall. As I threw my arms over my head, the gun came down and hit my shoulders. In reflex, I grabbed at it, my hands closing around its barrel.

The skeleton-bot extended its arm, a needle snapping out of its thumb. As Althor swung around to face the robot, the Trader officer lunged at me. I had no time to think; I just pointed the gun and hit the largest projection on the stock, a black stud.

Light blazed, blinding light, making it impossible to see. Someone yanked the carbine out of my hands and wrapped an arm around my waist, forcing me to run.

As my vision cleared, I realized it was Althor. Twisting in his hold, I stared back down the corridor. A pile of fused armor smoldered in the center and a ragged hole rent the wall, one repeated through several rooms beyond it. No trace remained of the man I had fired at.

"Oh, God." I kept saying it over and over as we ran. I had just killed another human being.

Althor held the carbine by his shoulder and kept his other arm around my waist, pulling me so fast I could barely keep up. We activated every security arch we ran under, turning the corridor blood red. Periodically he fired down the octagonal passage, searing membranes into oblivion.

Two waroids strode out of a side passage up ahead, both armed with carbines. They fired to either side of us, obviously trying to stop Althor without damaging him. Althor had no such qualms; moving with enhanced speed, he shot straight at them, cutting through their armor. Then we were running through their remains. When I saw what was left of the humans inside that armor, I nearly threw up.

Switching to Annihilator B, the Jag thought. On the ghost schematic traveling with us, a ray stabbed out from the red dot and sliced through the fluted tube. Statistics swarmed like bees, data with stings. The ray depicted a neutralized antiproton beam; when it struck, it annihilated protons and created high-energy radiation and pion showers, followed by cascades of killer reactions.

The Jag avoided populated areas, instead targeting defense systems. Its choice to stay in the docking bay made sense: to hit it, Iquar's people would have to fire on the Cylinder itself. Nor were they likely to want it destroyed; together, the Jag and Althor represented state-of-the-art Imperialate military technology.

Use a transport car to reach me, the Jag thought.

Althor ran by reflex, under the direction of his web. On the ghost schematic moving with us, the transport conduits lit up in blue. Our progress showed as blips closing in on one of those conduits.

A sudden flare of violet light smeared across the schematic. When it faded, a gaping wound showed in the Cylinder, extending from the inner to outer hull and stretching out raggedly in all directions.

We were on this side of the blast site, the Jag on the other.

Anyone trying to reach a location on the other side would need to detour for hundreds of kilometers. As data came in, it became clear the explosion had destroyed transportation conduits throughout the entire area. Iquar had struck back, cutting us off from our escape. The fact that it meant killing large numbers of his people and destroying a section of his station apparently meant less to him than recapturing his valued property.

We reached the cross-passage that led to the transport conduit we sought. At the end of it, a bullet car waited quietly at a platform. Althor stopped, chest heaving, only a few hundred yards away from the glassplex wall that separated the platform from the passage. *Jag, can this car reach your location?*

No, the Jag thought. *The blast destroyed its magrails farther down the line.*

Althor swore. *You must go someplace where we can reach you.*

Thrusters firing.

On the schematic, the red blip moved into the hollow interior of the Cylinder. As soon as the Jag was clear of the hull, a missile shot out from another section—and hit the ship dead on. Yet the Jag continued to move as if nothing had happened.

Quasis released, the Jag thought.

Can you keep protecting yourself? Althor asked.

Errors are accumulating. I am safer in a docking bay. An area a few thousand yards from our location lit up in green on the schematic. *Go to bay 436-D.*

With no warning, a force knocked me away from Althor, throwing me against the wall as it spun Althor around. Neither of us had been hit; the target was the laser carbine. It flew out of Althor's hands, shattering, debris flying everywhere. Althor kept turning, under his own power now, until he faced the direction of the shot, a small passage that entered this one close to the glassplex wall.

Kryx Iquar stood there.

Had we been thinking more clearly, we would have taken warning: Why would the Eubian Trade Minister risk coming after us when he had other systems, living and mechanical, to do the job? At the time I assumed he and Althor were still fighting that war for control, Iquar determined to assert his dominance over a prisoner who refused, even in slavery, to submit. And a component may indeed have been that. But not all.

Althor's face twisted with rage. As Iquar raised a sedative tube-gun, Althor ran toward him with sight-blurring speed. He was too far away to reach the minister in time, but his web calculated well; in the instant Iquar fired, Althor dove to the side, avoiding the shot as he rolled across the metal-stripped deck and came back to his feet.

A shot cracked behind us and a blast of air slammed Althor against the wall only a few yards away from Iquar. The minister shouted, his meaning obvious despite the unfamiliar language: he didn't want his valuable property damaged.

I whirled around, facing the direction we had just come from—and saw an officer only ten yards away. Far down the corridor behind him, a quartet of mirrored waroids were jogging toward us. The officer still had his gun raised, but he hesitated to shoot, his attention fixed on a point behind me. Turning, I saw Iquar and Althor in motion, Iquar smacking his hand on a wall panel as Althor lunged for him.

A shimmering curtain fell from the ceiling, a membrane tuned to hold a human being. It draped over Althor, molding to his body and pinning his limbs. His momentum still carried him forward, so that he knocked the minister down. Then Althor's hand ripped through the membrane, his arm shooting up like the periscope on a submarine. As Iquar scrambled to his feet, Althor tore the membrane off his body. He grabbed Iquar's arm and swung him around to face the officer and oncoming waroids. Locking his arm around Iquar's neck, he shouted in Eubian, words with the sound of threats.

Iquar should have been worried, having his neck cranked back that way by a man he knew hated him. His calmness worried me far more than the officer or oncoming waroids.

"Tina, run!" Althor hissed. "Get in transport."

I ran for the car. The glassplex wall that separated the passage from the platform reflected the scene behind me: the officer was aiming his gun at Althor, but he couldn't fire with Iquar in the way. Althor gave the minister a shove, then took off after me as Iquar stumbled forward and fell to his knees. I ran to the car and spun around. Iquar was between Althor and the other Traders for only a few seconds, but it was long enough for Althor, with enhanced speed, to reach me. He banged a panel on the car and the door whisked open. As we scrambled inside, Althor yelled and the car surged forward even as its door closed.

It sped down its rail—taking us away from our rendezvous with the Jag.

"Why did you let Iquar go?" I gasped, trying to catch my breath. "He was the perfect hostage."

"Too perfect." Althor gulped in air. "He read me too well. It was a trap." He held out his arm, the one that had been around Iquar's neck. "His skin was doped with a sedative keyed to my DNA. On him, it does nothing. On me, it becomes active."

"It didn't work," I said. "You haven't passed out."

"Not yet. I realized the trap before I got a full dose. But it won't be long before it takes effect."

An alarm sounded. Althor strode to the console and studied the displays. "We're approaching the zone where the explosion broke the magrails. We have to get out."

I have moved to compensate for your new situation, the Jag thought. *Go to docking bay 412-Q.* The ghost schematic around us changed to show a close-up of the area damaged by the explosion. In one section of the broken region, a square glowed green.

We can't go through there, Althor thought. *You have to come closer.*

I can't risk it, the Jag thought. *I won't survive another hit. This is a good site: security in this sector is gutted and it's close to your location. Althor, you only have five minutes before your mode failures become so widespread you can't function. In six minutes the sedative will have spread enough to knock you out.*

A beep came from the controls. The car stopped and opened its door.

We stepped out in chaos. Crowds massed on the platform, pushing into cars as fast as they arrived. Voices over a speaker system gave what sounded like instructions alternating with words of reassurance. Uniformed officers directed the evacuation, shouting to be heard over the rumble of voices.

An officer pushed his way over to us. He spoke harshly to Althor, and for one blood-freezing instant I thought we had been caught. Then I realized it was only the rough sound of the language that made him sound threatening. He hadn't recognized us. The officer motioned for us to return to the car and frowned when Althor shook his head. But he didn't push it; in the turmoil, his attention was needed in too many other places.

Leaving the terminal was a struggle; we had to push our way against a dense flow of human traffic. More people crammed the octagonal corridor outside. The crowd was poised on the edge of panic, but it didn't go over; instead, the evacuees followed an obviously well-practiced evacuation drill. Officers stood on raised platforms, directing traffic and reinforcing the reassurances from the speakers. We pushed our way against the flow toward one of the octagonal arches. The schematic came with us, showing the route to the Jag's bay. It wasn't far, but to make it there we had to get through a packed mass of humanity.

You have four minutes to reach me, the Jag thought.

We passed under an arch—and an alarm screamed. As the arch turned an all too familiar red, Althor swore, then grabbed my arm and tried to run. We made little headway, barely managing to reach the next arch, and its alarm went off as well, adding its clangor to the noise. People surged around us, order threatening to explode into panic.

An officer was trying to reach us, shouting in Eubian, and another appeared at the mouth of a cross-passage only a few yards away. The crowd grew more agitated and dragged us with them, back toward the terminal, taking away what little ground we had gained. If it hadn't been for Althor's holding me up, I would have fallen and been trampled. Officers were converging on the area, shoving their way through the turbulent throng.

You have three minutes left, the Jag thought.

The loudspeaker kept talking, trying to calm the people. Then the disembodied voice changed, its tone firm, carefully calculated, like a wronged friend seeking help from loyal companions. A familiar string jumped out of the harsh words: Althor Vyan Selei Skolia.

I stiffened. *Althor, what is it saying?*

His face paled. *A description of me.*

A woman shouted and pointed toward us. Another person took up the cry, then a third and a fourth. The crowd surged, shoving us against the wall. It was terrifying, like being trampled against a wall rather than underfoot.

Suddenly, they drew away, leaving us in a pocket circled by a wall of people. And they stood, staring at us, the prospect of seeing a captive Rhon heir overcoming even the razor edge of mass panic.

That calm lasted only a moment. The crowd surged toward the terminal again, and a gaunt woman stumbled into the open space around us. She laid her hand against Althor's chest, as if to verify he was real. Then the crowd caught her and swept her away.

You have two minutes, the Jag thought.

More people pressed in on us. No one offered help. Not a single person. They all wanted to touch Althor, put their hands on him, feel him as if he were a talisman, but no one even tried to help. He struggled to shove them away, his efforts growing more and more disjointed. Even if his biomech hadn't been failing, he couldn't have pushed them all off; hundreds of people filled the corridor now, with even more shoving from behind.

Then I saw it: a line of four waroids was making its way forward with the crowd, a moving wall of mirrored armor stretched across the passage. They were coming from the direction Althor and I needed to go to reach the Jag.

You have one minute, the Jag thought.

Jag, we can't! I thought. *We can't get through.*

With dizzying speed, my perspective changed: I was above the corridor, looking down on the scene. I saw Althor and myself shoved against the wall while people moved past us. It looked like I had passed out; Althor was struggling to hold me up and stay on his own feet as well.

Odd mechanical thoughts came into my mind. Humans come in frangible casings. The Pilot and his Mate. Vulnerable. Fragile. Easily disrupted configurations. Difficult to repair. Erratic. Emotional.

Priceless.

Jag? I thought. *Is that you?*

I'm running your brain on my web, it answered. *Right now you're in an observation unit above the corridor.*

Below, the line of waroids reached us. They formed a break against the crowd, protecting us in a hollow, like a bay sheltered from the ocean. Althor sagged to his knees, his arms wrapped around my body. He pulled me into his lap and sat on his heels, bending his body over me with his head bowed. At the terminal platform, a phalanx of officers jutted into the corridor, like a boat pushing through a sea so viscous it could barely make headway. They were pointed at us, slowly advancing against the tide of humanity. In the corridor, both Althor and I were unconscious now, slumped on the floor.

How can I be seeing this? I asked.

Since we first linked, back at Earth, the Jag thought, *I have been mapping your brain cells and replicating their function and firing patterns in one of my simulation moods. I just now used the Kyle Afferent Body in your brain to upload your consciousness into that simulator.*

Why?

I will transfer you into Althor's web. It needs a conscious mind to direct it. If I load myself into it, that will worsen his brain damage. You are human and already part of him. You also have a sympathetic resonance with the neurological mappings of his brain activity.

I didn't understand that last one, I thought.

The two of you have compatible personalities. Then: *Transfer initiated.*

Suddenly I was kneeling in the corridor. It was disorienting to look at what I perceived as my own body and see Althor's bulky form. My real body lay in his arms—my arms—eyes closed, black hair streaming over the floor. I saw everything through the gold sheen of his inner eyelids. As I stood, holding my/Tina's limp body, the waroids turned their helmets. Their surprise at seeing me get up made sparks in the air.

Tina, the Jag thought. *I'm going to cut the corridor with a laser.*

No! You'll start a panic. We'll be trampled.

Panic, yes, the Jag answered. *Trampled, no. We're close enough to the inner hull for the laser to breach it. The passage you're in won't lose enough air to cause suffocation, but the resulting chaos will aid your escape.*

You better be right, Jag.

I didn't see the beams, but I heard the screams, both of people and alarms. The stampede started back in the corridor. Within seconds it reached us, the crowd bursting forward in a tidal wave of humanity. In that instant a brilliant flash made me clamp my eyes closed. I opened them to see three of the four waroids who had been guarding us fused to each other and the deck, their armor melted into mirrored pools that were already solidifying. I swallowed, struggling against a sudden nausea. The fourth waroid backed away, its arm fused off at the elbow, and the panicked crowd swept it down the hall. The only reason the two of us weren't trampled was because the fused remains of the other waroids made a break against the tide of humans.

Run, the Jag thought. *Run to me.*

The shot had blown out the wall in a ragged hole. Holding my/Tina's body, I stepped through it into a small corridor. *Jag, what weapons do you have left?*

Lasers and Annihilators are exhausted, Impactors are destroyed, and I've used my store of small missiles. I have four tau missiles, but I can't launch them inside the Cylinder. You must make it the rest of the way on your own.

I ran. It was easy carrying my body; it hardly weighed anything. The sheer physical power of Althor's body was exhilarating. How could he take it for granted?

The schematic of the Cylinder, which I could see even more clearly now, highlighted the path to the Jag in blue. *Follow,* I thought. The biomech web took over, directing my legs. The few people we passed were running in the opposite direction, some holding masks over their faces. We followed a twisting route through side passages—and came out into a large octagonal chamber fed by passages from seven directions. The eighth side consisted of two large doors with *412-Q* written in bold print.

Jag! I ran to the doors. *We're here! Open up!*

I cannot, the Jag thought.

I laughed and was startled to hear Althor's voice instead of my own. *We made it! Open the doors.*

I cannot. The Cylinder has reestablished control over this section.

I stopped smiling. *What?*

I've been purged from the Cylinder web.

Then how do we open these doors?

With explosives or lasers.

But you don't have any more.

This is correct. Its thought sounded subdued.

A man ran out of a cross-passage—and froze. His emotions were a battering ram; he recognized Althor. He slapped his hand against a band on his wrist and spoke into it, words I neither understood nor knew how to translate.

Jag, I thought. *We have to get in that docking bay.*

I'm trying to override the Cylinder protocols.

A voice came out of the man's wristband, cold and harsh, either asking questions or giving orders.

Jag! We can't go back to Iquar. You know what he'll do to us. Open those doors!

I cannot. Then, quietly: *I have four tau missiles remaining.*

My hope leapt. *Can you use them?*

Tina, one tau missile could destroy half the station.

For a second I couldn't absorb what it was saying. Then I understood: it offered us suicide. And vengeance.

A woman ran into the area, a Trader officer with a sedative gun. She nodded to the man, then spoke into her wristband, her attention fixed on me. I watched from across the octagon, my feet planted wide, my/Tina's body limp in my arms.

If we destroy the Cylinder, the Jag thought, *the Traders will no longer have access to a Jag or Jagernaut. They will no longer have a Key, Kryx Iquar will die.* It paused. *But we also kill the only known Rhon woman with no genetic tie to the Ruby Dynasty.*

I don't want us to die.

The Jag's thought was calm. *As long as the two of you live, the chance exists that you might someday escape again. And as long as you live, Tina, so does the hope that Althor's family won't become extinct.*

The Traders watched us, waiting for reinforcements, knowing they were soon to reap the glory of making the capture. They stared as if we were beautiful animals escaped from a zoo and then trapped, waiting to be caged.

Tina, the Jag thought. *You must decide.*

I can't. I felt as if I were shaking, even though my body—Althor's body—was rock solid. *I don't want to die. I don't want Althor to die. But God, Jag, to be Iquar's providers—that's worse than death.*

You must make the decision.

I can't.

And then I went insane. That's the only way I can describe it; I lost rationality. In times of crisis, the human body can exhibit strength far beyond its normal capability: a man holds up the roof of a collapsing mine shaft, a woman lifts a truck off her child, a mountain climber holds back a boulder many times his weight. I blasted Althor's biomech web past the known upper limits of its capabilities.

Spinning around, I kicked my leg above my waist and slammed my boot into the doors, again and again, with teeth-jarring force, like a high-speed drill, so fast that the motion blurred. Again, again, again. The force of the impacts jarred through Althor's body, vibrating to his bones. The web's timer said a mere fraction of a second had passed.

I heard a gun fire, felt the shots hit my chest, knew sedatives flooded my blood. It made no difference; Althor had already been knocked out. His body was operating on pure biomech now. I kept at the doors—and with a screeching groan of metal they buckled, the huge serrations where the two sides joined crumpling inward. My foot slammed through the opening, up to my thigh, ripping Althor's uniform. With enhanced speed, I pushed my/Tina's body through the opening and squeezed through after it. More shots hit my side and legs, and shouts sounded behind me, echoing eerily in my boosted state.

Then we were in the bay, a small one located on the torus

rather than the fluted tube where most ships docked. The Jag already had its airlock open. The outer doors of the bay were also open—*wide open.* We were running full tilt into the vacuum of space.

Even as I swore out loud, I saw the shimmer of a molecular airlock in the open doors. I ran to the Jag and shoved my/Tina's body inside, then scrambled in and fell across the deck. The airlock sucked closed behind us.

Download, the Jag thought. The rumble of engines vibrated in the deck.

Download, the Jag repeated.

I lifted my head, still in Althor's body.

Tina, get out of his web! the Jag thought.

Download, I thought.

Then I was in my own body again, sliding along the deck as the Jag accelerated out of the bay. A huge metal arm unfolded from a bulkhead in the cabin, gathering up Althor's now unconscious body. I felt metal against my own skin, too, and the warmth of a membrane, as a second arm lifted me off the deck. A familiar cloying mist blew against my face.

Preparing taus, the Jag thought.

Jag, NO! I fought to stay conscious. *Millions of people live on the Cylinder!*

Cannons primed.

NOOooo . . . I tried to shout it, but sleep closed around me like a moth folding its wings.

Just before I passed out, the Jag's thought whispered through my mind: *Taus fired.*

Darkness and warmth.

Gradually, I registered sounds, the noises of a ship in flight.

Jag? I thought.

Attending.

Where are we?

Traveling in inversion.

How is Althor?

I am attempting repairs.

Will he be okay?

Pause. *He will function again.*

But?

His web needs reprogramming. His degraded memory files must be restored. He may have lost some forever. His structural components must be repaired. Some must be regrown. He will need surgery. A sense of sorrow came from the ship. I didn't know any other way to describe what it communicated to me. *He also needs treatment to heal his emotions. I cannot give that.*

Can you make him forget?

This would require erasing extensive sections of memory. Much more would go than his memory of Iquar. More gently: *Deleting parts of himself is no good, Tina. He needs to heal if he is to be whole again.*

I just don't want him to hurt.

The Jag's answer had a sense of softness. *Nor do I. Neither of you.*

Jag—

Sleep, Tina. Mist curled around my face.

No. Wait. I fought the drowsiness. *What did you mean on the Cylinder about my being Rhon?*

Althor suspected it almost as soon as he met you.

Back at Earth, you said you didn't know my rating.

I said I couldn't determine a numerical value. The Rhon have ratings too high to quantify.

Why didn't Althor tell me?

He felt you would be incapable of hiding that knowledge were you put into a situation such as the one that occurred.

He was right.

At Epsilani, I linked your Kyle centers to my EI, the Jag thought. *When the mercenaries shut me down, they also damped your Kyle fields.*

You should have protected Althor.

I couldn't do you both. It would have strained my resources too far. Its next thought came with a sense of pain. *I had to choose.*

Why me?

You needed it more. And they already knew what he was.

Jag—
Tina, sleep.
Mist wafted over my face. *Jag, wait. The taus* . . .
Sleep, it thought.
I slept.

18

The Abaj Tacalique

The Raylicon sky glowered red above the horizon, its streamered clouds lined with fluorescent pink. Directly above us the sky calmed into gray and at the opposite horizon it deepened into black.

Althor and I stood alone, surrounded by desert. Low red hills rolled out in every direction as far as we could see. In the distance, claws of rock stretched like skeletal fingers up to the angry sky. The horizon was closer than on Earth and the gravity weaker. Although it looked like how I imagined Mars, Raylicon is actually a darker red than Earth's neighbor and has a more complex biosphere. Her atmosphere is oxygen rich and dense, giving the daytime sky a pale blue color.

Althor still wore the pants and boots of his dress uniform, with a black knit pullover. He had given me his flight jacket, and it hung down over my dress to my hips. Made from the same insulating material as his regular uniform, it even carried its own web system.

We stood staring at the sky. The receding spark that had been the Jag was gone now. "Do you think it can make it back without a pilot?" I asked.

"I don't know," Althor said.

I wanted to offer comfort, to take away his haunted look. But in the few minutes since the Jag had revived us, Althor had remained distant and closed.

"The Jag was right," I said. "We're safer here. Both of us."

"It needs a pilot." He looked no more accepting now of its decision than he had when it first told him it was going solo.

A rumbling finally registered on my mind. As I became aware of it, I realized it had been in the ground for a while, growing stronger. With it came the memory of that morning so many years ago in Chiapas, when an earthquake shook the ground until fissures opened. After it was over, my aunt and uncle had been dead, our home destroyed, our sheep lost, and our crops gone.

The rumbling grew stronger, shaking the desert, stirring dust. Thunder in the ground. I moved closer to Althor, but when I touched his arm he stiffened. So I dropped my hand. He wouldn't look at me, just stood staring at the horizon.

They came silhouetted against the crimson sky, hundreds of them, sweeping over the curve of the world like phantasms created from the burning horizon. In wave after wave, a horde of riders thundered out of the sunset.

"Go away," I whispered. "No more."

"These are friends," Althor said. "Abaj."

"Your ancient bodyguards?"

He nodded, his attention on the riders. The force of their coming raised clouds of dust.

"If these are bodyguards," I said, "why weren't they here when the Jag set us down?"

He continued to stare out at the riders. "The Abaj Tacalique control the ground-based, orbital-based, and interplanetary defenses for this system. They've one of the most extensive defense matrices in settled space." Dust swirled around his feet, agitated by the rumbling ground. "It makes no difference where we are on the planet. They have been guarding us since we entered the system." He motioned at the riders. "This is ceremony."

They came on, resolving out of the gathering shadows, tall forms on mounts. Long strips of cloth trailed behind their heads, snapping in the wind.

From a distance, their mounts resembled *Tyrannosaurus rex,* but differences became clear as they neared. About nine feet tall at the shoulder, the animals ran leaning forward, back legs thrusting against the ground like pistons. Their scaled forearms were longer than on a tyrannosaurus, enough so that every now and then one dropped into a four-legged gallop, a loping stride with front legs skimming the ground. Refracted light from the fading sunset made their hides scintillate with gold, blue, and glass-green glints.

Their riders were lean and angular, well over seven feet tall. Scarves covered their faces, except for their eyes, protection against the storm of sand they raised. Black cloaks billowed behind them, revealing glimpses of vivid gold, red, green, and purple clothes. They came on, line after line in the deepening crimson light, as if they meant to run straight over us.

Every animal halted at the same instant, the closest less than fifty yards away. In the sudden silence, wind ruffled our hair and whispered across our skin. A mount shifted its weight, another snorted, but no other sound broke the silence. Had someone on the horizon called, we would have heard.

A rider jumped to the ground. He released the scarf from his face and it blew back, its long ends rippling in the air. His legs devoured the ground as he strode forward. I recognized him: the cast of his features, his hooked nose, the angles of his face, his dark eyes. He was much taller than a man of the Maya, but that was his only real difference. If anything, with my small nose, I looked less Maya than he. Separated for millennia, across different universes and times, yet still I felt the kinship. Like knew like.

He stopped in front of Althor, towering over him. Then he knelt on one knee, his head bowed. Althor touched his shoulder and spoke in Iotic, the language I almost understood, words with the sound of ancient ceremonies.

Standing, the man answered, his voice deep and resonant, ringing with notes. His words had a sense of ritual, like a chant. At the time I thought he spoke a different dialect of Iotic, one harder for me to decipher, but in fact I understood Althor better only because he and I were more attuned to each other. All I picked up from this man was that he was called Uzan. I've since learned *Uzan* is his title, as leader of the Abaj. If he has a personal name, he has never told us.

The Uzan unsheathed the sword that hung at his side, a long blade with a curving tip. In form it was identical to the one Althor wore with his dress uniform. But this blade was a metal-diamond crystal grown in one piece from nano-bots, built atom by atom, with a razor-sharp edge. The Uzan raised it above his head, and its blade glinted in the dying sunset.

He brought it down at Althor.

Before I could shout a protest, the sword hit the ground and sent up a fountain of sand, one inch to the right of Althor's foot. Althor didn't even flinch. The Uzan raised it again, and this time a rush of air brushed my cheek as he brought it down. I made myself stand utterly still, my heart thudding in my chest. Its tip hit between Althor's foot and mine, spraying sand as high as my face.

The Uzan turned to his warriors and lifted his sword. In response, they raised theirs in perfect unison, hundreds of blades pointing at the stars. The Uzan lowered his and the Abaj followed suit, again in unison. I wondered how they timed it with such precision.

Althor slid his hand under my elbow and we walked forward with the Uzan. It was hard to see now, as the shadows deepened. A man appeared out of the enveloping darkness leading a riderless animal. It loomed over us, forearms reaching out with claws as long as my lower arm, daggers that could easily tear a human to shreds.

Althor ran his hand along the animal's side with a practiced touch. It responded by lowering its bulk to the ground, folding front and back limbs under its body like a camel. It smelled of sand and musk, with breath as sharp and bitter as lemons. The head came so close that I saw the scales on its face, blue prisms edged in green, with an echo of the sunset trapped inside. It watched me out of large gold eyes.

A bony ridge extended down the animal's neck, and another crossed its lower back from haunch to haunch, like a natural saddle. Althor grabbed the animal's neck ridge and swung gracefully up onto it. As soon as he was astride its back, the creature rose to its feet, higher and higher, until it towered above us. Althor spoke to the Uzan, and the Abaj bowed. Then he turned to me and knelt on one knee, his head bowed.

Flustered, I glanced at Althor. He just sat on his dinosaur, no help at all. So I did what he had done, touching the Uzan on the shoulder. The warrior rose to his feet and leaned slightly forward. I looked at Althor again, but he just continued to watch, his face shadowed, emotions hidden.

Then I realized the Uzan was actually listing toward the riders. I stepped in their direction and he bowed as if I had answered a question. I had in fact, though I didn't know it at the time. I had accepted his offer of a ride. As he led me to his mount, the animal settled to the ground, folding its legs under its body. Condensation rose from its snout into the cooling air.

The Uzan put his hands around my waist and lifted me onto its back. Startled, I grabbed its neck ridge. The Uzan swung up behind me—and the ground dropped away, lost in pooling shadows as the animal rose to its full height. When I started to slide, at first I thought I would plow into the Uzan and knock us both off the animal. But instead I settled into a smaller ridge across the middle of its back.

The Uzan spoke and the horde turned as one. Althor rode several riders down the line. I tried to decipher his mood: curiosity to see my reactions; approval of my calm; darker, more buried emotions about our capture and escape. I understood why he and the Abaj preferred I rode with someone, rather than alone, given how little I knew about the animals. But it puzzled me that he wanted me to go with someone else.

Then we took off. The animals ran in a loping gait, far faster than any horse. Althor leaned forward, his lips parted, his exhilaration flashing like the discharge from an iron arc. I pulled up my hood against the dust storm our passage created, but without a scarf I still should have been breathing sand. Yet I tasted none. When I touched my face, my fingers pushed through a molecular membrane within the hood; the jacket's web system had determined the need for protection and provided it.

Night soon overpowered the last of the sunset, leaving the

land dark. It reminded me of Nabenchauk. No city lights glared on the horizon, no city hum broke the silence. As we rode through the starlight, I wondered how the animals kept from stumbling. I later learned their vision extends into the infrared; to them, the desert is anything but dark so soon after sunset, when the ground is still warm.

I didn't realize we had reached a city until we were actually within it, among buildings that slept in shadow and silence. Our mounts slowed, picking their way through a forest of spires. Broken spires. These were ruins.

The riders dispersed, taking up posts in groups of five: at a tower, by a pyramid, alongside the path. We stopped at a tapering spire about forty feet tall, with a base fifteen feet in diameter. The Uzan dismounted, stirring up clouds of sand as he jumped to the ground. Clinging to the animal's neck ridge, I brought my leg over its back and slid off. For a moment I hung with my feet dangling. Then I let go and fell.

As I hit the ground, the Uzan seized me from behind in a bear hug utterly unlike his previous gentle, almost reverent, touch. I jerked away and stumbled on unseen rocks. As I staggered, he grabbed me a *second* time. Angered, I folded my arm and clenched my fist, ready to ram my elbow into his side—

Then I realized it wasn't the Uzan. It was Althor, trying to keep me from falling. I turned in his arms, looking up at him, and he grinned, the first good spirits he had shown since our wedding night.

The Uzan led us into the spire through a rectangular doorway. It was hollow inside, with a sloping roof that narrowed to a point about thirty feet above us. A crack stretched up the opposite wall, widening into a gaping hole that let starlight silver the interior. The Uzan spoke, ceremonial phrases, and Althor responded in the same singsong style, their rumbling voices accented by musical notes. At the time I thought they were chanting, but that beautiful exchange was actually how Iotic sounds when spoken properly by Raylicans.

Although all Skolians can trace their ancestry to Raylicon, four thousand years of genetic drift, often self-imposed, has changed them into new races. Althor is three-eighths pure Raylican: his mother is half, his father one quarter. His family are the only ones, after the Abaj, who carry so much of the original race in their genetic makeup.

After Althor and the Uzan finished speaking, the warrior bowed to us. Then he departed, his cloak swirling after him. When we were alone, Althor stood watching me, his arms crossed, his body silvered by the starlight. "You handled yourself well."

I didn't know what to say, so I just nodded, feeling awkward with the emotional distance that had opened up between us.

He went to the wall and knelt by a ledge. As he pulled two silvery blankets from under it, he tilted his head toward the remains of a partition that had once divided the spire into two rooms. "If we sleep behind that, it should help shield us from sand sifting in the break."

I looked around the spire. It seemed an odd place for the Abaj to put up their prince and his new bride, especially given the high level of technology Althor said they possessed. "Is this the only place they have for us?"

Althor glanced at me. "Why should we need more than they need?"

"You mean they all live like this, in these ruins?"

"At this time of year, yes."

"Can't they rebuild the city?"

He went over and set a blanket behind the partition. "Why should they?"

"It's falling apart."

"The Abaj have lived here for six thousand years. They won't change now, on the eve of their death." He sat on the blanket, looking more relaxed than before. When he held out his hand, I went over and sat next to him, cross-legged. He didn't stiffen this time when my arm brushed his knee.

"I've always had a fantasy to do what we did tonight," he said.

"You mean that ride through the desert?"

"That was not just any ride." He paused. "Five thousand years ago the Abaj were all women, as tall as the men you saw tonight, strong and fierce. When a Ruby queen brought a husband home from one of the colonies, the Abaj greeted her as they greeted me tonight. They guarded the husband while she went to ensure her holdings had remained secure in her absence."

"What if the man wanted to go with her?"

"He had no choice. Men had no rights then." He snorted. "My ancestors were barbarians."

"It sounds—different."

Althor laughed. "Don't look so intrigued."

I smiled. "What happened to her husband?"

"The Abaj took him to Izu Yaxlan. This city. He rode with the Uzan."

"You mean like I did tonight?"

"Actually, you were supposed to ride behind him. But I thought you might fall off the ruzik, so I asked him to put you in front."

"What's a ruzik?"

"The animal."

"And your fantasy was to switch the roles, to be the Ruby king bringing home his bride?"

I thought he would smile and say yes. Instead he stared into the darkness. It was a while before he spoke. "Those queens controlled an interstellar empire. To bring home a husband was a sign of their control over their lives and realms." He paused. "Of all nights, this was perhaps a good one for me to live out such a fantasy."

I understood. Iquar had taken everything from him, more than his freedom, even his control of his own mind.

"I was afraid you didn't want to ride with me because you were ashamed," I said.

"Ashamed? Why would I feel such a thing?"

"Because of—him." I couldn't say Iquar's name. "Because he touched me."

Althor put his arm around my shoulder. "Among my people, the shame at being Iquar's slave is mine, not yours."

I laid my head against his chest. "You have nothing to be ashamed of."

He sighed and murmured soft words with no meaning beyond the comfort of making them. After a while he said, "I think I recognized one of the mercenaries."

I looked up at him. "How?"

"The one who knew my military record sounded familiar, even through the filtering of his armor. My bioweb is processing the data." He paused. "Tina—when the Jag woke me, I scanned its weapons systems. All of its tau missiles are gone."

"It fired them at the Cylinder."

"Do you know what a tau missile is?" When I shook my head, he said, "They're equipped with an inversion drive. A starship engine. They move at relativistic speeds, with a huge kinetic energy. Four taus could obliterate the Cylinder."

I swallowed. "Maybe Iquar's people destroyed them."

"Some, probably. But all four? Not coming in at near light speed from so close." He pushed his hands through his hair. "Gods, Tina, I hadn't realized just how seriously the Jag's EI brain had degraded. It's lost all rationality."

"It knew exactly what it was doing."

"It couldn't have."

"Iquar hurt you, so it hurt Iquar." I could still feel the ice of its rage. "It wasn't just Iquar, either. *No one* helped us. I've never felt anger like the Jag's before. It wasn't human."

His incredulity flared. "My ship avenges me?"

"It loves you."

He stared at me. "What?"

"It loves you."

"A ship can't love."

"Yours does."

"That's impossible."

"Why? You're more than a man; why can't the Jag be more than a machine?"

It was a while before he answered. Then he said, "I need to think about it."

After that, we sat listening to the night. Musical clicks came from somewhere, like finger cymbals tapping together. Every now and then I heard feet shift, or the voice of an Abaj on guard around the spire. Their watch over us was symbolic: on a planet protected by the technology of a starfaring people, we hardly needed guards with swords. But I was glad they were there. I doubted I would ever feel safe again . . .

The scratch of cloth on my arm woke me. I was lying on one of the blankets with the other pulled over my body. Althor lay next to me, sleeping on his back. He jerked and his knit pullover scratched my arm again.

Suddenly he sat upright, his inner eyelids gleaming in the starlight. His mouth opened, as if he were trying to scream. But no sound came out. I sat up but didn't touch him, fearing his enhanced reflexes if I woke him too fast out of a nightmare. Instead I kept murmuring, "It's all over. You're here, with me."

Finally he made a strangled sound. His inner lids rolled up and he looked at me.

"It's all right." I put my arms around him and stroked his hair. "It's all right."

He pulled me close. "Gods, Tina—I can't—can't—"

I didn't know what to say, so I just kept murmuring nonsense words. When his shaking eased, he lay on his back again, pulling me with him. He spoke softly. "I hope an afterlife truly does exist. And I hope its spirits do to Kryx Iquar for all eternity what he did to his providers during his life."

I laid my head on his chest. "It's over now. He can't hurt you anymore."

Althor turned on his side, propped on an elbow, facing me. "You are like rain in the desert, so sweet and gentle. Thank gods he believed you were my concubine."

Although I was almost certain Althor had lied about the concubine business, it still made me uncomfortable. "It isn't really a supplement contract, is it?"

He grinned. "What if I said yes?"

"Althor!"

He touched my cheek. "It's a Rhon contract. It makes you a full member of my family, an heir to the Ruby Dynasty. For whatever that's worth." Dryly he said, "Statistically, it was supposed to be impossible that any of us would find a Rhon woman. I had to go to another universe to find you, but I did it." Lying down again, he wrapped me in his arms and spoke against my ear. "I didn't tell you the rest of the ceremony, when a Ruby queen brings her mate home from the stars."

My body warmed with the tickle of his breath. "There's more?"

"After she secures her holdings, she rides through the night to this city and goes to her husband. That's when they consummate the marriage." He bit my earlobe. "In my fantasy, my wife awaits my return, warm and sleepy in our bed, ready to take me into her arms when I come to Izu Yaxlan."

I traced my fingers along his lips. "She's waiting."

That night, in ancient ruins, on a dying planet with a dying sun, we finally consummated the union that would give new life to a dying people.

19

House of Flight

Dawn came with that hint of magic that hangs over the land before sunrise, when the sky has begun to lighten but the desert remains in shadow. I lay spooned with Althor, my back to his front, his arm around my waist as he slept. Morning sounds came from outside: quiet voices, the shuffle of feet, a clank of swords. Fragrant smells of cooking and incense drifted into the spire, and insects clicked at the dawn. The Abaj had hung a cloak in the doorway and weighted its hem with jeweled clasps. When wind tugged the cloth, the clasps bumped each other, making the musical clicks I had heard the night before.

A voice spoke outside, louder than the guards', but still quiet. I wasn't sure if its owner was talking to us or our guards.

Althor nuzzled in my hair. "Hmmm?" As I turned over to face him, his eyes opened. "What did you say?" he asked.

"I didn't. It was someone outside."

Althor spoke in a louder voice, in Iotic, and someone answered.

"Ah." Althor smiled. "They want to know if we want cacao."

"Chocolate? You're kidding."

"Chocolate?" He pushed up on his elbow. "What is that?"

"The drink I gave you in LA."

"That was good. But it wasn't cacao."

"They must have brought the word with them. Chocolate made from cacao beans was a favorite drink of ancient Maya royalty. They even had special pots for it, like Lord Smoke Squirrel's cacao cup."

"Let's see how you like ours." He pulled the blanket up over us, then spoke to the warrior outside. An Abaj entered and knelt, setting a pot and two cups on the floor. Red glaze covered the pot, accented by aqua hieroglyphs. Although I didn't recognize most of the symbols, that didn't mean much; I didn't know many Mayan glyphs either. There was one that was familiar, though, on the pot's lock-top cap: a comb, pronounced *ca;* a fish, also *ca;* and underneath that a symbol for *wa.* Ca-ca-wa. Cacao.

The warrior asked Althor a question. After Althor answered, the Abaj stood and bowed, then left, the curtain rustling with his passage.

"What did he ask you?" I said.

"If we wished witnesses."

"To what?"

He motioned at the two of us in bed. "This. That we consummated the marriage."

"*What?*" I flushed. "We most certainly do not want witnesses."

"I think it is a good idea."

"You can't be serious. They want to *watch?*"

He grinned. "Many millennia ago, when deemed necessary for political reasons, the Abaj did indeed witness in that manner."

"Althor!"

He laughed. "Today they just witness us together like this. They will take our word that everything else went as it should."

"But whatever for?"

"Proof the treaty is valid." He picked up the cacao pot. "I asked the Abaj to check the web last night. Stonehedge apparently delivered our contract to the Assembly himself. Our marriage has been public knowledge for days." Dryly he added, "So are the circumstances of our kidnapping. I want to avoid embarrassing questions."

"It actually makes a difference whether or not we consummated the marriage?"

"Legally, no." He poured a steaming dark liquid into one of the cups and set it in front of me. "But as a symbol, yes."

I took a sip of the cacao. It was wonderful, like raspberry-flavored coffee with cinnamon. "Don't they get lonely?"

"The Abaj?"

"Yes. Don't they want wives?"

"Some do." He poured himself a drink. "Those leave Raylicon. But most stay. They are all clones. The original templates were chosen from men believed suited to this life. I guess they learned to live without women." He shook his head. "I can't imagine it."

"Couldn't they clone their women too?"

"The women were already gone. That's why they learned to clone in the first place. They did save some genetic material, which is how Rhon created my grandmother." He took another swallow of his drink. "Healthy clones are difficult to make, though."

"The Jag told me about it."

He regarded me. "Will you let the Abaj geneticists analyze your DNA? One of their best genetics labs is here, underground."

I took another sip of my drink. "All right." It was hard to imagine a high-tech lab under the ruins of this ancient city.

Althor spoke in Iotic, in a louder voice. A guard outside answered, and I heard the booted tread of someone walking away from the spire.

As we were finishing our cacao, footsteps approached the spire. I rolled over under the blanket and Althor pushed up on his elbow, his front against my back.

The Uzan entered with five warriors, their robes billowing. They knelt before us and the Uzan spoke. In response, Althor kissed my cheek, a gesture more ritualistic than affectionate. I tried to imagine the Abaj as towering female warriors, me as an Amazonlike queen, Althor as my concubine. It was an odd image, hard to get my mind around.

The Uzan and four of the warriors left in a swirl of robes. As the curtain opened, revealing a dawn-washed sky, the sun raised its huge rim above the horizon. Then the curtain fell back into place and we were alone with the fifth warrior.

"This is the geneticist," Althor said. "He wants a skin sample."

I looked at the Abaj and he averted his eyes. He unhooked a tube from his belt and took out two spatulas, each smaller than my little finger. He scraped one along my arm, then dropped it into a vial, where it hung suspended.

"Your mouth too," Althor said.

I opened my mouth and the Abaj scraped the second spatula across the inside of my cheek. He dropped that into another vial, then closed up everything in a black pouch, hung it on his belt, and rose to his full height. He departed with a bow, sand drifting in his wake.

"How do they do that?" I asked. "They move so fast. And always together, as if they all know what the others are doing."

"They're empaths. Being clones makes their link stronger." Althor lay down and slid his hand under the blanket, over my breasts. He smiled. "Perhaps we should make doubly sure this treaty we've established is valid."

I laughed and pulled him into my arms. "Perhaps we should."

Izu Yaxlan. City of magic.

As we stepped out into the reddish rays of the morning sun, I had my first good look at the ruins. We climbed a pyramid near the spire, up stairs so steep we could put our hands on the steps in front of us without bending over. All that remained of the top was a platform two stories above ground. I turned around and around on it, my dress whipping in the wind as I absorbed the sights.

Half a mile away, a cliff rose up from the desert, and behind it mountains stepped into the sky. At the base of the cliff, the ruins of a palace basked in the sun. The building was long, three stories high and three times as long. Nine doorways were spaced along the front, none with doors. Had I drawn a line through the center, the two halves would have been mirror images. The remains of the roof angled in steep vaults made by overlapping flat stones. Faded murals covered important areas: stairways, walls, parts of the roof, the tower at each end.

Izu Yaxlan spread out in the desert beneath the cliff. Wide streets linked houses, plazas, and what resembled Maya sweat houses. The buildings with gaping beast mouths for doorways had to be temples. I even saw ball courts like those in ancient Maya cities. Pyramids rose here and there, with steep stairs. Other structures were less familiar: narrow spires reaching up many stories and bridges arching between upper levels of buildings, their spans built by overlapping stones. Cobblestone paths bordered by octagonal pillars wound through the city, and more buildings showed beyond the city center, smaller and more widely scattered, like suburbs.

"This is incredible." I stopped turning. "How can they let such a beautiful place fall apart?"

"Almost no one lives here now," Althor said. "Just the Abaj, and they don't spend the entire year."

"But they could do *something*. Send in robots, or nano-machines, or bring people from offworld."

"That is not what they want." Althor regarded me. "After the last Abaj dies, Izu Yaxlan will belong to my family. We will follow their wishes that it be left alone."

"To crumble back into the desert?" The thought was heart-breaking. "Why, Althor?"

He motioned at the city. "This is Raylicon. Like Raylicon, it is dying. The Abaj have accepted their death."

"If they wanted to die, they wouldn't have tried so hard to survive."

"They don't want to die. My family, all of Skolia, even the Traders—we exist out of their struggle to live." He spread his hands. "Some unknown race brought them here. They never had a choice. Now, in the sunset of their lives, they want no interlopers to take control again, either human or machine. They will die as they have lived for six thousand years. On their terms."

"I understand. I think." I motioned at the city. "It looks Maya. Has anyone from Earth seen these ruins?"

"Not many," he said. "Raylicon is closed to all but a few select visitors. And Izu Yaxlan is a sacred place."

"Has anyone ever sent pictures of it to Earth?"

"No. It would be sacrilege."

"There must be records about the Maya," I said. "Anthropologists love to study us, or at least they did in my universe. All that work couldn't have just disappeared."

"I thought the Maya didn't exist six millennia ago."

"Maybe your ancestors were brought from another universe, one with history shifted by thousands of years." I considered the thought. "Most Maya kingdoms collapsed around 900 A.D. Maybe it was because our ancestors were taken away." I shivered. "Maybe it happens over and over again in different universes, some race taking them from one and stranding them in another."

He stared at me. "For what gods-forsaken reason? To see if we can survive? To concentrate Kyle traits in a race already strong with them?"

"Maybe." I couldn't think of a better reason.

"Then they failed."

"Your family exists."

"Just barely." His expression softened. "Though perhaps now . . ." He held out his hand and I went to him. We hugged each other, the wind twining my hair around our bodies.

Eventually we returned to the stairs, where two Abaj waited on the steps, out of sight but close enough to hear if we called. They descended before us, like a human safety net. Althor took me through the city to the cliff, a pitted wall thousands of feet high, with a staircase switchbacking up its face. If a railing had ever protected the stairs, it was gone now. Cave entrances showed far up on the cliff, great beast heads carved into the mountain. The stairs reminded me of a toy I once saw, a frame with chutes that went back and forth. You put a marble in the top and it ran down one chute, dropped to the next, rolled down in the other direction, and so on, to the bottom.

"You go first," Althor said. "I'll come behind you, in case you slip."

His emotions made a gentle amber glow around us, colors of

hope and love. I cupped my hand in the air, filling it with that luminous mist. Then I started up the steps, resting one hand against the cliff face at my side.

Gusts tugged at us, growing stronger as we climbed higher. The two Abaj followed, their long legs taking the steps with ease. I looked back once, but it made me dizzy. After that I kept my gaze on the stairs, trying to forget the drop-off next to us.

At the first switchback, though, I couldn't resist looking down at the city. It spread out for miles, radiant in the bronzed sunlight, timeless and mysterious. I could easily believe ancient warriors had become legends in this place.

When we started up the second switchback, I said, "How high are we going?"

Althor answered from behind me. "To the House of Izam Na Quetza."

"Izam Na Quetza? That sounds like Itzamna and quetzal."

"Who?"

"Itzamna was the Maya god of wisdom and knowledge." I kept talking, trying to take my mind off the long fall to the ground. "A quetzal is a bird. It's gorgeous—green, red, white, and yellow, with long tail feathers. Royalty and warriors wore them. The feathers, I mean. In some places the penalty for killing a quetzal was death. It angered the god Kukulcan. Also the Toltec god Queztalcoatl. They're the same god, really, a feathered serpent who rules on Earth. Sometimes Kukulcan disguised himself as a wind god, though."

"Izam Na Quetza is the Raylican god of flight," Althor said.

The wind grew stronger, enough to make balance difficult. When we reached the second landing, we looked out at the city. Izu Yaxlan lay far below now. A black bird lit on the tip of a red-gold spire and cawed, its lonely call flying out into the desert.

We started up the third switchback. I faced the cliff, using both hands to search for handholds, not so much because the stairs were any steeper but because we were so high I felt the need to hang on. Wind sang across the cliff, its voice chill as it threw tendrils of hair into my eyes. The Abaj came behind us, walking steadily. I could imagine how we looked, four tiny figures far up on a vertical cliff.

My hand slid out into empty air and I *fell*—

And hit ground, landing on one knee. Althor tripped over my leg and caught himself on his hands and knees. We were inside the mouth of a cave. Literally. The entrance had been carved into a beast head with its mouth open in a roar. Huge stone fangs framed the opening.

Both Althor and I turned and sat on the edge of the opening, our legs dangling over the lower teeth. Far out in the desert, dunes rolled for mile after mile to the horizon. Scraps of clouds drifted through a porcelain sky. Out in the distance a sand devil whirled across the red sands.

The Abaj appeared, bending their heads to fit under the fangs as they stepped inside the beast's mouth. Wind tugged their cloaks, revealing bright clothes with gold embroidery, then hiding them again. They bowed to us without missing a step. It was impressive. I hoped they hadn't seen our far less graceful entrance.

As Althor and I stood, one of the warriors went to the wall. From a hook there, he took a bundle of what looked like dried branches tied together with cord. Then he pulled a tube off his jeweled belt. A spark of light—and the end of his torch flared with flame. The yellow glow mixed with the bronze sunlight, giving the cave an aged look, like an old photograph.

A rectangular tunnel stretched into the cliff for several yards, then bent sharply to the left. Hieroglyphics covered the back wall, drawn with black, red, and brown paints. The paint looked fresh; I later learned that the temple was one of a few sites in Izu Yaxlan the Abaj scrupulously preserved.

They led us down the tunnel. At the turn, they gave Althor the torch, then bowed in unison and withdrew back to the entrance. There they stood looking out at the desert, two gaunt figures in black framed by giant teeth, silhouetted against the sky. Wind keened past the entrance, high and lonely.

Althor took my hand and we continued down the new branch

of the tunnel. Behind us, sunshine lit the space where the tunnel turned, but the farther we walked the more darkness folded around us. After a few hundred yards the tunnel turned again, plunging deeper into the cliff. After that, only the torch lit our way. It was cool, too, the heat from the desert only a memory. Hieroglyphics covered the walls. Torchlight made shadows dance across them, so that the glyphs seemed to move.

"Here." Althor raised the torch. A staircase descended from our feet; at the bottom, a chamber curved out, disappearing into the darkness beyond the pool of torchlight. The air felt heavy. Ancient.

We descended the stairs together. At the bottom, he slid the torch into a claw that gripped the wall, its talons carved in stone. He took a second torch from a claw next to it, lit it with the first, and set it in a claw on the opposite wall. Four more times he repeated the procedure; when he finished, six torches lit the chamber with dim light.

My memory of that moment I first saw the House of Izam Na Quetza remains vivid even now. A sense of magic lives in that place, a memory of ancient kingdoms, of legends distilled until their essence became a part of the temple. Blocky friezes covered the walls, painted with dyes as blue as the sky and as red as the desert, their colors vivid even in dim light. The shadows were motionless that day, flickering only if the torches sputtered or we stirred the air. Gemstones embedded in the walls glittered in the radiance from the torches.

A bench stood in the center, carved with winged creatures. One was a square-faced beast with horns that spiraled around his ears. He had six legs, three on each side, and a tail that also curled in a spiral. Wings lifted from his back in a magnificent sweep of outstretched feathers. Another showed a woman with tufted ears, or at least she was a woman from the waist up; her body was that of a hunting cat with a feathered tail. She held a spear over her head, her breasts lifted high, her wings spread in flight. Even carved in stone, her hair seemed in motion, tossed by the wind. Statues stood against the walls, beasts with wings opened wide, their heads thrown back as they shouted to the sky. Flight, frozen into rock.

No statues stood on our right. Instead, the wall was sculpted into a man's face, his visage nine feet tall. The simple concentric circles of his eyes gave an impression of gentleness. His nose jutted out from the wall in a hook and his mouth was a long rectangle with square teeth. His chin came out parallel to the floor in a ledge six feet long and one wide, supported by stone columns. Incisors bent out from his mouth like armrests. A set of stairs led up to the wall, ending at the face, the top step even with the chin.

Althor was watching me. "What do you think?"

"It's beautiful," I said. "Harsh too."

"Like the desert."

"Yes. Like the desert."

He took me to the bench in the center of the temple and I sat with him, the carvings on it sliding smoothly against my legs. "How long has this been here?" I asked.

"Over five thousand years." Althor motioned at the winged statues. "Izam Na is our god of flight and transcendence. He rises above the ills that plague humans. He nurtures. The Abaj came here after battle to seek healing, not necessarily of physical wounds but those that killing inflicts on the spirit."

I brushed my hand across a carving. "What are these?"

"Each is a spirit companion to a goddess or god." He indicated the winged woman. "'Chak'."

His pronunciation surprised me. He started the name with a perfect glottal stop and ended with a glottalized *k*. Although most Skolian languages use glottals sparingly, both Iotic and Eubian are full of them, more even than my native tongue, Tzotzil Mayan. That's why the Trader language sounds so harsh. However, the musical quality of Raylican voices renders the glottals pleasant. It's one reason Iotic is such a difficult language; to speak it properly, you need vocal chords that can produce musical notes.

"Who is 'Chak'?" I asked.

"Spirit companion of the fertility goddess Ixa Quelia," Althor said. "She wields the ax of lightning and brings rain to the desert. She's also the goddess of war."

"There is a Maya diety we call Chac, a spirit of rain and war." I touched the carving of the beast with spiraled horns. "And this?"

"Azu Bullom. Spirit companion of Izam. You have this one also?"

"I don't think so. But *balam* means jaguar in Mayan." I looked up at him. "We have spirit companions too. Animals. The jaguar is the most powerful."

"Bullom is also a spirit of great power."

I regarded him. "It's not myths to you, is it? This is real."

It was a moment before he answered. Finally he said, "The Jagernaut in me knows it is mythology. Deep down, though, despite my logic—a part of me believes it is more."

"But you were willing to marry me in a Catholic ceremony."

His voice gentled. "Your spirituality is part of you. That we express our faith in different ways—to me, this adds to rather than detracts from what we have together." He slid his hand into my hair and trailed his fingers through to the ends. "I married you by your ceremony. I ask now that you marry me by mine."

"Here?"

"Yes." He indicated the temple. "My ancestors couldn't heal the sickness in their genes. At first they didn't even understand why they were dying. So they developed this ceremony as an offering to Ixa Quelia, goddess of fertility, and Izam Na Quetza, god of healing. The newly married couple came here to petition them for fertility."

I took his hands. "Then we should too."

Althor spoke in Iotic, a chant that rumbled, piling up against the walls and rolling back to us. Even after he stopped speaking, my skin tingled like a drum ready to tap. He released my hands and touched the neckline of my dress. It opened, separating down the front as he ran his finger along the seam.

As he took off the dress, I averted my gaze, still self-conscious in front of him. When I finally looked up, he touched my hair.

Then he got up and went to an arched niche in the far wall. A flint scraped, and the recess began to glow, warmed by the flame in a bronze lamp. After that he walked across the temple, to the stairs. He doused the torches, and then the only light came from the niche, giving the chamber a shadowed honey color, dim and mellow.

Finally he returned to the bench, where I sat with my legs dangling over its edge. He held objects he must have taken from the niche: a necklace strung with emeralds and rubies, two bracelets, and a vial. He set the vial and bracelets on the bench, then slid the necklace over my head. As he laid the largest ruby between my breasts, his fingers trailed over my nipples and they hardened. He knelt on a ledge in front of the bench, bringing his head even with mine, and pulled me into an embrace. I hugged him back, wrapping my legs around his waist.

After a moment he picked up one of the bracelets, a ring inset with blue and green gems. He clicked it open on a hinge, then took hold of my wrist and snapped the ring around it under the bracelet I already wore.

I pushed back his sleeve, revealing his wrist guard. "Now we both have them."

He gave me a guilty look. "Actually, the woman puts wrist guards on the man. But last night I asked the Abaj to bring up more delicate rings. For you." He took the second bracelet and snapped it around my other wrist. He reached behind his waist for my leg and set my foot on the bench, bending my leg so that my knee was by my shoulder. Then he leaned down and kissed the inside of my thigh.

"Hey," I said.

Althor lifted his head, smiling, his eyes half open. "My addition to the ceremony."

I pulled at his sweater. "You too."

He undressed standing in front of the bench, more relaxed than in days. After he sat down, he pulled me into his lap so that I was sitting sideways with my right shoulder against his chest. He picked up the vial, a delicate bottle glazed in swirls of gold, red, and deep blue, with a top shaped like a bird's feather. When he opened it, a fragrance curled around us, sweet and tangy, like spices or night-blooming flowers.

He poured oil into his palm and massaged my torso, holding me with one arm around my waist. I laid my head on his shoulder. Scents tickled the air, jasmine and honey. When he moved his hand lower and his fingers slid inside, like silk, my mind created a gold radiance. I saw it both within my mind and the temple, mellow and smooth, as if he were anointing both of us, banishing the lingering remnants of Iquar's soul that had tried—and failed—to envelop us in shadow.

After a while, he said, "You're supposed to say the Oath of Quelia."

I raised my head. "How does it go?"

He spoke in Iotic, and my mind swirled the words into ruby dark streamers, blending them with scents of oil and incense. I heard the lament of a pipe, its song drifting like the distant voice of a spirit roused from a millennia-long sleep. Slowly, stumbling over the words, I repeated the chant. He continued in Iotic, and I repeated it as best I could.

Then he said, "Come to me, husband."

"Is that the translation?" I asked. When he nodded, I said, "Come to me, husband."

"May Quelia give us embers that grow in warmth."

"May Quelia give us embers that grow in warmth."

"Bless the new—" He hesitated, his face blanking. "The new slate."

"Slate?"

"This is closest translation I find in English. Delete the slate? Start with a clean file?"

"Wipe the slate clean?"

"Yes. That is the soul of the new child. A clean slate." He touched my necklace. "Ixa Quelia takes a soul freed from the spirit of an ancestor. She cleans, burnishes, and blesses it and puts it in the child."

"That's lovely."

His voice softened. "Bless the new slate."

"Bless the new slate."

"Let the night sky come down."

"Let the night sky come down."

"Let the night sky wrap us in her ruby-dark cloak."

"Let the night sky wrap us in her ruby-dark cloak."

"Let the night sky grace us with her spirit."

"Let the night sky grace us with her spirit."

He stood up, holding me, and walked toward the face on the wall. I smiled. "Is this how Ruby warriors carted around their husbands?"

Althor laughed. "No. The husbands were too big. They just walked." He watched my face. "Does it bother you?"

It was like asking if I minded my husband treating me to a candlelit dinner on a romantic island. "Why would it bother me?"

He spoke carefully. "Imperial culture encompasses a huge range of courtship rituals. And of course legally, women and men are equals." He paused. "Despite claims to the contrary, though, the overriding culture retains remnants of a time when men were property. Some women would be uncomfortable with this reversal of roles."

I touched his cheek. "It's fine."

He set me down on Izam Na's chin, my back against the wall, my arms resting on the incisors. The stone felt cool under my thighs, with a dusting of sand. Althor climbed the steps and swung his leg over the bench so we faced each other. Incense curled out of the niche in wisps, bringing a scent of lost kingdoms. It felt as if we were caught in an instant stolen out of time, when ancient spirits still visited the city of Izu Yaxlan.

Althor had a gentle expression, the one that crinkled the lines around his eyes. With the two of us facing each other, he lifted me onto his lap. I laid my head on his shoulder and stretched my legs behind him. He rocked us back and forth, as if he too heard the distant pipe music. Perhaps he did; we were so close, it felt as if our minds nestled inside of each other.

He brought my hands between us and turned them so the palms faced outward. When he pressed the bracelets against each other, they locked together. Lifting my wrists, he framed my face with my hands, palms facing outward, "Izam Na's wings."

Then he bent his head and put his mouth around one of my index fingers. It surprised me how good it felt. I buried my face in his curls, inhaling his scent while he sucked my finger. After a moment, I heard him press several points on the bracelets. When they clicked apart again, I put my arms around his neck and hugged him close.

We made love slowly, taking our time. Althor held back this time, using our mental link to match his rise to mine. The music and fragrances my mind created blended together, mixing in a river of golden light. When we reached our peaks, they atomized that river into a mist of water-spray rainbows.

Gradually the music slowed, and the mist faded to an inner gold light. I lifted my head from Althor's shoulder. His eyes were closed, his breathing deep. I took a curl of his hair between my teeth and shook my head like a cat. "I liked that."

He opened his eyes. "So did I."

"But why this?" I touched the ledge under us. It seemed an odd place for lovemaking, ceremonial or otherwise.

"It's supposed to symbolize fertility." He yawned. "Probably it came about because most positions you end up on this thing increase the chance of conceiving a girl."

I almost asked if he wanted a son to carry his name. Then I remembered he had his mother's name. "It's hard to get used to, all the differences between us."

He smiled. "It makes life more interesting." Rubbing his eyes, he added, "If we stay here any longer, though, I'm going to fall sleep and topple onto the floor."

I laughed. "Don't do that."

He walked down the steps, his contentment filling the air with a mellow bronzed haze. When I started down, he picked me up and carried me to the bench.

I've sometimes wondered how it would have felt to live during the Ruby Empire, when women won the choicest mates through combat with other women. I wouldn't have had a chance against a towering Abaj warrior. It was just as hard to imagine Althor forced into marriage with an Abaj queen. And I would have had competitors, despite his aggressive nature. His sheer physical beauty and sexuality would have more than compensated for any "flaws" the Abaj saw in his personality. He would have been a challenge, a prize to conquer, or some such sexist business. I would never have stood a chance.

"I'm glad this is now," I said as we dressed. "Not five thousand years ago."

"I too." Althor pulled on his boot, watching me fumble with the seam on my dress. He showed me a loop on my neckline. "It's a sensor. When you press it, molecules on the seam change state, becoming little hooks."

It would never have occurred to me to look for such a thing. That has been the most difficult part of adapting to his universe; not the big changes, like interstellar travel or star-spanning computer webs, but rather the details, like learning how to dress.

We found the Abaj waiting at the cave entrance. As Althor smiled amiably at them, I wondered what they thought of him coming here for a ceremony no one had performed in centuries. They revealed nothing; living among a race of empaths, they had learned to shield their emotions.

But as they bowed, one glanced at my bracelets and an odd look passed over his face. I did pick up a wash of his mood then, a mix of wonder and something less definable. Althor later told me he had felt it too, a sense of puzzled loneliness from both Abaj, as if they felt the lack of something they couldn't define.

One of the warriors spoke with him, and Althor's unease rippled like colorless heat waves. When they paused, he turned to me. "The Uzan has allowed an ISC ship to land. But there is much tension, and the Abaj are refusing to let anyone disembark. Apparently Imperial Space Command believes we may be here against our will."

"Against our will? Why?"

He exhaled. "There's never been a situation like this. I disappear, reappear, am kidnapped, then sold. News of our marriage breaks, a Rhon contract, which means you're a Rhon psion. Then we destroy a Cylinder, assassinating a major Eubian political figure." He grimaced. "Right now the Traders must be screaming for extradition and demanding the Assembly honor the Paris Treaty. Of course the Assembly is refusing. They will threaten war if the Traders try to recover us, the Traders will threaten war if we aren't returned, and the Allieds won't know what to do because no details are worked out yet in our treaty." He spread his hands. "It's a mess. Basically, whoever gets us first, wins."

I swallowed. "What about Admiral Bloodmark? He knows we're the only ones who can reveal his betrayal."

"I don't know. The Abaj can't get messages offworld. Communication has been blocked." He exhaled. "Apparently three military envoys are requesting entry into the system: ours, the Traders', and the Allieds'. The Abaj let the one ship in because it came alone, is ISC issue, and gave proper security codes." He looked out at the city. "We better see what is happening."

Going down the cliff was easier than coming up, mainly because the wind had died down, but also psychologically, for me, because each step took us closer to the ground. At the bottom, as we were walking through the city, we saw a red cloud of dust on the horizon. We climbed a pyramid to see better, and the cloud resolved into a horde of warriors riding across the desert.

"They must be from Saint Parval," Althor said. "The port city."

The riders came on, several hundred, all in black, with flashes of silver beneath their cloaks. They slowed at the city limits, letting the ruziks pick their way through the ruins.

"What?" Althor said.

I looked up at him. "I didn't say anything."

"No. I mean, I know." He whirled around and strode to the edge of the platform. As he disappeared down the steps, I heard our bodyguards protest; when I reached the stairs, I saw them trying to hold him back. He gave a command and they reluctantly dropped his arms. He sped down the stairs, jumping the last three to the ground, and ran toward the riders.

I stepped down between the Abaj and we watched Althor run through the city. Other Abaj tried to stop him, with no more success than the ones with me. He passed the first of the approaching riders without even a nod. As they wheeled around their mounts, staring after him, a rider in the middle of the horde halted. He wasn't Abaj; although well built, he was nowhere near as tall as the warriors, and he wore plainer clothes, dark pants and a white pullover. For a mind-warping moment, as the man dismounted, I thought I was seeing double: Althor both running toward the ruzik and getting down from it, the same person in two different places.

The man ran toward Althor. They met and embraced with so much force they almost knocked each other over. Together, their differences were obvious; the man was a few inches shorter, with longer hair that brushed his shoulders. As he and Althor separated, one of the Abaj next to me spoke. I looked at him, and he motioned toward the stairs. A question. I nodded.

We descended to the ground and walked through Izu Yaxlan. When we drew near to Althor and the other man, I saw tears on the man's face. He was laughing and crying at the same time. He pulled Althor into another embrace and they hung there for a moment before releasing each other.

When we came up behind Althor, one of my bodyguards spoke. Althor spun around, then grinned and grabbed me by the waist. He pulled me so hard against his side that I went "oomf" as my nose hit his chest.

"Hey," I said.

Althor laughed. "You all right?"

"Fine." I rubbed my nose.

The unfamiliar man watched me with a gentle look, his violet eyes and sun-streaked purple hair so familiar that my breath caught. He didn't have metal-tinted skin, though. Althor spoke to him in another language, one that took beautiful advantage of his musical voice. The man answered in the same, his voice even more musical, a work of art itself. Althor spoke a phrase that finished with " 'Akushtina Santis Pulivok kya Skolia."

To me, he said, "Tina, this is my father. Eldrin Jarac Valdoria kya Skolia."

The man took my hands, pressing them between his as he spoke. I feared he would find me lacking, given what Althor had told me about Abaj women. At the time I had no idea how much I resembled Althor's mother. Not all the Kyle genes code for tallness, but among pure Raylicans they do all code for dark hair and skin.

Althor said, "My father asks that you call him Eldrin. It is his personal name, as I am called Althor and you are Tina." He smiled. "He says he is pleased to meet his new daughter."

I smiled tentatively. "Tell him I'm honored to meet him." It felt strange to say the words. And wonderful.

Finally I had a father.

20

Machines of the Ruby Dynasty

We rode to Saint Parval accompanied by both Eldrin and Althor's escorts. Althor offered to ride with me, but by then I had realized his love of racing the ruzik. If he took me, I knew he would worry about my falling off. So in the end, I rode with his father. I think we both hoped it would offer a chance to become acquainted. Given that we had no common language, though, and were sitting in tandem, we had little chance. Eldrin was also as tense as a board; he shares none of his son's enthusiasm for tearing across the desert on an iridescent dinosaur.

Sitting so close to Eldrin, though, I picked up a lot from his mind, especially his relief at Althor's escape and his contentment at seeing his son happily married. Beneath that, his mood was complex, layered with concerns of political intrigue, as well as anger over the Allieds' apparent role in our kidnapping. His mind felt disconcertingly similar to Althor's, yet different, too, more refined.

I didn't realize then the honor he did me. Trained as a Kyle operator since childhood, he guards his emotions with firm control, more so even than Althor, who by nature tends to be moody and volatile. Yet that day Eldrin relaxed his barriers, letting me absorb a great deal about himself and his family.

His appearance is classic for a native of the minor but well-protected planet known as Lyshriol. It was founded as an agricultural colony during the Ruby Empire. To help the colonists adapt to low levels of ultraviolet light, the Ruby geneticists engineered a lower melanin content in their skin, making them white, a color as unusual to them as Althor's metallic skin is to me. Their eye and hair color was an unexpected but harmless side effect.

The Ruby Empire relied on barely understood technology, so it's not surprising many of its fledgling colonies lost that technology during their millennia of isolation. The Lyshriol settlement regressed to a pre-steam-power stage. It almost disappeared, its people leached of fertility like their Raylican ancestors. Over the millennia, as the number of women dropped, the laws that made men property gradually fell by the wayside. The population rebounded when its gene pool lost the Kyle traits and settled into a more balanced state.

The Kyle alleles didn't completely vanish: Eldrin's father had been a Rhon telepath. But he was a rare exception. That was why Eldrin's mother, an offworld member of the Rhon, married him. She chose to live on Lyshriol because she loved its untouched beauty. Eldrin grew up in a rural community. Uninterested in the subjects taught by his tutors—physics, math, political science, literature, and so on—he spent his youth learning hunting, swordplay, and archery instead. His frustrated parents finally sent him offworld, at the age of sixteen, to attend a private Imperial school. He reacted strongly against the overreaching culture of the Imperialate, baffled and angered that it placed more importance on his undeniable physical beauty and spectacular singing voice than his prowess as a warrior.

In contrast, Althor's mother grew up steeped in the heritage of the Ruby Empire. Imperial culture is generally well balanced now, though it is true what Althor says, that it retains vestiges of its matriarchal past. He notices it more because his mother descends from its most conservative lineage, one that traces its roots directly to the Ruby queens. Although she is a woman of the modern age, that inheritance runs strong in her veins. The differences between Althor's parents explain a lot about him, why he is such a complex mix of machismo and a son of the Ruby Dynasty.

Eldrin already knew how Althor and I met. The Jag, rather than risking the gauntlet of intrigue surrounding Imperial Space Command, went to Lyshriol and landed on a farm belonging to one of Eldrin's brothers. The brother contacted Althor's parents, using a secured web channel designed for exactly such a crisis. It was Eldrin who gathered the military force to come to Raylicon, putting it together with his most trusted people, officers he knew were loyal to Althor, including, of course—

Damn.

I twisted around on the ruzik to face Eldrin. "We have to stop!"

He gave me a reassuring smile, apparently believing I too felt uneasy on the animal.

"I'm not scared!" I said. "We have to stop!" I turned back and pounded the ruzik's neck ridge. The animal didn't even slow. I might as well have been a bug flying around its head. A few Abaj glanced over, surprise flickering around them that I panicked now after riding so well the previous night. I felt pressure on my mind, as if they were knocking at the door, too respectful to enter without permission I had no idea how to give. I felt Eldrin, too, but had no idea how to "invite" him in either.

I searched the horde; Althor was far ahead, riding like a maniac. I concentrated, but his mental doors were closed, part of the courtesy and protection trained Kyles automatically assumed among a race of Kyles. He was far enough away, too, that I couldn't gain the immediacy of contact we shared when we were closer together.

One of the riders called out. A moment later I saw it: a city of chrome spires rising out of the desert. These were no ruins. A modern metropolis grew before us, metal, ceramic, and glassplex, gleaming in the bronzed sun. We had reached Saint Parval, and the starport.

"No!" I shouted.

Eldrin leaned his forehead against the back of my head and the sense of mental pressure increased. I made a picture in my mind, showing him the marble room where the mercenaries had first taken us, Althor sitting with his hands bound behind his back, Ragnar Bloodmark standing over him, his face contorted with anger as he told Althor he would never again bow to his family.

Eldrin made a choked noise. Then he shouted in Iotic.

Every ruzik in his escort stopped. In a delayed reaction, Althor and his escort halted a few seconds later, wheeling around to look at us. Eldrin played his fingers across our mount's neck ridge like a pianist. The animal took off again—headed back into the desert, away from Saint Parval.

The Abaj stood by their mounts like narrow statues. The red-gold sun hung above the horizon, hugely bloated, and dunes stretched out around us in giant ripples of sand. I sat with Althor and his father on a crumbling bench by a fountain where no water had flowed for centuries. A few yards away, a pyramid graced the desert, its steep sides stained red in the slanting light.

Althor's father spoke Iotic, pausing as Althor translated. "I told Ragnar everything," Eldrin said. "He arranged for the ISC warships. They're outside the system now, waiting for permission to enter. Ragnar ordered me to stay on the ship." He touched Althor's shoulder and said something Althor didn't translate. But I understood. He had needed to see himself that his son was safe.

"Ragnar played his part well," Eldrin continued. "He told your mother and me that he feared betrayals in both ISC and the Abaj. He counseled us to remain silent about his involvement, lest we warn the conspirators about his work against them. That's why I didn't tell the Abaj he was on the ship." He shook his head. "We believed him, Althor."

"How could you have known?" Althor spoke first in Iotic, then in English. "By the time we learned of his part, the mercenaries had shut down the Jag. During the trip here I was unconscious and Tina was only awake for a few moments." He shook his head. "If Tina and I had boarded his ship, Ragnar would have isolated us and arranged for an attack by the Traders. He could have been rid of us before we had a chance to reveal him." He regarded his father. "Now that you know, he has to get rid of you too."

A vivid flux of emotion came from Eldrin, born of a fifty-year-old memory, one worn by time but still vivid: fear, anger, loathing. I remembered what Ming had told me, that Althor's father had been captured by the Traders in the last war.

All Eldrin said was, "Ragnar can do nothing. Too many know we are here. Perhaps that one ship is crewed by his people, but certainly not the entire force we brought. Perhaps not even that one ship."

"That's all the more reason to fear him," Althor said. "He's desperate."

"He can do nothing," Eldrin said.

"No?" Although Althor spoke sharply, he translated his words as, "Father, you are a brilliant bard. Military strategy is my expertise." Eldrin stiffened, though, and I caught the sense of what Althor really said: *Father, what does a folksinger know about modern military strategy? Absolutely nothing.*

That was my first experience with the grating side of Althor's attitude toward his father. I've since realized his lack of respect for Eldrin's intelligence was a legacy planted and nourished by Ragnar Bloodmark. The wounds have gradually healed, as they've come to understand how Bloodmark used Althor, driving a wedge between parents and son. It is a testament to the strength of Althor's family that their love survived even after so many years of manipulation by their close "friend."

"A hundred ways exist for him to arrange our recapture by the Traders," Althor said.

"That wouldn't be enough," Eldrin said. "The Abaj also know his guilt."

Althor grimaced. "If the Traders break the system defenses and fire on the planet, no witnesses will survive to tell the story."

"They can't break through," Eldrin said. "And they would be fools to destroy Raylicon. I can't think of a more inflammatory act of war."

"Without help, no, there's probably no way they could do it. But they have help. An ISC admiral. And, Father, the act of war has been committed by Raylicon. It's the Abaj who refuse to give us to ISC."

Listening to them, I wondered what would have happened had

we never escaped Iquar. Once he realized I was Rhon, he would have forced Althor to reveal how we met. He would have learned about my Earth, alone and vulnerable, like a succulent fruit ready to pluck. For the first time it hit me how severe the consequences could be for my universe if the Traders ever recaptured us.

Althor and Eldrin had fallen silent, both watching me. Belatedly I realized I was probably broadcasting my emotions.

Eldrin spoke gently, with Althor translating. "I've also been with the Traders, Tina. I understand your fear."

I spoke. "But they let you go."

"They agreed to an exchange of prisoners," Eldrin said. "Me for an Aristo youth. The boy was Jaibriol Qox III, now Emperor of Eube. I still don't understand why he arranged the trade."

His comment surprised me. Why wouldn't the Eubians want the trade? They had the better of it. Although Eldrin was a member of the Rhon, he wasn't the same rank as an emperor. Of course, that was before they discovered one of their military units had captured a Lock.

Eldrin was watching me. "No one knew Jaibriol II had a son. He was hidden on Earth, going to high school, for gods' sakes. After his father's death, he went to Delos, an Allied planet with both Skolian and Eube embassies. He simply walked into the Eube embassy and offered himself for trade. They verified his identity with genetic tests and had me brought to Delos within a day." He spread his hands. "Why a trade? He was a free man. Why not just claim his birthright?"

Althor shrugged. "Of course they traded. The Allieds wouldn't give up Qox for nothing."

Eldrin frowned. "I was there, Althor. That trade wasn't orchestrated by the Allieds. The boy did it himself."

"The Allieds say otherwise."

"The officer in charge was protecting himself." Eldrin snorted. "You think he would admit such an exchange took place under his nose without his knowledge? Of course he claimed credit."

Behind Althor, in the direction of Izu Yaxlan, a spurt of dust showed in the desert. "Someone is coming," I said.

The red plume neared, resolving into a rider. He reached the ranks of Abaj and jumped off his mount. As several Abaj led him to the fountain, the three of us stood up. The messenger knelt before Althor's father. When Eldrin touched his shoulder, the man rose and spoke with deep respect, the regard Althor should have been giving his father. Eldrin nodded, then tilted his head in my direction.

The Abaj knelt before me. When I touched his shoulder, copying Eldrin's gesture, he stood and spoke to me. I glanced at Althor.

"They've finished the genetic tests," Althor said. "This man has the results."

My pulse leapt. "What does he say?"

As Althor spoke with the Abaj, Eldrin's incredulity spread out in a glittering mist. Finally Althor took my hands. "You are Raylican. The pure strain. Your father must also have been Maya. Your ancestors were the original seed." He stopped. "Or not yours, but Maya from a time-shifted universe. It explains why we've had so much trouble identifying our ancestors. We've looked for a people who lived on Earth six thousand years ago. But the Abaj estimate that only about a thousand years have passed since your DNA branched into a different evolutionary path from that of the first Raylicon settlers." He took a breath. "And, Tina—you don't carry the CK complex."

"That's good, isn't it?" I asked.

He squeezed my hands. "It's a miracle."

Eldrin spoke, and Althor nodded. After a moment I asked, "What did he say?"

"That the existence of the Maya may be moot if Ragnar kills the Raylicans."

Eldrin continued. "I doubt the Traders wish to start another war. They would rather recover the two of you according to the Paris Treaty. If it were anyone else, Jaibriol Qox would probably let it go. But any of us could serve as a Key, and both Althor and I have been bred for it. It's why we exist. That makes recapture more worth the risk."

The Uzan spoke to Eldrin. He listened, then motioned to his son. Althor just shook his head. It was frustrating not being able to understand them.

"What is it?" I asked.

Althor turned to me. "The Uzan suggests we copy our neural patterns into simulators and load them into the net. That way, if we're killed here, we might survive in the web. If cloning Rhon psions ever becomes possible, they could create new bodies and transfer our simulations into them."

"That's horrible," I said.

More gently he said, "It wouldn't work. Even the best neural simulations are less than the human mind they come from."

"The Jag did it with me."

Althor nodded. "I've a record of it. It was a good simulation. It also included a Kyle transfer of your consciousness. But that was still a poor substitute for your mind. It was already degrading when you downloaded back into your own brain."

I rubbed my fingers on the hinge in his hand. "Even if they figured out the cloning, wouldn't it fail for you? Or not fail, but . . . ?"

"Yes." Althor pulled away his hand. "They would have to rebuild me. Again."

When Eldrin spoke, Althor didn't translate, but I understood anyway: he didn't want his son to suffer the pain of his childhood a second time. Althor looked at him, love gentling his face. Bloodmark may have injured their bond, but nothing could destroy it.

"Ragnar has cut off our access to the electro-optic webs," Althor said. "We can't send out eomail via starship, either. And he has a V-class cruiser sitting in port. From Saint Parval it could destroy this entire region. From space he could slag the planet's surface. It's a standoff; his ships are blocking us from sending anything out and the Abaj are blocking them from entering the system."

"We can't use the psibernet?" I asked.

He shook his head. "I've worked with his covert operations agents. He has high-rated telepaths working as telops. They're blocking psibernet transmissions. It's the equivalent of cutting electronic or optical lines in an eoweb."

"Become a data line yourself," Eldrin said. "If you are a living part of the web, it makes no difference if someone cuts you off from the system. You simply move elsewhere."

Althor made an exasperated noise. "Father, what are you talking about?"

"I think he means put your whole body into the psibernet instead of just your mind," I said. "Then you can go anywhere you want."

"That's ridiculous," Althor said.

I reddened. "Well, it was just a thought."

Eldrin smiled when Althor translated, as if I had made a joke. I suppose it sounded that way. Either that, or he was giving me the benefit of the doubt.

Eldrin spoke to the Uzan. The Abaj responded at length, and when he finished, he asked a question. This time I guessed the meaning: *What do you want us to do?*

Eldrin spoke: he wanted them to go ahead.

Althor shook his head, angry. *No.*

"Althor?" I asked. "What is it?"

Taking my hands, he sat with me on the bench. "My father claims my mother once transferred herself, mind and body, through the net. The Uzan also says it is possible, at least for a Rhon psion. It has to do with this equation my mother has named after her." He frowned. "They are both crazy. She must have used the net in a manner my father didn't understand and he interpreted it in this strange way."

"Why would he do that? And why would the Uzan agree?"

"I don't know." Althor hesitated. "As an equation, it works. But that is math. It isn't a physical process."

"How does it work?"

"You know quantum theory?" When I shook my head, he said, "It's all wavefunctions. I have trouble with it myself. In school, I barely passed."

In truth, he knows theory better than he gives himself credit for. It's in his genes, after all; his mother is one of the great math-ematical geniuses of her time. He described the wave-particle duality: matter sometimes behaves like particles and other times like waves. Macroscopic objects don't act like waves because their wavelengths are too small to measure, but human beings are still wavepackets propagating through space.

"I can locate a packet by its coordinates," Althor said. "If I want to describe where you're sitting, I need three numbers, say your height from the ground, your distance from me, and your distance from the fountain. Your coordinates. Every point has three. It's the same as saying three mutually perpendicular vec-tors specify a point in space. Those vectors span our three-dimensional universe." He paused. "But suppose you exist in a space where it takes an infinite number of vectors to specify 'lo-cation.' "

"Places like that exist?"

He nodded. "Mathematically. They're called Hilbert spaces, after an Earth mathematician. The 'vectors' are wavefunctions."

It sounded crazy. "What do they do?"

Althor snorted. "Torment engineering students who have to take classes in quantum theory." When I laughed, he smiled and cupped his hands as if he were holding a universe. "The wave-functions are building blocks. They depend on physical quanti-ties, like position, time, or energy. In other words, Hilbert spaces are built out of blocks from our universe. The math has been known for centuries. Your friends at Caltech probably studied it."

"But there's more?"

"Suppose your blocks don't depend on physical quantities. Suppose they depend on thought."

I blinked. "Wouldn't that mean that your location in that uni-verse depends on what you're thinking?"

"That's exactly what it means."

"Althor, that's weird."

He laughed. "This is why I like engineering better than the-ory. My mother loves this stuff, though."

"What was the equation she discovered?"

"You know what is a transform?" When I shook my head, he said, "A transform takes a mathematical function from one space to another. You can Fourier transform an energy function into one that depends on time. The reverse transform takes it back to an energy function. You go from energy space to temporal space and back again. Children here learn Fourier and Laplace transforms in school. They study Selei transforms later."

I had heard Joshua talk about the first two. "What's a Selei transform?"

"It takes you from our universe to psiberspace. My mother figured it out when she was a teenager." He exhaled. "The Abaj claim they can transform the wavefunction of our bodies into psiberspace and send us to another node. We would have to reverse the transformation ourselves: with communications blocked, there would be no way to notify anyone we were coming." He shook his head. "It's crazy. Suppose they actually turn our bodies into a mathematical function? Suppose it degrades while we're in the net? What if we can't transform back? What if we only partly transform on one end? Or both? What would we be, semi-transparent humans? Missing parts of our body? I can't even guess."

"Althor, it doesn't sound any crazier than when we went from my universe to yours through that thing—what did you all call it?—a branch cut on a Riemann sheet."

"That made sense."

I smiled. "To you, maybe. Not to me."

An Abaj out in the desert shouted. Turning, we saw another red plume racing toward us, this one from the direction of Saint Parval. It resolved into four Abaj warriors. They were escorted to the Uzan, who conferred first with them, then with Althor and Eldrin.

Althor translated. "Ragnar has told the Abaj that by refusing to 'surrender' us, they are committing treason. He gives them one hour to release us. Then he will begin destroying sites on the planet."

I tensed. "Are they going to give us up?"

"No." Althor looked out at the warriors, some astride their ruzik, others tending their mounts or simply standing by them. "Six millennia of fealty do not vanish with one threat."

"Can't we take a ship up from another starport?" I asked.

"The Jag put us here because Saint Parval has the only functioning starport on the planet." He shrugged. "We probably don't need a port to take off. But Ragnar will attack any ship trying to escape. And he has a state-of-the-art V-class cruiser."

"Which do you think is more likely?" I asked. "We try to escape and are recaptured or destroyed, or we use the psibernet and don't make it?"

He grimaced. "Both are suicide."

"We have to do something." I squeezed his hands. "Your father says his way has been done. Have you ever seen an Abaj-type ship escape a warship like Bloodmark's?"

"No."

"Then shouldn't we try the method that's worked?"

"I don't *know* it's worked, damn it."

"Your father—"

He made a frustrated noise. "He doesn't know what he's talking about."

"Did you ever think that maybe your opinion of him has been poisoned by Bloodmark?" More gently I said, "You're acting just the way Bloodmark would want."

Althor stared at me, his emotions so intense I felt them despite his barriers: denial, shame, anger, guilt. Underneath all of that he hurt, both from Bloodmark's betrayal and from the wounds in his relationship with Eldrin. Despite their prickly interactions, he loved his father deeply.

Althor stood and spoke to him. Eldrin nodded, and they walked away, to the other side of the fountain. They spoke quietly, Althor sometimes dropping his gaze, unable to look at Eldrin. A tear ran down his face and he quickly wiped it away. Eldrin watched him gently, with a love nothing could ever wash away, neither the years of struggling to make a child whole nor the years of an interloper poisoning their lives.

Finally they returned to us. Althor said, "We'll try the psi-bernet."

Tiqual rose out of the desert, a solitary pyramid hundreds of feet tall. The setting sun gave it a luminous bronze glow, accenting the shadow that stretched out from its base into the darkening desert. Its name gave me chills, so like ancient Tikal on Earth, the greatest of the great Maya cities, a metropolis of glorious temples and legendary dynasties.

I rode with Althor this time, Eldrin at our side and the Abaj all around. We approached Tiqual at a stately pace. No city surrounded it, only a courtyard tiled with close-fitting triangular bricks the color of terra-cotta. Wind blew across the courtyard, ruffling sand into the air and letting it down in wings of red dust.

Several hundred yards from the pyramid, an arch glowed in the aged sunlight. Its sides were fluted blocks nearly three meters tall, its top a long stone. The Abaj rode through it two abreast. As we came closer, the sides resolved into statues; each was a woman, a muscled warrior with her arms stretched over her head to support the top stone. Neither wore anything except the Abaj sword hanging from her belt. They showed no shyness, with breasts lifted high and heads thrown back, their faces proud in the bronzed light.

A statue as tall as a man stood near the arch, one of the mythical spirit companions. He had a powerful body similar to a mountain lion, but longer. His head was human, with a hooked nose and heavy-lidded eyes that watched the desert, sensual and forever half-closed. Instead of ears, horns spiraled in his luxuriant hair.

We rode under the arch and across the courtyard to the pyramid. The entrance was a ruzik's head with its mouth open in a roar. In truth, I've never heard a ruzik roar. But it created an impressive doorway, one over ten feet tall.

From far away Tiqual looks like a Maya pyramid. It has the pyramidal base with terraced sides and a steep stairway that climbs the front of the temple. At the top is a chambered sanctuary, and on top of that a roof comb, a high-reaching crown of masonry hollowed out by airy vaults. But up close, its differences show, from the ruzik's gaping mouth at the base of the pyramid to the intricate designs made from the red, gold, and yellow bricks used in its construction. Yet its differences only accent its haunting similarities.

We dismounted, the Abaj jumping down around us. Wind had swept the courtyard clear, but the cobblestones felt pebbly under my soles. Althor's hair stirred, glinting bronze in the slanting sunlight. Eldrin stood next to him, arms crossed, staring up at the pyramid.

The Uzan and ten warriors ushered us through the yawning beast mouth. It faced away from the setting sun, so we entered darkness. A light flared, then a second, then a third as the warriors took up torches from claws on the wall. Yellow radiance surrounded us but it barely extended past the edges of our group.

They took us deep into the pyramid, following a rectangular tunnel. Carvings on the walls jumped into focus as we passed, and receded into the darkness behind us. Eventually we reached what felt like a larger place, though it was hard to tell with such meager light. The warriors doused their torches, plunging us into chilly blackness.

Light flooded the pyramid.

A vast cavern spread out before us, wide and lofty, as high as Tiqual, its sides sloping to a point far above our heads. Mammoth generators made from ceramic and precious metals hummed. Crystal columns rose up for hundreds of feet, lights spiraling within them. In one corner, a gigantic maze of mirrors and panels reflected the light. Other machines resembled the intricate workings of a huge watch, with gold and copper gears, glass levers, polished ebony. In another place, they could have been the innards of a fantastic antique submarine, its cables woven from flexible crystal.

Modern science neither designed nor developed psiber technology; it all comes from the Ruby Empire. Tiqual and the three psibernet Locks are the only functioning Kyle machines left. Althor's people have barely begun to deduce how they work.

Eldrin seemed stunned, but Althor looked relaxed, familiar with the surroundings. The Abaj led us to a dais that supported three gold boxes with transparent lids. They looked like coffins. The warriors stopped in front of the center one and turned, their black-cloaked forms reflected in the polished surfaces all around us.

Althor looked at his father. "I'll go through." When Eldrin protested, Althor said, "Father, it makes sense. You and Tina are more valuable to the Rhon, and the Abaj don't have high enough Kyle ratings to manage it."

They spent almost ten minutes arguing. Althor quit translating after the first few sentences, but it was obvious Eldrin had no intention of letting his son risk his life. Finally Althor made an exasperated noise and raised his palms in a gesture of surrender.

As Eldrin stepped toward the boxes, Althor glanced at the Uzan. The Abaj leader barely moved, but Eldrin suddenly slumped, falling face forward. Althor caught him and gently eased him down to lie on a bench near the dais.

"What did you do to him?" I asked.

"Nothing," Althor said, looking guilty.

"Then what did you tell the Uzan to do to him?"

"It's a mild sedative. He'll wake up soon." Althor took hold of my shoulders. "Tina, he's the true Third Key, trained all his life for it. I'm expendable."

"No, you aren't. Let me do it."

Softly he said, "You're the miracle. The least expendable of all. Besides, no one knows you. Why would they trust you? Nor do you have any psiberspace experience."

I made myself take a deep breath. I knew he was right. "Just be careful."

He squeezed my hands. Then he walked to the dais. As he mounted its steps, I murmured a Zinacanteco prayer, also forming the words in my mind, for Althor:

> *Holy Vashakmen, my father,*
> *Holy Vashakmen, my lord,*
> *In divine unison, then,*

In divine accord, then,
  Will you stand up in holiness,
  Will you stand firm in holiness,
    Behind the lowly backs, then,
    By the lowly sides, then,
Of your sons,
Of your children.

Do not yet lose them for me,
Do not yet abandon them for me.

Althor glanced back at me, his face gentling. Two warriors turned a crank on one of the boxes, and with a protest of long unused hinges, the bronze fittings on the lid retracted. They opened the coffin and Althor climbed inside, lying down on his back.

They fastened finely tooled leather straps across his legs, chest, hips, and arms. At first I wondered why, but as they worked, the mental shield on the mind of one slipped and I glimpsed one of his memories, a time one of the Abaj had experimented with the boxes. I saw the warrior twisting in panic, arms flailing to open the lid as he disappeared. One arm remained after he was gone.

I shuddered. Although Althor was calm, his inner turmoil brushed my mind. In part, the symbolism of the coffinlike box agitated him. More than that, though, the procedure echoed his memories of being fastened into Iquar's framework. That he went ahead with it despite his feelings, and despite his well-founded doubts, spoke eloquently to me about his courage.

The Abaj closed the lid and cranked its fittings into place. Seen through the translucent lid, Althor looked calm. But his claustrophobia made a gray mist around the coffin. Please make it fast, I thought. Get it over with.

The Uzan turned to a pillar of brass-bright metal and pulled a lever. At first I thought nothing happened, that the ancient machinery was broken. Then I realized the lid was turning opaque, like moonstones on a beach. Lights flickered inside, flashes of white and blue, and glitters ran along the edges just inside the lid. I could no longer see Althor, but his claustrophobia felt like tar on my skin.

Then I didn't feel him anymore.

The Uzan pushed up the lever. The coffin became translucent again—revealing an empty interior.

Eldrin and I sat together on the bench. Two Abaj worked at a console, monitoring communications from another site on the planet. The others stood quietly, the eternal bodyguards, positioning themselves around us yet keeping enough distance to give us a bubble of private space.

Eldrin had awakened only minutes after Althor disappeared. He hadn't said much, just stared at the coffins. I felt his anger, and his fear for his son. If we could have talked, the interminable wait might have been more bearable. But we had no language in common. We didn't even know what we were waiting for. Had Althor made it through to an ISC ship? For all we knew, he had died as soon as he disappeared.

Five warriors suddenly strode into the cavern and crossed to the Uzan. As they spoke to him, Eldrin tensed.

"What is it?" I asked.

Eldrin spoke in Iotic, then paused, watching my face. When I shook my head, he averted his eyes, concentrating. Words came into my mind, but in the unfamiliar language. The Uzan glanced at us, then continued to confer with his warriors. Eldrin's sense of urgency tightened the air. A picture formed in my mind, an alien image, as if he were running a movie in my brain. It felt strange, intrusive; my initial reaction was to shut it out. I resisted the impulse and concentrated until it became clearer.

First he made an image of Ragnar Bloodmark. Then a picture of a Raylican sundial. Another picture of Bloodmark. Then the sundial exploding, followed by Bloodmark giving orders to people in uniforms. Next he showed a ship taking off from a red planet. Then a ship in space firing on that planet. He finished with images of the Abaj dying in the inferno.

I understood. Bloodmark's hour deadline was closing in. If the Abaj didn't surrender us to him, he would fire on the planet.

There must be a way to stop it, I thought. But what escape could exist for the Abaj? No matter what we did, Bloodmark still had to kill them and destroy any site where they might have left a record of his betrayal.

I made an image for Eldrin, trying to evoke an Imperial military officer. Since I only knew Jagernauts, I based it on that and hoped he understood. I showed Althor talking to the Jagernaut, then the Jagernaut locking Bloodmark's hands behind his back.

Eldrin spread his hands in an *I don't know* gesture. A blue mist spread out from him, the color of grief. I understood. He feared his son had already died.

Eldrin formed another picture: He and I standing together, facing Bloodmark. Another man was there, one with shimmering black hair and red eyes. *Jabriol Qox III,* Eldrin thought. He showed me Bloodmark giving us to the Trader emperor.

My unease at the picture was muted by an odd effect; the emperor looked familiar. I couldn't place why. I shook my head, then showed the image blowing up.

Eldrin responded with the imagine of an unfamiliar Aristo. A rush of emotions came with it: fear, anger, shame, hatred. He knew this Aristo, hated him with an intensity that burned. Eldrin shuddered and the picture disappeared. That's the only time I've ever known him to "speak" about his capture by the Traders. I understood what he meant: he would rather die here than become a Trader prisoner again.

No, I thought. I showed an enraged Jagernaut locking Bloodmark's hands behind his back. Then the admiral on trial. Then his execution.

Eldrin shook his head and showed a Trader ship firing on Raylicon. That one was obvious; Bloodmark would help the Traders break the Raylican defenses, letting them do his dirty work and take the blame.

But that logic had a hole. Attacking Raylicon was no use to

the Traders unless they retrieved us. Otherwise they risked starting a war for nothing. Even with help, breaking the defenses would be no easy task, and they would have to get in and out fast, before ISC forces caught them. Unless we had already surrendered, getting us would take too long. So all we had to do was refuse to surrender.

Eldrin was watching me. He made a new picture. Althor's mother. Seen through his thoughts, she was warm and vulnerable. In truth, that delicate exterior hides a steel cable. Dyhianna Selei walks the Imperial halls of power as a mover who knows every nuance and convolution of its intrigue. Spectacularly beautiful, a power among powers, yet caring and nurturing to those she loves, with an awe-inspiring intellect—it was no wonder Ragnar Bloodmark wanted her.

Eldrin added a second person to the picture: Bloodmark. The admiral was leaning over her, pulling her head back, with a knife against her neck. That image dissolved, replaced by one of Eldrin and me surrendering to him. Another image of Althor's mother, this time showing Bloodmark comforting a bereaved wife and mother.

So. There had been more in Bloodmark's ultimatum than Althor realized, threats couched in terms meant only for Eldrin: if we didn't surrender, Althor's mother would suffer Bloodmark's revenge. Eldrin had showed a knife, but I had no doubt the admiral's methods would be far more subtle.

I reformed the image of Bloodmark threatening Althor's mother. Then I showed her rolling him into a tiny ball that she chewed up and spat out.

Eldrin smiled dryly. But he spread his hands. Neither of us knew if Bloodmark could make his threat real. One thing was obvious: if we died on Raylicon, it would devastate Althor's mother. And she still trusted the admiral. Eldrin showed another possibility: Bloodmark comforting her. As she cried, he tilted up her face up and kissed her. Eldrin exploded the image into shards.

The Uzan came forward and spoke. Eldrin nodded, then turned to me and motioned first toward the starport, then toward the sky. He made two images, one showing us going to Blood-mark's ship and the other showing us dying on Raylicon. Next he tilted his head: a question. It was time to decide. Give ourselves up or die here?

I shook my head. I had an idea, perhaps insane, but better than the alternatives. I got up and went up onto the dais. Laying my hand against one of the coffins, I regarded Eldrin. He stood up, next to the Uzan now, watching me. I made an image of the Abaj stalling Bloodmark, telling him we were about to give ourselves up. Then I showed Eldrin and myself climbing into the coffins. Even if only one of us survived to warn ISC, it would be worth the effort. If we both failed, as Althor apparently had, the result would be no different than if we died at Bloodmark's hand.

Eldrin made an image of me in a coffin. Then the Uzan pulling the lever. Then an empty coffin. He tilted his head: a question. In answer, he spread his hands in an *I don't know* gesture. I understood: once I was in psiberspace, I would have no idea how to reverse the transformation and return to normal space.

At least this gives us a chance, I thought to him. I took hold of a crank and tried to undo the lid's fastenings. It was harder than the Abaj made it look.

One of the warriors took over, opening the box. I made myself climb in and lie down. Soft material lined the interior, but it felt claustrophobic even with the lid open. As they strapped me in, I had to make a conscious effort not to thrash. To distract my attention, I lifted my head—and saw Eldrin climbing into another box. He glanced at me and nodded. Then he lay down, disappearing from view.

When they closed the lid, panic hit. I struggled against the straps, twisting as the lid fogged over. A strange sensation came over me, a sense of dissipating. Dissolving.

Disintegrating . . .

The last thing I saw, before I lost touch with the physical universe, was Althor's face above the lid, his mouth forming the words, *Tina, no! Come back!*

21

Integration

Sea of blue light. Shimmering.
Bessel function.

I am a Bessel function.

Spherical Bessel function. Circular hill. Concentric rings surround center peak.

Drop a stone in a lake, ripples round, round it makes.

Smells: sweet, sour, roses, sulfur, urine, honey. Sheep on a hill. Gunpowder. Althor's seed on my thighs. Tortillas baking in the dawn.

Sounds: rings, jangles, booms echoing, echoing, fading. Cries overlapping. Song: louder, sweeter, harsher, fading, fading, fading.

Textures: liquid on my skin.

I have no skin.

Pricks of fire. Hands on breasts. Scrape of bark. Wind on face. Grass under feet.

Tastes: honey and mustard, salt, cloves, beans, corn, maize as sweet as the sun . . .

Disturbance.

Waves in the lake. Other waves.

Ripples spreading, interfering, spreading.

I am two Bessel functions. A sum.

Losing symmetry.

Infinite sum. Ripples crossing, disappearing, spreading.

Spreading . . . spreading . . .

Tina?

I grasped at the thought. *Eldrin?*

Another Bessel function appears. Violet and glimmering. Compact. Secure. He knows this place, has visited often, in mind if not body . . .

Tiiiina . . .

I am spreading.

Spreading.

Spreading throughout the stars . . .

One thought in millions . . .

Trillions . . .

Infinity . . .

I am . . . ?

Swirls of light.

Streamers. Streaks. Swirling. Coalescing.

Around, around, around.

Streaks of light against my consciousness.

Colors resolve into solid streamers.

Smells fade, until only the antiseptic scent of machinery remains.

Universe hard under my body.

Universe arched over my head. Metal/plastic/I don't know what.

Around and around.

I was sitting in a chair, in a laboratory. Lights flickered on the cage of equipment over my head.

The chair was turning. Rotating. I strained to see the lab. A panel jumped into focus as I swung past it. I made out a web console. People were here, too, bent over the equipment. When I concentrated, the chair's rotation slowed; when my mind wandered, it increased.

Around and around.

The lab moved slowly past, its display panels, control banks, and consoles in focus. The upper half of one wall was made of glass.

Beyond it, I saw people standing. Watching me. As my chair rotated, they moved past my field of vision.

The glass came into view again. Althor was there, watching. On the next rotation, he was still there.

On the third rotation—or was it the fifth?—there were two of him. After several more rotations, I realized it was Althor and Eldrin.

I lost track of the number of times the chair went around. Althor was always there, sometimes standing, other times slumped in a chair sleeping, other times reading.

People came to watch with him. I recognized Eldrin, but none of the others. Except maybe the woman with black hair and green eyes.

Around and around.

The rotation gradually decreased, until the chair barely turned. I wet my lips, trying to speak. A tube clicked into my mouth and cool water ran down my throat. Patches were attached to my arms, which lay on the chair's armrests.

I tried to lift one arm. It barely moved, squeaking on the smooth surface.

A voice spoke Skolian. As the chair rotated, a face appeared in front of me. A woman. She caught the armrests, stopping the chair's motion.

"Can you hear me?" She spoke English with a Skolian accent.

I tried to speak. A croak came out.

"It's all right," she said. "Don't push it. Just relax."

"I'm . . . out? Of the net?"

"Not completely," she said. "We've done 85 percent of the inverse transform. You were so spread out, we've had to integrate over the full volume of psiberspace."

Around and around.

I opened my eyes and saw a knee nearby. Gradually I absorbed the fact that I was lying stomach down on a bed. Soft blankets and sheets covered my body.

A snore rumbled and the knee twitched. Looking up, I saw Eldrin slumped in a chair, sleeping, his arms crossed, his feet planted wide. Behind him, someone was sprawled on a cot, also asleep.

"Eldrin?" I said.

He kept sleeping. I tried to push up on my arms, but dizziness hit and I collapsed onto the bed. As I closed my eyes, a blur of movement came from behind Eldrin.

A hand pressed against my forehead. "Tina?" It was Althor.

I opened my eyes and looked up at him. "Hi," I whispered.

His eyes had a funny look, wet and full of water. He squeezed my hand. "Hi."

"If I had come a minute earlier," Althor said. "Just one *minute.*" He was sitting on the divan in the bedroom where I had woken up, in the house his parents kept on the planet Parthonia. "When I saw you disappear, I thought I'd lost everything."

I finished sealing up the jumpsuit he had brought me, a snug lavender coverall. "We thought you hadn't made it." I sat next to him. "What happened after you disappeared?"

"It was eerie." He shook his head. "I was a wavepacket, similar to the diffraction pattern produced by a circular aperture, but multidimensional. I saw the net as hills and valleys made from a grid. They must have been potentials created by the thoughts of users in psibernet."

"I thought it was a lake," I said. "I kept spreading out."

"I'm not surprised. I had trouble orienting and I've been using the net almost since birth."

"How did you get out?"

Wonder touched his voice. "I finally realized that when a telepath jacked into the net, I could 'see' it as a small hole. The first two I found were together in psiberspace, but linked to consoles fifty light-years apart in spacetime. Eventually I found a psiphon linked to an empty console seat on *Assembler,* one of the ISC ships Ragnar brought." He grimaced. "I had to alter the wavefunction of my body so that when I transformed back into spacetime, I ended up localized in that chair. I did finally manage it, but it isn't something I ever want to try again." His face relaxed. "It was worth it, though, to see the looks of the crew when I coalesced out of nowhere."

I smiled. "What did they do?"

"Took me to the captain. Maurisa Mettledawn." Dryly he said, "It's a good thing I know her, because I was almost incoherent by then. But when she finally understood what I was telling her, she acted immediately."

I took a breath. "And Bloodmark?"

"He escaped." Softly he said, "A part of me wants him to die. Another part is grateful he didn't."

I took his hand. "You can't just turn off the love you felt for so many years."

One of his memories from childhood washed over my mind: Ragnar Bloodmark, laughing as he threw Althor a ball. Then the image vanished, like a light turned off. Althor sat staring at his hands as if they still held the ball.

I wanted to offer comfort, but I knew he didn't want to talk about it. In the years since, he has spoken some about Ragnar, but more often he keeps his thoughts private. Sometimes in the night, I wake to find him staring at the ceiling. He pulls me into his arms and buries his head in my hair, seeking solace even in his silence.

Ragnar Bloodmark lost almost everything: his home, position, wealth. But he's kept his freedom, remaining a specter in our lives. To me, Althor's loss seems worse. How do you give back the ability to trust? For the sake of greed, Ragnar threw away Althor's love and admiration. Now he has nothing. Wherever he is, I hope he suffers for that irony.

All I said then was, "Are you going to be all right? The Jag said you needed a lot of repair."

"They've been working on me since Captain Mettledawn brought us back." He sounded subdued. "They say it will be a while before I'm whole again." His face gentled. "The doctors have asked about you, too, Tina."

"Me? What for?"

"They want to know if you would like to see a therapist." He paused. "Not just because of Iquar. You had been to hell and back before I even met you."

Did my life really seem so terrible to him? I couldn't talk to a stranger about it, or at least that was how I felt then. Perhaps that's why his moods have always made sense to me; we are alike in the way that such experiences turn us inward.

"I've been reading about your century on Earth," he said. "Trying to understand what this must be like for you. There is a phrase from then." Softly he said, "Healer, heal thyself." He squeezed my hands. "Let us do something for you."

I hesitated. "I'd like to go to school. I probably have to start all over. But I want to learn." After a moment I added, "I'd like to know what happened to my ancestors too."

"We'll get you private tutors until you catch up, *querida*. Then you can choose any school you want." He drew me to my feet. "Right now I want you to meet someone. She may be able to tell you about the Maya."

Belatedly, I realized what he said. *Querida*. Sweetheart. So formal and sweet. I raised his hand and kissed the knuckles.

He led me through a house. Everything in it was soft and airy. Holo-art graced the walls and cloud carpets softened the floors. Arching doorways, arches in the walls, and vaults in the ceilings made elegant open spaces. We ended up in a large atrium. Trees filled it, their feathery branches drifting in the air currents. Flowers bloomed everywhere: rose-colored bells, blue stars dusting the moss, vines with green blossoms that followed our movements. Birds flew among the trees, parrots with red, gold, and green feathers. A woman stood on the far side, looking out at a mountain grotto with a waterfall.

Althor brought me over to the woman. "Mother?"

She turned to face us. In person, she's even more striking than her holos. Her face is perfect, so classically beautiful it's hard to believe she is real. Some of that beauty is bio-sculpted, but she comes by most of it naturally. The vivid green of her eyes never ceases to startle me. Although traces of gray show in her hair and faint lines surround her eyes, she doesn't look much older than her son. But in her presence you feel her age: Dyhianna Selei is more than two centuries old.

She spoke to me in English. "My greetings. I am Dehya."

I nodded, trying not to look as clumsy as I felt. "Hello."

As she drew me over to sit on a bench, Althor went off to another part of the atrium—and I nearly panicked when I realized he was leaving me alone with my new mother-in-law. Pale colors swirled around her, pastels my mind created out of her emotions. I know now that she controls those swirls with a finesse no other Kyle operator can match, even among the Rhon. All I knew at the time was that I picked up only a faint sense of her mood, polite curiosity, what she chose to show, no more.

I took a breath. "I want you to know I'll do my best to make Althor happy." It seemed the safest opener.

She regarded me coolly. "Your marriage contract with my son is—interesting."

From what I remembered, the "contract" was no more than a few lines: our names, the date, Althor's job as a Jagernaut, mine as a waitress, his parents' names, my mother's name, the base where he was stationed, and my address in Los Angeles. We neglected the most intriguing part, which was that my Los Angeles was in another universe.

"Interesting?" I asked.

"These terms Althor worked out with Director Stonehedge."

I tried to recall what Althor told me. "He said he had a little land he wanted me to have if he—if anything happened to him. And something about a minor title."

She sat with her hands folded in her lap, face composed. "Althor gave you full rights to everything he has. Everything." Softly she said, "My son has made you a spectacularly wealthy and powerful woman, 'Akushtina Pulivok. What do you offer him in return?"

I swallowed. Apparently Althor's title wasn't so "minor" as he would have me believe. His mother asked a fair question. But how to answer? Although I have come to love Dehya, even now she flusters me. That day, I had no clue what to say.

One thing was clear: she loved her son. It sparkled in the air like white light and lilted in a soft melody. She glanced past me, her face gentling. I turned and saw Althor across the atrium, grinning at an incensed parrot that glared at him from its perch in a tree. He laughed and the bird squawked, as if outraged that a human found it amusing. Although Althor didn't seem consciously aware of his mother's colors and music, I sensed an inner peace in him that I hadn't felt before.

I looked back at Dehya. She was watching me again, her face unreadable. I wanted her to know I loved him for himself, not for what he could give me. So I said, "I didn't know anything about Althor when we met." I smiled. "In fact, at the time I thought he was a fruitcake." As soon as the words were out of my mouth, I wanted to die. I had meant it as a lighthearted joke, but it bombed like dough thudding on the floor.

Deyha's face remained cool. "How much do you understand about his position?"

I spoke more carefully this time. "That your family descends from the Ruby Dynasty."

She nodded. "Your scholars translate my title as pharaoh. However, in this day and age, the title is merely honorary. The Assembly now governs, a council of leaders from our twenty-six strongest planetary governments. The Ruby Dynasty has no power."

The years since have revealed a far more complex situation than what she claimed that day. Many believe the Rhon rule Imperial Skolia, quietly, behind the scenes; others see them as prisoners of a cynical Assembly that uses them for its own ends. About one thing I have no doubt: Dyhianna Selei controls the psibernet with an unmatched reach and skill—and in Althor's universe the fluxes of power all tie to that ever-evolving web which has become an entity in and of itself, one that spans the stars and more, dimensions beyond space and time as we know them.

That day all she said was, "Althor is my only living child. My heir."

I didn't know how to respond. It was no wonder she was wary of me, given my background, or lack of it.

"I have seen the Jag's records," she said. Then she surprised me. She took my hand. "To say my son is a moody, complicated, contradictory man is an understatement. You seem, however, not only to genuinely understand him, but to like him just the way he is."

"Well, yes. I do."

"Althor has high standards." Dryly she said, "A person might be tempted, in fact, to say no woman could ever meet them. If he has decided that you do, you deserve a medal."

"But?"

"He is repeating history. My history. And I didn't do so well with it." She exhaled. "My ex-husband was far more experienced in the politics of power than you, Tina. William Seth Rockworth was a high-ranking Allied naval officer from an elite Earth family. He was also a strong Kyle operator, though not Rhon. There were no known available Rhon men at that time." She paused. "When the Assembly arranged the marriage and treaty, they neglected to tell Seth the 'minor' detail that I could take more than one husband. He didn't appreciate it when he learned the truth."

I thought of Bloodmark's lack of success with her. "But you wouldn't have."

"It isn't that simple. After the Rhon produced more males, the Assembly wanted me to have their children. If Seth and I had still been together, the Assembly would have chosen a Rhon man to sire my children."

I stared at her. "That's awful."

She sighed. "You are so young. So unguarded. You must learn to cope with a way of life so complex that at times it will seem nothing could ever make it worth the trouble."

I felt a pit opening up under me. "Are you trying to say you don't think Althor and I can make it?"

She considered before answering. "If all I knew were the facts of your background, I would say yes." Her face gentled. "But seeing the love you two share—it may be that my initial reaction was pessimistic." Her silent laughter made a spray of sparkles in the air. "After all, you treated him well even when you thought he was a 'fruitcake.' "

I winced. "I'm sorry I said that."

Dehya squeezed my hand. "Both you and Althor seem comfortable with this reversal of roles you have chosen. But whatever roles you take, you still each come, in your respective cultures, from the side of the union expected to compromise, to adapt, to please. Put two people like that together and they just might make each other very happy."

Despite what Althor had told me, I hadn't really thought of our relationship as role-reversed. She was right about compromise, though. For all Althor's intimidating demeanor, he has always been flexible with me, adapting to my differences as I try to adapt to his.

"Have you found anything out about the mercenaries who kidnapped us?" I asked.

"We captured one, an officer who was Althor's CO years ago. Althor thought he recognized the man's way of speaking."

"Do you think you'll get the others?"

She regarded me steadily. "Yes."

Watching her, a chill ran along my spine. The mercenaries would pay for their crimes against her son. I wondered if she suspected what Bloodmark had intended to do with her if his plan succeeded.

The soft colors of her mood shredded. "I have my spots of . . . blindness."

That was all she said. But her reaction was so intense that I picked up more despite her defenses. She had loved Ragnar Bloodmark, not in the way he wanted, but as a friend. The wounds of his betrayal went too deep to ever fully heal.

"I'm sorry," I said.

She just shook her head, dismissing the subject.

"What will happen now?" I asked.

"Threats will be exchanged among our governments—Imperial, Eubian, and Allied. Impassioned speeches will be made. But if we remain calm behind the posturing, I think we will avoid war." She paused. "Restitution will be demanded and must be given."

"Restitution?"

She regarded me. "Minister Iquar's defenses destroyed two of the Jag's tau missiles and the third failed to explode. The fourth hit." Quietly she said, "Kryx Iquar is dead. A third of his Cylinder was destroyed. The civilian sections weren't hit, but his military force was wiped out. Several hundred thousand people died."

I stared at her. "I tried to stop the Jag. It wouldn't listen."

"Yes. We know. Your protest is in its files." She shook her head. "We don't yet fully understand what went wrong. The EI link between Althor and the Jag has evolved to a more advanced level than previously achieved, more even than believed possible. Its brain is a new model, and Althor has more extensive biomech than any other Jagernaut. He's also Rhon. Apparently in combination, they attained a remarkable symbiosis."

"It loves him," I said.

"Yes, it appears so."

"Are you going to destroy it?"

"We must. We can't have Imperial warships bombing colonies."

She was right, of course. Although they didn't physically destroy the Jag, they reworked its entire brain. It was several years before it returned to duty with Althor, and ISC now periodically checks all Jags to ensure they remain rational. Althor's passes every test. I have to admit, sometimes I suspect it simply gives them the answers they want, and that if Althor were ever harmed again it would seek vengeance with the same single-minded intensity as before. If that is true, though, I have no proof.

Dehya also told me that as soon as Jag notified her people about my Rhon genetics, the Assembly charted the history of Mesoamerica from 1987 onward. Virus wars in the late twenty-first century wiped out a quarter of Earth's population. When the United Nations finally established peace, Earth was exhausted, her people grateful for the respite and terrified of losing it. So after centuries of fighting for lands lost to the Spanish in the sixteenth century, the Maya reached an agreement with Mexico, Guatemala, Belize, El Salvador, and Honduras. Large tracts of our ancestral lands were returned.

Under the Isolation Act of 2192, the Maya formed a closed nation, choosing to live independent of Earth's international community in much the way the Abaj sought isolation on Raylicon. In a sense, they ceased to exist as far as the rest of Earth was concerned. That was why Ming, and many others, mistakenly believed they were extinct. The Imperialate was the first government the Maya Independent State agreed to open relations with, and that was only because of the Abaj. We still don't know what universe the Abaj's ancestors came from or why they were brought here.

"Even so," Dehya said softly. "Just to know the identity of their ancestors means much to the Abaj. Eldrin and I, Althor, all of the Rhon—we feel it too. We have found our lost siblings."

"Your kin. My kin." I tried to absorb it. "Or not kin, but our people."

"For you, Tina, kin. Your descendants are spread throughout the Allied Worlds."

"Descendants?"

She regarded me. "Althor didn't tell you, did he?"

"Tell me what?"

"He discovered it when he checked the Jag's files on the Caltech students. We verified it. Heather James discovered the inversion drive in this universe without prior knowledge of it. No record exists that an alternate Althor came here in 1987." She paused. "Perhaps the Ragnar of his universe never betrayed him. Or perhaps Althor died as Ragnar intended." Pain touched her voice. "Or he may never have existed. Given the genetic problems Eldrin and I bequeathed to our son, a good chance exists that in other universes he never lived. Whatever the reason, he never came here. You married a man named Joaquin Rojas. He wasn't Rhon, so none of your descendants are either. But hundreds of them are alive now."

Jake and I married? It made sense. But after knowing Althor, I could never imagine a life without him.

Dehya glanced past me. Turning, I saw Althor and his father a few yards away, talking to each other. As they came over, Althor regarded his mother warily. "Well?"

"Don't frown so," Dehya said. "I haven't been terrorizing your bride."

Althor snorted. "I'll bet."

Her face gentled. "You chose well, my son."

Althor smiled and held out his hand to me. "*Bienvenido, ?Akushtina.* Welcome home."